LOCKE
MC SHIFTER ROMANCE
VERA FOXX

FOXX FANTASY PUBLISHING

First paperback edition: August 2024

Book design by: Etheric Designs

Model: Hunter Hobbs

Photographer: Jane Ashley Converse

Publisher: **Foxx Fantasy Publishing LLC**

DEDICATION

This book is dedicated to Emm E. Goshald.

To a beautiful soul that deserves so much more.

You're tough as nails and deserve an equally tough, commanding, a little psychotic book boyfriend to go with that sass of yours. I hope you enjoy this as much as I squirmed in my seat writing it.

Because it was for you.

But not in a weird, awkward way. We have similar tastes, and I knew you would enjoy it.

Gonna shut up now.

K bye.

DEAR READER

Take note:

This book is different from any other book I have ever written. The male lead is psychotic, feral, and very much obsessed with his female all while dealing with running a broken pack.

Locke is darker than any other male I have written. It was challenging but I feel I did convey both of these characters as perfect fits for each other.

That being said, some triggers need to be known.

Please visit the author's website and click on the book for a full list.

authorverafoxx.com

CONTENTS

PROLOGUE

Locke

My wolf tugs on the chains, his howls echoing in the cell and down the hallway of empty rooms. No one is down here, and even the cameras appear to be turned off tonight. The thunder rolls from the outside. It must be a powerful storm for me to hear it down here.

My wolf's menacing growl resounding as his bared teeth glisten with frothy saliva. The scent of wild determination intensifies as he gathers his powerful muscles, preparing to exert one final forceful tug.

Death would be much better than this. Why won't they let me die in peace?

Part of me knew why, they didn't want the Iron Fang to lose hope. If their president died, what the hell would they do next? Who would step up? Who would have the balls to continue any of what was built?

Grim wasn't the most talkative fucker and any other alpha in the club were small-timers from small packs. They weren't strong enough to handle a group of rowdy rogues or know how to read a room.

Our head violently collides with the cold, unforgiving silver bars. The metallic clang reverberates and the sharp pain pierces through our alpha strength, aching deep within. The warm, sticky sensation of blood slowly trickles down our face, clouding our vision with a crimson haze.

Just let me have peace. I've done enough.

The rogues have a warm place to sleep and solace before they all go rabid, unless, with the blessing of the Goddess, they survive long enough to have a mate. Except for the ones that have kept me alive all this time; forget them. They should have killed me weeks ago, because I can't fucking take another administration of medicine.

That means you Bram, you warlock asshole. It was all your idea and you got everyone to agree. If I could I'd bite your hand off first.

Anyway, it's over, done with. I've become too feral; rabid.

My inner circle throws meat into the cage, sprays water into the trough for me to drink. What do they think they are going to do? Bring random women down here to see if they are my mate? Is Journey gonna go find me a lady friend?

My mate would take one look at me and run, and I wouldn't blame her. My fur and teeth are missing, my claws are long and soaked in the blood that seeps through the pad of my paws. I look like a bloody hellhound, ready to take anything that breathes to the Underworld.

No one is safe around me. They don't even put a guard down here anymore. Another damn mistake!

For Goddess' sake, have I taught them nothing?

A baby's cry pierces our ears, like nails on a chalkboard, and our body rears back just enough to pull the brackets from the cement of the floor. My wolf's elation causes it to howl loudly, shaking the chains from our back and letting the cuffs clink on the floor where they still connect to our bodies.

They should have killed me.

Our body becomes a battering ram. He takes a running leap and hurls our body into the silver bars. They rattle more with each strike of our body, as we leave singed hair and meat on the bars. It doesn't deter my wolf, but I feel the burn as our body tries to recover.

Rabid shifters are unpredictable. They grow stronger as their will to live - to kill with no reason and to survive - multiplies tenfold. With no soul there is no moral meter, and the thoughts of the human inside vanishing completely, now have me rethinking all of that entirely.

Now I'm the passenger; watching as my wolf has complete control of my body, and there is nothing I can do to stop it. Hell, what did the other rabid members think when we had to take them down, so they didn't destroy the rest of us?

When the light left their eyes, did they see Grim and me? Did they know we hadn't wanted to do it?

Nausea turns in my gut at the thought of letting them down. I was a fucking failure, just as my father had said all those years ago. I never could make the right decision; never could be the alpha I should have been.

My wolf's haunting howl reverberates through the dimly lit corridor, blending with the sharp sound of its claws scraping against the smooth, cold floor. With a sense of urgency, the wolf taps into my mind, guiding me through the labyrinth of interconnected cells. Its powerful claws relentlessly tear into the pin pad, shattering it into fragments as the metallic wires snap and crackle. The odor of burnt electronics assaults our nose, mingling with the musty scent of confinement.

With a heavy push, the doors open and he gazes around our torture chamber, ready to strike any guards.

There are none. *Fucking Idiots!*

The baby's cries make him freeze - listening and instantly I know what his body language means. *Easy, tender prey!*

I panic and grip the imaginary handlebars in my mind. I shake him out of it, trying to steer him to the upstairs, to the door and to our freedom.

The woods where he could run and be free; away from the chains, the bars of the cell, the guns and the shifters that are ready to put him down.

He hesitates and I yell at the bastard to run. Then, run he fucking does, leaving a mess in his wake. Shifters scream as we turn over tables, ruin the bar and tumble around the floor. We are like a weakened fawn as I continue to push him to the door. The baby's cries are a distraction, but hell, I will not let Hawke's baby be the first victim.

Get to the forest.

The very few that were left in the bar look on strangely. Pity hangs in their eyes as I glance toward them, but I sling myself out the door, taking half the wall with it.

Why aren't they coming after me? I need to be put down. I would hurt innocent lives. They would all be in danger.

But not a single person steps out of the building. Not one wolf or bear emerges to take me on; to head me off, to kill me.

I knew I was strong, and would be difficult to manage, but it should have never come to this. Never! They knew my wishes - it was an order! They disobeyed a fucking direct order from their alph... president.

I was never their alpha. I was just... a president. My word is like a human's. They could choose to obey it, or not, because I didn't really hold any authority. None. I held no authority over any of their animals. Nor over them.

The woods smell fresh and cool to my wolf as he bursts into the forest, leaving the bloody chaos of the bar behind. His body races with a wild, primal energy that I'm sure he hasn't felt in years. Each breath carries the promise of freedom and a chance at redemption.

But little does he know it isn't coming. Nothing is coming. This is the beginning of the end for the both of us.

With every step deeper into the trees, the nauseating guilt and self-loathing gnaw at me. The memories of my failure hang heavy, like a net trapping me and reminding me that I'm not a wolf running free; that I have gained my animal again and I will soon be human once more.

None of that will happen.

I was once a leader, a president responsible for the safety and well-being of a band of rogues that had nowhere to go. This is how they repaid me. To let me suffer. Was I ever really a leader to them? Or was I just the fucking scapegoat the whole time? I just was here to watch everyone suffer and let my guilt eat me away because I couldn't do a fucking thing about it. They wanted me alive to watch it all go to shit.

My wolf's paws hit the soft earth and he feels the discomfort of his deteriorating body; the hair loss, the uncontrollable hunger and the gnawing loneliness.

Finally, my wolf is seeing that not all is fucking sunshine and roses.

My wolf howls a mournful cry, a mixture of pain and loss echoing through the forest. He will now have to accept the truth that he is alone. We can never connect; to speak to one another.

He will only know me as... a feeling.

As we continue deeper into the forest, we see a doe and its fawn. My wolf's hunger surges at the sight, and he watches them as they graze, taking in their every movement.

I groan, not wanting to watch. I have hunted many times in my life, but I always spared the fawn. At a young age, all shifters were taught to spare the young so they could grow and bring new offspring, but I know immediately what my wolf is going to do. And I'm not going to like it.

My wolf snarls as his sorrow has gone and hunger has taken over. Primal animal instincts rise above the training we had done together over the years. He is a rabid alpha. He is truly an animal, one that I no longer recognize as part of my soul.

The doe senses it as well, and suddenly realizes its danger. It turns to bolt, but the fawn is slower.

My wolf lunges at it, tearing its throat out in a single swipe. It is brutally efficient, leaving behind a mess of gore and broken bones. Its cry for help is short-lived, being silenced by the vicious beast that had once been me.

But, as I watch the fawn take its last breath, I realize I have lost more than my wolf. I have lost myself. I'm not a leader, a president or anything else. All of that is gone. All that remains is the animal.

CHAPTER ONE

A month and a half later...

Emm

I rubbed my right eye as it did that funny twitch when I've been awake for too long. I slapped my hand on the wheel and wiggled my hips to bring the blood flow back to my butt. If the numbness wore off, then the pain in my lower back would come back and would help me stay awake.

Not that I should have trouble staying awake, as it was broad daylight. But I've been driving for days, and I haven't had over four hours of sleep at a time.

A week ago, I got on the dark web and hunted through the hundreds of bounties for my next target. I knew I had to be smart about it. I needed a load of cash, and the smaller jobs wouldn't do. It would take longer, but the payoff would be big.

The problem was that it was a bigger risk, but it was a risk I was ready to take. My experience was better than most. I'd never been caught, not ever left a trail and I wouldn't start now. I scrolled through the listings one night as I hunted for the perfect job, and it popped up, practically highlighted on the screen.

No picture, just a name, a few details about them and a chunk of change beside it. There were big, bold letters struck out as well that would further complicate things.

Locate target. Wanted Alive.

There was no picture, plus a live capture wasn't easy. I could request a few extra zeros once he's captured if they wanted him alive so badly.

I didn't care if the target was dangerous, unhinged or that I may very well lose my life for his capture. I *needed* that money.

I pulled the energy drink from the cup holder, took the reusable straw and sucked in a large gulp of the now-flattened carbonated drink. I slapped my lips together, my brows furrowing.

Ugh, hours old.

Coffee was my go-to. A good Columbian roast reminded me of my abuela and my younger years, but the gas station I visited had mud water coming out of the dispenser. And, I wasn't about to drink...mud.

Hours ago, I stepped into that gas station with aching muscles and cracking bones. The air was heavy with the scent of gasoline and behind the counter stood a man who looked like he was from India. His wary eyes scanning me as I inspected his coffee machine. I crinkled my nose in disdain at the sight of coffee grounds lingering at the bottom of a cup; a blasphemy to the coffee gods.

"Anything else I can help you with?" he said with a thick accent.

I had gazed around the counter, looking for some old-school maps for the back roads I was taking. The cell service was patchy around here and I was sick of getting turned around.

"Yeah, I'm looking for Forest Falls, it's a small town—"

The man pushed back from the counter and shook his head. "You don't want to go there."

I curled my nose up, snatched my energy drink and dropped a five on the counter. Typical reaction for any of these tiny little gas stations and an unknown customer waltzing up in here.

Well, tough cookies, mate. All my research to find this guy was leading to this small podunk town in the upper north-west and I wasn't going to give up the price on his head. I never did—I was good at what I did.

"Well, I'm going." I opened the can and took a sip. "With or without your help, but it would be a hell of a lot easier if you just told me."

The man's eyes narrowed as he watched me defiantly take a sip of the energy drink. "Fine, it is your funeral."

He gave me directions, and at first, I didn't know if he was leading me on a wild goose chase or not. I didn't have a choice though, and if he was wrong, I could come back here and kick his ass. At least his gas station was on this map.

Why the hell would they not put this freaking town on a map, anyway?

The man's eyes darkened, a shadow passing over his face. "Before you go," he began in a low voice, "let me tell you something about Forest Falls: it's not a place for outsiders. They say beasts roam the woods and convicts run the town. Bad things happen there, and it's best a woman like you steer clear. Once people go to that town, they either never leave, or run out screaming." His words were full of warning, but it didn't deter me.

I fluttered my lashes and put my hand over my hip, brushing the Glock on my side. The cashier looked down and cleared his throat.

"I'm sorry, a woman like me?" I mocked.

If only he knew what kind of life I'd been through, he'd know a town full of urban legends was the least of my worries.

"Thanks for the warning, but I can handle myself," I replied, turning to leave. As I reached the door, his voice stopped me in my tracks.

"There's a darkness in those woods; a darkness that devours all who dare to enter. You may find more than you bargained for in Forest Falls."

Ignoring his ominous and cliched words, I stepped out into the blinding sunlight and walked back to my car.

Whenever my phone caught a signal, I tried to search for Forest Falls again.

Nothing.

The only thing that came up was people claiming, on a popular forum, that they had been to this town accidentally, passing through for gas or a place to eat. They were unable to get a strong signal with their carriers, and encountered rowdy bikers who chased them out when they overstayed their welcome. The townspeople who lived there didn't show any concern when the bikers chased them out.

'*It was strange. I almost felt the heaviness of something dark there,*' one person had written.

I scoffed and tossed the phone onto the passenger seat. It was just a town, probably full of doomsday preppers that wanted to have an off-grid community. It was a perfect place for someone to hide: criminals, runaways and any other people who wanted to stay hidden.

Well, it wouldn't stay hidden for long. This hunt had consumed me. This would give me a break, a chance to relax, but right now, it was driving me to the edge of exhaustion, and I pushed forward with a determination that bordered on obsession. I had to find this guy, and if my suspicions were correct, he would be there.

Who knows, maybe I'll hit a jackpot and find more bounties on the dark web, and bring them all in. Then, I'd be really set.

As the small town came into view on the horizon, I couldn't shake the feeling of unease that settled in the pit of my stomach. It wasn't small, it was of average size. How the hell is this town not on a map? Not on Wikipedia or Google, or some shit?

One hand hung on the wheel, the other hung out the window to feel the cool breeze. The sun dipped behind the rolling hills, filled with tall trees. You could smell the fog coming in. The sun cast long shadows that seemed to dance and taunt me as I navigated the winding roads leading into Forest Falls. The town appeared quaint and peaceful at first glance, with charming houses, before I rolled onto the main street lined with old-fashioned shops—the older part of the town. But, as I drove deeper into the heart of the town, an oppressive atmosphere descended like a suffocating shroud.

It sat on my chest, like it was warding me away.

The streets were eerily quiet now that the sun had fully set. The street lights were lit, but not one person walked up and down the sidewalk. The restaurants were closed, and the corner liquor store didn't even have a light on inside.

I stopped in front of the two-story motel connected to the other shops on the street. *No Vacancy* it read, not that I was going to stay there anyway. I traveled with Marlow, my black truck and trusted fifth-wheel RV, that I've had in my possession for more than a decade and a half.

I continued to creep down the street, the lights now brighter the further I went, and took a right at the stoplight that was blinking red like it should in the middle of the night. It appeared to be a bar; bikes lined up and down the street, and loud music played. I could feel its vibration through the windows. It shook Marlow violently, feeling the bass from the outside.

Four bikers wearing vests, which sported their club logo on the right breast, were holding beers and watching me intently from outside the bar. Their gazes never wavered, while they watched as I continued on past.

I huffed, tapping my fingers on the wheel, and shook my head. It was just a town and the happenin' place to go was a bar; a biker bar. That's all this was.

I cocked my head to read the signs on the road. During my travels I learned to spot RV parks, and if this town wasn't into having visitors, I doubted they had one - or a campground - if they believed beasts roamed in the woods.

Looks like we are going off-roading.

Into the woods that the Indian man told me not to venture into. *Ha! Look at me now. I'm gonna go spend the night in it. Because I'm a cheap ass.*

Once I found trees spaced far enough apart, just outside of the town, I took a deep breath and began maneuvering Marlow off the main road, and onto the rugged terrain of the forest. The wheels of the RV jostled and bounced over rocks and fallen branches, causing me to grip the wheel tightly, as I navigated the unfamiliar landscape. The moonlight filtered through the thick canopy of trees, casting long shadows that seemed to reach out towards me like ghostly fingers.

Okay, maybe a little creepy.

As I finally found a clearing large enough to park, I shut off the engine and stepped outside, inhaling the crisp scent of pine and earth. The silence of the woods was deafening, broken only by the rustle of leaves in the gentle breeze. I set about unhitching the truck; my movements quick and efficient. I'm not stupid. I may not believe in beasts and monsters in the forest, but I believe in wild animals.

My fingers brushed over the Glock on my hip when I stood from unhitching the RV. I inspected the clearing, trying to imagine how I was going to set out my space. I knew hunting this guy down would not be quick and easy. He obviously wanted to be hidden, so, I'd be here for the long haul, which meant getting involved with the locals and becoming their friend.

Ugh, friends. That means talking to people. Gross.

I grabbed the machete from its sheath in the bed of Marlow, which was tucked neatly away. I then began hacking away the branches, from my traveling home, to make space. As I rounded the truck, cutting one large branch, I noticed the moonlight reflecting over water.

It caught my eye more than it normally would. I've never been into nature; I've never had time to sit down and partake in what it offers. I'm about survival, taking care of me and what was left of mi familia.

I pushed away the brush, and stepped out into the clearing to gaze upon the large lake. How I didn't see it before when I came barreling into the woods was idiotic of me. I wasn't paying attention to my surroundings at all.

The lake was so clean, so pure, untouched and unsoiled by humans. And I had driven my truck and RV right into the middle of this peaceful spot, which had been the sanctuary of all the animals.

I groaned, threw the machete to the ground and sat at the water's edge.

For the first time in a long while, I just sat. Listening to the sounds of nature, which was now very little since I came barreling in here. It was—peaceful. I think the moon was part of it, dancing on my skin, not knowing who I was or what I've done.

It almost made me feel like an angel myself.

I was far from that!

The moon did not know how much blood was on my hands, and how much more bloody they were about to become.

CHAPTER TWO

Emm

I didn't sleep well that night. I felt like I was being watched through the windows of my home. Yet, each time I went to the window, there weren't any peering eyes, or tracks below the window. The night was empty and the fog had rolled in, covering most of the moon's rays.

With the lack of sleep, I woke early and tidied up the RV, then planned out my day. If any of the posts online about this place were correct, I was going to have a hard time fitting in, and I needed a good rapport if I was going to get any information out of anyone.

I couldn't snoop if people were going to be suspicious of me the entire time.

As I steered my truck into town, the bustling scene overwhelmed me. The streets, previously deserted, now teemed with an array of vehicles: cars, bikes and even pedestrians on the sidewalks. The desolate roads from the night before, where no one could be found, contrasted starkly with the vibrant sight of people going about their day. The scent of exhaust mingled with the aroma of freshly brewed coffee wafting from nearby cafes. The transformation was remarkable; a complete departure from the eerie stillness that allowed a tumbleweed to roll through the town unnoticed the night before.

The biker bar, known as The Iron Fang, stood eerily quiet. Its sign loomed overhead, casting a dim glow on the door. The absence of lights and people made it seem even larger than before. The two-story structure dominated the empty street. Behind the bar, a bustling garage functioned as a real mechanic shop. The air was filled with the scent of oil and metal. The constant whirring of drills and the clattering of tools created a symphony of loud noises that reverberated through the space.

Overall, in the daylight, a seemingly normal town.

I buzzed through town, picking up supplies. Mostly food and water, but I also picked up a burner phone and quickly deposited it in my pocket for safekeeping. The people were not judgmental of me like I'd feared. They were genuine and downright nice, and that put more worry in my gut than them showing hostility.

"Are you staying or passing through?" one cashier asked. He was young, maybe eighteen, fresh out of high school. He had an innocent look about him, but his eyes looked old. That didn't stop him from putting a smile on his face, showing a friendly front and looking genuinely happy.

"Ah, not sure yet. I've been road-tripping for a while. Tired of the corporate world. Wanted to travel around the country for a while." I smiled, letting the lie roll off my tongue.

The boy grinned and put the canned beans in my paper bag. "Yeah? Well, you won't get more nature than this. Just make sure you don't go out at night. The animals around here are savages." He rang me up and told me my total.

As I rummaged through my wallet, I leaned on the counter. "What do you mean by savage? What animals?"

The boy shrugged his shoulders and put the bill in the till. "There are stories, but lately, there have been noises. It's scared the whole town. The mayor has put on a mandatory lockdown at dusk. Everyone has to be in their homes until the animal is caught." He leaned forward to whisper like it was a big secret. "Personally, I think it's a werewolf. You should see some of the damage it leaves in the town sometimes. Huge claw marks on the bricks, loud howls down the alleyways and sometimes, even blood all over the roads with no corpse left behind."

The kid's face went pale, while I just stared at him expressionlessly. I didn't know if he was trying to scare me or himself.

"What about those bikers? They were standing outside the bar last night, past dark." I grabbed my bag from the counter and balanced it on my hip.

The cashier leaned back and glanced around the room like the other stock boy was going to go tattle on him. "That's the Iron Fang. You don't mess with them. They do what they want. Like, they have the cops in their back pocket."

I rolled my eyes. "So, for all you know, it could be the bikers acting like a werewolf or some beast, and getting away with crimes in the middle of the night?"

His lips parted and that little bit of imagination he'd created in his head was crushed.

Gah, way to be a bitch, Emm.

"Look," I glanced at his name tag, "Garret, it could be a werewolf, alright, but why don't you look at the entire picture first, before you get all excited about the prospects of some magical creature taking over the forest and the town?" I turned my back to walk away, but the boy grabbed my arm.

I ripped it away from him quickly, dropped my groceries and pinned his wrist to the table. Garret's face turned pale, his heart beating through his chest.

"Hey, you forgot your change?" his voice shook.

"Sorry," I snapped. "A woman has to know her self-defense. Sorry I did that." Heat flooded my cheeks.

He nodded and dropped it in my hand. "Just so you know, the Iron Fang, they wouldn't do anything malicious like that. They may have the police in their back pocket, but for good reason. They help people. Help women mostly, but they have helped guys, too." He blushed. "They help them get out of tough situations."

"Situations?" I asked.

The boy leaned his head to the side, but his eyes wouldn't meet mine. "Just situations too embarrassing to talk about. Just take it from me. They are good guys. They are here to protect the town. I trust them—with my life."

I hummed, taking in the information Garret had shared with me. It seemed like there was more to this town than ghosts and goblins. Now, we have goblins, werewolves and now, savior bikers?

And what of the townspeople? No one had been mean or unwelcoming—yet, anyway. I hadn't worn out my welcome, although I was trying my hardest not to show my resting bitch face.

I walked out of the small grocery store, into the sunlight, and then I felt it. The hair on the back of my neck rising, with a sense of unease washing over me. As I left the store, I couldn't shake off the feeling that someone was watching me. The paranoia from the previous night resurfaced, so I quickened my pace back to Marlow and drove at a not-so-suspicious pace back to the RV.

Of course, I passed the bar on the way. It was bustling on the outside, now. Men and women coming and going out of the tavern-like bar. The apartment building across the street had women swarming around the outside, waving, linking arms with some of the men, mostly bikers.

It couldn't possibly be a brothel they had going on, could it?

My eyes narrowed and the high hopes I had for the biker gang vanished.

As I made my way back to the RV, with my heart pounding, I tightly gripped my bag of groceries and swiftly closed the truck door. Despite the silence that enveloped the area, an eerie sensation prickled my skin, as if unseen eyes were fixed on me. With a mix of trepidation and curiosity, I anxiously scanned my surroundings. The stillness was almost palpable, not even a single melodious chirp from a bird broke the silence, and the gentle breeze barely whispered against my skin.

I cleared my throat, adjusted the bag on my hip and unlocked the door of the RV, slamming it shut and quickly locking it again.

I don't get spooked easy, and I'm not sure why I was letting those foolish tales get to me.

It's the lack of sleep.

I sat at the small table, unpacking the groceries while deep in thought. My mind was fuzzy, and I needed sleep. Taking a sleeping aid was the only thing that was going to help.

My mind kept going to Iron Fang bikers instead of my target. They piqued my curiosity. If they were truly as involved in helping people as Garret had mentioned, perhaps they would know where the target was.

Then, those women coming out of that apartment building, and the men that surrounded it with guns at their sides. Were they protecting them? Or just making sure they never leave?

Between the internet post and Garrett's confession, that the Iron Fang was important to the town, I couldn't make sense of it. It was distracting. I shouldn't care, I was here for one thing.

Then again, they could be connected. This male could be involved in the gang. The description of the target included strong leadership skills, cunning, tactfulness and even psychosis.

I huffed in annoyance, feeling a headache growing, and pulled the burner phone from my pocket. I plugged it into the outlet, using the RV battery reserve. I waited a few minutes until there was enough charge so I could use it, and quickly typed in the number I had memorized years ago.

It rang three times before they picked up.

"Hola?" The voice was small and meek, and instantly I knew who it was.

I smiled instantly. "Hi Luis, how are you doing, mijo?"

"Good. Mama is walking a lot today."

I let out a sigh of relief and played with the paper in front of me. "That's great, Luis, that's really great! Is she taking her medicine, like she's supposed to?"

"Mmhm, the nurse is nice. She's helped a lot. She lives with us, now."

The muscles in my throat constricted.

Thank God.

"Yeah, she should stay there with you, now. Is the apartment okay? You are still going to school?"

Luis is quiet for a moment. I pulled the phone away to make sure the phone hadn't died on me. "Luis?"

He sniffed. "Si, school is bueno. When are you coming to visit? You haven't come to visit in so long."

I tried not to frown. Somehow, kids can always sense a frown. "Oh, mijo, I wish I could. I have this big job, and if I finish it in time, then I will have a big, big surprise for you."

Luis groaned. "That will take forever."

"Luis, who is on the phone?" my sister, Elena, called. Her voice sounded strong, but there was a hint of pain that only I could recognize.

"It's Tia Emmie! She is going to give me a surprise after her job." His voice faded and Elena's giggle came into the phone.

"Emmie, you can't be making a promise to Luis. He will hold you to them," she chastised.

Doctors diagnosed Elena with MS ten years ago. It wasn't so bad back then. She had symptoms, body aches, fatigue. She has her good and bad days, but they have been worse as of late. Especially since she had Luis.

When her no-good on-again, off-again boyfriend found out she was pregnant, he took off. He didn't want to deal with a child. Elena stayed with Abuela all this time and I've taken care of both of them financially since we all left Mexico. I came to the States, since I had a bounty on my head, and they went south to Venezuela. It was safer for me to stay away from them.

"I promise to come visit." I laid my hand on my chest. "And if I don't visit, then I promise to bring the family up here."

Elena was silent, I could almost hear her grip the phone.

"What?" she finally uttered through the phone.

"I'm onto something big. If I can secure this job we will be set. I'll get you all up here with a green card and everything. Make it legit. Abuela will be happy, you can be more comfortable, Luis will get better schooling—"

"You can't keep doing this," Elena said, sadly. "Abuela is getting older, she just wants to see you, she doesn't want you doing what you've been doing—"

"I can't visit much more; it's dangerous," I interrupted. "Every time I come it's a risk."

I make my family meet me in the countryside of Venezuela at a cottage. I can't take the risk of them to getting caught with me. My enemies could find them, hurt them, kill them. I would never let that happen.

"It's for the best to get you all up here. I'm going to get this done. Give me a month and I'll have this guy."

I could hear Elena's big, hooped earrings clinking against the phone.

"Sí, chica es loca, you know that? I can't believe I'm related to you."

I scoffed. "Yeah, your older, cooler sister, who is going to kick some major ass. Now, are you ready for the name of this guy?"

My sister had one request of me when I started the job: she wanted to know their names. It was like she wanted to bear part of the burden; of knowing who was going to come into custody with me, or die.

"Yup, let's hear it." She perked up.

"I only got a first name. He apparently doesn't have a last name."

"Makes it all that much better. Might be a code name."

I snorted. "Lame. Anyway, the name of the guy I'm after is—Locke."

CHAPTER THREE

Locke

Our mouth tasted coppery whenever I came into consciousness. I'm out most of the time, but when I wake, I taste the remnants of what my wolf has consumed. Mostly meat, horrifyingly, rotten meat.

I don't know if he's killed an animal or a human. It tastes terrible and maybe that's why I haven't come to the surface to see what he has been doing. Plus, it's too hard to fight him.

I've lost track of time. I don't know if it has been days, weeks. Hell, it might have been months, but I'm tired of living. Maybe my wolf is, too, because he's not been taking care of himself.

Insects have infested us, causing our hair to become manged, falling out in clumps, and our teeth to ache.

An unquenchable appetite, a relentless craving that fuels his wrath, consumes him. Always on the prowl, his growls echo through the eerie silence of the night. Perhaps, fatigued from ceaseless pursuit, he reluctantly feasts on carcasses.

I groaned inside him, frustrated with it all. They should have killed me.

Our bloody paws trampled the leaves. They left the crimson droplets of blood behind us as we took our large, mangled body through the woods.

I could smell something different, something strangely feminine yet tropical, as we came closer to the lake we like to lie by during the day.

I've smelled it before while I've slept, but this was the first time I've had the nerve to be awake for it.

Struggling for breath, he quickened his pace; blood trickling down his forehead. Seeking respite from the scorching mid-day sun, he found solace in a dense bush, with its foliage shielding him. He wedged himself snugly between two towering bushes, felt their roughness against his skin and exhaled a weary sigh, finding a moment to relax.

My wolf was completely still, not normal for him - unless he was hunting. Yet, his heart was not racing, he wasn't on his haunches, ready to strike. He was staring out at the lake, watching the ripples of the water spin outward like someone was swimming in it.

Who the hell was swimming in the lake? Let alone in the fucking forest?

I gritted my teeth. My wolf must have noticed my agitation because I felt the hair stand up on his neck.

Could he feel my emotions?

But hell, the club can't do shit without me. I told them, explicitly, not to let anyone in the forest if I somehow got out - if any rabid got out - and look at this. Some fucking person—

My wolf crawled forward, our snout pushing through the bushes to see what exactly was swimming. He must have known who, because he was whimpering, and when his head pushed out he cocked his head and saw *her*.

A female.

She glided across the water, like a smooth, light-colored amber stone. The light reflected off her bare back as she was wading in the cool water.

My wolf's silence, and his claws digging in the dirt, told me one thing—he was interested, but he wasn't interested in hunting her. He was stalking her.

If it was for prey, he didn't let on. He was more interested in watching her, I still had yet to know his true intentions, but I knew one thing—I needed to be more conscious from now on, with his interest in this female.

Hell, she was pretty to look at, not a burden upon me in the slightest.

She stepped forward, her back toward us, and I got the view of the most perfect, round ass I had ever seen. It wasn't one of those skinny human females we usually rescue, none of their fault because they have been abused for so long—this female has been well-fed.

I wanted to sink my hands into that bountiful ass. It was meaty and soft, and her hips were wide, perfect for fucking and bearing pups. If I was in my human form, I knew I would be able to get it up.

She slung her dark hair over her shoulder. The tips of her hair held a pink hue.

My wolf inched forward to get a better look, and she stopped once her feet hit the dirt. She turned to look around her as if she knew someone was watching.

Smart girl.

And fucking gorgeous.

My wolf's eyesight is strong. I can see her big brown eyes from here. Thick lashes, pouty lips and fuck, she's got a rack that hangs low. I wanted to do nothing but beg the Goddess to hold her breasts up for the rest of my days.

Does her back fucking hurt with those? I feel it is my duty to help this blessed human.

My wolf's claws sank deeper into the soil. His mouth salivated and a low purr resonated in our chest.

She turned her head slightly to the side after she put a towel around her body. Her gaze fixed on us lurking in the bushes. I felt a surge of panic and excitement run through my wolf as she stepped the rest of the way out of the water, her eyes never leaving us. She didn't seem scared; rather, she appeared curious, intrigued even. A small smile tugged at the corners of her lips, and my wolf's heart pounded in response.

I tried to push him back, to take control and assess the situation, but her presence captivated my wolf. He wanted to explore, and to discover more about this enchanting creature that had wandered into our territory. It was not just lust driving his actions; there's a deeper connection, an inexplicable pull toward her.

Fuck, fuck! No fucking way.

As she approached closer to the bushes where we were hidden, a subtle fragrance wafted towards us. It was a heady mix of coconut, like a Pina Colada. I'd always liked those since arriving to the Earth realm.

I would never tell a soul, but Pina Coladas were my favorite drink.

And, I wanted to drink *her*.

Her smell was like a witch's spell; bewitching my wolf. He inhaled deeply, and his nostrils flared with the scent of this mysterious woman.

I tried to regain control, to push back against the growing hunger in my wolf, but, it was a losing battle. The longer I had been in this form, the more he had control. He took over completely, his instincts overriding any feeling I tried to push toward him.

With a sudden burst of energy my wolf rushed from the bushes, startling the woman. She stumbled back in shock, her eyes wide with fear and confusion. But, my wolf didn't attack; instead, he circled her.

He paced around her slowly, sniffing her hair and her skin, but leaving enough room so she couldn't touch him. She stood frozen, unsure of what to do as my wolf continued his inspection. Our head stood close to her breasts; we are large for a shifter and I was surprised she hadn't tried to run.

Then again, she wouldn't get very far.

He brushed against her leg, his tail wagged slightly, in a sign of his amusement.

I struggled against him, trying to regain control over my body. But, he ignored me, too consumed by this woman. She tentatively reached out a hand, her fingers trembling as she hesitantly touched the fur of my wolf's back.

A low rumble escaped my wolf's chest, a sound that was both threatening and inviting. The woman pulled her hand back quickly, and her eyes narrowed in confusion. But, instead of running away in fear, she stayed where she was, watching my wolf with a mixture of wariness and curiosity.

My wolf suddenly sat down in front of her, his gaze never leaving hers. He tilted his head to the side and studied her intently.

Goddess, she is fucking beautiful. And, nearly naked.

If only my wolf had some sense in him and pulled that damn towel off her, she could do nothing about it.

Yeah, I'm a sick fuck.

But, I'd bet my left testicle that her tits are pierced or she has some weird tits. I'm all for weird, but pierced tits are hot as fuck.

"Are you the animal everyone is talking about?" She tilted her head to match my wolf.

My wolf made a pathetic puppy sound and I nearly died of embarrassment.

"You don't look that dangerous, except for the blood all over you. Are you going to attack me when I turn my back?"

My wolf snarled at that comment, and she jumped back a little.

"Dios Mio! Well, I'd like to get some clothes on," she snapped back at him. "And, you could go wash up or something?" She pointed to the lake and made a shooing sound.

Did she just fucking shoo us?

She picked up the flip-flop she was about to put on after exiting the water and held it up. "Go on!" She waved the shoe again, so my wolf lowered his head and ears, and trotted to the water.

I don't fucking believe this.

I sat in the back of my wolf's mind, absolutely stunned. This female just ordered my wolf to go bathe—and he did. He *listened* to her. He won't listen to me!

I snarled, and my wolf snarled with me. He shook his head as I do and dunked his head into the water. I tried to grab the reins of my wolf and for a few moments I had them. I moved our legs and our head, got the blood off of us, and pulled us back to shore to see where our female was.

But she'd gone. She'd closed the door to her RV and turned on the light.

I smirked, while my wolf took back control of our body and shook our wet fur.

I laughed inside my wolf's mind and I could feel the confusion inside him. He could hear me, feel my emotion and it made me laugh more.

Holy shit, this was too fucking comical.

The female looked out the window, her hand brushing the curtains, and stared down at us. My wolf put his paws up on the RV to get a better look at her face.

She watched us with apprehension. Her gaze flickered between my wolf and the forest, and I could sense the wariness in her demeanor. But there was also a spark of curiosity, a hint of something more beneath the surface.

As my wolf continued to peer up at her, his tail wagged excitedly. Despite the initial shock of our encounter, she didn't react with fear or hostility like most others would have. There was a boldness in her actions, a defiance that both intrigued and captivated me.

And now I knew exactly why.

She was my fucking mate!

CHAPTER FOUR

Emm

Peering through the thin, tattered curtain of my cramped RV, I locked eyes with the wolf—or at least, I believed it to be a wolf. Its fierce gaze pierced through me, as if I were nothing more than a succulent piece of meat.

I shut the curtain and dropped the towel, going along with my business and getting dressed. I went for a swim to clear my head, and get my mind off the animal that haunted the woods, and any other weird paranormal activity. I even went swimming during the day which is something I wouldn't normally do.

Skinny dipping wasn't something I do often, but the lake looked so clean and refreshing.

The woods during the day weren't as foreboding as at night. I thought I would be safe from predators, but once I felt the hair on my neck rising like someone was watching me again, I waded to shore and covered myself, hoping to find maybe a curious rabbit or a small deer.

Regrettably, the sight that greeted me was that of a repulsive-looking creature. It loomed before me, its size surpassing that of any ordinary wolf. Its snout reached up to my shoulder, a testament to its immense proportions. And, as if its appearance wasn't unsettling enough, its gaze on me was hungry and added to the sense of unease.

Blood smeared across its face, missing teeth, scratches and scars were embedded along its body, and the worst of it was a severe case of mange that had caused it to lose clumps of fur.

I could have easily been attacked, and of course, I was foolish for not having my gun near me, but I didn't think I would need it in broad daylight. However, I won't make that mistake again.

Yet, he wasn't aggressive, just curious.

I dried my body quickly, putting on a pair of stretchy jeans and a black top. I fluffed my hair and let it air dry as I checked my laptop to see if the listing was still there for Locke.

It was; no one had reported catching him yet and my lip curled in excitement. I closed the computer and shoved it, along with my burner phone, into my heavy fireproof lockbox underneath one of the kitchen seat compartments.

It was getting late in the day, and my goal was to head to the Iron Fang bar and take a look. I was hoping not to stick out too badly, but being a newcomer, it would be inevitable. I had to become part of the town and be friendly.

I rolled my eyes at that. Usually, I stay under the radar and hide. My targets usually hide in big cities and I go unnoticed by so many. This town would really test my skills.

With the sun hitting the tops of the trees, the shadows hovered over the camping area. I took one quick look out the window to see if the wolf creature was present, and damn if he was.

I reached out and firmly gripped my Glock, feeling its cold metal against my palm. With a slight click, I toggled the safety switch on and off, ensuring its readiness. Confirming its loaded magazine, I carefully slid it into my holster, leaving my hand on it as I felt the weight now resting against my hip. I approached the door and opened it, ready for him to barge inside. Instead, I found him patiently waiting. His curious gaze meeting mine, and his tail swished into the dirt.

Weird.

"Whatcha doing there?" I tried to give him soft voices to not provoke the animal. He looked better after a dip in the lake. He didn't have the deranged look in his eye and the blood had been washed away from most of the fur that was left.

He cocked his head and whined, then glanced at the gun I was holding.

"If you stay back, I'll let go of it." I spoke to him like he understood me. I wasn't sure why. I'd never been a big nature person, but then I never had time. This animal, though, I felt was different.

Why I thought that, I wasn't sure. I should shoot the thing and put him out of his misery. I bet the thing has fleas and ticks all the way up his asshole.

The wolf didn't move, and even dared to lay his head on his front paws. So, I slowly let my hand go of the gun in my holster, covering it with my leather jacket. The wolf stayed and wagged his rat-like tail— since it held no fur.

Huh, guess I have a little companion for the time being.

As I continued to walk away, the beast's whines became louder.

"Easy there, just going into town for a bit."

Hopefully, you'll be gone by then.

"I'll be back. Just—stay over there." I put my hand low to the ground, and the beast lay his head back down.

Smart thing.

I revved up Marlow and she roared to life. As I put her into gear the beast was already at my window, his green eyes shining brightly into mine.

"Damn it!" I exclaimed, my hand instinctively clapping over my racing heart. The monstrous creature locked his gaze with mine, his eyes unnervingly resembling human orbs, rather than those of an animal.

Surely not.

"D-down, boy," I muttered.

It took a few long seconds before his claws fell off the truck so I could get out the hell out of there.

Those eyes stuck with me the entire drive to the Iron Fang.

I couldn't keep them out of my head and I couldn't figure out why. I leaned my arm against the window and rubbed the side of my head. There *was* nothing weird about that forest. It was my lack of sleep, and the townspeople putting crazy ideas in my head. That beast could just be my imagination or just an enormous sick wolf that needed some care and was looking for someone, anyone, who would give it attention.

I could go to the town vet and ask for some meds for it?

I shook my head, and parked on the other side of the street from the bar. I wasn't really thinking about helping that animal, was I? I was here to get Locke. Get the bounty, get paid, bring my family to the States and hopefully be done with this sort of thing. Get a real job and then do... what? What would I do?

I blew out a breath and stepped out into the late afternoon sun. I got here at a time that would allow me a few hours before dusk, to show my face and get to know some patrons so I could start asking questions.

As I approached, the sound of laughter echoed through the open window. Pushing open the door, a vibrant melody poured out from a nearby DJ stand, captivating the room. Against the wall, a guy leaned casually, exuding an air of nonchalance. A silver vape dangled from a chain around his neck, emitting a faint scent of sweet vapor. He clutched a beer bottle by its neck, his mischievous smirk fixed on a girl who held his undivided attention.

No one turned to look at the door to see me come in, which was good, since I needed as few eyes on me as possible. As I walked closer to the bar, the bartender, tall, slim and muscular build, approached the side where I now sat and looked me up and down.

He poured two beers into glasses and shoved them at two patrons. He gave them both a wink, tapped the bar and let them know he would be right back.

"You aren't from around here." He flipped his blonde hair back with a flick of his neck. "And, I know everyone, so who are you, gorgeous?"

I gave him a fake laugh and leaned on the bar with my arm. "I'm Emm, and you are?"

The bartender leaned on the bar toward me and smirked. "Name's Anaki. Best bartender here; always ask for me, and I'll get you the best. Now, pick your poison or do you want me to guess your drink?" He wiggled his eyebrows.

I sat back and smiled. He was quite refreshing, and I haven't smiled in quite some time. "I'll have you guess my drink."

It should be hard for him. I was a mood drinker, and I was in a mood that might surprise him for the night.

Anaki narrowed his eyes playfully, sizing me up as he leaned back, tapping a finger against his chin. "Hmm, I'd say, right now," he played with his chin, "you're wanting a whiskey; neat. How did I do?" he grinned, pouring a glass of amber liquid and sliding it over to me.

I raised my eyebrows and lifted the glass in a toast before taking a sip. The burn of the whiskey down my throat warmed me from the inside out. "You hit the nail on the head. I'm impressed."

Anaki beamed proudly, polishing a glass with a towel. "I have a talent for reading people," he boasted before leaning in closer, and lowering his voice. "And you look like a very interesting person. So, what's your story, Emm? How did you come to this bar in the middle of nowhere?"

He was certainly straight to the point. I dressed as best I could to fit in with the locals, and I wasn't far off. I wore jeans, a simple top and a leather jacket because of the cool breeze that would come late afternoon.

The atmosphere was filled with women confidently embracing their fashion choices; donning dresses and jean shorts that accentuated their figures. Not a single soul felt the need for a cover-up, and amidst the vibrant scene, I noticed a blonde-haired woman in the corner of the bar, tenderly breastfeeding her baby.

What in the Sweet Home, Alabama is this?

I bit my cheek when I saw it. I could not say one damn word.

But, a baby? In a bar?

And, the bikers may look rough on the outside, but some of them were actually cute with the women they were with. Holding their hand, kissing their cheek.

—and wait, I saw some making out. Or what, were they having sex in the hallway?

I guess a single woman in the bar does stand out.

"I'm just traveling around, right now." Taking another sip of my drink. "Tired of the corporate world and just wanted to travel around the country."

Anaki bobbed his head. "Yeah, I get that. Being a paper-pusher would have to get boring. That's why I'm behind the bar, I get to talk to people all day—learn about their lives." He looked me up and down and I knew there was a hidden meaning behind it.

He was trying to figure me out as much as I was him. Anaki's body language suggested that he just might not believe me.

Before I could utter a word, a woman, approximately my height, gracefully approached. She was adorned in a sleek black trench coat, accentuated by a vibrant purple corset. Cascading from her neck were intricately designed long necklaces, garnished with brilliantly colored stones and talismans. Behind her stood a dark-skinned woman, who discreetly concealed an unmistakable assault rifle beneath her own trench coat. My gaze inadvertently landed on the weapon, but she quickly concealed it, catching my curious stare.

I sat up straight, narrowing my eyes at her and letting my other hand drop to my side, but continued to sit in the chair.

"Your kind isn't welcome here," the woman with the corset said.

Anaki's brow furrowed as well as mine, and I waited for her to continue.

"You come here with bad intentions. I can feel it. Finish your drink and leave."

I downed my whisky and stood up from my seat. "I'm Emm. Sorry, I didn't catch your name?" I held out my hand and smiled to look pleasant, but the woman just stared at it.

"Tajah, what gives?" Anaki hopped over the bar and stood between us. "This is Emm, she's new in town. She's traveling—"

Tajah waved her hand in front of Anaki. He pretended to bite her finger and I held back a smile.

"She's an outsider is what she is. An outsider with bad intentions." Tajah glared at Anaki and the fire he had to keep me here, faded.

"Emm seems harmless to me," Anaki weakly argued back. "We were just getting to know each other."

"Hi! You must be new. I'm Journey." A smaller woman with brown hair and caramel-colored eyes interrupted the tension. She held out her hand, and I took it just to get away from the thickness invading the room.

When I got a better look at her, I saw a blue crescent moon on her head. The artistry of the tattoo on her forehead was so beautiful. It was bold to tattoo your face, I had to hand it to her, but it matched the beauty she held.

"Nice to meet you, Journey. It seems I'm not welcome today. Maybe we can chat another time." I kept my hand held at my gun as I turned toward the exit.

I could feel the stares from others in the room, and I did not need to stir up trouble. Not yet anyway.

"No, you are most definitely welcome." Journey scowled at Tajah, who was clenching her jaw. "Tajah was just about to apologize."

"I wasn't—"

"Excuse me?" A rugged biker joined. He stood behind Journey and put his hand on her shoulder. He had death surrounding him; I could feel it. Tall, imposing and his voice was like timber. This man was dangerous, and I prayed he wasn't the one I was looking for.

Tajah cleared her throat. "I was telling Journey that Emm isn't welcome. She's an outsider, she even wields a gun in our establishment." She nodded her head toward my hip.

"You all have guns," I argued back. "Why can't I, as a female, protect myself?"

Ha, yeah, I pulled the weak female card.

"Grim, it's perfectly logical that Emm would have a gun. She's traveling on her own. She needs to protect herself," Journey sided with me.

Grim's intense gaze locked with Tajah's, and a wordless exchange passed between them. Tajah let out a low grunt, the sound filled with frustration, as the woman trailing behind her shot daggers at Grim. With a swift motion, they hurried away, leaving Grim behind.

Journey let out a long sigh until she smiled back at me. "See, no harm done. Come back to the bar, next drink is on me."

I continued to stare at the fleeting back of Tajah and her guard. I would have to be on the lookout for those two. I'd never had to watch my back much, since my targets were usually easy to find and acquire.

As we sat at the bar, Journey apologized for Tajah and her partner, Beretta. Journey explained that they weren't keen on outsiders. It was a small town that the club, the Iron Fang, protects and a lot of the town now included transplants.

Transplants meaning people that the Iron Fang rescued from sex trafficking rings, kidnappings and other assorted crimes, who were looking to get back on their feet as Journey explained.

A club that fights for the weak? I guess it isn't unheard of. I've seen clubs fight against drugs and help domestic violence victims. But, whole sex trafficking rings? And... why the hell are they telling me that?

And why did that mean that Tajah had to be so cunty to me?

One thing was for sure. They were apologetic about Tajah and wanted me here. Did they think that me carrying a gun meant I was helpless?

I wasn't fucking helpless. In fact, if there was truth in anything Journey had told me about the club, I was certainly the bad guy here. Tajah had every right wanting to kick me out of this town.

Shit, just what I needed. A nice biker club that does community service, and a bounty hunter that wants to hunt out a bastard hiding in the town.

I took the water that Anaki had already poured for me and drank a few sips. What if this Locke character was a runaway and was here because he needed help? And I was hunting him down to put him back with his captor?

Wouldn't be the first time I've dealt with some shady shit on the dark web. I've had to kick the original poster's ass, too.

Dammit.

There were too many variables and that was just one scenario. I'd have to keep digging. Which meant more lying to these bikers, who might just have hearts of fucking gold.

"So," Journey took a sip of a Margherita next to me, "what kind of job did you leave, again?"

CHAPTER FIVE

Locke

As our mate drove off in her truck, my wolf was consumed by sheer panic. He snarled fiercely, his claws digging into the earth with a desperate force. I tightly restrained him, feeling his wild energy pulsating against my grasp. The scent of fear hung heavy in the air, mixing with the lingering exhaust fumes. In that moment, I held on, my determination to stay awake overpowering any fatigue. I felt a surge of life coursing through me, a newfound zeal for existence like never before.

She was here, in the flesh.

I suppose Journey was right. It only took how many of my club members to receive their mates before I got my own? Hell, I fucking prayed to Her as soon as it was confirmed by Grim, but now that she was here– it felt good.

I didn't deserve this female. I knew I didn't. I was one of the worst of all the rogues here in this club. If roles were reversed and another alpha was interviewing me to join, I'm not sure if I would be accepted.

Then again, I'm the one with the money and strength. They'd needed me.

My wolf continued to thrash against my mind. He was confused and shit, so was I. She came to us like a bat out of hell, and she had a fire in her I knew would burn me alive. She was no timid thing, that was for sure. This female would stab me in an instant, but damn, those eyes. I'd let those brown eyes do anything she wanted to me.

I'm a sucker for pain, and I bet she'd like a good hand necklace from time to time.

My wolf, becoming more anxious by the minute, needed to be calmed. I forced him to move his head to the RV and saw that she didn't lock the door. A misstep on her part, most likely because of our presence, but fortunate for us.

I planted the idea in his head that her scent was covered in the RV, and our heart leaped as he raced toward the door, with our nose and claws tugging at the handle. It opened with ease and as we entered, we saw a neat living area. She lived here permanently, it appeared. The area was well-worn, filled with her scent that lingered and faded into the walls. Groceries sat on the counter of a small kitchen, which also had a humming refrigerator and a small dining table.

My wolf meticulously sniffed the air, his nose twitching as he absorbed the alluring aroma of tropical paradise. With each step, the room became a symphony of growls and excitement. Together, we leaped onto her bed, feeling the softness of the covers against our bodies as we playfully rolled around.

It was like drowning in her scent, drowning in her essence. My wolf nuzzled deeper into the blankets, trying to merge his being with hers, trying to claim her in every way possible. I could feel his desperation, his yearning to make her his. Yet, I knew I couldn't let him take over completely.

He was still an animal; he couldn't rut a human.

We sat up on the bed, feeling the softness of her sheets beneath our paws. Her presence filled the room, along with her warmth. It was a stark contrast to the cold emptiness that had consumed me for so long. She had brought life back into my damned soul.

She was utterly mine, and she didn't even know it.

When I gazed throughout the room, however, I noticed it lacked the touches of a female. Females liked to make their home theirs through decorations, pictures and small tokens, but this whole RV lacked it all. It only held necessities; blankets, clothing, food, and—ammo?

The corner table, with its worn wooden surface, was adorned with a haphazard stack of magazines, their glossy covers reflecting the dim light of the room. As our wolf approached, his sensitive nose twitched, catching a whiff of the lingering scent of gunpowder. With a sudden sneeze, he continued his investigation, his paws gently padding across the floor. Bending down, he discovered an assortment of knives; their glinting blades catching the faint glow from the nearby lamp and coils of rope, their coarse texture grazing against his fur as he brushed past.

Well, lookie here, we have a little hellcat.

My mate had some sort of agenda, or she was a freak in the bed. I wouldn't mind; either way I think she would put up a fight. One I could perfectly put up with.

I smirked to myself, and my wolf jumped back onto the bed. He rubbed his neck into the blankets, rolling his entire body so our scent would rub off on her.

If she was staying in town, and she better fucking be, then everyone at the Iron Fang would notice my smell on her. They'd know she was mine, and they'd know I'd be coming back, soon. At least, I hoped so.

For all the fuck I knew, I may be stuck like this and never be able to shift back, but one thing was for certain. No male would ever touch her again.

She'd have to masturbate the rest of her life, while I sat there and watched from the floor. I wonder if she'd be kinky enough to let her new pet wolf watch, maybe get closer. Maybe a tiny lick?

I groaned, as I could feel my wolf's dick becoming hard at the thought.

Humans wouldn't care for that; she would think I was an animal. Not a shifter. She'd find it repulsive.

I couldn't wait until I got her to trust me enough in my animal form. I wonder if she'd let me inside her home, to see her naked again? Curl up next to her?

As I settled into my seat, the soft cushion enveloping me, a sudden and distinct snap of a twig shattered the stillness outside. It wasn't the familiar sound of a deer, or any other creature. Not even the delicate footfalls of the light-footed fae that now inhabit the distant reaches of our land.

We lay still in the bed, our heart racing as my wolf's ears perked up at the sound. There was a human lurking outside the RV.

"*Easy,*" I whispered to my wolf, trying to think this through. He slowly stepped off the bed with the soft steps of his paws. Pissing in the corner to claim her bedroom would have to wait until later.

With our ears tuned in, we pinpointed the intruder's location amidst the silence of the forest. Their stealthy footsteps echoed faintly by the crackling of pine needles and twigs beneath their feet. The scent of fresh pine, mingled with the earthy aroma of decaying foliage, filled our snout.

This wasn't an ambush. They obviously could see her vehicle missing. They knew she wasn't here. They were scouting the area, looking for ins and outs. It was the only logical reason they were here. Or maybe searching for something else?

The sun was far behind the trees, casting dark shadows over the campsite. I could see the silhouette of a figure approaching the RV, and hear their footsteps crunching on the loose twigs. The instinct to pounce rose inside me, but I fought to keep my control.

As the figure came closer to the side of the RV with no door. I saw it was a man, dressed in dark clothes and carrying a weapon. He walked with stealth, eyeing his surroundings with precision.

I padded across the RV and pushed the door ajar. I let my tail take the brunt of the door so it didn't slam and rushed around to the back. I watched with dark eyes, as the intruder came around with their gun raised, as their other hand reached for the handle.

They tugged, expecting it to be locked, but their head rose in surprise seeing it open.

That isn't the only surprise you're going to be getting.

Our snout went into the air, getting a better idea of what we were dealing with. Male, dirty, had his natural scent overpowering days-old human deodorant. Fuck, it was potent.

We crept up closer and could hear him taking steps through the RV. "I'm in, she isn't here." His voice was quiet as he spoke on the phone. "There's a wet towel and fresh tire tracks. I'm guessing she went to town. I'll check for a burner."

He still had the phone up to his ear, though I couldn't make out what the other person was saying, if anything at all. He walked to the back, away from the kitchen and into the bedroom. This turned on my wolf's primal instincts. The logical thing to do was to keep this clean. Let him come and get what he's looking for and then pounce on him once he leaves. But my wolf was blinded by rage; furious that this male was in our female's bed—nest.

"She may have taken it with— what the hell!?" The intruder's eyes widened in surprise, then a mixture of fear and anger. The metallic clatter of the phone hitting the floor echoed in the room. With trembling hands, he reached for his assault rifle, but his sweaty palms caused it to slip from his grasp, crashing against the cold, hard ground.

My wolf snarled. He was overcome with pure rage and the need to protect our mate's territory.

With a mighty leap, we soared through the room, our claws digging into the intruder's chest with a resounding thud. The impact sent him hurtling towards the wall, his body colliding with a bone-rattling crash. Gasping for air, he crumpled to the unforgiving floor, while the metallic clang of his weapon echoed in the RV. The acrid scent of fear permeated the room, mingling with the stale stench of the intruder's sweat.

Our eyes glinted with a murderous gleam, reflecting the sunset as we loomed over the defeated man. The metallic scent of blood fills the room, mingling with the tang of fear. Our fangs, sharp and menacing, glistened with anticipation, while our teeth dripped with frothy saliva. We emitted a low, guttural snarl, our body quivering with an untamed, primal determination.

This was our mate's—our territory.

The intruder tried to scramble away, but we were too quick for a pathetic human like him. With a single leap, we pounced; our claws raking down the man's back, leaving deep, bloody gashes in his flesh. The man let out a gut-wrenching scream, and his voice echoed through the small space.

In that moment, the scent of blood filled my nostrils, and the adrenaline coursed through our veins. The smell of his fear and pain intoxicated us, pushing us further into a primal state.

We vigorously shook our head from side to side, causing crimson droplets of blood to splatter across the floor in a macabre dance. A wicked grin stretched across our maw, revealing our dark delight. The sensation of the intruder's life force seeping into the fur brought a warm and chilling satisfaction.

Our wolf's instincts took over, and we tore into the man with relentless force. We were driven by an animalistic need to dominate and claim our territory and prove our power and dominance.

He invaded our mate's space. He came into our territory. He was asking for this—this was a death wish, being in my forest.

The once-defiant man now lay still on the floor, lifeless eyes staring into the abyss. A pool of blood formed around him, marking the spot where we staked our claim and showed our true nature.

As the last breath left his lungs, our wolf howled in triumph, echoing through the RV and out the door.

I have always been fond of the old ways. It was one thing I missed about my old home. The simpler way things were. I have destroyed an enemy that has come into my future mate's home, killed him and proven my place as a suitable mate and protector to her nest. However, she is human and will not perceive this in the way of my ancestors. She will be terrified, or will she just be annoyed?

There was a reason why she was paired with me. Surely she will see some happiness in my protective nature?

Blood continued to pour out of the body, where my teeth had ripped out part of his throat. My lip curled in disgust and I reached down to pulled off the hood of the intruder. It was an unknown faceless male—human as I thought so before, but you could never be too sure with all the mixing of genetics and that bastard dark fae still prancing around.

More questions floated around my mind. Was my mate a runaway of some kind? Was she being hunted? I licked my maw and the coppery taste of his blood. We both had much to learn about each other, but even if she was the prey or the villain, one thing was for certain: she was mine.

I was going to keep her.

She would not run.

With no opposable thumbs to help with cleanup, I pushed my way through the door and pulled the body by the ankle out of her, our, home. The body landed with a thump outside and I winced at the mess of blood inside.

She wouldn't be happy about the mess.

I left the body where it lay, happy that the blood wasn't ruining her floor and headed over to the wheels of the RV. I encouraged my wolf to elongate his tough claws and penetrate the tire. It made a long hissing noise and we watched the tire go flat.

We repeated this with each tire, then went to the spare that hung on the back and pierced that one for good measure.

Once my mate returns and night has fallen, we will go to the Iron Fang and make sure all the tires for an RV, at the mechanic shop, are pierced, too.

I couldn't have my mate getting scared and running off now, could I?

CHAPTER SIX

Emm

I came back from the bar with my social-meter deflated. The people there were certainly different than I anticipated.

A typical biker bar: they had the tattoos and the cuts-vests-they wore; they had a code, rules and regulations and they had their old ladies, who in this case they called their mates-as in soulmates. I wasn't sure if I wanted to think it was sweet or make me gag.

The longing to have something like that was there, but I've been through enough relationships to know soulmates do not exist. At thirty-seven years old and not finding anyone remotely close to what I want doesn't give me much hope that there is some sort of magical soulmate.

Good for them, though, they all looked happy in the bar with their partners.

The men were rough around the edges and appeared to have gone through some shit. They had their tattoos and scars, and some had obviously gone through emotional trauma. If the ladies have gone through something, they never showed it. They smiled at their men like lovesick teenagers while their men kept a possessive hold on them.

Red flags waved around all these bikers, but the women looked too enthralled with them to care.

On the outside, everything looked okay. I'd be sure to keep an eye out for the women, though, just to be safe. Journey was a kind soul, and she had pain behind those eyes, like most of the town, but her strength and resolve shone through. She wasn't afraid of her partner. Grim, I'd come to find out was the head of the club, was the roughest one of all. And, thank God he wasn't the man I was looking for.

He would put up a good fight, though.

The woman holding the baby was Delilah. Her partner, Hawke, was part of security. His eye was constantly searching but kept most of his gaze on me. Figuring me out like I was doing with them.

The women of the bar, especially those two particular ladies, made me feel guilty. I'd lied all about my life, and they sat there like I'd hung the moon for them. I told them all about my fake life of being in the corporate world and sold stationery. Wedding and party invitations, dealing with printers and ordering the right card stock. It was easy, the same lie I've told a hundred times and shouldn't have an issue letting it roll off my tongue.

This time my tongue swelled, with regret seeping through my pores as I told them.

I felt like I was betraying all of them, and the men especially eyed me a few times, but would just drink their beers and say nothing. The women didn't care too much about the job, but asked about my hobbies. At first, I was reluctant to tell them, no one has ever really asked what my hobbies were. Besides, what was I going to say? I enjoyed going to the shooting range on the weekends? I enjoy martial arts, kickboxing, sparring and eating my weight in tacos while downing bottles of tequila when I'm alone?

That didn't make me sound great at all. It made me sound 'rough and unladylike', my father used to tell me. As the drinks kept coming I let the truth slip by several times—especially about the tacos and tequila. That perked a lot of them up, especially when I told the truth. Was it possible they knew when I was lying? How could they possibly know I was?

A large guy, with a thick beard and such muscles that he could knock me over with just a finger, tapped my shoulder and told me I was welcome into his gym anytime. I was even welcome to spar with any of the guys, and he wouldn't be surprised if I kicked some ass while I was there!

Shock must have been written on my face because the girls all giggled, and pushed another glass of whisky in front of me. I shot it back quickly and hid my flushed face because I knew I was messing up far more than I should have with this trip.

But, I just... have never felt so comfortable.

I didn't get to spend much more time with them because dusk came quickly and to keep up with the pleasantries, and the curfew that was imposed on the town, I made promises to meet with the women much earlier the next day, and for the first time I felt excited about meeting up with them.

And I shouldn't. I really shouldn't.

I needed to remember I had a mission to accomplish, and that was to find Locke. None of the men met the brief description given. This Locke was supposedly dangerous, which was why I took the job. Every single biker in there was talking loudly, arm wrestling, curious of the newcomer and too damn friendly.

Would Locke be hiding in a bar like that? Or was he psycho enough to pretend he was some innocent guy and playing a game? I'd have to continue to become friends, get in deep and find out more.

I ate a burger, on the house from Anaki, to help sober me up enough to go home. I tried to pay, but he glared at me with a twinkle in his eye and told me I could pay him back in some other way.

I didn't like owing anyone anything. "It better not be anything sexual,"

I said with a smirk.

Anaki's eyes twinkled with mischief. "But what if it is?"

I shrugged my shoulders and rolled my fingertips on the bar. "Then, you better be ready to go on an adventure, because I have a cave you can explore." I fluttered my lashes and blew him a kiss.

Anaki pretended to grab the air kiss and instead of putting it in his pocket, he put it into his pants. "Oh, my sweet Emmie, you do not know what you have just done to me." He bit his lip.

My heart caught in my throat when he said Emmie, but I smiled and gave him a wave as I walked out the door.

I must have had too much to drink, because these bikers—who I believed were just putting on an act in the beginning—were now wiggling their way on my I-don't-need-to-fuck-them-up list? They were making me forget the reason I was there.

When I arrived home, I expected to see an empty campsite with just my RV and the small campfire, with fresh wood and stones placed meticulously around it, but instead the enormous wolf was there, still waiting. I groaned, pushed Marlow into park and switched off the engine right when the sun dipped behind the horizon.

"You just won't leave, will you?" I put my hand on the side where my gun sat.

He didn't whimper this time, but just pointed his snout to the ground and continued to look at the same spot. Curiosity got the best of me, so I walked forward, still cautious, and as I heard the last twig break, I gasped when I saw what sat in front of me.

A hand. A bloody human hand.

I took a step back, my eyes widening in disbelief. My gaze darted back and forth between the menacing wolf and the mysterious hand. The air was heavy with tension, and only the faint rustling of leaves from the breeze broke the eerie silence. I could feel my heart pounding in my chest as I anxiously awaited an answer.

Like he could answer.

"Where did you get that?" I asked, my voice barely a whisper.

Upon closer inspection, it became clear that the area contained an excessive amount of blood, surpassing what would be expected for a hand. The unmistakable scent of metallic tang filled my lungs. It was evident that the hand belonged to a male, as scars adorned the knuckles. The fingers, thick and weathered, showed evidence of being bitten, with the nails being noticeably short.

It was so much blood I felt my stomach flip inside itself. I covered my mouth and pinched my nose to get rid of the stench.

I've been around blood, caused blood myself but I never had the stomach for it. I usually wore a mask, to hide the smell, but this–*ugh!*

Did that damn beast kill someone from town and bring it to my campsite?

"And where did all this blood come from?" I spoke more to myself and followed the trail, which went right to my RV.

Shit!

I leaped over streams of blood with quick, adrenaline-fueled jumps. My hand trembled as I reached for the door, pulling it open with a creak. An overwhelming sense of frustration washed over me as I realized it was unlocked. I cursed myself for my carelessness, knowing that my fear of the relentless wolf had caused me to leave it vulnerable.

This entire mission was nothing but mistakes.

With a low, guttural grunt, I forcefully swung the door open, revealing a shocking sight. My eyes widened at the sight of a vast pool of crimson blood, vivid against the cold, tiled surface of the kitchen floor. As my gaze traveled further, I noticed a small, steady stream of blood that had previously gone unnoticed, slowly trickling out of the door and onto the weathered step outside. The blood continued to drip, each drop landing with a disturbingly audible plop.

A wave of relief washed over me, realizing that my recent meal, a heavy burger, had already settled deep within my intestines, sparing me from the urge to retch at the gruesome scene before me.

"Shit, what happened?" I stepped inside and saw things misplaced. The intruder moved things in my home; my space.

An intruder violated my home, which I had lived in for so long. Instead of crying over it, I pulled back my shoulders and marched over to the bed. I bent over and pulled out the fireproof lock box that held my computer and burner phone. I shook it and pulled on the door. The lock was still engaged, and two items remained inside. Thank God.

I took the key out of my pocket and shakily put it into the lock. When it opened, I pulled out the burner phone and snapped it in half. I threw it on the floor and stomped on it several times.

They were most likely looking for the burner phone. The number that would lead them to my family—the innocent part of my family.

I leaned over my knees, rubbing my hands down my face. What the hell was I going to do now? There could be several people after me now, and I don't know who. Another bounty hunter trying to take out the competition? My father's men? Some rando?

The wolf came in the door, taking careful steps around the pool of blood. His head hung low and he edged to me. His fur was clean, but there was one spot he missed and it was on the side of his face. Blood was still spattered on his maw.

"Did you do this?" I pointed to the floor. "Did you kill the intruder?"

The wolf, of course, didn't answer. Instead, he kept his head lowered and came closer. I slowly reached out to touch the wolf's head. He didn't move. He watched me with those green eyes that looked far too much like a human's, and I touched the center of his head.

Why I was doing this I wasn't even sure. There was blood in my house, and a gnawed-off hand just outside, that he most likely chewed off.

Wait! I took that back, he'd brought it in here and put it on the kitchen table.

I made a fist and gently tapped it on my head.

What. The. Hell?

The wolf came closer and pulled on my jacket sleeve with his teeth. He pulled it away so I was no longer tapping my head with my fist. He stared at me, trying to get my attention and I just stared back.

"You killed someone in my house." I gently shook my head.

He didn't answer, because why would he? He was an animal. Probably the beast that'd been roaming the forest, and, for some crazy-ass reason, had decided to be my best friend.

I let out a heavy breath and put my hand under his jaw to stroke it. There wasn't any fur there, but it was mostly clean of blood. He was damp, like he just bathed in the lake, too.

Well, at least the thing has some manners for a savage beast.

It's official. Not here twenty-four hours, and I've got a biker club I can't make sense of, a beast that thinks I'm his best friend and a hand.

I should cut my losses and leave. Take up two jobs and go somewhere else.

With someone finding me here, I would have to move my RV. Drive ten-twenty miles out of town and drive in back into town when I needed. It would be a nuisance. I could try to work it out but I couldn't stay here.

The only problem is getting this wolf to understand that.

"Please don't eat me," I warn the wolf, "and I won't shoo you off."

The wolf's head cocked to the side, and I lifted my lip up into a smile.

The wolf backed away as I got up to grab some supplies for cleaning. I took the severed appendage with a gloved hand and tossed it outside. The wolf huffed in annoyance and trotted outside, while I began the job of cleaning out the RV.

It didn't take me long; I have a lot of bleach for accidents and before I knew it, I was done and my RV smelled like the inside of a chlorinated pool.

When I stepped out, I saw my wolf holding the hand and wagging his tail, as if I was supposed to take it.

"Yeah, I don't want that thing." I shook my head. "Thanks for protecting the fort, but ah, yeah, we should dispose of that." I pointed to the hand he was holding onto, by its middle finger.

Well, excuse you.

"Where did you put the body, anyway? Maybe I can see if I recognize the guy." I stepped over to the bushes where the leaves and twigs had been disturbed and saw just a pile of shredded clothes. The wolf trotted up beside me and sat down, gazing up at me.

"You... ate him?" I made a face of disgust.

He growled at the tattered clothes like they were going to harm me. He scratched at it and started digging. The dirt beneath the clothes was displaced, and I saw that the soil was loose and fresh.

I sighed in relief, "Oh, you buried it." Then wiped my nose with the back of my arm.

I kneeled and ruffled through the scraps of clothing. This wolf was smarter than he looked, and I looked him up and down again.

Maybe he *was* a werewolf.

I shook my head. *No, he couldn't be. He really couldn't. Most animals like to bury their stuff. He just buried it for later. Then, he would come back and eat it.*

I dry heaved, and the wolf looked at me with a cocked head.

"Sorry, I can't stand the smell of blood."

I went to pick up the clothes, but they were nothing but rags. Pulling out my phone and switching on the flashlight, since the moonlight wasn't enough, I dug around in the dirt, and looked around more. Closer to the trunk of the tree I saw a small square.

Bingo! We have a wallet.

I found the ID and pulled it out. The face meant nothing to me and neither did the name.

I tucked the ID into my pocket for later use and looked around the area for anymore items. The only thing left were bullets and a phone with a cracked screen. I'd have to go through that, and then destroy it. If it had a tracker in it I might need to drive out of town and dispose of it.

I stood, satisfied with my find, and grabbed the scraps of clothes to throw away in town. The wolf followed me closely, and I watched him as he took the same strides as me.

Why was he so close to me? Why so attached to a random human?

Was it because I was a female? A reminder of an old handler?

I glanced upward, and with the brilliant moon casting its glow above, I directed my gaze towards the RV, searching for any trace of blood spatter on the side of my home. Seriously, this day could not get any worse and as soon as I thought that, I discovered that of course it could get worse.

"That goddamn mother-fucking bitch!" I threw the clothes to the ground. "That prick slashed my tires!" I ran up to the RV and looked at each one. There were deep, gash marks in each one. I kicked my foot at the tires and swore a few more times, while the wolf stood behind me staring at me, probably thinking I'd gone off the deep end.

I was stuck here now. I couldn't move my camp somewhere else.

I threw my hand out in exasperation and muttered to myself, "I guess I'm stuck here for the night, dammit!"

And, I swear I thought I saw the wolf's maw lift into a smile.

CHAPTER SEVEN

Locke

"I figured you wouldn't have any of these tires but, seriously, two weeks for a shipment? That's insane!"

My mate leaned on the counter next to Hammer. He had biceps as thick as a typical female's leg. He was checking out my mate, who I came to know as Emm when she introduced herself to him.

I couldn't wait to scream it when I finally claimed her, but right now, I was teetering on the edge of leaping from my hiding place and putting my maw around Hammer's neck. He was staring right into her cleavage, which **was** abundant. She didn't shy away or try to cover up those beautiful hunks of curves and, damn it, I was happy with that.

Her breasts would easily overfill my hand and mouth; fuck I'm a lucky bastard.

"Again, I'm sorry. My supplier usually does cars and bikes. I'm going out on a limb here using another supplier for this type of tire." He kicked the spare she'd brought in.

It was a lie; I could read it by his heartbeat. Either someone told him to keep her here longer, or he's fucking with her to go out on a date. Which I highly recommended to all members that they didn't. No one should go around dating humans unless they believe it is their mate. Too much is at stake—like their damned lives.

If they got caught by their second-chance dating someone else—well, let's say they don't want that drama.

Hammer leaned in, his face inches from my mate who didn't back down. With a swift flick, his pen tapped against the desk. I fixated my gaze on the movement, and my wolf eyes narrowed with intensity. The sound reverberated in the silence, a sharp click that echoed through the room. I could feel the tension building within me, a surge of adrenaline pulsing through my veins. My wolf was dangerously close to the surface, on the edge of seizing control and plunging forward without thought. You better pull back, you bastard.

"I can call the next town over and—" He turns his head, taking a long whiff of her hair.

Hammer backed away suddenly, taking two steps back until he fell into the tire display behind him, knocking over a tool case and sending a cascade of wrenches clattering to the floor. Startled, Emm took a step back, her eyes widening in disbelief as she witnessed Hammer's fall.

I chuckled darkly in my spot behind the overstock tires in the far corner of the room. My claws scratched against the cold cement as I licked my fangs.

Ah, finally he smelled it. My scent.

Emm leaned over the counter, and her breast spilling over her top.

Well. Fuck. Me. Please.

"Dios Mio! Are you alright?"

Hammer looked up, avoided her gaze and cleared his throat. "Uh, ah, yeah! Yeah! I'm fine, fine. Just, uh, slipped there." He got up nervously, wiping away the dirt from his white cut-off and looked everywhere but at her. "Listen, I'll call around to different towns. See if I can find something.

You said you needed four, five if you wanted to replace the spare, too?" His pen shook as he took down notes.

Now the fun will really begin. I wondered what he would do now? Was he gonna yell out to the crew that he smelled me? Tell everyone I'm back or hide in fear that he hit on his president's mate?

The possibilities. I licked my maw from the shadows. *Endless.* I couldn't wait to play this game.

"Yes, five," my mate said, warily.

Hammer kept his distance, not even keeping eye contact with her now. In fact, he was bowing his head, showing submission.

Because he knew she was his Luna.

Pride swelled inside me, my fur bristling at the thought. Yes, my luna, my mate. She would be the key to the club becoming an actual pack. The last stone to help the rogues have a home, and to give them a chance to find their mates; for me to be alpha and to save them all.

A purr resonated through me. The men who were working on bikes and cars slowed their tinkering. They eyed one another but continued their work. Their hearing or smell not as attuned as it should be because of their dormant animal,...hell, they can't smell me either, but their natural instincts know there is something unfamiliar in the room.

"Call me with updates. Or I'll stop by." Emm broke the silence and took a card off the desk with Hammer's number. "I'm going to need to bring my truck in for some maintenance, too."

"Yes, Lu— Emm. Anything you need. On the house. For the wait and all." She eyed him and went to step out the door. "And, uh, do you want us to tow your RV? Keep it here in the shop? Where it's safe?"

Emm paused and I kept the growl from settling in my chest. *Do not take up on that offer.* I bored my eyes into her, trying to reach some sort of invisible connection. She rubbed the back of her neck, looking nervously around the room.

It would not bode well for my men if she allowed them to retrieve her RV. I would protect her home, I would maim—even kill to keep her in the forest until I had claimed her as mine.

The old ways would allow me to do so.

Emm kept quiet for a time until she tilted her chin up. "No. I'll leave it where it is."

Good girl.

Or, she's worried about the blood that has soaked into her campsite. People would see her as guilty. Anyone could see and smell the blood bath left behind.

As my mate exited the shop, the bell above the door chimed, filling the air with a tinkling sound. The sight of her enticing, round behind, set my desire aflame and caused my mouth to water. I let out a deep, longing groan and rose on all fours, emerging from the shadows cast by the spare tires at the back of the shop.

A wrench fell, making a clang and the mechanic room went eerily silent.

As I emerged from the shadows, my presence froze everyone into place. I could feel my aura overwhelming Hammer as his eyes widened in fear, unable to move. The scent of my mate lingered, driving my wolf's instincts wild with desire and possessiveness.

Without breaking eye contact with Hammer, I let out a low growl that reverberated through the room, causing tools to rattle on their shelves. The other men in the shop exchanged wary glances, sensing the primal energy that surrounded me.

I took a step forward, my muscles coiled with tension as I approached Hammer. He stumbled backward, knocking into a workbench and sending more tools clattering to the ground. Fear radiated off him in waves as he realized the danger he was in.

"Locke...Pres,—" he stammered, his voice barely above a whisper. "I'm sorry. I didn't—"

I bared my teeth in a silent warning, that his pleas would not sway me. My focus remained solely on him, my primal instincts driving me to assert dominance in this territory, where my mate had set foot.

As Hammer cowered before me, I could see the realization dawn in his eyes. He knew the significance of my physical presence, the message it conveyed to him and the others in the room.

I held his gaze for a moment longer, imprinting the memory of this encounter on his mind before finally shifting my attention away.

With a flick of my tail, I turned and made my way towards the entrance, the bell above the door jingling softly as I passed through. The men in the shop remained frozen in place, their gazes following me until I no longer felt them, as I disappeared from view.

Instead of just the witness of my scent, the entire shop knew I was there. Along with Hammer's testimony that Emm held my scent, it would soon spread like wildfire that she was their luna.

If some of the club believed it or not, that remained to be seen. The mechanics were... a different breed.

Would the club treat her differently? Most likely, yes, but I believed they had already begun to do so long before they had seen my weary body. She'd smelled like the Iron Fang when she returned home last night, mostly like Journey. I guessed Journey already had a plan in her head, and I was sure she'd spoken to Tajah to make sure the club didn't run her out of town.

Tajah could be one scary fucker when she senses someone new has evil intentions.

I smiled to myself as these puzzle pieces came into place. I had more things working for me than I cared to admit. I thought I was over and done for, that there would be no redemption, but here we were, a mere month

and a half later, and my mate came striding into my life when I'd hit rock
bottom.

Oh, that Goddess could be a heartless bitch, just as Grim always said. She
was toying with me, pushing me down to my lowest, so I could pay for my
sins of my past. Hell, the things I did were the way things were always done
long ago. I followed Ares' law, and I should not be responsible.

Or, perhaps I was being punished for putting my fellow rogues out of
their misery too soon.

My heart ached for those that my brothers and I had to put down, who
had already gone rabid too early, but there was no way I could know. I still
stood by my orders and I would not falter when brought up amongst our
club. But, deep down, I thought I'd always resent myself.

I stayed among the shadows as I followed my mate-no, stalked
her-through the streets of the town. She was memorizing, not the street
names or the shops, but rather the alleyways and the obscure. She dipped
inside the dark corners, and her hands trailed up the bricks and walls. Her
hands tugged at fire escape ladders, feeling their ability to move up and
down on the platforms.

I ducked lower into the shadows as more humans walked by. She acted
oblivious to the fact that someone was watching her, but every so often she
would nonchalantly observe her surroundings.

She was good, I'll give her that. Hunting her would be a challenge in the
town. In the forest? Mmm, I could find her scent easily. The sweet tang of
her scent was a tantalizing lure, The delicate blend of coconut and citrus
swirled around her, only adding to her mysterious appeal.

Who was this exotic woman and how did she come to the upper north-
west of the country, where the sun hid in the clouds, and her sun-kissed
skin now must hide on cold, rainy days?

She wasn't so hidden when she was skinny dipping.

Last night I tried to get inside her home. I had to speed up the bond, to have it heal me so I could become human. Killing the intruder was justified. It was only fair that as an animal, a shifter, she should shelter me and let me sleep next to her in her nest. I even saved a trophy of his hand. Any female from the old ways would be enthralled with such a gift being won from their enemies.

My endeavors, however, were just met with a pat on the head and an old sub sandwich.

My mate was human. I had to remind myself of that. Just like the other rogues, I would need to be patient. But, an alpha's patience only goes so far, and I was sick of not being in my human body. I had not only my mate to conquer, but a club to run.

There were other ways to gain her attention, and I was to find out soon enough how to win her over besides an intruder's hand.

CHAPTER EIGHT

Locke

I followed my mate through town. She went in and out through several shops until she made her way to a small park with a playground. Emm continued to pay attention to her surroundings without making it painfully obvious.

Children ran past her, screaming happily. She watched while they headed toward the swings as mothers and fathers went along and played with them. She gazed after them, with a sad look in her eye. A twitch of jealousy sparked inside me.

She didn't have a male, did she? Or a child she has left behind? The child would become mine, but the male would have to be dealt with swiftly. Any male that let their female wander away from them was, of course, an idiot.

Emm could handle herself, it appeared, but with a mate by her side she would be unstoppable. A male like me would fill that role.

Because I was fucking Locke—who was better than me?

My mate strode to a park bench which sat back toward a thicket of trees. It was cloudy today, and the air was crisp, carrying a faint scent of rain. I sat hidden behind her in the brush, my eyes scanning the playground as children laughed and played. Emm leaned against the wooden bench, her loose hair cascaded behind the wood backing and gave me the perfect spot to nuzzle my snout into it. The warmth of her body sent a wave of contentment through me, while she had no idea of the predator that was just inches from her pretty little throat.

My mate wasn't one to sit idle. I've noticed that about her in the days leading up to this. My wolf felt conflicted as she sat here. Why was she sitting? We continued to scan our surroundings, our senses were coming in stronger. Our hearing and sight strengthened as long as we stayed near her.

Emm ruffled through the plastic bags from her purchases and pulled out a phone. She ripped the packaging away swiftly, pulled out a portable charger and hooked it up to the block. She tapped on it several times, her leg bouncing up and down as she waited.

A child screamed in excitement in the distance. My mate looked up and smiled when she saw the little boy jump off the swing and land into the mulch. She shook her head and when the phone turned on, she took a heaving breath and quickly began dialing.

Standing tall I pushed my face through the leaves of the brush and watched as the numbers filled the screen. I committed them to memory as she dialed and when she pressed send, I fell back into my hiding spot.

"Hello?" a tired voice came from the other side.

"Elena? Are you alright?" My mate's voice said, laced with concern.

"I'm fine, just exhausted. Luis finally fell asleep after a marathon tantrum. How are you holding up?"

My mate's head turned to so I could see her features softened, and a hint of relief flashed across her face. "I'm doing okay, just needed to hear your voice. It's been a strange few days."

Elena chuckled lightly over the phone. "Strange, for the great Emmie? Do tell."

Emm glanced around the park once more before leaning in closer to the phone. "I think I'm being followed, maybe even hunted," she whispered, her eyes darting to a squirrel skittering across a nearby branch.

There was a brief silence on the other end of the line before Elena spoke again, her tone shifting to one of concern. "Followed? By who?"

Emm hesitated. Her lips rolled in and out of her mouth. "I... I'm not entirely sure. But I can feel eyes on me, Elena. It's like someone is watching my every move." Her hand subconsciously moved to her hip. I could smell the powder of the gun that was concealed beneath her jacket.

Elena's voice lowered to a serious tone. "Get out of there, Emm, it isn't worth it. We are fine down here. I don't know why you keep doing these jobs. We haven't been bothered in years."

Emm grunted and shook her head. "No, I need to do this. Besides, I can't go anywhere for at least two weeks. Someone slashed my RV tires and I'm not about to abandon the thing."

Elena gasped on the other side. "Is it another bounty hunter?"

My eyes widened in surprise. *A bounty hunter?* This was getting more and more interesting.

"Maybe, but, what if it isn't? Maybe it is you know who? There is something else, Elena, and I need you to ask Abuela about a name." Emm reached into her pocket and pulled out the ID of the male I'd ripped to shreds. She fiddled with it for a moment before Elena answered.

"Anything, what is it?"

"I need you to ask her if she has heard of the name Reyes Claudio." She tapped the card several times on her thigh. "See if it rings a bell."

"You don't think they found you, do you? I would have thought they'd have given up. It's been years. I think you are just being paranoid."

Emm put the ID back in her pocket. "It's either them or another hunter trying to get rid of the competition. This isn't a closed service. It's whoever can get this guy first."

Elena groaned on the other side. "Emmie, you said you wouldn't take those. There is too much at stake. We are fine here. Get a normal job, get a life. We are fine where we are. Abuela has friends, and Luis is in a good school. I do not need this nurse, we are fine—"

"No," my mate snapped. "I will take care of mi familia. I'm bringing you up here to get you better care. Abuela will not live forever and then what? What if you have a bad day?" Emm argued.

Elena growled on the other side of the line. "I take care of myself just fine. Luis is growing like a weed. My online business has taken off. I don't need your money!" she screamed.

Emm pulled the phone away from her ear.

"Elena, listen to me, please. Listen," Emm pleaded.

Elena huffed on the other end.

"I cannot call again until this is over. I will not risk the family," Emm said softly. "No matter how nice these people seem to be."

Elena hummed. "This place is different, where you are at, this Forest Falls? The little town?"

Emm nodded, knowing well enough that Elena couldn't see. "The people are nice. I just hope the people I'm talking to have nothing to do with this Locke guy."

I grinned wildly inside my wolf. Ahh, so we are both hunters. The question is, who will eventually become the prey?

I wetted my maw, mouthwatering with anticipation. I wouldn't object to my partner holding me down, a sharp blade grazing against my throat as their enticing curves hovered tantalizingly close to my dick. In fact, if it meant I could press them down onto my throbbing cock, I'd willingly surrender to the sensation of having her touch me anywhere.

Fuck, this is the ultimate turn on. Maybe I'll forgive the Goddess, after all.

"And what if he is? Maybe this Locke guy isn't some criminal, Emmie. That means you will let it go, right? You don't hurt innocent people, you said that from the very beginning."

Emm leaned her head back on the bench, her head mere centimeters from my snout. I took in a long, deep breath and inhaled her wonderful scent.

My cock stirred, and my tail wagged violently while she took a long breathless pause.

"I've gotta go, Elena. It might be a while before I can call again. I'm going to be using different burner phones, so always answer unknown calls."

"Emmie, you better not hurt a hair on that man's head, if he is innocent— ¡O te juro, te patearé el trasero!"

Emm forcefully ended the call, emitting an exasperated groan. With a swift motion, she snapped the phone in half, with the sharp crack echoing in my ears. Her movements were jerky as she grabbed a nearby bottle of water and poured it over the broken device.

My wolf licked our maw while we watched Emm gather her things. There were so many interesting revelations that have appeared before me, I wasn't sure which one I was more excited about.

My mate was a hunter, a strong female who has strong roots and believes in protecting a family—a pack. If I had my doubts before, which I didn't, she certainly had solidified my approval of the Goddess.

Now, she wants to trap or kill me which is a fucking turn-on. I wonder if she would try to harm me. Strangle me? Tie me up? Would she do it if I tried to seduce her? Would she take the bait, bring me back to her RV and somehow tie me to the bed? Or better yet, would she use my body then fucking stab me when it was all over, like some black widow shit?

Oh, the possibilities.

My mate took another look at the playground before departing. She traveled back to her truck and the only other place she could go would be her campsite.

I felt confident that she would be safe and, with the bond helping me heal, I knew I needed to make my presence known to the Iron Fang. They would need to know things were about to change, and new protocols would need to take place.

I huffed and trotted toward the back alleys, taking the darkest corners I could find.

The shadows swallowed me whole as I darted through the forgotten streets, the smell of iron and decay clung to the damp air. I knew this place like the back of my paw, every crevice, every alleyway. It was my hunting ground, my sanctuary. But now, it was also the perfect place to plan my next move.

As I made my way deeper into the maze of buildings and abandoned lots, I reached the back of the Iron Fang bar. The rusted door was left ajar, where the metal of the old tavern that stood once before us still hung. It cast a grotesque shadow from the streetlamp that twisted and turned with the afternoon breeze.

My large body pushed through the door, and my hulking form swung it wide until it slammed it shut behind me. I took a slow and steady pace through the halls, my claws clicking on the clean cement floor as I took my steady steps to the main area of the bar.

I heard my club's laughter and the clinking of their glasses. Aromatic smells of meat, alcohol and cigarettes wafted toward my nose as I came closer.

When I stepped into the main dining hall, it was Grim and Hawke who first saw me. They lowered their forks, their eyes widening in surprise.

"Shit, Hammer and the guys were right," Hawke muttered and stood from the stool.

Ah, so they still didn't believe the mechanics. Of course they wouldn't. I could shift back into my human form.

My low growl reverberated through the room, causing a sudden silence to descend upon everyone present. The dimly lit space was filled with tension, as the men's hands instinctively gravitated towards their waists, gripping tightly onto their weapons. However, Grim's fierce command to stand down cut through the air like a bolt of lightning, quelling any further aggression.

"I told you!" Hammer ran through the crowd. "He's here. He's found his mate. Emm! Emm is his mate!"

Grim glanced at Journey, and her features brightened.

Why does everyone have to be cryptic and shit? Damn stupid Goddess and priestesses, and their fucking agendas.

"We need to bring her here, then, to have her protected." Surkash stood from the back. "More outsiders are infiltrating the town." Others nodded in agreement, and the room became a chaotic symphony of noise.

I bared my sharp fangs and let out a menacing snarl that echoed through the bar. The low rumble of a growl reverberated from deep within my throat, and I shook my head vigorously. With an air of darkness, Grim, my second, stood steadfastly by my side.

"We do nothing," Grim announced. "Locke is in charge of his own mate. He's done fine thus far. If he wants us to do something he will let us know. As for outsiders, watch them. Chase them out."

Damn, I hope he didn't scratch up his throat with that whole speech. I gazed up at my companion and gave him a wink. He shook his head with a grunt and pulled on his beard.

"We will make her feel welcome, just as we have," Journey said as she walked up to me. "Tajah was not as welcoming and still has her reservations. You should know that Emm does not have good intentions—"

I snarled in annoyance and nodded my head once in confirmation.

"Of course he already knows, it's Locke," Hawke said, pulling out his knife. "He's probably going to get off on it, too." He leaned against the bar, the blade going under his nails to scrape at the dirt.

Well, he wasn't wrong.

CHAPTER NINE

Locke

The next few days I continued to suffocate my mate with my presence. I was her constant companion when she was at her campsite, and as the hours turned to days, she accepted me as part of her new life.

Last night, as the sun dipped below the horizon and cast a warm, orange glow over the forest, Emm sat by the lake lost in her thoughts. I watched her from the shoreline, my keen eyes picking up on the slight furrow of her brow, and the way her fingers absently traced patterns in the dirt.

Without a sound, I padded closer to her, the soft leaves cushioning my steps. As I settled down beside her, my head towering over hers, she glanced at me, and surprise flickered in her eyes before a small smile tugged at her lips. I could sense a shift in her energy, a subtle understanding passing between us that transcended words.

She was trusting me. It was moving slow as fuck, but she was.

Emm, initially, acted annoyed that I was in her presence, and I feared the bond wasn't as strong with her because of my animal form. However, as the days progressed, my hearing improved, and I realized her heart rate sped up in excitement when she saw me, especially in that moment by the lake.

Of course, she would be excited to see me. I was a looker, even if I was an animal.

She had not yet touched me, willingly, and I believe that was because I killed the intruder in her home, but we were making progress. When my body brushed up against her, clothing wasn't enough. Seeing her bathe in the lake tested my resolve. I needed the heat of her skin, her ass in my hand, her breasts in my face.

I needed her so fucking bad it was painful.

My mate's days were spent securing her camp. She pulled security surveillance cameras from her RV and hung them at points around her home. My mate even made rudimentary tripwires with bells attached to them to ease her mind.

The cameras won't work, though. Not with the magic that Tajah and Bram had woven through the forest. Soon, the elves that live in the territory would have their vines crush and destroy the mechanics. Emm's constant presence was the only reason the RV hadn't been overgrown with vegetation. The cameras—well, we couldn't have information leaking to the public about what goes on around here, could we?

Tajah's magic had grown and strengthened with the human technology, just as Idris continued to yield his witches and warlocks to his cause. Emm would see the recording now, but later...she will be one pissed-off female when she realizes it will all be erased.

Good thing I like my female feisty.

My mate had also spent time at the bar. My intuition told me she liked it there, being around our club, but part of it was she was hoping to have them trust her enough, so she could find out where I was.

They wouldn't tell her, or they would at least give her a run-around answer, until I had my way of dealing with her.

I was fond of her tenaciousness. She was trying to protect her family, wherever the fuck they were. With the intruder in her home, I knew she worried about her family more now. I snorted. She won't have to worry for long once I take care of it. My mate will see me as a complete asshole once she realizes what I've done.

Like most people do, but that is no loss there.

Currently, she was at a table with Bones, asking boring-ass questions about what he does for the club as he nursed his drink. There was tiredness in his eyes. He's got more white in his beard. My mate smiled at him. It only fueled a deep, primal aggression inside me. To rip Bones apart, to dig into his chest and eat out his heart. I let out a snarl and Grim set his hand on the side of my furless body.

"I get it," Grim grumbled. "But you can't let her know you're here, and I'd prefer not to find another doc. He's actually pretty good."

I grumbled and set my enormous head on the table. The darkness at the back table, where I normally sat in my human form, is dark enough that a human would have trouble seeing, but the members knew I was here.

The bar was busy. Glasses clinked, laughter echoed over the shouts, balls at the pool table smacked together. It was still hard to zone into Bones and my mate's conversation with all the background noise. It was like I was a fucking pup all over again.

"Duke Idris hasn't moved since you'd gone rabid. No new humans in or out of the mansion in New York. Delilah and Nadia put together a map of all the hidden passages. I assume Idris knows about them, but then again, he may not. There is one that leads in and out of the mansion that comes out by a river. That was completed four years ago and left off any blueprints. Delilah's ex-husband ordered the people, who constructed the passageway, to be shot once they completed it. All evidence destroyed."

Yeah, Delilah's ex-husband, Shane, was an absolute prick. Her step-brother made her marry him into the family mafia business on the eastside of the country. Duke Idris, the Dark Fae, took control of Shane's estate, after Shane was ripped to pieces by Delilah, Grim, Hawke and myself, before we finally beheaded him. The aftermath has been a mess since then.

I licked my maw and continued to stare at my mate making small talk across the bar. The smoke haze made me crave for a cigarette, but my wolf heaved, not liking the idea.

Fuck, he's back, so now that means I have to give up my vices.

I grunted and nudged Grim to continue. He chuckled toward my mate and took a drink of his beer.

"Anyway, we got in touch with a coven. We have partnered with them and they are willing to help."

I lifted my lip, showing my fang in disgust.

"I know you don't like it. Most blood suckers don't like us, but apparently, Idris stole some of their own. Besides, this coven came to Earth to start fresh, not to live the old ways of Elysian with fighting and bickering. They came to Earth for peace; a do-over."

I raised a brow at that. Were more and more supernaturals leaving the Elysian realm? Has it gotten that out of control? The Royal Council have always been pricks, but it was usually those who were in higher ranks that got the short end of the stick.

"Anyway, the elves plan on doing a stealth mission, with some of the mated shifters and the Heaven's Raiders Coven, to bring the innocent back here. I didn't feel comfortable leaving, but if you feel in control?"

I nodded my head once. I was more than capable.

And, what the hell? Heaven's Raiders Coven? That was a stupid name.

"Hawke and Dede are staying, obviously, because of the pup. But, I wouldn't be surprised if she was knocked up again, already."

I chuckled. The bastard would. And without Delilah knowing too.

It isn't a horrible idea, either.

My mate laughed again, and I took my enormous paw and stepped forward. Grim thrust his hand in front of me and placed it on my chest to pull me back. "Easy, man. Easy. You got this."

"Honestly, I'm surprised he hasn't ripped Bones up, yet. He's being a complete douche. He knows Locke is back here." Hawke strode up with a beer in his hand. "Hey, Fluffy, how you doing?" Hawke chuckled, and I stuck my tail out.

Hawke didn't pay attention since he was taking a sip, and fell forward. He tumbled onto the ground, and I couldn't help but snicker at the sight of my brother struggling to catch his breath, the beer spilling out of his mouth.

Grim pulled me back, and shook his head. "Easy, Locke. We don't want to draw attention."

I glanced at my mate and Bones, still engaged in conversation. They were both too focused on their discussion to notice the commotion at our end of the bar.

"You guys see that!" Anaki yelled. "Hawke only had one shot of a blow job and he's already falling over. Come get a blow job, made by yours truly!"

My maw opened and closed, and Grim and Hawke barked out in laughter.

What the hell is going on in this bar?

The bar erupted into laughter, and men and women walked up to the bar, grabbing shots filled with whipped cream and throwing them down their throats.

Delilah called for my mate, who shoved several glass bottles from Bones into her messenger bag. She waved Bones goodbye, and I watched her stride over to the bar. Anaki held out a shot for her and winked. Again, my throat let out a growl and my claws scraped the floor.

"I'm getting a blow job from you, Anaki?" My mate says sweetly. "You're awfully frisky tonight, giving those things away for free."

Anaki's eyes were wild with mischief as he leaned over. "You should see me on Thursdays. It's ladies' night. I've been known to dance provocatively on this bar." He patted it reverently with one hand and ran his hand up and down the pole with the other.

What the actual fuck have they been doing to my bar?

My mate downed the shot in one go, not taking her eyes off Anaki. He smirked and made her another quickly, but she shook her head. "I gotta drive Marlow back. I gotta stay sober."

Delilah groans. "You are such a party pooper. You never get drunk, not even tipsy. What about girls' night, next week? Will you let loose, then?"

Emm's lips pouted, her brow furrowed. "You know, maybe I need to let loose a little. But, only a little."

"Yay! I will pump and dump, that night!" Delilah shouts, holding her boobs.

Emm made a disgusted face. "I'm not sure what that means, but, yay?" She laughed, and I truly knew it was a genuine answer and not a lie.

CHAPTER TEN

Emm

I spent a lot of time with the members of the infamous biker club. I don't know what it was about them, but I felt drawn to the group. They were nice. I don't know if it was because they were trying to draw me in to get to know me and who I was, to find out the real reason I was here, or if they were genuine.

They were pulling away the bricks I'd built around myself, though. The women made me laugh, and the men weren't intimidating like I thought they were in the beginning. They were giant, golden retriever cinnamon rolls to the ladies they were dating, and I wasn't sure what to make of it.

Grim, for example, scared the shit out of me at first. Big red beard, tattoos and muscles. He was huge with a constant scowl on his face, but when he saw Journey, you could see the wrinkles soften around his face, and he followed her around like a helpless puppy, touching her, everywhere she went.

For the first time in my life, I felt a pang of jealousy. I've never, ever wanted a man. I've even toyed with the idea to become a lesbian. I even watched a few pornos to see if I would get into it, but unfortunately, my body didn't react like I'd hoped. It wasn't in me. I still liked dick far too much.

I think my ovaries just about exploded when I saw Hawke holding his baby while Delilah served drinks around the bar. The woman was a fairy, prancing around, and Hawke looked at her and his child-like they both hung the stars.

Yet, these women took the time out of their day to become friends with me.

Nadia was another that was hell bent on getting to know me. She was a tiny thing that barely came up to my shoulder. I think if I sat on her she'd disappear, but the woman ate as much as I did, which I had to give her credit for.

"You should come by Bear's gym." She cut up part of her steak. "You said you really liked kickboxing. They are starting up classes soon. If you stay, maybe you can be the permanent instructor. You look like you have powerful legs."

I tried not to smile and brushed the napkin down my lap. I don't remember ever being complimented so much, especially about my body.

"Uh, thanks, I'll think about it. I don't know if I'm staying here that long."

Nadia wrinkled her brow. "Why not? You fit in here great. Everyone loves you here. I think you'd be a great addition. We could get you a vest, too."

I took a sip of my whisky. "To be a part of a motorcycle club, I think you need a bike."

Nadia smirked and stuffed a hunk of meat into her mouth. "Well, you could always ride on the back of one of the guys'?"

My lips parted, my eyes narrowing at her until a man, not of the Iron Fang, strode up to the both of us at our two-person table. He leaned toward me with his hand on my shoulder to steady himself.

"Hey, baby. Did you sit on a box of Lucky Charms? Because that booty..." He looked down at my ass, which was hanging slightly over the chair. "Looks magically delicious."

A long, deep growl came from the shadows of the bar. I turned my head to find out where the noise was but as I did, Nadia stood and gripped her hand around the man's neck who was at least a head and half taller than her.

"This is a safe space," she declared, her voice filled with determination. With a forceful shove, she propelled him backwards, causing him to slide on his rear. The sound of his body hitting the floor echoed through the room, as he collided with the table next to us.

What. The. Hell.

I stood with my mouth hung open. There was beer all over the man, and the club members rushed toward him and pulled him up.

"Whoa, dude, the fuck is your problem? You know the rules in here," Karma, one of the members, snarled. He hovered over the now-standing man with a stern glare. "This is our bar, and we don't take kindly to that kind of bullshit and disrespect, especially to Emm. What's your name?"

I blinked in surprise.

"Beck," he said, and looked around nervously. He clearly realized that he'd made a huge mistake. "I'm sorry, I meant nothing by it. I just thought it'd be funny to mess with the new girl in town, you know?"

Nadia shook her head, clearly disgusted with him. "I suppose you learned a lesson about not treating a woman with disrespect like that. Now get, and don't come back."

Beck hesitated for a moment, clearly contemplating arguing or trying to play it off as a joke, but then he turned and swayed out of the bar.

With the tension broken, the group of Iron Fang members returned to their normal chatter, laughing and joking. Nadia sat back down and offered me a weak smile, clearly embarrassed by the incident.

"Sorry about that," she said, gesturing to the table. "Sometimes people can't help themselves, especially when they see someone new."

I smiled back, still a little shaken by the experience. "It's alright. I just didn't expect that kind of reaction from you."

Because you are so damn small.

Nadia nodded. "I know the club can be intimidating at first. We've tried to be really welcoming, and we are. We really care about you, and we want you to feel welcome here. If you're looking for a sense of belonging and a group of people who will have your back, I don't think you'll find a better place to settle down than here. Even if I do look small, I got some fight in me." She held out a fist and waved it in the air.

As we continued talking, I couldn't help but feel a swell of gratitude for the acceptance and warmth that these people had shown me. It's a stark contrast to the loneliness and isolation I've felt for so long, and I wonder if maybe, just maybe, this place could be a new beginning for me.

But, that isn't why I'm here. I'm not here to find a home. I'm here to find Locke, which I was not any closer to doing.

Now I felt too guilty to even ask where Locke was. No one has brought up his name, and it would be far too suspicious now if I brought it up. They would know I've used them and played them. And I didn't want to do that because, finally, I felt like I belonged.

The sun was high and the days were getting warmer. It was close to summer and the water didn't feel as cold anymore. It could very well be I was getting used to the cold dips in the lake, or the heat I felt on my body when I stepped in.

I took my caddy, one that floated in the water as I waded out about waist deep. I dunked my head under the water to soak myself and rose above the surface. The sun heated the skin on my back but also another heat filled me; from eyes watching.

I turned to check my surroundings, but the only eyes I could see were those of the wolf that had not left my side when I stayed at the campsite.

"Hey wolf," I said. I didn't shout at him, I figured he could hear me. Animals had excellent hearing, right?

He tilted his head, his eyes gazed upon me with a fierce intensity, like he always did when I bathed or he saw me naked. Do animals realize when people are naked? Do they know humans are at their most vulnerable?

"Watcha doing, big boy? Just going to sit there?"

He didn't wag his tail. He continued to stare at me, inching closer and closer to the water.

I haven't purposely touched the wolf. I've been far too scared since that one night. The wolf has taken plenty of times to brush up against my leg, begging me to touch him or give him some sort of companionship, but I have been far too reluctant.

But now, as the wolf crept closer to the water's edge, something within me shifted. Maybe it was the newfound sense of camaraderie I had experienced with the Iron Fang members that made me more open to connection, or perhaps it was the isolation of living in the wilderness that drove me to seek companionship in unlikely places. Without overthinking it, I extended my hand towards the wolf, offering a tentative gesture to come forward.

The wolf paused, his eyes meeting mine in a moment of silent understanding. Then, with a sudden grace that belied his wild nature he took tentative steps into the water. The wolf was large, so walking out toward me wouldn't drown the beast, he would just stand right beside me.

When he came closer, he dipped his head and nuzzled my hand. A rush of emotions flooded through me - surprise, joy, fear - as I felt the warmth of fur beneath my touch. It was comforting and not as scary as I thought it would be. The thoughts of blood running over its body when we first met, of when he killed an intruder weren't there now. Only calmness and trust.

This wolf wouldn't hurt me. This animal was here beside me for a reason. Maybe he was my spirit guide? My alebrije? Because he was a canine, I would consider him as a symbol of loyalty and protection. I wondered if anyone else could really see him?

I let out a huff of laughter. He looked up at me with questioning eyes. "Yeah, I think I've gone loco."

The wolf came closer and his nose nuzzled in between my breasts. I stilled, and watched as he did so, worried I had made a wrong movement. But, he did nothing except purr.

A purr?

I stroked his head and reached for the caddy that continued to float. I pulled out a bottle that I had asked Bones to get for me; for a wild dog I'd found and started to befriend.

This wolf had mange, and I'd have to treat both of us if we were to be close to each other from now on. *Maybe I had all along thought I would get close to this animal, if I'd put the soap in my caddy.* Anyway, this wolf was going to be treated for fleas, ticks, scabies and, if I could, I was going to get him vaccinated, too.

Bones said he wouldn't get near any sort of animal, and that I'd have to do it on my own.

"Easy now," I cooed at the wolf. "I'm just going to soap you up, and get you feeling and smelling better."

The wolf didn't move; he stayed contentedly between my breasts as I massaged the soap into his fur.

It was an odd feeling, the warmth of the sun on my skin, the water around me and the weight of the wolf's body resting between my breasts. I tried not to focus on it, knowing that I was doing the right thing for both of us. We were forming a bond, a connection that I hadn't felt in a long time.

As I massaged the soap into his fur, I couldn't help but feel grateful for the wolf's presence. It was as if the universe was sending me a sign, and letting me know I wasn't alone. For a moment, I really felt like I belonged in this wilderness, like I was part of something bigger.

The wolf seemed to enjoy the massage, purring softly as I worked my way through his matted fur. I could see the difference already - his skin was looking healthier, and his fur was regaining some of its original shine.

As I rinsed the soap from his fur, I noticed, again, the wolf's eyes had a human-like quality to them. It was as if he was looking into my soul, understanding the complicated thoughts and emotions that churned within me.

I finished rinsing the soap from his fur, and carefully wiped his face with a clean cloth when I led him out of the water. The wolf let out a small whine, and I realized I had grown quite attached to him myself. I didn't know washing your pet could be so—intimate, but it was.

I pulled a towel around myself now that my wolf was dry, and he let out a whine again.

"Well, I'm cold now and you're all dry," I told him, pulling out the glass bottles of medicine for him to take. It was some antibiotics to help with any open wounds he might have that I couldn't see. Bones said it was important to give it to the wolf I'd found, because it would really speed up his healing process.

I knelt to the forest floor and tapped his nose. "Open up, Bones said this would help you heal faster. It won't taste good, but if you're good, I'll give you some meat he gave me. Wild animals don't like dog food."

My wolf's lip curled in disgust and I shoved the syringe in the side of his mouth.

He gagged, and I laughed, falling backward. He jumped on top of me, his large thick, warm body hovering over me. He licked my neck and pawed the towel away. His smooth tongue went between my breasts, and my body instantly heated.

Oh shit.

His tongue grazed over my pierced nipple, and I yelped in surprise.

"No, no, bad boy." I went to push him off, but again, he licked my nipple. "No!" I slapped his nose and he stopped, his eyes boring into mine.

"We do not lick those! Off!" I pushed him away and he retreated with a sad face.

I stood, readjusting the towel and pushing the leaves out of my hair.

My pussy was drenched and my body was on fire, all because my pet wolf licked me in places where he didn't know any better.

When was the last time I practiced some self-love? Maybe that was the problem? Dios mio, I'm fucking drenched.

"I need—a moment." I said breathlessly to him, turned on my heel and rushed to the RV.

CHAPTER ELEVEN

Locke

She darted out of my presence like a bat out of hell.

My mate forcefully swung the door open to the RV, causing it to crash down with a resounding thud. Our faces twisted in pain, and we let out small, pained whimpers as the sound echoed in our delicate ears.

But, that couldn't stop my surge of excitement, because my mate did something so fucking simple and practical to her, but meant so much more to me and my wolf.

She fucking groomed me.

It was an ancient tradition amongst the wolves. One that had died out ages ago and I had often wondered why. I used to tell Grim how much I learned about the old ways of living from hundreds of years ago, when we first met and established the Iron Fang. If we ever had a chance to make this club into a pack, I'd want to run this pack like how it all used to be.

The forgotten ways where the women and men of the packs were equals, and they relied heavily on traditions in their mating rituals. They hunted and gathered together and they ruled together. There was no fucking hierarchy with males being the only dominant figures, like there was in the packs of Elysian. There wasn't just the pull, the bite, the knotting, and the claiming. It was more—it was a longer drawn-out process. It was to prove to one another that your bond was strong, that your bonds were tightly woven around each other.

Could it be that the Goddess gave me this female because she knew my mate would do these things for me? Bring this pack into the old ways?

My body thrummed with desire at the thought.

My mate combed her fingers through my matted fur. She'd pulled and brushed out the knots. She fucking bathed me even when, I knew, I did not look or smell my best. Then, she let me lay my head upon her chest and let me relish her comfort, and she knew she would get nothing in return.

Well, maybe my protection.

But she and I both knew what we were sharing was so much more. There was a connection, and it was intimate. I knew she felt it because, as she looked into my eyes, I tried to convey every bit that I was grateful to her, and wanted her. Even as an animal.

Then, my wolf had to take it a step further. He couldn't help giving her thanks, by licking her neck to return the favor. He wanted his chance to bathe her not just to clean her but in his scent. He released our pheromones scenting her deeply and directly onto her skin. Her body warmed and responded instantly.

With her naked beneath us, and the towel loose, I couldn't help but push it away and see the supple meat. It was game over when those glorious tits were right there in my face once again.

Goddess! Those breasts.

The barbells gleamed in the light and, hell, we were all over that. She was heavily endowed. They fell partly to the side. I wanted to bury my face back into them but of course my wolf took it a step further, and I swear I tasted the coconut on her skin as he took long slow licks over those tight nubs.

Best of all, it turned her on.

By us licking them.

I whined again, pacing.

A sudden thud echoed, followed by a series of tripping and thumping sounds reverberating through her home. The noise drew our attention towards the back where her nest was located. Intrigued, our ears perked up and we trotted closer to the door, eager to investigate.

We pushed our snout to the door and opened it enough so we could get inside. We stayed hidden, not that our mate was paying attention, anyway. Her bare ass was situated high over the bed, and she was shuffling through some boxes.

I wonder if she's been taken in the ass? I'd take her there; I'd take her in all her holes.

We crept closer, making sure our claws didn't click on the floor. That was when she pulled out a thick dildo in a rusty red color and hell, if it didn't look about my size in girth.

Good, I won't have to stretch her as much.

As for my knot, that might be a different story, but we will get there.

Her alluring figure reclined on the bed with her legs parted, granting me an exquisite view of her intimate region. A tantalizing aroma filled the air as she glistened, drenching the sheets beneath her. My mouth watered as I was captivated by the desire to taste her; fuck her.

She leaned over to the nightstand, opened the drawer and got out a small tube of lube. I shook my head. There is no way she needs any of that, that fucker would slide right in on its own but she did it, anyway. She dribbled it on top of the head, and pressed something on the base of the dick.

They didn't have dildos back in Elysian. At least not this—advanced. I've done my research here in the Earth realm. They have a lot of little toys that humans play with and this one also came with its bells and whistles. It rotated several times and my mate bite her bottom lip and turned it off.

"I just need to get off," she panted. "I just need to get off."

I watched intently as she spread her lips; she stuck the head in and arched her back.

Oh fuck, this was too much. My wolf was sinking his claws into the floor, surely leaving holes inside.

She slid it in, feeling a satisfying click, then gently pressed the sleek On button. A soft hum filled the room as she let out a subtle moan of pleasure. Her other hand delicately tugged at her pierced nipple, she shivered, most likely sending a tingling sensation coursing through her body.

With her legs spread wide, I had the perfect view of her fucking herself. My wolf is going mad, wanting to push to the surface, but, damned if I was going to have him jump on the bed and fuck her in this form.

But then, I felt my front leg snap.

Panting, my mate turned off her vibrator and looked around the room. I ducked behind the table so she couldn't see, and became completely quiet. You could hear a pin drop. With her lust-filled eyes, she resumed her ministrations, pumping the giant dick in and out of her pussy.

Hell, you can hear it sloshing in and out of her.

I gazed at my front leg and saw it was out of place, but from where it was broken I knew all too well it wasn't to change into my human form. It was into a form I'd only done once before—.

I kept the low growl to myself and slunk onto the floor. Her bed was shaking, her arousal had filtered through the RV, but if I was going to leave and not watch her finish, I was taking a souvenir.

There on the floor lay a pair of her yellow underwear. I grabbed it with my claw, slowly backed away out of the RV and shut the door slowly. I felt another crack on my other leg and I fell to the ground with a thud.

I snarled, unable to move my two front legs. Another crack and another. My back was no longer hunched over, it was rearranging, my hind legs longer while my front legs grew shorter. But my claws, they were retractable, I felt them sinking in and out of my body as the rest of the transformation completed.

I stood up straight, on just two legs, my paws were wide and sunk into the mossy earth. My chest was broad, fur covering most of my body and I could feel the power hum through me. I wasn't completely healed. I could still feel the aches and pains from my transformation, but as I looked at myself, I knew I was changing all the same.

The last time I felt this sort of power, I destroyed—

I shook my head. My mate was on the other side of that RV. Fucking herself. I could hear her, could damn near taste her arousal on my long tongue. I licked my large fangs and breathed heavily, gazing into the window.

The rod between my legs was a testament that the bond was working. I couldn't remember the last time I was able to get it up, let alone get it this fucking hard.

For the first time in ages, I took my alpha lycan's cock - long, thick, throbbing and a knot ready to be planted into my mate - in hand. I rubbed my palm across it, feeling the tightness of the skin. I groaned, my wolf growling in my chest at that exact moment and I leaned our wolfish head on the window where we could still see our mate fucking herself.

A glistening layer of sweat illuminated her face, reflecting the dim light. She ceased her self-pleasure, her fingers toying with her adorned nipple bars. Envious, I observed as she bit her lip, gently rolling her nipples between her fingertips.

She was edging herself! She wasn't allowing herself to come.

What a naughty, sweet female.

I picked up her underwear, from where I had dropped them, and lifted them to my nose. I took in one long whiff, smelling the sweet musk coming from it. It brought me and my wolf to a frenzy, a dire need to just go into that RV and rut her.

I knew what he did. He forced this shift, just like the time before—

This time for better reasons: to claim her.

But I still held on to some strength. We couldn't go in there. I would not fuck her like this. Yet.

I took her underwear and wrapped it around my cock, letting her scent engulf it.

I groaned as I felt the fabric rubbing against my throbbing erection, and my wolf groaned in pleasure. I took a deep breath, my chest rising and falling with my labored breathing. The lust in me was overwhelming, and I struggled to maintain control.

My heart raced as I heard the soft moans from the RV. I did my best to watch, see her face, the way her body moved as she took the implement and shoved it inside her. I leaned against the RV and felt the muscles in my body tighten. I wanted to be inside her, to feel her warmth and tightness around me.

Soon I will take her.

It wouldn't be soft and loving, it would be fucking animalistic. My mate would like it, she's tough, strong. I could feel it.

I'll take her in this form, and in my human form. It's what they did in the old ways.

As I held her underwear tightly in my hand, I felt a sudden surge of power coursing through my veins. My wolf was urging me to break free, to transform once more, to let me be human again and claim her as mine. But it was too soon. I knew I would fail the shift.

Pushing the urges aside, I took a deep breath and let it out slowly. I needed to calm down and to think clearly. I couldn't risk our lives or our bond on this desperate need for her. I watched my mate closely and focused on the sound of her moans and the scent of her arousal seeping from her home. I needed to focus my energy on the reality before me.

I sped up my pace on my cock, watching as my mate came closer to her orgasm. She was going to come; she couldn't handle anymore. She was finally going to reward herself.

Sweat dripped from her brow, her breasts heaving, beautifully shining in the dim light of her room. My cock leaked, dripping on the forest floor below as she moaned, flicking her clit as she stopped the continued thrusts of her fake cock.

It took all my restraint not to howl into the forest when I finally let my seed fall into her underwear, to the forest floor and all over my hand. I kept coming, letting years of my seed, that was waiting, be released. I panted heavily, my knees buckled and I landed in the dirt.

My bones cracked, my body seized. My elongated body shortened and I returned to the wolf I was once before. I huffed out in exhaustion and my mind clear for the first time in years.

This must be the post-nut after glow all the mated ones talked about.

After several minutes panting and regaining my strength, I heard the door to the RV opening. I took my paw and shoved her underwear under the trailer.

"Hey there," she muttered, still flushed from her self-fucking. "Sorry, I got you all clean and left. Now that you are clean and less infected, you want to come inside tonight?"

She gave a small smile and waved me forward. She was wearing a robe and her RV smelled like her.

Of course I'm coming in. I jumped up, and I felt my joints crack. I stretched them and my mate made a face of pain. "Maybe I need to get you some joint meds for senior dogs."

I jerk my head toward her.

The fuck?

I just shifted twice in twenty minutes and nutted all over the side of your RV, I'm going to be damn tired.

"Come on, I've got steak." She waved me in with a smile.

I huffed, trotted up to her and hopped into her home. At least I was here, invited this time, and with this simple invitation I'll make sure I'm here every time she is.

CHAPTER TWELVE

Emm

"She slept in this morning," Luis whispered into the phone. "Abuela took me to school."

I sighed and leaned on the table. I wasn't going to call my family anymore during this mission but I couldn't help it. I missed them and, having been around so many people being nice to me, well, I felt nostalgic. Call me selfish, I guess.

My wolf was happily eating the chopped-up, raw steak, on the floor beside me, off my nicest plate. Which I got from a thrift store ten years ago. He was eating like a king.

"I heard that! Emmie doesn't need to know my business, now give me the phone!" Elena's English was thick with her Spanish accent, and I couldn't help almost spitting out one of my microwave meals.

Luis screamed happily and ran off, and Elena picked up the phone and huffed. "I stayed up late last night editing a blogger's article. Of course I slept in. It wasn't because of the pain."

I rolled my lips, biting back any sort of retort. She needed sleep, at least eight hours, or she would feel the pain again. "I said nothing. Luis just worries about you, as any child would about their mother."

Elena sighed into the phone, her frustration evident in the way her breath trembled. "I don't want him to worry, but Abuela always has to bring it up. She keeps making these tonics, shoving them down my throat. I'm scared of what's in them, Emmie," she whispered harshly into the phone. "What if she put some of her 'shrooms in there? I can't be hallucinating right now."

I snorted and took another bite of the overly-cooked meatloaf. "She's just trying to help. Is she playing with her rocks again?"

"Crystals!" I heard my abuela yell from the background. "They are crystals and they have healing properties and they can pull destructive energy from one's body!"

I could hear her chanclas hitting the bottom of her heel from here and I winced. I remember too many times where she smacked me in the back of the head as a child, when I did or said something wrong.

"Ey, don't hit me!" Elena shouted. I could almost see Elena putting her arms up in surrender, but Abuela laughed.

"I won't, but you stop talking about my rocks—I mean crystals. They are keeping us safe in this godsforsaken place. Why do you think we have never been ransacked by any of those Venezuelans? Why do you think no one has ever beaten-up Luis? The magic!"

I put down my fork and stared into the phone.

"Are you practicing voodoo, again?" I snapped. "You said you would stop that nonsense when you left Mexico."

"She's done it the entire time we have been here! Ouchie!" *Smack, smack.* I can hear the chanclas hit my sister a few more times.

Better her than me.

"I told you not to worry her! Now, go rest before I hit you again!"

Elena swore under her breath, and the chair made a long noise, scooting back. "You will get yours, you old bat," I heard Elena say in the distance.

Suddenly, she screamed out. "The hell! How is your aim so good?"

I burst out laughing, my food falling out of my mouth.

"Years of practicing on your sister. Now go!"

I rubbed the back of my head. I think I can still feel that bump when she really got me, before I left and told her I'd be a bounty hunter. I hope she couldn't throw this far north.

"Now," Abuela started.

I groaned and leaned my head back into the chair. Here it comes. She was going to lecture me. Elena couldn't keep a secret, not with Abuela. No one could, she would get it out of you, and I wouldn't be surprised if she had a secret tonic she put in the food or drink.

"What is this that I hear about you liking it up there? Having second thoughts?" She hummed excitedly.

I lifted my lip up into a snarl and hunched my back over my food. "It's fine. Just a quirky town. Nothing to get excited about."

Abuela's voice filled with excitement as she let out a joyful hum over the phone. I could almost see that mischievous grin in my mind. "And what do you think of him? He compliments your personality, si?"

I paused, hearing a licking sound, and as I looked down at my feet I found my wolf licking the dildo I had used just an hour ago. I gasped in horror and left the phone.

"No! Dios Mio! What are you doing? Give me that!" He growled as I grabbed the base. He clamped down on it with his teeth and I swatted his nose. He whimpered and I pulled back. "Bad dog, you don't do that!"

"Emmie? What are you doing? You have a dog?" Abuela cackled over the speakerphone.

I'm glad one of us finds this amusing.

"It's a wolf," I retorted, placing my now pierced-with-holes dildo on the table. "He's grown attached to me so I let him become my companion. For now. I'm thinking about kicking him out, though."

The wolf whimpered, and Abuela laughed again.

"Don't be so hard on the animal. I am surprised you are even toying with the idea of letting it around you. Never thought of you as being the nurturing type."

I snorted in agreement, staring face to face with my new pet. I wasn't one to take on pity projects, but then again, it wasn't pity. It was something else I couldn't put my finger on.

"Hey, what did you mean earlier? About what do I think of him? What are you talking about?" I pushed away my meal, no longer feeling hungry.

"Oh, you know, the man you are supposed to meet? He is your soulmate, Emmie, the one I made you and your sister pray for so many years ago. It's about time you met him. I feel it in my old feeble bones. I was promised you would find him before I passed and I'm getting close."

I wrinkled my brow. My hand landed on the table with a smack. My wolf put his head on my lap, nudging me as if to comfort me.

"What the hell are you talking about? You're not dying."

Abuela groaned. "Remember the bonfire? The moon was full? The sky was clear? It was the perfect night. I can sometimes feel the forest spirits inside my body when I take just enough mushrooms."

A groan escaped my lips as I massaged my temples, trying to alleviate the pounding headache. She was probably tripping on acid that night.

"Abuela, you took us camping when Elena and I were kids, and you were as high as a kite. If I recall correctly, you were topless." I closed my eyes and leaned my head back. "A memory I keep trying to forget," I whispered.

My wolf snorted, and I rubbed the top of his head.

"I was not high! I was filled with a gift of discernment, Mija. You are to do great things with your soulmate. He's close, you've met him already. You just have to open your eyes and see."

I tapped my finger on the table. "Are you high right now?"

"Yes!" I hear Elena's yell come from the other room. "Ouch! How the hell can you throw a chancla around the corner?"

I snorted out a laugh and held my wolfs' head close to me.

"I'm telling you, Emmie," Abuela warned, "Elena and you both prayed to the Moon Goddess that night. You both asked to open your souls to her blessing. You wanted a love so powerful, so strong that nothing could break it."

"Abuela," I muttered, "we were children. We didn't know what we wanted. We didn't know what we were saying. Real love doesn't exist, look what happened to papa and mama".

Abuela's hand slapped the table. "No. It is true. I have seen it. Your match is there. Stop the head-hunting and open your eyes. You are where you are supposed to be. All will fall into place, and, mija...?"

As I fell into silence, a tear betrayed my feelings, cascading down my face.

"Yes, Abuela?"

"My time is short."

I shook my head. "No, it is not. You are using your crystals, remember?" I huffed out a laugh.

"Mija, my time is short and even crystals and tonics cannot keep me alive forever. Just know that I love you, and try not to fight so hard. You are a stubborn woman and, honestly, your soulmate might like that a little, so yeah, play hard to get. But, only a little."

I rolled my eyes and laughed. "Okay, okay, whatever you say," I humored her.

She was a crazy woman, but she had a heart of gold. She practically raised us and I wasn't about to argue with her. Her throwing skills were pretty amazing, too, so I would not chance it.

"Well, you get some sleep. I want you well rested once you meet him, you hear me? And, no more hunting. Promise me?"

I pursed my lips together and crossed my fingers. "Sure, sure."

"Mija," she growled. "Don't make me get another chancla."

"Alright, I promise!" I squeaked.

If there was anyone I was truly scared of, I think it was my abuela.

She hummed into the phone and hung up so I didn't have time to smart back.

Little did she know, I didn't have a decision on the matter, until I'd met the target. And, I definitely didn't believe her in this whole soulmate thing. I was thirty-seven and hadn't met any men that made me feel like my soul was on fire.

They were all boring and not worth giving up my lifestyle. I needed more excitement. None of them would live up to my expectations in the bedroom, even if I thought they were promising in the beginning. Had they never heard of foreplay?

Who the hell wanted to just fuck? Can a woman get a little foreplay? A few red flags? Like tie each other up, hunt each other down, play rough?

Ugh, I have to stop reading those BDSM romances.

I huffed out a breath, grabbed the lock box and threw the burner phone inside. I'll destroy it in the morning.

It was pitch black in the RV. The curtains were closed, and the fridge was humming quietly. I could hear the wolf's soft snores when I woke up suddenly, from the jingling of a bell from one of my rudimentary traps.

Why didn't the camera alarm turn on?

"Shit," I hissed, and tried to move.

Tried being the word here, because the sweltering heat of the wolf was on top of me.

He was supposed to be sleeping on the floor.

Another jingle came from the outside. It was quiet enough the intruder may not think I had heard it, but I most certainly did. The wolf's growl was deep in his chest. He stood up on the bed and covered my body.

"Get off, mutt, or I'm gonna stab you!" I muttered and pulled a knife from the drawer beside me.

He eyed me, annoyed, but did what he was told and watched me with curiosity. I stood on the bed and unlocked a hatch above me. It didn't creak, not when I oiled the shit out of the hinge. I had to always be prepared if I ever needed to use it as a getaway or in this case, sneak up on whoever was outside.

I squeezed halfway through the top, cursing myself for the extra fries I ate the night before and peaked out the other side. The intruder was tall, thin, lanky, wearing all black and, from eyesight alone, did not yield any weapons on the outside of his body.

I put the blade in my mouth and squeezed through the rest of the way. My nightgown pulled lower on my breasts. Poor intruder might get a show before all this was said and done.

I crouched on the balls of my feet, watching where he was going, and I saw my wolf walking out the front door like it was a fucking Sunday afternoon. The intruder didn't see him, but I'd be damned if my wolf got to him before I did.

Before I could wave my wolf off, the intruder surprised me and he came to the back of the RV where the ladder was. He started climbing, coming straight for me.

Well, this will be fun.

The wolf sat and watched. He didn't seem to be worried or territorial, he was just wagging his tail! I shook my head. *What the hell is up with this stupid animal? Is he protective or not?*

Once the intruder came closer, I saw he was wearing night vision goggles, but he wasn't paying attention to what was in front of him. I leaned forward and put the blade to his neck.

"Lookie what I found? A little squirrel climbing up my tree," I cooed, pressing the blade closer to his neck. "Climb down, otherwise there will be more than nuts you'll be missing."

CHAPTER THIRTEEN

Locke

S witch, the little prick.

What the hell was he doing here?

Switch wasn't an in-the-action sort of wolf. He was a young wolf, reject-ed far too early by an older female who didn't want to have a young wolf as a mate. Granted, she wasn't that much older than him, but she wanted someone stronger. Switch was weaker, but he was as smart as a whip.

I took that back, now, because he was on the wrong edge of a blade. Worst part was, my mate was turning me on with how fucking sexy she looked when she threatened to cut off his balls.

I swear he was about to piss his pants.

I should not get horny about this. He's a pack member, I should inter-vene.

But, it is so entertaining.

She followed him down the ladder. I stepped up, my teeth bared and a low growl reverberated around him. As soon as he landed, his eyes widened in fear and his night vision goggles clattered to the ground. The musty scent of damp earth filled the space, intensifying the tension. He stumbled, his body hitting the cold, hard ground.

"Yeah, let's not piss off my friend here." My mate played with her blade. "Not to sound cliche, but I need to know who sent you before I run this over your throat."

Switch squeaked and shook his head, pulling off his ski mask. "No, please, don't do that!"

My mate lowered her knife, her eyebrow rising. "I've seen you at the bar. Squat? Swat?"

"Switch," he said plainly. "It's Switch."

"Whatever. Why the hell are you on my roof and how the hell did you find out where I am?"

Switch went to stand, brushing himself off. "Well, we all know where you have been staying. We wouldn't be a good club if we didn't know when an outsider was hanging around our town."

My mate narrowed her eyes, the muscles in her arm tightening.

"That so? So, why hasn't anyone else come to visit my humble home?"

"We were told to stay away," he grumbled, and shoved his hands in his pockets. "Except one person can't let it go, and frankly, she scares the shit out of me."

"Tajah!" my mate said, without missing a beat.

Switch's gaze didn't meet hers, and I puffed out my chest. Fuck yeah, my mate is smart.

"I know she has been out to get me from the start. Now, what does she want? What were you doing?"

Switch shuffled his feet and stared at the roof of her RV. "You've got an electronic scrambler on top of your RV. I was gonna disable it, so I could get into your computer and phone, and see what you've been doing and why you are here."

Emm snorted. "Yeah, works a little too good right now. My cameras are out, and you tripped a simple wire to let me know you were coming. You kinda suck at sneaking around, you know that?"

Switch's face turned red. "I know." He rubbed the back of his neck. "But, Tajah knew I was the only one that would do it. Everyone else is following orders to leave you alone. To give you a chance."

My mate's eyes softened before they hardened again. "If Tajah's threatening you, you should have told me. I'd talk to her." She gripped her knife. "I don't like bullies and if you feel uncomfortable in your own club, your president, who is supposed to protect you, should take care of it."

Switch's mouth opened and closed, and then he shook his head. "I'm a guy, I don't—she didn't—"

"You all helped a guy named Garret at the grocery store. He says he owes the Iron Fang his life."

"That's different. He was fifteen when he was saved. A child."

"So?" my mate snapped and stepped forward. "If the Iron Fang is all it's cracked up to be, then it should be able to take care of its own members." My mate jutted out her jaw and crossed her arms. "I'll talk to her. I won't tell her or anyone else that you said anything about her being a bully or that you were here, but I'm gonna put her in her place."

Switch shook his head. "Nah, you don't wanna do that."

"Why? Think I can't handle the witch?"

Switch gasped in surprise. "You already know she's a witch?"

I groaned and leaned my head back, cursing to myself.

"Ha, she thinks she's a witch, huh? Let's see her cast a spell on me."

Shit, shit, shit. This is not good.

"Yeah, I'll take care of her and her little guard dog that follows her around all the time."

"Cat, she's a guard cat," Switch corrected.

My mate made a face. "Okay? Now why did you need to get on my computer? What are you looking for?"

Switch gazed at me and back at my mate. He swayed back and forth, awkwardly shaking his head.

He was already in a shit pile so deep when I got my human form back, he better not lie now. I stepped forward, and he screamed.

My mate let out a laugh and petted the top of my head. "The wolf won't hurt you. At least, I don't think so. Just don't do anything threatening."

Switch kept his hands out, ready for my attack, but I stood in front of my mate trying to cover some of her cleavage. As much as I enjoyed the view, she was close to a nip slip.

"H-have you named him, yet, or do you just call him Wolf?" he asked.

Dammit. What is he doing?

My mate tilted her head. "I haven't, but I have one in mind." She crossed her arms, lifting her heavy breasts.

I'm sorry, what were they talking about?

"And...?" Switch prodded.

"Fenrir." She scratched behind my ear. "He's fierce, and monstrous in size. I think it's the perfect name."

"Oh," Switched nodded. "Hawke will be disappointed," he whispered. "Don't you want to name him Fluffy? Something nicer?"

My mate scoffed. "Why would I name him Fluffy when he has patches of hair missing? If anything, I should call him Patches."

Switch snorted and laughed, his arms going to his stomach.

I snarled at both of them, leaving them to laugh amongst themselves, and stood away from them.

Those little pricks.

Once they were done, Emm stood closer to Switch. "I don't think you have bad intentions, Switch. I know you are trying to get information for Tajah, but I can't let you in my computer. Besides, I've got a firewall you can't beat once you get past my scrambler."

Switch huffed, "Bet I can."

"Doubt it, but if you can, I'll teach you how to be more stealthy in the forest. Because you are terrible," she giggled.

Switch kicked the dirt and pouted. "I'll show you."

Emm ruffled his hair. "Anyway, no, you can't know what is on my computer."

"So, you do have something to hide?" he challenged.

My mate frowned. "Are you going to give me every secret of the Iron Fang?"

Switch shook his head.

"Then, you don't need to know mine. Now, what do you need to tell Tajah to keep her off my back for twelve hours, before I have a talk with her?"

"Don't worry about that," Switch said. "She's out of town. I don't know when she will be back."

My mate nodded. "Fine, gives me time to prepare for my little meeting, then." She grinned. "Now, go on home, and I'll take care of everything else. Don't worry about a thing."

Switch's body relaxed. "Thanks, I—owe you."

Emm waved her hand. "Don't worry about it."

Switch turned to leave and the knife she'd been holding all along went flying. The hair on my back stood straight up and my claws dug into the dirt, ready to protect my idiot member, but it sailed past his head and into the tree next to him. He jumped with a squeal and stared at the knife just inches from his head.

"Hey, Switch. Don't come back here unannounced, okay?" My mate smirked at Switch and he nodded his head shakily.

"Y-yes, Lu—I mean Emm."

Shit, I think I'm in love.

Emm waited until she no longer heard his footsteps. It didn't take Switch long to leave the woods and step on the road. I could hear him start up his bike and rev it several times before speeding off.

I must have been in too deep of a sleep to even hear his bike. Emm wouldn't have been able to hear it with her human ears, but since I've become stronger, I should have noticed.

My mate woke me. She was the one that brought the intruder to my attention. It was the first time I slept where I did not have nightmares of my past, my wolf running aimlessly through the forest thirsting for hunger.

It was because of her, she was helping my body rest but I could not rest like that again. Not when she had—for the second time— an intruder in our territory. She needed to be protected, even though she was quite strong for a human.

There were other things lurking. Magic, shifters, hunters, hell, even myself.

Emm let out a long sigh and walked up to the tree, pulling the blade from the splintered wood. She flicked it back and forth, running her thumb across it.

"What happened to my protector, huh? Are you getting lazy now because I'm giving you free steaks?"

I said nothing, my ears drooping with guilt. She was right. I had been careless, but when you sleep beside, well, on top of a beautiful woman's breasts, why would you want to wake?

She let out a happy huff and rubbed her hand across my maw. She took her thumb and went over one of my scars several times. "You've been through the wringer, haven't you, Fenrir? Just like me?" She said the last part so quietly, I don't even think it was meant for me to hear, but of course I did.

My mate walked past me, took slow steps up the RV and opened the door. I stayed sitting, ready to take my punishment. I was supposed to protect her—warn her, and I didn't. I deserved to stay out in the darkness and let it swallow me alive.

Yet, she stayed at the door, rapping her fingers against the metal of her home. "Come on, you can make it up to me by keeping me warm. I have to admit I was sleeping pretty hard, too."

My ears perked up and again she tapped the side of the RV.

I'm a selfish bastard and would not say no. I bolted inside before she could change her mind, and her laughter filled the inside. My nails clicked on the hard surface of the floor and I jumped on her bed, rounding the soft blankets several times and waited until she arrived in the bedroom. She leaned on the door frame and shook her head.

"For a wild animal, you know how to make yourself comfortable." I huffed out a breath and pawed the covers for her to come over. She smiled, put her knife on the bedside table and curled up under the covers. I took the chance to curl around her and she didn't push me away, she didn't show she was afraid and didn't tell me to get down.

"Strange towns, bikers, big wolves and witches, what else am I going to find?" She yawned and closed her eyes.

As she drifted off to sleep, my mate let out a contented sigh, her hand finding its way to my fur as she buried her face against me. I could feel her heartbeat steady and her breathing slowing into the rhythm of dreams.

I gazed over her body and memorized as much as I could; her shape, her smell, the shade of her hair. I took in long deep breaths, making sure I kept her scent to memory; if for some reason I ever lost tabs on her, I would always find her. Even if we had not bonded, I knew I would.

I watched her hand pause as her sleep grew deeper. The tops of her hands, her arms and even parts of her shoulders held scars from the Goddess knows what. I don't know what fights she's had before she met me. No longer will she fight alone. She has me now, and I will be by her side during it all.

The first fight she would deal with would be Tajah. I understood Tajah was looking out for the pack as a whole. She wanted to know why my mate ultimately came here, but obviously, I already knew. I'm a step ahead, like always.

Just follow my fucking orders.

It was hot as hell that my mate wanted to put the witch in her place. If she knew she really was a witch, would she even dare? But, her sense for danger, the unknown, is strong. She knows something is off about the town and club. I hope that will make it easier for her to know what we all are.

I smirked to myself and gazed down at my mate, knowing that our body chemistry would spark to life during this one night alone, as her face was buried deep within my fur. Her body would crave me, and it would be one hell of a confusion for her.

I would never fuck her in this form. I prefer to use hands to sink into her tender flesh, watch my nails, my claws, sink into her soft skin. Besides, humans find it too taboo, but hell, I was a human under this fur. I could still have those feelings.

My wolf purred, his tail swishing back and forth on the bed.

But, in our lycan form— mmm, that will be fun.

My wolf growled approvingly and my excitement grew. He could hear me!

We were so close, so damn close, to being human.

I took one long lick of her bare shoulder, up to her neck. She let out a needy moan, her back arching and her ass pushing into my side.

My wolf groaned when we smelled her arousal seeping from her body.

It looks like we needed to practice our shift for the big night. There was going to be one hell of a reckoning when I was through with her.

CHAPTER FOURTEEN

Emm

For the next few days I did my usual. I continued to infiltrate the town, concentrating more on the townspeople than the Iron Fang this time. Although, somehow, the ladies of the club would lead me back, or my body gravitate, toward the bar by the end of the day for a last meal.

I talked to Garret again at the grocery store. I frequented the establishment, but made sure to use their self-checkout, more often when I had to buy another burner phone, to make sure I didn't look too suspicious.

Garret was more than happy to talk about the Iron Fang the more he saw me. He praised the cult biker bar for keeping the town clean and saving his life, but never went into more detail that I really needed. None of the townspeople did. They either didn't know or gave roundabout answers.

They seemed rehearsed, giving the same vague answers repeatedly. Should it surprise me? At this point, no it didn't, because this whole town was something magical, just like the subreddit page said. There was a magical mist to the town and everyone in it. I had become Alice in this messed-up scenario.

After becoming stressed and, beyond, frustrated that my search was coming up with nothing, I asked Garret if he knew of anyone named Locke. He paused, like his brain had to reboot and finally, he drew in a long breath and rung up my bottles of water for the day.

"You know, it sounds familiar, but I can't say that I know him."

When he told me that, I wanted to shake the kid. This job was going to take more than a month: it was going to take longer because now I was beginning to understand why the price was so high on this man's head. He was untraceable. This was a dead fucking end.

On top of it all, when I spoke to Elena the night before, she'd been able to bring up in conversation with Abuela, who Reyes Claudio was– the male that was buried out back behind my RV.

Abuela did not know, and she told Elena she better not fall for another man soon, because her soulmate was going to come find her.

I could only handle so much crazy right now, and I was at my tipping point. Not that it mattered because tonight was Ladies' Night at the bar, and on this Ladies' Night, the men were welcome to come entertain said single ladies.

Well. Fuck. Me.

And literally, because I was a hot, wet mess down south, and I think if I could find me a man tonight to let off some frustration, it would be better for everyone.

It didn't help that my libido shot up ten points in the last couple days and with Fenrir wanting to be by my side when I was at the campsite, I couldn't very well take care of business with him there.

Or could I? Do animals notice that sort of thing?

Not that I could fuck myself with anything. Fenrir put holes in The Prolapser, and I did not need an infection from wolf saliva. No offense to Fenrir, even though he's been getting heavy doses of antibiotics.

I was sure one biker would have some big-dick energy that I could satisfy myself with tonight. I'd shaved in all the right places and put on the sexiest pair of lingerie I could find. I just hoped I would find a man that could handle all of this.

When I stepped into the bar, the party was already going. The sun had already set and, since the lift on the mandatory curfew days ago so that people could stay out past sunset, I wanted to be fashionably late.

The atmosphere was electric, with pulsating music filling the air and pulsing lights illuminating the room. The dance floor was packed, filled with individuals moving and swaying to the rhythm. The live band on stage was delivering an energetic performance, captivating the crowd with their talent and infectious energy.

As I made my way further into the bar, I noticed vibrant signs scattered throughout, boldly announcing "Ladies Drink Free" in eye-catching fonts and colors. The bar was buzzing with excitement and laughter. It was clear that this was the place to be for a night of lively entertainment.

The one strobing light crossed the dance floor. Men sat talking amongst themselves around wooden tables. Their eyes were fixed on the dance floor, watching the women but not intervening. Women, radiating confidence, gracefully pulled men from their seats, hopping and jumping with excitement with each step. With warm smiles, the men obliged, while their faces lighting up as they relished in the attention.

The women were comfortable. It was good to see that.

When I found a seat at the bar, I searched for Anaki. He wasn't behind the bar, but this time on top. He didn't have a shirt on, he was sweating and damn pole dancing. My eyes went wide as he and several other guys were humping the different poles spread out on the bar, and the ladies were eating it up.

As Anaki caught sight of me, he swiftly ducked behind the gleaming bar counter, his agile movements accentuated by his glistening, oil-slicked skin. Beads of sweat cascaded down his face, adding a subtle sheen to his features. Leaning over the counter, he locked eyes with me and playfully winked, his voice carrying a hint of mischief. "Well, hello there, sugar. You made it."

I cleared my throat and looked away. He was a good-looking guy, but he didn't make my pussy flutter. He had become a good friend, someone fun to joke around with and seeing him—like this - was different.

"Aw, come on, can't handle me at my worst. You don't deserve me at my best!" Anaki rubbed his hand down his abs. "But, really, I think this is my best."

I snorted and pushed at his bare shoulder. "Just get me my drink, you perv."

In a few short minutes, he returned to my side of the bar and held out a Pina Colada. I raised my eyebrow and took the fruity drink. "I know you have more than one drink. It depends on your mood."

My lips parted, but he tapped the bar before he hopped back on it again and started rubbing his body up and down the pole, with the women in the bar going wild for him.

Ten minutes passed and I saw people continue to come through the door. The bar was packed, filled with mostly women and the bikers who stay here. The men of the town weren't allowed in, only the club members. Which I found strange, but I guess this was a haven for women to let loose and party since the men here are supposed to be saviors.

It didn't take long for Journey and Delilah to find me. They were in way too deep already with their alcohol and luckily Delilah's baby isn't here. Nadia told me earlier she wasn't going to make it because she had a hard time with loud noises. Bear and Nadia volunteered to watch Hannah and take her up to their cabin in the mountains.

"Another!" Journey handed me another shot.

I'd lost count how many I had drunk, but I knew I was feeling tipsy and that I shouldn't drink any more. I needed to still know my surroundings; at least try to work.

"Here, have a blow job, too!" Delilah yelled over the music. A shot glass with whipped cream slid down the bar and Delilah shoved it into my mouth.

"Dios Mio, I'm not as young as you two. I won't wake up in the morning!" I licked the whipped cream off my face.

"You're not old!" Delilah licked the salt off her hand. "You are like a few years older than us, right?"

Journey stared at Delilah like she was crazy, and I shrugged my shoulders.

"Sure, hun, whatever you think." I took a sip of water to cleanse my palate. "I'm going to go run to the ladies' room."

Journey grabbed my arm and shook it. "Be quick! They are getting ready to do body shots!"

Delilah squealed and clapped her hands. "Oh, these are so fun! Yes, hurry and come right back. Right here." She poked my leather skirt several times and then finally the wood of my seat.

I laughed, slid off and made my way through the throng of people. I cut through the dance floor; the bodies were moving enough that it was easier to slide through. But, when people rubbed up against my body, I felt my skin light on fire.

I should have taken care of myself before I left the campsite.

Why was I so damn horny?

As I reached the hallway that held the bathrooms, I pushed my skirt down to straighten out the wrinkles, hoping to regain a sense of composure. The dimly lit hallway felt eerie, casting long shadows that seemed to dance ominously on the walls. The air was heavy with an unsettling stillness, and a sense of unease washed over me.

In the darkness, I couldn't shake the feeling of being watched, causing the hair on the back of my neck to stand straight up. A sudden gust of cold air sent shivers down my spine, as if invisible hands were wrapping themselves around my breasts, tightening the grip on my chest. Goose-bumps formed on my arms, and a primal instinct urged me to flee from the mysterious presence that seemed to lurk in the shadows.

My breath caught when my hand wrapped around the doorknob and the heat of a body enveloped me. My hand reached back, an instinct to grab the assailant and switch from defense to offense. But, they were quick as lightning, faster than I have ever encountered. They pulled my hands behind me with one of their hands, their hips pushed into my ass and I felt a very large, prominent erection digging into me.

I gasped, but I didn't scream. Not when the sense of wilderness, un-tamed nature and raw masculinity invaded my senses. The arm snaked up between my breasts and their hand wrapped around my neck. The hand was thick and muscular, and instantly I felt my body wanting to surrender to the dominating aura pressing me to the door.

What. The. Hell.

I blinked several times, trying to regain my composure. I tried again to turn around to see who had me pinned against the door, but his grip tightened, stopping me in my tracks.

I moaned and there was a sense of familiarity in this body, this heat. I continued to struggle and I heard a low, reverberating chuckle in his throat.

I froze, my heart pounding in my chest as I struggled to find my voice. "W-who are you?"

He said nothing, but kept me pinned against the door. He prevented me from seeing what he was doing, but I could feel it. His head dipped and his teeth pulled at my top so my shoulder was bare. The heat from his breath traveled between my cleavage and I let out a whimper.

Oh no. Do not submit.

He breathed heavily, his lips pressed against my neck and trailed down my shoulder.

"Oh, oh, what are you doing?" I pressed my thighs together.

Because, God, I was going to come just from him kissing my shoulder. Why was I that desperate? *What was wrong with me?*

My underwear was soaked, I could feel my heartbeat in my clit, all because a stranger had me pinned against the bathroom door.

The Iron Fang was supposed to be a safe place, but was it safe? They had a perv back in the bathroom area rubbing up against me!

But, you want it, Emmie. You want this faceless man to keep up with these ministrations; you are just too chicken to admit it.

Did that bother me, right now? Obviously not, because I had one needy pussy and I let intuition go out the window. The tension in my body released, and I let him pin me against the wall further without fight. With his cock nestled between my ass cheeks, he let go of my wrists and used his hand to cup my breast.

I whined, needily.

My breath hitched as I felt his rough fingers tweak my nipple, sending shockwaves of desire coursing through my body. My eyes searched the darkness, trying to determine the identity of this mysterious man. His body was muscular and powerful, with muscles that rippled beneath his clothes. A faint scent of smoke and sweat hung in the air, adding to the allure of this forbidden encounter.

I've had my share of companions over the years, but I haven't had one this muscular before. Few men want a woman as extra as me.

As his lips traced the line of my jaw, down to the sensitive spot below my ear, I panicked. What was I doing? I was risking everything, including my safety, for this fleeting moment of sexual hunger. But the pleasure I was experiencing was too intense to resist.

His hand trailed from my breast and across my soft stomach, but before he reached that sacred space his hand disappeared. The warmth of his body, his lips from my shoulder—all gone.

I turned, hoping to see him still standing there, but there was nothing. Just me, in an empty hallway and with an extremely upset vagina.

I turned to the wall and balled my fist, punching the thin wall. I left a hole there and let out a menacing growl.

What the hell did I just let happen?

This wasn't me, not me at all! I let someone grope me, and I freaking liked it. I, at least, know the face, know the person before I let anyone ever touch me. But, the touch, and the fire they had in their fingers. It was like he knew what I liked, even knew who I was.

I don't know if I found that disturbing or a turn-on.

I snarled and kicked the door in to use the restroom. First, I gazed into the mirror and wrapped my hand around my neck. There were no bruises, no marks showing that they were ever there. I was almost disappointed. But I think I was more disappointed that I didn't know who the hell that was.

Because if I knew who he was, I would go find him and tell him to meet me out back and get a real party started.

Hmm, does he want that? For me to find him?

Because, I most definitely would.

CHAPTER FIFTEEN

Locke

With a wicked smile, I savored the sight of my mate storming out of the bathroom, her footsteps echoing amidst the bustling crowd. The unmistakable scent of smoke lingered as she pushed through the throng of people, determined to reclaim her seat at the bar.

"I don't think that was wise," Bones drawled and shoved a large needle into my arm.

I didn't even wince. I watched her from the shadows as she swayed her hips. I could still smell her. Her arousal was potent; the pheromones she leaked were mouthwatering, and it was taking everything inside me from finishing what I started.

My fingers itched to slip into that sweet leather skirt she was wearing and graze her clit to a taste. Just a small one. Hell, I bet she would orgasm with just the flick of my finger.

Granted, I thought she would fight a little more with me but we were both hanging on by a thread there. Night after night we were so close to each other, and we had the bond weaving us tighter together, trying to get us to complete the inevitable.

Doing something so wicked with an animal never crossed her

mind—and I didn't blame her. To her, I was nothing but an animal. A beast, a wolf. She would never think to do anything like that with me.

In her sleep she nuzzled deep within my fur. She moaned and withered against me. If she was awake I'm sure she would have been mortified.

"When have you ever thought anything I do is wise?" I smirked and rubbed my arm where he'd injected the thick serum. It was similar to the medication that was given to me before I went rabid. It was to help suppress my wolf, but it wasn't going to work. I was far too strong now.

Do I tell him that?

Nah.

I'm doing it to appease him. He was such a damn worrywart, and I had to keep some of my members from losing their heads.

"I'm just saying, Anaki might not enjoy having to patch up holes in his bar." Bones eyed me as he put the syringe away. "And as for upsetting Emm, you don't want her going off her rocker and punching one of the guys if she thinks it's them."

I growled and balled my hand into a fist. "She wouldn't dare think it was someone else. She knew it was me."

My mate had to know my scent by now. She knew my touch, my warmth and my body. She had been with it every night while she slept. That was why she submitted to me. If it was anyone else, I knew she would overpower any unmated, soul-broken person in this bar. She was that strong.

"Never—that wouldn't happen," I said, more to myself.

Bones eyed me warily and pulled out a blood pressure cuff.

"Get that damn thing away from me. I don't need it." I pushed him away and gazed over the railing. Watching her.

"I need to make sure you aren't gonna shift when you get down there. When your blood pressure rises, you shift. Just let me get a base on what you are right now."

I leaned over the railing. Bones did his thing while I watched the club chant over the music. Everyone had hovered around the current couple doing shots. Savannah was laying on the bar. Her belly button was being used as a shot glass and the valley between her covered breasts had a trail of salt. The male in question sucking and licking her skin was Surkash.

As soon as Savannah jumped on that bar, Surkash claimed her so no one else would. We all knew they were mates. Everyone could feel it, but he had yet to claim her as his. Members had tried to get them together but, for some reason, he wouldn't take the jump.

Yet, he wouldn't let anyone else touch her but him.

If anyone knows about not feeling worthy, it's all of us. Yet, Surkash's resolve is stronger than anyone's.

Savannah arched her back when he went between her breasts and grabbed his head, pulling it closer to her breasts. Once he was done, he stared at her and pulled away, leaving her behind and alone on the bar.

Embarrassment flooded her face, and she covered up. Her friends were there to cheer her on, but you could see she was upset.

Fucking bastard, I'd have to threaten him.

"You mean talk to him?" Bones raised a brow.

"Said that out loud?"

Bones nodded. "Blood pressure is stable," Bones said and ripped the Velcro off my arm.

I shifted a few days ago. It was one of the most painful shifts I've had since I was a pup. The worst part was I could only hold my human form for an hour at a time and the clock was already ticking. I needed to get down there and touch my mate, better yet taste her.

When I walked into the bar buck-naked, no one flinched. My men gathered round, slapped me on the back and handed me a beer, and it was back to business as usual. Yet, when I shifted back into my wolf again suddenly, that was a reason for concern, but Bones made sure everyone gave me space.

My wolf was still unpredictable. He wasn't speaking to me, and could have times of complete control, usually at dusk when I needed to hunt. When we were around our mate, I had the control. She soothed him, but around the club, with all these unmated idiots, could cause a reason for concern. That was why Bones was up my ass.

Hammer almost got his leg bitten off, when I spontaneously shifted and he came over to pet me just this afternoon. Good thing Grim had some quick reflexes.

Why the fuck Hammer tried to pet me I wasn't sure, but those mechanics were separated for a reason. They were born on Earth, not in Elysian. Earth-born shifter traditions were different. All that had to change, though. We all needed to be integrated and understand each other.

"It's my medical advice that you don't pursue her yet, Locke." Bones followed me to the stairs as the next woman got up on the bar. This time it was Journey lying on the bar and Grim hovering over her, pouring a shot in her mouth with his own. "You might shift in front of her, then what?"

I sighed, my mouth coming into a frown, and stopped halfway down the stairs. "She's my mate, and I'm the president here, Bones. I know how to handle what's mine," I snapped.

Bones snapped his mouth shut and bowed his head. "I'm sorry, Pres. Didn't mean to offend you, it's just—" He paused and darted his head to my mate, who was sitting at the bar, laughing. "Just don't want your shot messed up. We can't go on without ya."

I stepped up onto the same step as my medic. "Don't you think I know that?" I blinked at him. "Don't you know how much I think about the decisions I make, every day? About the club, about me, about her? It's all about everyone else, but you know what?" I shot my head to my mate. "It all boils down to our happiness, too. It comes down to our connection. If there isn't any of that—there is none of this." I waved my hand out over the members' heads. "And, she and I have our own demons, Bones. We have our own shit to deal with. It ain't gonna happen as fast as you want it, it ain't gonna happen the way you want it. So, back the fuck off and let your alpha handle it the way he sees fit, and worry about your damn self instead of everyone else."

Bones bowed his head again and bared his neck. A complete sign of submission. I huffed, my mood nearly ruined when I walked down the spiraling metal staircase. When I reached the bottom, Hawke was leaning up against a pole, watching my mate and his.

"Finally, Bones needed a new asshole."

I grunted and took in two long, calming breaths. Being questioned made my wolf angry, even if we weren't alpha status, yet. I built this bar from the fucking ground up, gave Bones a place to stay, which helped him live longer. Now, we were getting mates. How fucking dare he question me.

Just like fucking Tajah.

"Is Tajah back?" I muttered to Hawke, watching as Journey and Grim continued their show on the bar.

"Yes." Hawke took a sip of his beer. "She's at the cabin with our new guests. She will remain there and she was given a warning to behave."

I gritted my teeth and glanced over at the private door near the bar where Switch hides. He had the door open, per my request, so Grim and I could keep an eye on him. He was hunched over the computer, a bag of chips on the desk, his hand buried inside, scrounging for more food. I shook my head and straightened my shoulders.

"Good, let her know she isn't to come back to town and to watch over the guests until I say. After her job is finished, she still may face more punishment."

Hawke smirked. "Good, can't believe she went against orders."

I hummed and tried to calm myself, gazing at my mate's backside. She was glancing around the bar—trying to find *that* someone who could have touched her. She was failing, and disappointment was showing on her face, but Delilah kept bringing her back to the show on the bar.

My mate shifted her legs, crossing and uncrossing. She could feel my heat. I just knew it. At least her body knew of my presence. She just didn't know my face. Fuck, what if she didn't like my face?

Not that it mattered. She was mine, and she didn't have a choice.

If she didn't like it, I'll just make her sit on it.

Oh, so fucking soon, I was gonna make her squirt on the bar. *It wouldn't be the first time the bar had been defiled.*

"Tajah might be powerful, but once I gain alpha status, she won't be able to use much of that magic shit on me. She needs to know her place." I crossed my arms and watched Grim take his mate off the bar. It was almost showtime.

"You ready for the big debut? What happens if she refuses to get up there?" Hawke nudged me and gave me a wide, fanged smile.

I jerked my head toward my mate. Delilah was leading her up to the bar. They already had a stool ready to go to sit her up there.

I knew she wouldn't say no. She was fucking horny *before* I started sucking on her neck minutes ago. Hugging her breast with my hand was just icing on the cake.

The auction would begin soon and that was when I would seal our fate. The auction was rigged. Only the males that were destined to be mated to the woman on the bar were allowed to be up there. If we knew a woman didn't have a mate in-house, she was refused politely, and told there was a sign-up list and would have to try another night.

I'm a fucking genius, I tell you.

My mate hopped up on the bar, smiling. Anaki made her lean her head back and poured a mouthful of tequila straight into her mouth. Some dripped down her neck and instantly my tongue swiped across my lips.

Showtime.

I took a deep breath and headed up to the bar, my club mates cheered, not by my name, just a general cheer to keep my name hidden—for now.

My heart pounded in my chest as I made my way toward the bar, my eyes never leaving my mate. She was beautiful, her laughter infectious, and I couldn't help but feel a surge of protectiveness wash over me when Anaki grinned and blindfolded her.

"Let's make it interesting," Anaki announces. "Let's make her blind!"

Emm let out a loud gasp, laughing, but holding the blindfold in place. "That isn't fair!" She shook her head, but Anaki whispered in her ear it would be worth it.

"Alright, who's ready to claim the lady for the night?" Anaki called out, his voice laced with mischief, as a wild dragon grin crept across his face.

I stepped forward, leaning on the side of the bar next to her thick thigh. I nodded my head in confirmation to Anaki.

My eyes locked on my mate's lips. I could feel her excitement, the trepidation, the hint of fear at losing one of her senses.

"You got it, brother," Grim said, clapping me on the back. "Remember, bid for her."

I took a deep breath, squaring my shoulders and stepping up onto the stage. The room fell silent as I raised my hand, and I heard a murmur ripple through the crowd. I could feel their eyes on me, judging me and watching me like a hawk.

"Start the bidding at $20," Anaki called out.

It was a low bid, but it always was. We were a low-class biker bar. I was the only one with the money, so the business helped keep food on the tables and a roof over their heads. The extra cash they earned on their own.

I sucked in another deep breath, my heart pounding in my chest. This was it. I was doing this. The introduction of our luna, and she didn't even know it. I raised my hand, I didn't even yell it across the bar. I was close enough she could hear it, and that was all who needed to know the bid.

"One grand."

The room erupted in gasps and murmurs, and then silence. But I didn't care. No one was going to bid against me, no one ever did bid against the other mate, but they always gave as much as they could.

Anaki broke the silence, and the rest of the bartenders banged the bottles on the table. The music started again, and Journey and Delilah laughed and squealed in Emm's ear telling her what a catch I was.

Fuck yeah, I was a fine catch.

I stepped in front of my mate, spread her legs and placed myself between them. I put my hands on either side of her hips giving them a strong squeeze. I could feel the heat of her cunt on my stomach as I leaned in close to her ear.

Goddess, she smelled just like a Pina Colada.

"Hey, Princess, I couldn't help but stare at those gorgeous lips all night. Now, what can those beautiful lips do?" My mouth grazed her earlobe.

Her breath hitched but without missing a beat, she replied, "Hurt your feelings, probably."

CHAPTER SIXTEEN

Emm

It was him!

I couldn't pinpoint the exact reason how I knew, but something in the air told me. Maybe it was the warmth radiating from his body, the electric sensation of his touch or even the intoxicating scent that enveloped him. His voice, husky and filled with desire, stirred a deep longing within me. In that moment, I had never felt more turned on and wanted in my entire existence.

He bid a thousand dollars on me, while the other women got a few hundred. Who was this guy? And why did he want me out of all the women here?

Journey and Delilah said this was just about the night; the bar and a consent to having him drink a shot off my body. More things could happen if I wanted to—which, hell, I wanted them to. I was so fucking wet my skirt was getting really uncomfortable, and I worried that my deodorant just would not be enough.

I sensed the gentle tug of Journey and Delilah, their delicate touches pulling at my shoulders, urging me to lay on the bar. However, a resounding N*o* echoed from the male standing in front of me. I felt the weight of his thick, calloused hands as they trailed down my leg, sending shivers of anticipation through my body. The scent of his musk lingered before me as he wrapped his hand around my ankle, his fingers playfully toying with the strap of my shoe.

The crowd's deafening roars filled the bar, the glasses clink and drinks were swiftly placed around me. Splashes of alcohol cascaded onto my legs and arms, leaving a sticky sensation. With a sudden jolt, he positioned the shoe beside my hip, prompting Anaki to release a startled yell, "Oh shit, this is completely unexpected!""

My muscles tightened as the man before me gently spread my thighs apart. His hand settled on the innermost region of my leg, sending a shiver of pleasure through my body. I surrendered to the touch, and a gentle moan escaped my lips.

"You like that?" he whispered into my ear, his breath warm and tantalizing.

Surrounded by a roaring crowd, their cheers sounding like the roar of the ocean, my indifference remained unbroken. My attention remained fixated solely on this man, with his fingertips delicately exploring the tender flesh of my inner thigh, evoking an electrifying sensation that sent waves of bliss cascading through my body.

As his warm hand ventured higher, I was acutely aware of his thumb gently grazing the moist fabric of my underwear. A rush of adrenaline coursed through my veins, quickening my heartbeat and causing my breath to hitch. This long-awaited moment filled me with a sense of anticipation and desire that had consumed me all night.

Suddenly, I heard a commotion behind me. Journey and Delilah were arguing with Anaki about my consent. I heard them yelling my name over the music but I couldn't focus on their words. I was too caught up in the rush of desire that was coursing through my body.

"It's okay, it's fine," I managed to whisper, my voice barely audible over the roar of the crowd.

I could nearly feel the smile on the man in front of me. "Is it now? You trust me?"

"I trust I will get what I want," I retorted. My heart was pounding, but it was not from fear. It was anticipation, excitement and something else – something darker, more primal.

He leaned in closer, his breath warm on my skin as he whispered, "Well, trust me when I say this, then: you and I will both get what we want."

His scent was intoxicating, a blend of the outdoors and desire that was making me drunk. I could feel his breath on my neck, warm and heavy, a low, husky whisper against my skin.

"And, I don't think one night is going to give me everything I need from you."

Did he really think he was going to get one more night than this? I didn't do more than one night—wasn't my style.

"And what is it you want?" I asked, the timbre of my voice low and sultry, a promise of the pleasures to come. "What is it that you want from this?"

I was genuinely curious about what he wanted. This was supposed to be just a one-time deal, but his touch, his breath fanning my skin and the mystery of not seeing him, piqued my interest.

I couldn't see his eyes with my blindfold, but my mind flashed a deep, dark green with gold flecks inside. I saw the hunger there, devouring me. With my senses heightened, I felt his fingers trace my dampened panties again.

He leaned down and whispered in my ear: "I want to taste you. Every inch of you. And, if I'm going to take my time with you, I'll need more than just a night."

His words sent a rush of heat straight to my pussy, and I felt myself melting against the bar, my body trembling. He was going to do it; he was going to follow through with his promise.

He pushed my skirt higher, and suddenly the crowd cheered even louder. I felt his warm tongue lick the inside of my parted thighs and I leaned my head back.

"Open!" Anaki shouted and placed a lime wedge into my mouth, the pulp facing out and tapped my chin to close my mouth.

Delilah screamed and gently tugged my shoulder. "He's putting salt where he licked you, oh Goddess, that is so hot!"

My chest heaved, the sound around me becoming louder, the taste of the lime exploding in my mouth. And then, that was when I felt his hand wrap around my lower back and pull me towards him.

"Hang on there, Princess. I'm gonna take care of you."

He leaned in, his hand reached behind my neck and pulled me into his lips. He sucked on the lime, but I felt the heat of his mouth. His nose brushed against my skin, and I was lit on fire. It was all I could do to sit up straight, and not moan and wither under him.

As he released his grip, a rush of air filled my lungs, and the warmth of his presence dissipated. Curiosity tingled within me, wondering where the alcohol would find its path. Suddenly, a sensation trickled down my leg, a cool liquid tracing a delicate path down my calf, eventually reaching my feet. His touch remained gentle, as he clasped my ankle softly. Then, in an unimaginable act, his lips enclosed around my toes, sending shivers down my spine.

"Total submission!" someone cried out.

The bar went wild, and for the first time in my life, my mind went blank.

He was tasting my feet.

He wasn't shy; he was sucking and licking, and, it was so fucking hot to have a guy do that.

Suddenly, the blindfold came off and I was able to see the man who had my body tied up in knots. He'd got those dark green familiar eyes that I had pictured in my head, and his tongue was slowly licking up my leg. He reverently sucked on my ankle and gave me a wicked grin.

Holy fuck balls!

He slowly continued to lick the remnants of the alcohol up my leg until he reached my widely spread thighs. The salt was there, I looked at him and back at my leg and I nearly shook my head.

Nearly.

I wasn't a quitter, and I wouldn't get all shy just because I was in a bar.

He palmed his crotch and bit his lip as he lowered his head. He took long, slow licks and my eyes rolled into the back of my head. With each tantalizing lick, I imagined him just moving his tongue centimeters to the apex of my thighs—to lick just where I wanted it.

He took a deep breath, inhaling my scent, and then with a low growl, he pressed his mouth against my panties, his tongue licking the outside of my underwear.

He. Did. Not!

My body curved, my back arching as I pressed my heated core towards his eager mouth. My hands tightly clutched the cool edge of the bar, the sound of the bustling crowd fading into a distant hum. A soft, not at all embarrassing moan escaped my lips, blending with the roughness of the bar. His firm grip on my thigh sent shivers over my skin, while his daring finger slipped beneath the fabric of my skirt, effortlessly tearing my delicate lace underwear. The touch of his skilled tongue danced over my pulsating nub, igniting every inch of my hypersensitive skin, and unleashing a torrent of pleasure that drove me to the brink of madness.

I was lost in the sensations, my body writhing under his skilled touch. I glanced over at my friends, wondering how they were taking this turn of events. But I was quickly lost in the rhythm of his tongue when I came crashing down in a mind-blowing orgasm.

The biker stood with remnants of my arousal on his lips. He licked it clean as the patrons of the bar passed around more beers, excited about the entertainment. As I was getting over my orgasmic haze, he stood up, his erection straining against the fabric of his jeans.

Shit, what the hell was that?

And can we do it again?

Without a word, he pressed his lips to mine, his tongue sliding into my mouth, tasting the sweetness of the lime I had held there earlier, along with my arousal. His hands gripped the back of my neck, pulling me closer to him as our tongues danced together.

As our kiss deepened, the man slowly made his way down my body, palming my backside. I could feel my body responding, my nipples hardening under his touch and my arousal building with each whisper of his breath.

The crowd was wild, cheering him on as he continued his lovemaking using his mouth and tongue. I was lost in the moment's ecstasy, my body writhing under his skilled touch.

I pushed him away, the heat of the moment being far too much. There were people here, and if he didn't stop now, I'd probably fuck him on the bar.

"Too much, Princess?" He gave me a crooked smile that would have made my panties melt if I had some.

"Never," I panted. "Just figured you might need a moment."

He raised his eyebrow, then cupped my face and gazed at me like I was something precious, and not just a fuck buddy for the evening. It was a feeling I wasn't sure I liked or not.

"Funny, you weren't worried about me complaining when my head was between your thighs."

My face heated and I pushed him away. "I was caught up in the moment! I never thought a man would ever do that in front of his friends." I smiled.

"There are a lot of things I'll do in front of people to show off my claim." His face went dark. "And I mean a lot more." The darkness from his face faded and he pretended to bite my shoulder as I laughed. "And—you should smile more. It suits you."

I pushed down my skirt and threw a lock of hair over my shoulder. "Hey, don't let this smile fool you. I can go from zero to fuck everybody up, real quick."

"Princess, you are speaking my language. I like a woman with fire."

"Funny, I thought you like women's toes the best."

The man pouted his lips and nodded. "Only certain toes, and let me tell you, you have perfect toes. I wouldn't mind sucking on them later." He wiggled his eyebrows, and I playfully shoved him again.

We both laughed, but our eyes never left each other. I was drawn to him like a moth to a flame. He was dangerous, that much I knew. He had it written all over his face, the scars on his hands and his arms. He was trouble, but my body wasn't getting the message.

When the silence became thick I realized this stranger had me completely under his spell. He was not only a master of pleasure, but also knew how to make me feel comfortable and desired.

Maybe it was the booze, or maybe I just needed a good time. But I needed something, and this guy was going to give it to me.

I grabbed his arm and pulled him closer, our bodies pressing against each other. "Take me to your bed," I whispered, my voice breathy and husky.

He raised an eyebrow, a smirk on his face. "Are you sure you can handle this? I'm an animal in bed." He laughed at his own joke.

I snorted. "Yes," I replied, never more certain of anything in my life. "Just promise me we won't stop until we're both completely satisfied."

He nodded; his eyes filled with a fire that mirrored my own. "What the princess wants, the princess gets."

I shimmied my skirt down my leg. My face reddened at what the hell I just let happen. He smirked, holding out his hand and helping me off the bar. We made our way through the crowd who were cheering us on as we left. We stepped onto the metal spiraling stairs, and once we reached the top you could see the entire bar. It was the perfect view to see everyone partying. The dancing, the drinking, the laughter, I had come to love every part of this place—but I still had a nagging feeling in the back of my mind.

My own family. My flesh and blood. I still needed to save them. One night; just one night, then back to work.

My mystery man - I still didn't know his name - led me down a corridor full of doors; apartments I realized, and he jiggled the door handle to the first one. He pushed it open and shoved me inside, pressing me against the wall and slamming his lips against mine.

The door shut with a slam, but the bass of the music outside vibrated within the walls. My toe-licking male groaned into my mouth as his hands roamed up and down my body until they rested on my ass. He massaged and squeezed, feeling the fullness of my backside.

"Fuck, this is the best ass I have ever seen or felt. I can't wait to bury my face in it."

Oh, an ass man. Finally!

His sharp teeth pierced through my tender lip, sending a jolt of pain that made me release a throaty, pleasure-filled groan. In that moment, it was as if a switch had been flipped, transforming him into an entirely different being. Gone was his gentle and playful nature; now, he exuded an intense forcefulness, like a primal creature driven by raw instinct. Every movement he made was harsh and unyielding, his determination palpable in the air around us. The scene was charged with a mix of excitement, pain and the musky scent of our bodies blended in this wild encounter.

And I was here for it.

He wasted no time taking off my top. He didn't comment on the bra I wore and how it had to hold up my heavy breasts. He gazed at them with such intensity I swore the bra would melt at his stare. "I've been waiting to hold you beautiful girls," he spoke to my breasts, as he unclasped the front. They fell in front of me, and he was there to hold them, while he groaned in happiness.

"Fuck, fuck, fuck, all mine. Shit, Emm, I'm gonna come in my pants, right now."

I wasn't a crier but, hell, did it feel good to have a guy tell me how much he loved my body? The stubble on his cheek grazed my sensitive nipple and he sucked it into his mouth. The barbell clicked against his teeth and I grabbed his hair, pushing his face further into my chest, like he could take the whole thing in his mouth.

"Easy, or I'm gonna hump your leg," he mumbled, and I laughed.

He traced my nips and bit between the two breasts; biting hard

Unlike most men, he didn't only care for my curves, he relished my thick thighs and my large breasts. He buried himself in them and touched every single inch of my body as he worshiped, kissed, nipped me.

He released his grip, yet rather than undressing me further, he focused solely on my ample chest. With a feverish intensity, he traced his fingertips along my skin, leaving a trail of goosebumps in their wake. The sensation of mixed pleasure with a hint of pain, as he gently sank his teeth into my flesh, imprinting his ownership upon my breasts.

The teeth marks, the hickies and scratches, and the pain that came with them, all raised my pleasure higher. I wanted more; I wanted to see him and I wanted to touch him.

He took a hard bite around my throat. I squealed out in pain, arching my back. He paused, staring to check if I was okay, but the only word that would escape me was, *more.*

More bites, more scratches. Hell, I wanted him to slap my skin and leave marks, and if there was a next time, maybe I would tell him all my fantasies because it seemed like he was more in tune with my body than anyone else ever was.

"Perfect; every inch of you. I haven't even thrown you on the bed, yet." He lowered himself and picked me up, my legs wrapping around his waist. I felt his prominent erection and my mouth watered.

Oh shit, he was large. Dare I say, he could surpass The Prolapser.

I gyrated my hips, rubbing my pussy across his cock, and he sucked on my neck hard. "Princess, you can't be doing that, yet."

"Why is there a schedule?" I giggled.

He laid me down on the bed, my breasts bouncing as he crawled on top of me and planted a sweet kiss on my lips.

"As crazy as it sounds, yes, there is a schedule," he curled his lip into a smile. "And I'm very particular in what order I have my meal."

I shook my head, rubbing one of the bruises he'd left on my chest. "You're crazy."

He chuckled, "I've been told that a time or two."

CHAPTER SEVENTEEN

Locke

I pulled at the barbell on her nipple with my teeth and she pulled my hair, causing me to let go with a click.

"Damn it! Please," she begged.

She wanted my name to scream it on her lips. I wanted to give it to her, so bad, but it would ruin the moment. She'd do what most women did; *think* and use that mind of hers.

Thinking was bad, especially right now.

All I wanted to do was sink into her cunt and let us succumb to the bond that had us clawing at each other like savage animals.

"Mate, call me that." I snarled, showing indifference.

I scraped my nails down her leg to leave a sting and let my fingers dip between her folds. Damn, she was wet; so fucking wet.

"All this for me?" I purred. "Fuck, this is hot as hell." I pressed kisses down her soft stomach, rubbing my face along her neatly trimmed pubic area, and took a tentative lick at her clit.

She took a hard grab of my hair and pulled me away. "I'm not your mate—" She took in a breath.

My mate's eyes met mine and I swear there was a longing in those narrowing daggers. I've seen her stare at the other women in the bar. It was a feeling all too common that I have felt before. To want to be wanted, to feel loved and cared for. But Emm was not a woman to be trifled with. She had a hell of an attitude, senses that put my brothers' to shame and she needed a male that could meet her sort of crazy.

A male like me.

A strong alpha, headstrong enough to tame a luna and, so fierce, yet soft enough to let her be free to be her own person.

I inserted two of my fingers into her wet core, feeling the intense grip as it clenched around them. She arched her head back, releasing a soft moan into the air.

"You bastard." She gritted her teeth.

With reverence, I passionately embraced her, sensing her body convulsing with pleasure. Her rhythmic hip movements guided me as I became her support. Oh, her beauty was breathtaking, as I witnessed beads of sweat trickle down the crevice between her breasts. I delicately traced my tongue between them, savoring the sweet tang of the alcohol left on her skin.

"You're fucking beautiful, Emm." I added another finger, and she whined, feeling me stretch her. "I bet you could take another, couldn't you? Take four of my fingers?"

She shook her head, and I bit my lip teasingly. "Look at me and tell me you don't want it."

Her eyes opened, and no words left her lips. If I added a fourth, it would be near the equivalent to my knot. Did I want to stretch her that far yet? Or would I rather use my knot to do such a devilish act?

"Who are you?" She breathed and wrapped her arm around my neck.

We were centimeters from each other's lips, staring straight into each other's souls. Fuck, I never thought I could love someone, not after what I've been through. I'd been betrayal by my previous mate, and pack, but looking into her eyes knowing that she was hunting me down didn't deter me wanting her. It fucking turned me on.

The bond was nothing but a tool of evil, and I was going to let it consume me.

"Someone you will never get rid of." I pumped my fingers harder and faster into her cunt; rubbing that spot where she squirmed just a little more than usual.

She screamed.

Ahhh, found it.

My mate's body released a torrent of fluids, while my cock strained hard against my jeans. Fuck, I didn't think I could hold it back much longer. I might just come right now.

She breathed heavily, the sound echoing in the room, as her hips persistently gyrated against my hand. A low moan escaped her lips, urging me for more. With a passionate force, she slammed her lips against mine, fueling the intensity of our connection. In response, I gently pushed her down onto the softness of the bed, surrendering to the electrifying sensations that enveloped us.

Instead of ripping off my jeans, I slid down her body to lick up her slick. She grabbed her breast, and I licked up the inside of her leg.

"Oh my god, oh my god," she repeated over and over.

"There is no god, just your mate," I mumbled as I sunk my tongue deep inside her pussy. "And you're mine, Emm."

With a renewed vigor, I plunged my tongue into her depths, exploring every inch of her, relishing the taste of her arousal. Her soft moans filled the room, every sound driving me wild with desire. I thrust my tongue inside her, hearing the wet sound it made as I withdrew, only to plunge back in again.

Her body trembled, her sweat-slicked skin glistening in the dim light. Her passion and desire mirrored my own, fueling my need for her even more.

Her back arched, and one of the legs that hung over my shoulder suddenly went under me. She rolled her body and pinned me against the mattress. Her pussy was in my face, and I stared up at her wide-eyed, a smile on my face.

"Fuck, Princess, if you wanted to ride my face, you should have said so." I tried to move my arms, but she firmly planted her shins against my biceps, as she reached underneath the pillow and pulled out some rope.

Where did that come from? This was getting as kinky as fuck!

Emm's firm grip tightened on the coarse rope as she skillfully bound my wrists together, weaving them into a secure knot. I could feel the rough texture against my skin as she expertly wrapped it around the sturdy metal bed frame. With a meticulous eye, she ensured its stability, her fingers brushing against the cold, unforgiving metal.

She gracefully left my body and picked up her clothes on the floor.

Woah, woah there.

My cock pushed shamelessly against my jeans. My mate took one tentative look and sighed. She took her hand and rubbed up against it, her eyebrows rising when she felt the hard metal bars along its length.

"Hey, Princess?" I grabbed her attention. "What do you think you are doing?"

Emm remained silent, her actions speaking louder than words. She gracefully slipped into her skirt, the fabric gliding over her smooth skin. As I watched, she discarded her lace panties, revealing her bareness. The sound of the clasp echoed softly as she fastened her bra, accentuating her silhouette.

"Well, you haven't told me your name. Meaning, there is a significance to it. I don't fuck people I don't know. So, you can tell me your name, or I'm going to leave you here, tied up and naked, and let one of your friends come find you in a strange predicament." She stuck out her hip and put her hand on it.

My mouth dropped open. I couldn't help the smile that came after it. "You are sensational."

She raised a brow and crossed her arms. "Name?" She walked over barefoot and unbuttoned my pants. Panic struck because that was one thing I wasn't ready for. For her to see my knot. If we had fucked, I would have done it from behind, or blindfolded her and kept my knot out of her body.

"Alright, alright!" I wiggled away from her.

She laughed. She fucking *laughed!*

I never saw this coming. I see everything coming. I'm two steps ahead so why the hell did I not see this?

Because you were tongue deep in her pussy that's why.

Mates, dammit, they put you in a lust-fog and you can't see for shit.

"My name's Locke," I said frankly. There was no use hiding it. Now, I just had to act like I didn't know who she was, and that she was hunting me. Granted, I had hoped to have gotten under her skin more, but this will have to do.

Emm uncrossed her arms and stared at me, the color draining from her face. "What?"

"The name's Locke. Not unless you wanna call me something else, Princess?"

"W-why didn't you want to tell me your name before?" She pulled down her shirt over her head and fixed her hair.

I shrugged my shoulders. "I was trying to be all mysterious and shit. Women like that, right? I mean, you enjoyed it when I pinned you to the bathroom door."

If smoke could come out of her ears they would have. She growled once and turned her back to me.

"Hey, aren't you going to untie me?" I tugged on the ropes.

"No, get out yourself, you pig!" She slung the door open and marched down the hall.

My wolf's eyes widened in fear, our sharp canines glistening under the dim light. As we tugged on the coarse rope, it strained against the weight, emitting a metallic creak that reverberated through the room. The tension grew unbearable, causing the sturdy bed frame to groan and buckle until it finally snapped.

Frustration consumed us, manifesting in a low, guttural growl that echoed in the air. Determined, we swiftly leaped out of the broken bed, our hearts pounding in our chests, and stormed out of the room, our footsteps echoing down the hallway. The urgency to find Emm overwhelmed us, a desperate desire to prevent her escape. The irrational part of our mind took control, urging us to ensnare her, to keep her captive in this space with us.

As I reached the railing, peering down at the bustling bar, I could see the members' gaze fixed on her. She stormed through the crowd, determinedly, and made a beeline for the exit. Only the music played, no one spoke and I refrained from calling out, not wanting anyone to interfere. However, the unmistakable scent of her arousal wafted through the room, causing the males to search for me. It triggered an intense fury within my wolf, and without hesitation, we leapt over the railing, gracefully landing on the cold floor with bare feet.

The surrounding people stood back, shocked by our quick landing. I was about to take off when a large round of fire flew across my path. Sizzle held alcohol in his mouth and blew across a torch, causing an enormous flame.

I took a step back, my breath catching in my throat as I beheld the immense inferno before me. The scorching heat licked at my face, and the acrid smell of burning wood filled the air. My heart thundered in my chest, echoing in my ears like a pounding drum. Beads of sweat formed on my forehead, trickling down my temple. Small fires were manageable, their flickering flames often captivating my attention. But this colossal blaze had a power that transported me to haunting memories, places I desperately longed to forget.

I stepped back, my arms covering my face. Hawke shouted for Sizzle to cease the fire—his parlor trick when I am not around. Sizzle's face morphed into horror when he saw me backing away.

Gasping for air, my breath came out in ragged bursts, the sound echoing in the room. My heart pounded relentlessly, as if trying to escape the confines of my chest. Trembling, I continued to retreat, my body instinctively seeking distance. Despite the overwhelming fear, I summoned the strength to turn my gaze towards the door, desperately hoping to find my mate standing there. But, to my dismay, she was nowhere to be seen. The door stood ajar, allowing the cool summer breeze to seep in.

Fuck.

"Shit!" I let out a roar, my voice reverberating through the crowd as frustration consumed me. Gripping my hair tightly, I felt the strands slipping through my fingers. With a surge of anger, I clenched my fist and slammed it forcefully onto the sturdy oak table laden with glasses and plates. The resounding thud echoed in the corner, mixing with the sound of shattering glass and the clattering of dishes as they crashed down onto the cold, hard floor.

The music went silent as everyone turned to look at me. I could feel their disappointment and their confusion. But, in that moment, the only thing I could think about was tracking down Emm, to be close to her.

I bolted out the door, not caring about the shattered remains of the wooden table behind me. The crowd parted like the Red Sea as I made a beeline for the exit, my wolf's senses heightening to track Emm's scent.

Outside, the night air was heavy with the anticipation of rain, carrying with it a distinct earthy scent. It stood in stark contrast to the hazy, booze-infused atmosphere of the bar. And Emm's scent was slowly fading.

I heard the rumble of Emm's truck roaring to life, its engine growling like a beast awakening. In a heartbeat, I sprinted towards it, my muscles tensed for the run. With each stride, the cement beneath my feet scraped against my heel.

But, as I surged forward, a cascade of fiery images and anguished screams crashed upon me, assaulting my sight and ears. The screeching sound of her tires turned to screams as she departed. My vision blurred, and before me, materialized the haunting figures of the pack that had once betrayed me.

Overwhelmed and paused in the middle of the road, I felt the comforting presence of Grim and Hawke, which was reassuring anchor amidst the chaos.

"Let's get him back to his room," I heard Grim say over the screams.

The fire roared in my ear, the screams for help, the apologies that came too late, the sin that needed to be taken to hell; it all came rushing back, along with my wolf screaming at me to take what was ours.

CHAPTER EIGHTEEN

Locke

I found myself back in a time I didn't want to revisit. It often comes in the form of nightmares while I sleep. I'm always in the foulest of moods those days when I wake, but this time—I couldn't control the movie playing in front of me.

Surrounding me, there were rustic cabins and humble huts, forming what appeared to be a quaint village at first glance. Some of the dwellings were engulfed in raging fires, their flames dancing wildly in the air, while others now stood as mere remnants, resembling nothing more than empty husks. The scene was filled with the crackling of burning wood, the acrid scent of smoke, and a lingering sense of devastation.

Surrounded by thick smoke, I sensed the scorching heat of the raging flames grazing my fur. The pungent odor of burned timber and flesh overwhelmed the air, suffocating me. With each beat, my heart throbbed in my chest. What was left of the pack stared at me in horror—their faces pale, their bodies burned, broken and no longer healing. I observed the ruins before me, a harrowing sight that instilled fear in those around me.

They all deserved it, well most of them, except for the ones I let go free. These wolves deserved to suffer. I felt it with the very core of my being.

I stumbled forward, my eyes darting around, scanning the remaining wolves concealed in the shadows. The once bustling village now lay in ruins, engulfed in an eerie silence that hung over it like a heavy shroud. As I cautiously navigated through the wreckage, my foot abruptly collided with a small metal object, causing me to teeter on the brink of falling to the ground.

Looking down, I saw a glint of metal buried in the ashes. With trembling claws, I brushed away the debris to reveal a small pendant, its surface scorched but still recognizable. It was hers - a token of our bond that had obviously meant nothing to that whore.

I held the pendant in my paw and bent the metal, letting it topple to the ground.

The Blood Rose Shadow Pack was vicious. If pups appeared weak when they were born, the pack disposed of them, throwing them into the forest where wild animals feasted upon them. Any sickly or old wolves were shunned to the edges of the pack, the first to be eaten if there was ever a breach. The elders did not rest. They still worked weaving baskets, cooking for the warriors, and the healthier ones often hunted or gathered.

Our pack had no time to take care of the weak. If any could not take care of the pack or themself, then they would be dismissed and have to find another pack.

In those days, it was hard to find a willing pack to take any member of Blood Rose. Parents had instilled viciousness in their children. They trained day in and day out and fought for their right in line for rations. The best fighter got the bigger portions, the best meals. Most parents encouraged brawls with the siblings to teach them to fight for themselves, to show who was the stronger sibling.

All were taught to obey the gamma, beta, and most of all, the alpha. The alpha was law, giving out duties, punishments and unjustifiable deaths, to his circle. That didn't mean that the alpha didn't do a lot of the work himself.

I doubt the king of the shifters understood what went on, but as long as the alpha put out the strongest warriors, maybe he didn't care.

These wolves were the most untamed compared to the majority of the realm. But, they were the strongest, most cunning and the largest in size, second to the King of the shifter's guards. Although they did not get along with others, the alpha and the king taught them to obey them alone.

You would think everyone would want to leave a loveless pack such as this, and you would find that to be wrong. Wolves love power. They received praise for their aggression and were constantly tested on their strength and training.

The king would often take the strongest from the Blood Rose pack to use in his armies, for rogue missions. Wolves were treated better with the king, and everyone wanted a taste of being next to the strongest of all the shifters.

The alpha of Blood Rose was a bastard. It was as simple as that. Before Alpha Mordecai, this pack used to be prosperous. It had traditions of taking care of mates, raising children in the ways of the gods, and caring for many shapes and sizes of wolf shifters. They did not have the recognition of the king, but this pack flourished.

Mordecai saw unlocked potential. He wanted to seep his claws into the ripest fruit.

Beating his pack into submission and raising a new generation of wild wolves, was his thought of a good idea. He wanted to be seen and heard, to get into the King's good graces, and hoped he would soon become part of the king's inner circle.

That day would never come.

His day of reckoning was here.

Now, I stood before him in the nightmare that I'd dreamed so often; risen above him in my lycan form. The first Lycan in over a thousand years.

"And what magical entity helped procure this form for you, because surely you didn't do it yourself?" Mordecai spat as the flames of his pack danced around us. "I bet you have no strength, no power to defend yourself, that it is all but a ruse to scare me off." Mordecai clenched his fist and took a step forward.

Snarling, my grip tightened around the flaming torch, its searing heat radiating against my palm. With a fierce motion, I hurled it towards the neighboring hut, its crackling flames illuminating the darkened night. The acrid scent of burning wood filled my nostrils, mingling with the distant cries of the outraged family who had dared to pilfer from our elders.

"Isn't this what you wanted? A powerful male to take over Blood Rose? Isn't this what you planned all along so you can advance to the king's side?" I crooned. "Now you have it, a son that has risen to a power stronger than the great Alpha Mordecai. I've been beaten and tormented by you, for years. Now, you will get a taste of your own training. But first, I think we should tell what's left of your pack how you have come to your position—illegally."

Corpses burned in the dirt, the rest were ash or already being picked by the buzzards. Soot and ash covered the remaining bodies. Those who were left had hardly any fight left to give. They had lost, they knew they had sided with the wrong wolf. They had their chance to follow me before this massacre began.

Those who had decided to follow me in the end; I let them live. They had scampered off already fulfilling their duties, as I required. The rest here will die. But I had to monologue, and to monologue to just one person was boring.

"You liar!" Mordecai's heart skipped a beat.

I snarled, my claws extending and clinking against one another. I cautiously stalked around him. My lycan form towered over him, boasting elongated limbs and sinewy muscles that rippled beneath my thick fur. The air was heavy with the scent of primal power, a heady mix of sweat and dominance. Rows of razor-sharp teeth glistened in the dim light, ready to tear apart anyone who dared to challenge me. This vessel, this embodiment of my true nature, was so flawlessly designed that it almost felt cruel to unleash its destructive force upon him. Especially now, as the sting of rejection from my mate still lingers fresh within me.

"You forcefully mated with my mother, the true alpha of the pack. She was not your true mate. You raped her, forced her to mark you so you could claim this pack as your own. To defile it, to use it against all things sacred to the bonds. You, along with every other damn leader like the king, planned to destroy all traces of holiness, traditions of the wolf and mate bonds." I snarled. My arm rose back and sliced across his chest.

He roared in agony.

"You wanted mates for status and glory, not to calm your souls!"

I let out a guttural roar, the piercing sound echoing through the stillness of the night. As I howled, my laughter erupted, a cacophony of eerie amusement filling the air. I gazed up, witnessing my breath materialize into delicate wisps, intertwining with the darkness of the night sky. The crisp chill of the air prickled my skin, intensifying the sensation of pain coursing through my body.

I was the product of a forced bond; I wasn't meant to be here. Yet, here I was, one of the strongest wolves, only to eventually die because my mate rejected me for another—one with a higher status.

Well, look where she is now, amongst the ashes of her pack.

Mordecai's eyes revealed the pain and anger, but he knew he had lost the battle. He could feel his own heart slowly giving out. The poison from the wounds I had inflicted was finally beginning to take its toll. He fell to his knees, a snarl still lingering on his lips.

"You're not going to get away with this," he growled, his voice weakened by the blood loss. "Your reign will be short-lived. You will go rabid and die."

I simply laughed, the sound echoing through the night.

"Do you honestly think I care?" I asked, raising my claws high above my head. "Haven't you heard that the truth shall set you free?" My wolf chuckled. "I'm free of you Morti, I'm free of this pack and the toxic wolves you lead."

Mordecai growled and shifted, his body breaking, but before he could fully shift, before he could become his alpha wolf, I pounced on him and sunk my claws into his back. I pulled the meat off his bones, his fur, his hair, skin and muscle were instantly fileted from his body.

As Alpha Mordecai fell, his last breaths fading into the night, the remaining pack members began to scatter, their once unwavering loyalty now faltered in the face of something more sinister.

I stood tall, my lycan form engulfing me as I roared into the sky, signaling my dominance over the Blood Rose pack. The wolves that remained, the ones who had not yet been banished, now fled.

My animal took over while I shut the human part of me away. Sick, evil, menacing wolves raised by an evil alpha were all that was left of Blood Rose. They would not survive, they would not continue through the night.

I watched in the back of my mind as my animal ripped apart more pieces of bodies before me. He threw them into the fires of their homes, letting the flames engulf the entire territory. Not one home was left untouched. Each tree that stood in the territory burned to ash to leave no remaining evidence that Blood Rose ever existed.

The only ones who would ever remember it, were the wolves who actually wanted to forget the pack and me; the heir of Blood Rose who wanted to just remember my mother and my sister.

CHAPTER NINETEEN

Locke

"I'm so sorry, I didn't know he was coming out. I thought he was with her—"

"How could you not know, man? Everyone stopped talking!" Hawke snapped.

Sizzle cleared his throat. "The music was playing, I couldn't decipher voices and the music, I just—shit."

I groaned, rolling my head from side to side. My body was soaked, and there was a chill entering the room from the open window. I blinked several times, rubbing the heel of my hand on my right eye. "Ugh, why am I wet?"

"Bones threw some water over you," Grim mumbled. "Said you were overheating."

"We're wolves, of course we are going to overheat." I sat up on the cold exam table and shook my head. Water droplets flew through the air, propelled by the force, and landed on my closest comrades. The room echoed with their groans as they hastily wiped the wetness off their faces and clothes.

"He was fevering. He was far warmer than he should have been, even for a wolf. He had to be cooled down. I swore there was smoke coming off his body. You smelled the cinder, right?" Bones ran his hand through his salt and peppered hair. Worry lines were etched in his face, and long gone were the playful smiles he threw at me when he talked to my mate earlier the week before.

Sizzle laughed, "Hey, it would be awesome if he was a fire wolf, huh?"

Hawke groaned, "Those are old fairy tales. No such things as elemental wolves."

I waved my hand at Bones and steadied myself, resting my elbows over my thighs. "It's fine, don't worry about the water. I've never flashed back like that before. It was so vivid, damn near felt like I was there."

The lingering sensation of heat radiated on my face, mingling with the metallic taste of blood in my mouth. I could almost see my old pack's eyes, once brimming with life, abruptly vanish by my claws. The weight of their deaths, though justified, would relentlessly haunt me. I derived no pleasure from taking lives, especially those of the innocent. But, for those deserving, a surge of adrenaline coursed through me as I witnessed their blood staining my hands, fur and chest. Their anguish was a twisted satisfaction that got me hard when it shouldn't.

At night, I still hear their screams, an after-effect I didn't care for at all.

"Maybe it's the bond? Now that you are getting better?" Hawke offered his piece of advice.

Grim gave a shake of his head and crossed his arms. "A bond heals, a healthy bond anyway. He shouldn't have flashbacks, or so my mate says." He rubbed his chin pensively.

Journey's direct line with the Moon Goddess has given us more information than we ever could have obtained alone. Sometimes it's a pain in my ass, because Journey could only give us small pieces of information, as the Goddess slowly dealt it out.

Bones slowly retreated, his steps echoing against the cold linoleum floor.

He sought solace by leaning against his cluttered medical counter, cluttered with an array of tubes, sterile medical supplies and various items I'd paid for. He rested his weight against the counter and his head sank. The look of remorse was etched across his face, as clear as day. "I know why your dream felt so real."

Sizzle, Grim, Hawke and I stared at him, curiously, waiting for his explanation.

"Those shots that your mate has been giving you aren't just antibiotics. They have steroids in them. It's a drug that humans use a lot in their health care. It's used in a wide range of physiological functions, including growth, development energy and metabolism. Since we are part human, and we are all waiting for Locke to gain his human form, I thought he would be the perfect specimen to try it out on. He's the strongest, even if he was rabid, and look what it did." He held out his hand and waved it up and down my human form.

I stared at Bones in shock; the pieces falling into place in my mind. The intense sexual feelings even in my wolf form, the bond between Emm and me developed far faster than I could have imagined, coming from a rabid state, the flashes of memory - it all made sense now. I clenched my fists, feeling a mix of anger and betrayal swirling inside me.

"You drugged me without my consent?" My voice was low, dangerous.

Bones held up his hands in a placating gesture. "It healed you faster, Locke. I didn't mean for this side effect. Half the club will be leaving, soon, going on a mission and members were hoping you would be human by then. I was trying to help!"

Hawke stepped forward, his eyes blazing with anger. "You put our pack at risk with your experiment! What if Locke went crazed after reliving that nightmare? You don't know what he fucking lived through! What were you thinking?"

Grim's expression was stone-cold as he spoke. "You will tell us everything about these shots, Bones. And, we will decide what to do next."

Sizzle stood silently in the corner, watching the scene unfold with a mix of worry and disappointment.

As the tension in the room thickened, I felt a growl building deep in my chest. The betrayal cut deep, and I knew things would never be the same with Bones. He had crossed a line.

I stood up abruptly, the hair on my neck bristling with anger. "You are out of your damn mind! Drugging me without my permission is un-forgivable. I trusted you, and you betrayed that trust for the sake of an experiment?"

Bones held up his hands defensively. "I didn't mean any harm, Locke. I was only trying to help our pack and to help you. I promise I had your best interests at heart. I wanted our leader back, I worried—"

Hawke snorted in disbelief. "That's rich, coming from the man who experimented on our president without our knowledge. You're supposed to be our healer, Bones, not a mad scientist. You should have come to us, not decide all on your own."

Sizzle stepped forward, the dragon still hanging his head from his own mistake. "I trust Bones." I eyed Sizzle suspiciously. Sizzle doesn't trust just anyone. He's a grumpy ass at times, doesn't talk much to anyone since Grim had his mate now. "I believe he wanted to help. It's been hard, Pres. He shouldn't have gone about it the way he did, but he helped you. He got you to shift, he got you with Emm. I'm sure he calculated the pros and cons of this drug."

Bones nodded, but kept his mouth shut. He knew he didn't have the floor any longer, and he had no say in anything, now.

I sighed and pinched the bridge of my nose, my anger slowly dissipating as I considered Sizzle's words. He was right. Our pack's survival depended on helping me complete my transformation, to gain my mate and form the bond with my luna.

I turned to Bones, my expression softening slightly. "Do the shots need to continue?"

Bones shook his head. "No, Pres. You've shifted, I can let Emm know—"

I snarled, my eyes narrowing as I lunged forward and my fingers wrapped around his throat. The sound of his gasps filled the room, mixing with the thud of his back hitting the wall. The sickening crunch echoed through the room as I slammed his head against it, leaving a visible dent. The metallic scent of fear mingled with the adrenaline coursing through my veins, fueling my actions. "You will stay away from my mate, and you will stay the fuck away from me. The only reason you are keeping your doctor title, and your life, is because of what you have done for this club. Do not make a mistake like this again, Bones or I will rip you apart myself." Spit fell on his face and he nodded.

"I-I won't." He choked. "T-thank you for your mercy."

I forcefully pressed him against the rough, cold wall once more, my voice filled with anger as I unleashed a stream of curses. With a final push, I released my grip, watching as he crashed to the floor. "A week in the basement cell. He only comes out to treat our guests at the cabin. Make sure he showers before he comes out."

Sizzle gave Bones a pitiful look before he wrapped Bones' arm around his neck, lifting him from the floor. Bones said nothing as he was taken from the medic's room and I wiped my hand down my face in frustration.

"You had to do it, Bones was over-stepping. Hell, a lot of them have." Hawke rubbed his beard and leaned up against the wall.

"Who else, I want names and what they have done. This is bullshit. I thought our club would stay in line, even with Grim. Hell, I even fear you, brother." I gave Grim a smirk and he shook his head.

"I'm not an alpha. My word isn't law," Grim grumbled. "I can only do so much, and take care of a priestess that is constantly being harassed by the members trying to figure out if their mate is coming."

I huffed in annoyance. "It stops, now!"

Every inch of my being tingled with an uncontrollable urge, as if invisible ants were crawling beneath my skin, desperately seeking escape. The sensation was maddening, a relentless itch that made me want to tear myself apart. The brief respite of my human form was slipping away, its frailty no match for the transformative power coursing through me. Time was running out, and I could feel the imminent end drawing near.

A knock at the door started us from our conversation and Hawke yelled for them to open. Hammer strode in, his cut the only thing he was wearing above his waist. "Yes, uh, Pres, sir? I just got a text from your mate. I wanted to let you know."

I raced over to the other side of the room and ripped the phone from his hand. He stood back by the wall and made himself appear smaller than he was. I know logically I shouldn't be pissed at him, but fuck, why did she text Hammer?

"I need my tires. Are they still on schedule for delivery?"

Fuck. She's gonna run.

And, not stab me? I'm feeling insulted.

As I heard the sickening snap, I felt an intense jolt of pain shoot through my forearm. A guttural grunt escaped my lips as I clenched my teeth. With a trembling hand, I reluctantly let go of the phone, watching it soar through the air before colliding with Hammer. "Tell her three days." My voice broke into a growl and fur sprouted on my forearm.

"Shit." Hawke and Grim shoved Hammer out the door and gave me enough space.

I could feel my wolf inside stirring, pissed off and angry that I hadn't gone after Emm yet. He was a silent bastard, not talking much, but would let me know if something pissed him off.

"Mate," he snarled inside me.

"Good to hear from you, too," I laughed maniacally as my knees fell to the floor.

I don't think I'd ever been so happy to hear his dark voice inside my head again. He was ruthless after we were raised by Mordecai, and he could be a scary thing.

"You let her go."

Again my bones cracked. The shift from human to wolf was getting faster, but still not fast enough. It was because I was still rabid. My wolf had control of me, not the human like it should be.

I grunted, feeling the bones breaking again.

"We go to her, stay near her."

Great, now with the Neanderthal shit.

I agreed, bobbing my head and fully shifted into a wolf. Thank the Goddess it wasn't my lycan form, because I don't think Grim and Hawke could handle the bar's chaos if they knew I could do that.

My wolf shook his fur, now mostly healed, and sauntered out the door. He stared down Grim and Hawke and took us the back way out of the bar, away from the crowd until we hit the cool night air.

As we reached the outskirts of town, his sharp claws dug into the earth, propelling him forward in a determined sprint to locate Emm. The scent of the forest filled our nostrils, intensifying his relentless drive to find her. Usually, when I was in this form, it was me that was in charge, but my wolf, Fenrir as Emm had called my wolf's body, was here and making the movements.

Anxiety, an emotion I am not familiar with, surged within me. My wolf brushed it off and continued to rush toward our mate's campsite. She was outside, her shoulders slumped, staring at the tires on her RV.

"I could leave it. Just get in the truck and go." Her hair was a mess, no doubt from our actions earlier. I could taste the air of her leftover arousal but also dried, salted tears.

As we reached the clearing, Emm abruptly lifted her head, her eyes scanning the surroundings. In the dim light, she spotted us standing amidst the eerie darkness. A jolt of tension coursed through her body, but soon her muscles eased and she cautiously approached us. The crisp scent of fallen leaves hung in the air, while the distant sound of rustling branches added an unsettling ambiance to the scene.

"Hey there, Fenrir, where have you been?" She sniffed and knelt on the ground.

My wolf buried his nose in her hair, rubbing his body over her as she dug her fingers through our fur. "I had a bad night, wanna come inside?"

My wolf whined. He whined! *"You hurt her."* My wolf snarled at me.

I couldn't argue with that statement. I did hurt her, but I didn't intend to. She was the one that wanted to hurt me. She was just upset that she was so attracted to her target.

I kept quiet and watched from the inside of my wolf as Emm led us to her room. I didn't have the heart to watch her strip off her clothes and put on a nightshirt before she wrapped her body around ours on the bed.

"What am I going to do Fennie? I don't think I can stay here anymore." She frowned and stroked our fur. "You are looking so much better. You don't need me anymore, really."

My wolf whined and pawed at her.

She huffed out a laugh and rubbed her face into our neck. "Would you miss me?"

He licked her cheek.

"You would, well, then that means I need to stay, then, huh?"

He yowled and pawed her again.

She huffed tiredly and laid her head on the pillow.

When my wolf looked around, we saw that the room was in shambles. Blankets, clothes, her knives and rope were all over the floor. She either had a break-in or she was angry when she got home.

After sniffing the air, I realized it was the former. She was angry.

I would be too, I guess. Having the enemy licking your cunt could be rather... invasive.

I snorted and my wolf laid his head on top of Emm. She was out faster than I expected. Maybe I would have to tone it down a bit. Show my true intentions, show her who I really am, rather than be a sneaky bastard.

One thing is for sure, though. She wasn't leaving, and I've already got the insurance to make sure of that.

CHAPTER TWENTY

Emm

I couldn't believe how stupid I was.

Of course, everything was too good to be true. Everything fell into place too perfectly.

I was having a great time. My body was being worked with magic fingers and a tongue. Hell, I came harder than I ever have on my own, and it was by the work of some guy.

Alright, not a guy, a man. A man who needed to have his ego knocked down a few notches, but I could do the honors of kicking him off his high horse. Especially, when that man was none other than Locke.

I tried not to show any look of surprise when he told me his name. I couldn't show him I was looking for him or had any recognition of his name, and I think I did a damn good job about it. I put on a facade like I always did, but instead of reaching in my bag and chloroforming the shit out of him, I had to walk away.

Why?

Well, I'm still asking myself that same question.

I stormed out of there. Not even the girls came up behind me. I saw them in my peripheral, they knew something was up but they knew not to approach. I don't think I can describe the feelings I had, right then. There are no words.

What was I going to do?

Take this guy in, get the money and free my family from one of the poorest and most crime-ridden countries of South America? Or let him go?

I didn't even know Locke, but he was part of the Fang. He was part of this club and everyone in it had checked out. None of them seemed devious or with ill intent, and this guy was part of it. Otherwise, he wouldn't have been in the club to begin with, and the girls wouldn't have let him lick me from head to toe. Literally.

When I arrived back at my campsite, Fenrir was nowhere to be found. I think that put me in more of a state of unease, because I jumped in my RV and threw all my belongings around. I had such rage, such fucking rage; because not only was I dealing with the inner turmoil to save my family, but now taking down someone who could be potentially innocent.

"We don't hurt the innocent, Emmie." My sister's voice echoed in my head.

And what if the innocent ends up being my family? They have lived in that country for far too long. They were playing a waiting game living in that hellhole, and someone is bound to get hurt, or even die. The only reason they stayed was because the Mexican cartel didn't dare venture into that country or they didn't know my family fled there.

When I'd half decided I was going to get the hell out of here, I texted Hammer from the business card he gave me with his number. Of course, it would be three more days for me to sit here. I contemplated leaving the RV here, start over, just live out of hotels.

I burst out of the RV cursing at the stupid tires again, but then warmth, that same familiar warmth, fell over my body.

Fenrir was staring at me from the shadows, and I just knew things would be okay. How an animal companion could have such an effect on me, I wasn't sure, but damn it, I needed that big ball of scary fluff, now, more than ever.

I walked toward him slowly.

His fur was thick and his scent was even more calming, and it almost reminded me of—I blinked several times and let go of him, constantly rambling until I led him to the RV.

No, he couldn't smell like Locke. That was insane. But, the more I thought about it, the more he did smell like him.

It was a very distinct smell. Forest-like but manly. I don't know; I wasn't great with words.

As soon as we stepped inside the cozy RV, I stripped out of my clothes quickly into a large shirt. I couldn't resist flopping down on the soft bed. It felt like my big Fennie instinctively knew what I needed. He slid closer, his warm body enveloping me. In an instant, I leaned into him, finding instant comfort. The worries that had loomed large just minutes ago seemed to fade away, replaced by a sense of peace and security. The faint scent of the RV's familiar mustiness lingered, adding to the soothing atmosphere.

Now, my problems were distant, barely registering on the radar of what I needed to do next.

Maybe I wouldn't run just yet. I could gather myself, figure out if Locke really was an evil bastard, then take him out. But, what would the girls think? Would they thank me for finding out he was a jerk all along? But, what if he isn't and I waste my time, leaving my family waiting for longer?

I groaned, rubbing my face into the now thick fur of my companion.

I didn't want to leave Fenrir, either. This was his home. How terrible of a person would I be if I took him away from the wild where he grew up?

Not a very good one.

My eyes grew heavy the more I thought, so, instead I took in that deep scent of forest and masculinity. Thinking of that man between my thighs, the electricity that made my pussy pulse and those stupid green eyes that I just couldn't get out of my head.

That stupid cocky smile was the last thing I remembered before I fell asleep gripping the fur of Fenrir, purring contentedly.

The phone rang four more times until it went to voicemail for a second time. I pulled it away and hung up, staring at the blank screen. It wasn't like Elena not to answer. It wasn't like for *someone* not to answer. It was eleven their time and someone had to be up, especially Abuela. She could have been making lunch for my sister, or doing some of her magic potion, or doing some sort of drug she wasn't supposed to be doing.

After fretting last night about their safety, my anxiousness doubled. Fenrir stretched from his spot on the floor and trotted over to me, rubbing his head on my hip.

"They aren't answering," I muttered to him. "They always answer." I rubbed my neck and dialed again. They didn't answer for a third time, and I huffed in annoyance.

What the hell was going on?

I rubbed my hand down my face, and jumped when I heard my other phone ring. When I glanced and saw it was Delilah, I weighed my options about whether I should answer it. If I didn't, they may come over here, since Switch told them, they all knew where I was anyway.

I sighed and slipped my finger across the screen. "Hello?"

"Hey, there's the bar wetter, did I wake you?"

I groaned and leaned my head back on the seat. "Did that really happen?"

Of course it happened. It was one of the best orgasms you've ever had.

"Duh, we all saw it and boy, that was hot. I think all the paired couples went home and got off on it. Maybe even some singletons." Delilah snickered into the phone.

"Dios Mio." I rubbed my forehead.

"Yeah. Anyway, a lot of us are getting together at the gym to do some sparring. You said you liked kickboxing and I thought you might want to join."

I let out a deep sigh, feeling the weight of the world on my shoulders. With a gentle motion, I began to rub Fenrir's head, his soft fur gliding beneath my fingertips. As I did, I could hear his purrs resonating in the room, a soothing melody. His snout brushed against my thigh, leaving a warm sensation. The faint scent of his fur filled my lungs, comforting and familiar.

It crossed my mind again this morning; I could take my belongings and leave, but with Fenrir right here in my lap I don't think my heart could do it.

Maybe beating the shit out of someone would help me get rid of my frustration, instead of fucking it out of someone.

"Yeah, sure. Is it just guys or can the women join, too?"

Delilah's laugh echoed through the phone. "The women can join too, alright. They can even mix and match. Nadia's kicked some tail before."

I huffed out a laugh and bent down to kiss Fenrir on the snout. "Alright, count me in.”

Delilah squealed on the other end and hung up promptly. My hand still clutched the burner phone with my family's number.

One more time.

It rang only two more times before it went to voicemail, and instead a text message came onto the screen.

> **Elena:** *"We're okay. Abuela and Luis have a cold and are sleeping. Try calling later."*

I wrinkled my nose in distaste and sent a quick message back.

> **Emm:** *"I expect you to pick up next time. I need to know you are okay."*

Instead of breaking the phone, I put it in my bag with me. I'd just make sure to keep the phone with me. Fenrir stood up with me as I changed my clothes, watching every move I made.

"I'm heading out. Do you need something to eat?"

Fenrir stood by the door, with his tail wagging. I shrugged my shoulders, and he stepped out of the RV with me and strode to my truck. He watched me with piercing eyes as I stepped up into Marlow and started the engine.

"Going to guard the fort?" I shouted at him as I rolled the window down.

He didn't reply, just stood there, watching.

As I tore my gaze away and began to drive, a heavy pressure gripped my heart, compressing it within my chest. Through the rearview mirror, I observed the campsite fading into the distance, my eyes fixated until a sharp turn beckoned me towards the rugged path I'd forged. When I stole another glance behind, Fenrir had vanished from the site, causing my shoulders to droop in disappointment. With a sigh, I navigated my way back to town, feeling a sense of deflation settle upon me.

Once I pulled up to the gym, I shut the door with a slam and was immediately greeted by Delilah with a mischievous giggle. "So, how did last night go? You left in such a rush, I didn't get to ask you."

I thought the look on my face was enough, but apparently, it wasn't.

"Not as well as I had hoped," I admitted.

Delilah frowned. "Did he not fulfill what you wanted? The chemistry was freaking—"

I cleared my throat, heat rushing to my cheeks. "Ah yes, he was great. Just maybe it was a bit much." *An information overload.* Was what I wanted to say, but I kept that to myself. What could I say?

While he's fucking hot as hell, knows all the right buttons to push, he's the guy I originally came to this town for, so I can free my family from poverty, get them citizenship in the US and live free from constantly looking over their backs?

"It's complicated." I finally sighed, and pushed the door into the gym.

Delilah tutted, wrapping her arm around mine. "I don't see how it's complicated when he ate you out on the bar, just fine, and led you to his room. The guys here are great, Emmie. You need to give the guy a chance. He might be a little crazy around the edges, but the men around here take care of their own. Especially Locke."

A knot formed in my throat when she led me inside. "How do you know that? That all these guys are good? A background check can only go so far.

I'm sure they have some pasts that aren't on record." I kept my voice calm and as I spoke, made sure it didn't waver. I didn't even look Delilah in the eye, to show my reluctance as I said it because part of me knew that wasn't the case.

Delilah sighed, understanding the weight of my words. "Emmie, you're right. But these guys are different. They fight to survive, not to hurt. We've all been through hell and back, and each of us has our own story. I can tell you that Locke is a good person. He's got the scars to prove it, but they're battle scars earned for the sake of our community. He's a fighter, just like you."

I tilted my lip into a smile.

Delilah squeezed my shoulder, her voice lowered. "Emmie, I know you're worried, but I've been around these guys long enough to trust them. They're good, I promise. Besides, Locke has been looking out for us since we got here. I wouldn't be here if it wasn't for him. He took me in and gave me a home when I had nowhere else to go. I trust him with my life." Delilah's eyes watered.

Damn it, I was fighting it. I was fighting it; hard.

But why wouldn't Locke tell me his name, last night? Was it really because he was trying to be mysterious? The entire night was a whirlwind full of booze, music and let's face it, me being horny.

Maybe I was being a little—rough?

But still, I had my family to think about, and if I did not pursue Locke I needed to find another job.

"You ready for this? Ready for some sparring?" Delilah waved me closer to the ring. Two men were already in position. Their knees were bent and their arms out in front of them, until one of them leaped and attacked the other.

It was brutal. Sweat was already covering their bodies, blood was coming out of one man's nose. Grunts, growls and even scratches marred one person's back.

This wasn't the typical sparring I usually saw in a gym.

"Damn," I muttered under my breath.

"Yeah, pretty cool, huh?" Delilah puffed out her chest. "I love seeing them rip each other apart. You should see my man. He really likes to make noises and dig into them." She rubbed her hands together.

Jesus.

"Hey! It's my favorite RV tires customer!" Hammer shouted from the other side of the gym. He waved and ran toward us.

I think I am his only RV tires customer.

"Damn, you really do look just like—" Delilah swatted him in the back of the head before he could finish saying anything, and I gaped at her violence. For a thin blonde girl she had quite an arm.

"Look like who?" I asked.

Delilah glared at him and Hammer stuttered, rubbing his head. "Ah, uh, well, you really look like Sofía Vergara, the actress, you know, when she was in her 30's."

I gaped at him.

I looked nothing like her.

"You know you are right." Delilah bobbed her head. "She really does."

"I do not," I argued back. "Nothing like her, at all."

"Maybe it's her skin. They have the same glowing skin." Hammer patted his cheeks.

I pinched the bridge of my nose, listening to two men grunt in the background until a body slam knocked one out. "Just forget it."

When I turned around to see who'd won the fight, I found myself not seeing a bloody mess but a male with no shirt, glistening muscles and a smirk that really looked good between my thighs.

Locke—staring down at me.

"Well, hello there, Princess."

CHAPTER TWENTY-ONE

Locke

I had just got done doing a warmup. Maxing out on some weights on the other side of the gym, just enough to get the blood flowing to my muscles, to make me look like I had some definition. I knew I was going to look slimmer than my normal form. Being a rogue for many years had made me less defined. Fuck it, I was going to work with what I had.

Emm's narrowed eyes glanced down my torso, toward my sweats and back up my body. It was quick, but not quick enough. I gave her a panty-dropping smile and she sneered, crossing her arms over her workout top that could barely hold up her breasts.

And, fuck me, she didn't even take out her piercings as they pushed at the fabric.

Is she trying to kill me and every male in this gym?

"What are you doing here?" She cocked her hip.

I huffed and crossed my own arms. "Same as you, here for a good workout. And I challenge you. I think we might have an even match."

I turned, giving her a good view of my backside, and heard the quickness of her heart racing. She was trying to give me the cold shoulder, but I could smell her. Her arousal was undeniable.

I climbed up on the boxing ring. She huffed and puffed in exasperation and followed behind me.

"I don't want to fight you. I'd rather fight someone else."

I stood and looked around the gym. Members were punching bags, and others lifting weights. I cleared my throat, loudly and announced, "Anyone want to take on Emm for a spar?" The gym went silent, they all looked at each other and shook their heads.

Emm gazed around, grunted and walked over to Hammer. "Why not you? Come on." She pulled on his vest and he pulled back.

"Nuh uh, your thighs would break me, girl. And, I mean that in the most respectful way." He backed away, bowing his head.

Emm rolled her eyes. "Delilah, what about you?"

She shook her head. "I'm breastfeeding. You might punch my boob and milk would just shoot in your eye." She pointed at her eye exaggeratedly.

Emm groaned and leaned on the ropes, contemplating. Her nose twitched, and she sucked on her teeth while she thought.

I couldn't wait to get into that head of hers to know what she's thinking. I bet her thoughts were complicated as hell.

"Fine then, what are the rules?" Emm climbed up on the elevated platform and grabbed the tape to wrap it around her hands and wrists.

I was impressed, as she'd done this before and quickly got to work on the other hand.

Quickly, I explained the very few rules, leaving out about groping each other because, hot damn, I was going to grab every part of her.

Emm pulled back her hair, braiding it down her back. "No pulling my hair, that's only for special occasions." She chuckled and got into her stance.

Duly noted.

We both circled each other and the gym went quiet. It didn't bother me people were watching, but obviously Emm was getting nervous. Her heart and her breath were no longer in sync with each other, and her arousal was also growing.

Does she like fighting? Was this some sort of foreplay?

I'm here for it.

I tried my best to let her make the first hit and let her get me square in the cheek. I thought I owed it to her considering I had angered her by withholding my name.

"You let me have that," she hissed. "Fight like you mean it."

I burst into boisterous laughter, the joyous sound reverberating through the room. As my cheeks tingled under my fingertips, I couldn't help but revel in the sheer delight of the moment.

She circled around again, this time not even crouching. She was standing tall, like a luna would be. How she didn't know she's got luna blood running in her veins was almost comical.

I darted toward her, spinning her around, grabbing her forearm and pinning it, and me, behind her back. She slung her head back, hitting my cheek bone and stomping on my bare foot.

I grunted. She turned around and decided kneeing me in the balls would be the best option, but I grabbed her knee mid-air, and flipped her on her back. I fell with her, my cock landing at the sweet spot between her thighs. Her skintight black biker shorts and my sweatpants, the only fabric between us.

I was hard, so damn hard, and hurting from last night's affairs.

One knee was pushed up to her chest, keeping her nice and wide, while my body hovered over hers.

"You're flexible. That's good to know."

She growled at me and used the strength in her lower body to roll us both to the side until she was on top of me. Her cunt ground into me, and she pushed my hands above my head.

"You like being on top, that's fine. I'm into that too." I chuckled.

"God, do you ever shut up?"

I tilted my head and stared at her. The lights overhead were bright; fluorescents, hard on anyone's eyes, and now harder on mine because of my wolf.

The light created a halo over her head, making her face darker as she straddled me. It was like she was an angel, here to take my soul, crush it and spit it out.

She had a hold on me, and she didn't even know.

"Goddess, you're beautiful," I whispered.

She blinked and sat back, letting go of my arms.

"Excuse me?" Her face softened.

"You're beautiful. Stunning. Fucking strong. Do you need more adjectives? I don't have that many, not much of a word guy."

She scoffed. "You sure? Because you talk a lot to me."

I shrugged. "That's cause you're special."

She eyed me. "We're supposed to be sparing right now. Why are we talking?"

"Because, maybe, you don't want to fight me; because I don't necessarily want to fight you. At least, not here." I wink at her.

She emitted a low, menacing growl, sending a shiver down my spine. Instantly, an intense surge of desire coursed through me. In a swift motion, she lunged at me, her arm swinging towards my face. Reacting instinctively, I seized her arm, effortlessly overpowering her. Rolling on top of her, a rush of adrenaline fueled my movements. My throbbing shaft found its way between her legs while I rubbed against her.

I grabbed her breast and slammed my lips on hers. She didn't fight it. She'd got her hands in my hair, moaning my name. The room became silent, the doors opened and the lights went out, a signal that Hawke had everyone out.

She moved her hips in tune with me pushing my cock against her pussy.

"Mmm, Locke," she moaned into the kiss.

I grabbed her ass, squeezing the succulent meat.

"Damn, Princess, my name is good on your lips."

"Don't call me that," she moaned, when I reached up under her top.

I played with the barbell, tweaking and pulling. "This top needs to come off, I need to see it again. It's all I think about. And, that wet pussy."

"Dios Mio, you are so bad. I love it."

"If you think this is bad, you might be in trouble." I lowered my head, hiding my fangs, and ripped her tank from top to bottom. It ripped easily, then I pulled it apart and her breasts spilled out. "I can't decide what I like more. Ass or tits. It's a toss-up."

She laughed, and I suckled and pulled. The harder I pulled the more she whined. My body trembled at how my mate responded to my touch and my eagerness to keep pleasing her.

My wolf howled, his pants pounding in my head. "I need all of you exposed."

"Locke, there's people–" She gazed around the room and saw we were alone.

Her words died on her lips as I reached for her tight shorts and ripped them apart. Suddenly, she felt exposed and tried to cover herself. I swatted her hand away.

"Never," I let my growl consume the empty room, and she stared at me with wide eyes. "Never cover yourself. This body is a fucking temple, and I am here to repent of my sins."

Her body stiffened. "I am no saint, Locke."

I laughed. "Didn't say you were. None of us are. I said you were a church and, didn't you know, all churches are supposed to be full of sinners?" Her lips parted and I brushed my damp ones against them. "So, let me fill you up, Princess."

I pressed my lips to hers, slowly and sensually. Just enough to let those thoughts sink in. Because I was going to take her, I was going to fuck her senseless, and I would not be soft about it.

I'd waited too long—far too long—for a mate. Fuck the traditions I've read, we couldn't damn well do them now like I wanted. Not when time was short

Emm was mine and I'd take what I wanted. She was there, naked; fucking bare for me.

Fuck, it was going to be hard not to knot her.

I lifted my mate into my arms. Her legs wrapped around my waist, and her fingers delved into my hair when I pinned her to the boxing ring pole. Thankfully, it was double-padded because she was going to fucking need it.

My cock was fucking dripping. I felt the wetness on the front of my sweats. Moans into my mouth distracted me as I fumbled with the tie on the front.

"You're mine, Emm. I don't care what you say after this," I mumbled into her mouth. "Once it's in, that's it."

She hummed in agreement; I don't think she cared what I said, not that it mattered at this point. She was mine, like it or not.

I pulled my cock out of my sweats, rubbing my hand down my shaft and felt the bars with my fingertips.

My Prince Albert was covered in pre-come and my Jacob's Ladder was ready to be soaked. I tapped the tip against the wet folds of her pussy.

She stiffened her legs around me and opened her eyes to see me; wild with desire.

"That's a b—" she breathed.

There was no way out of this. I could feel her shaking as she stared back at me, but I didn't show any weakness. The moment had finally arrived, and there was no turning back. I reached down and guided my throbbing erection to her entrance, pushing it forward with full force.

She gasped and buried her face in my neck, her nails digging into my skin. I could feel her pussy muscles tightening around my thick cock, gripping it like a vice. My heart raced as I thrust deeper into her, feeling her warmth enveloping me. We were truly becoming one, our bond strengthening with each thrust.

"Emm," I whispered into her ear, "you're mine, now. There's no going back."

She leaned her head back as I buried my cock into her. My hand snaked up between her breasts and wrapped around her neck. I gave her a gentle squeeze, my wolf prowling forward. He wanted to push our knot deep inside, but the human part of me—we just couldn't yet. Not when she didn't know.

But he didn't get that message.

He forced himself forward and squeezed our hand around her neck, to let her know he would never let her go. I expected some push-back. My mate was her own woman, she'd lived alone for years and taken care of herself. I expected her to thrash and fight, but do you know what my luna did?

She smiled.

She ran her hand up my arm as I slid my piercingcovered dick in and out of her body. Her hand squeezed over mine, having it go tighter.

"I like it a little rough," she moaned, so I squeezed a little tighter.

My cock twitched and I pumped my cock harder into her body, hearing the groans of the pole against my thrusts.

Her eyes locked onto mine and her lips parted in anticipation. The room filled with our ragged breaths, the sound of skin slapping and the scent of passion and desire. I could feel my wolf bristling at the edge of my consciousness, eager to mark her, but I held it back for now.

I couldn't, not yet.

I thrust harder, the pace increasing as Emm's hips met mine, her body eager for more. I could feel the wetness that coated her folds growing, a testament to her arousal. My hand tightened around her neck, a silent reminder that she was mine, and I would never let her go.

I watched her face, her eyes locked on mine, her lips parted in a silent plea for more. Her breaths came in ragged gasps, mingling with my own. I could feel the tension building, the pressure of our impending climaxes threatening to consume us.

"You're mine, Emm," I growled, my voice a low, primal rumble, "and you know it."

She moaned, her hips bucking wildly against me. "Fuck. Yes, more. God, you feel good!"

I thrust harder, my cock sliding in and out of her wet heat, my piercings rubbing against her sensitive flesh. Her cries echoed through the room, mingling with my growls of satisfaction. The room was alive with our sounds, our desire and our need.

I felt the familiar twitch in my groin, the telltale sign of my wolf's knot preparing to release. I held it back, not yet ready for that final, irrevocable bond. But my wolf was insistent, and I knew that soon, very soon, I wouldn't be able to help but plant it inside her body and make her fully mine.

Emm's body trembled, her eyes wide with pleasure, and I knew I could delay no longer. My wolf surged forward, demanding to mark her as his own. I squeezed her neck, prepared to unleash my seed and coat her walls.

She grabbed either side of the ropes, her body glistening with sweat as she threw her hair back.

And as I felt my knot swell, I felt her body shake, her muscles tightening around my cock. Her eyes locked onto mine and her lips parted in a silent plea.

"Take it," I growled. "Take me, take everything I have to give!"

I gripped her ass, and her pussy strangled me. I couldn't stop myself and buried my teeth into her shoulder.

My mate cried out, her pussy fluttering around my cock while I shot stream after stream of my seed.

Her body relaxed, after she experienced the first orgasm from her mate, and her legs fell from around my body. I held her up, though, my hips still lightly thrusting to push more of me inside her.

My cock was still streaming load after load into her pussy, it was running down her leg and the front of my pants—fuck, it was a beautiful sight.

I laid her on the boxing mat, as she was panting, with her arms wrapped around me. Her hips were pushing against me, begging for more.

I let go of her shoulder, watching the blood trickle down her skin. I licked it clean, feeling the sweetness of her blood in my mouth.

My mate moaned, pushing her chest up toward me. I kissed her breasts, letting my cock fall from her body. She whined in protest and I pressed my fingers between her legs, scooping up my come and pressing it back into her.

"Shh, it's alright. I'll make it all better." I rubbed my fingers around her clit and she rode them, being greedy. "Fuck, you want more?"

My cock had stayed hard, and my knot was sensitive. I didn't know if my wolf would let me take her again without putting it in her body.

"More," she begged.

"You're come-drunk, aren't you, Princess?" I chuckled and kissed up her breasts, to her neck. I admired the bite mark. It wasn't deep enough to mark her, but everyone will know I'm close.

It took a lot of restraint not to bite too deep.

"That was—wow! Yes, I want more." She reached down to grab my cock, but I pulled her hand away.

My knot was swollen, it should be rooted deep within my mate, seated in her tight cunt and nestled within her warmth. But, being a fit mate, I've kept it to myself and now I'm going to pay the consequences later.

"Why aren't you naked?" she sobered.

I rubbed the back of my head. "I just— little shy, I guess?" I continued to shove my come back into her body. "Today was about you and—" I pulled my sweats over my erection and my, still very tender, knot.

She pushed me off and got up - the come dripping down her leg - and she hopped down from the boxing ring. "Do you have some sort of disease on your dick you don't want me to see? Is that why you won't let me see it?"

I reared my head back. "What? What are you talking about?"

Emm, shook her head and grabbed a random shirt hanging on the ropes. *Some other male's shirt.*

I snarled and stood. "Take that off."

"No." She stood firm and pulled it over her body. She tilted the chair where the shirt lay over and it crashed, echoing into the empty room and walked toward the door.

I jumped from the ring and stalked toward her. "Take. It. off."

"Fuck you!" she roared.

I chuckled darkly. I didn't think I'd ever had anyone tell me that in all my years since I arrived on Earth. It was–refreshing.

I grabbed hold of her shirt, gathered it in my fists and ripped it from top to bottom. Before the shirt fell to the ground, she landed a punch right to my nose. I stumbled back feeling blood tinge the back of my throat, where she'd broken it.

I snorted loudly, letting out a haughty laugh and wiped away the single drip that fell from my left nostril. "I was going to offer you my shirt instead of that sweaty one."

Emm stood there, her beautiful body marred with my marks and bruises, completely unashamed. I turned, grabbed my black shirt and handed it to her.

She ripped it from my hand and stalked out the door. My wolf snarled and bashed against me. My skin itching and the fur on the back of my neck sprouting.

Fucking hell—what a time to shift.

CHAPTER TWENTY-TWO

Locke

"We'll be fine on our own," Bear said confidently, his footsteps echoing as we entered the old church.

The abandoned church, with its weathered walls and creaking doors, served as the sacred space for our official meetings. As I stepped inside after a long absence, a musty scent engulfed the air. The sunlight filtered through stained glass windows, casting colorful patterns on the floor. The echoes of our inner circle's voices resonated against the high ceilings, filling the space with a sense of familiarity and purpose. It was disheartening to see the place slowly crumble, but it matched the club so perfectly until I claimed Emm.

"I don't care—I don't like my members going on their own. I'll accompany you."

Bear, our most recent inductee to my inner circle, let his bear snarl at my words. I ignored it and stepped inside the old cleric room that held a rounded table. Sizzle, Hawke, Grim, Switch and Shhkuk, leader of the elf clan that now inhabited the woods, all waited for my arrival.

"I don't think it's wise to send you all alone to Duke Idris' mansion. It's been quiet, too quiet over at that house and with not enough mated couples to travel with you, you won't have enough back-up. I don't trust sending that many rogues without my help." I sat down in my seat with a thud and Bear groaned.

We still had the private plane from Delilah's ex-husband. It was one of the larger ones but it wasn't like we could send the whole club. Besides, rogues don't do well separated and I would only send those I feel were the strongest.

"My mate, as well as Hawke's, have been on our asses to get these humans out of that mansion. They've been in there longer than we planned already. If you were still rabid, we would have already gone." Bear pushed.

I snarled and pounded my fist on the table. "I am still rabid, Bear. And you will hold your tongue." I pointed at him. "Just because you are part of this circle, now, does not give you the right to speak your mind to your president."

I had my reasons. An alpha thinks of his pack, of the souls that live within it. Bear shifters think differently. They do not work as a unit, rather, they are individuals and come together in time of need. He will have to change his mentality if he is going to continue here.

With a heavy thud, Bear sank into his chair, his massive arms crossing and a deep, guttural grunt escaped his throat.

"Switch, I need the security details. Anything out of order. I mean anything; I want to know if a leaf has fallen the wrong way."

Switch cleared his throat and dropped some papers on the table held by paper clips. We each grabbed the stacks and dispersed them amongst ourselves. "I haven't seen the Duke. This could be because of a glamor he has put on himself, or he simply isn't there. I have seen his followers are taking orders by ravens, with scrolls attached to their feet. They are no longer using electronic communications.

"Humans are not being escorted out of the facility, but they are being brought in and being put into cells. From the rudimentary camera feeds, they are being fed, watered and cared for. Better conditions than Nadia ever dealt with." Switch glances at Bear, who has a stoic expression on his face.

Nadia had it the worst. No food for days, and she couldn't sleep. At least the women were fed, but their unknown was almost just as bad.

"They're collecting. They are getting ready for a sale." Hawke said. "Question is, when and where is it? We can't sit around waiting much longer. We also can't take them all out at the same time. It looks like there are at least a hundred bodies in there."

"Locke—may I suggest something?" Shhkuk slowly rose from his seat, the soft rustle of his light green linen outfit catching the attention of everyone in the room. His ears, sharp and alert, protruded from his head, while his pointed face commanded attention; he stood out amidst the small crowd.

"With spring and summer upon us, my clan will be at their strongest, even without a mate. Most of my people are not rejected; they are simply looking for a peaceful life. To repay you for your kindness and haven, we can ensure the safety of these humans and set them free in the least bloody way possible. Our abilities to manipulate the Earth's life force can be of great help. We can remove the grass and soil, have brand new tunnels dug and put back together before any of the guards would know we are there. We can come from within the Earth and bring back the humans from under their noses."

The table grew quiet as they awaited my answer.

My fear was not only my people, but Shhkuk's people as well. They had become part of the Iron Fang a few months ago, before I had become rabid.

They didn't wear a vest, but they were part of my protection. I could not bear to lose anyone. Going into a mission so deadly, dealing with Duke Idris, as powerful as he is, as a Death Necromancing Fae without me, made my worry increase.

"You understand the risk here, don't you, Shhkuk? I will not be there. Grim and Journey will be heading this mission. Hawke cannot attend, and leave his mate and pup. You will not have the eyes you need from above. Tajah and Beretta will accompany you, but even Tajah's magic is limited against a necromancer."

Shhkuk nodded solemnly. "We understand the risks. Kraven's power of the soil has strengthened since his bond with Nadia's mother was completed. We will do well sneaking out these women to avoid conflict. That is why I wanted to speak."

No bloodshed. A clean steal under the Duke's nose. It could work. But what about getting them there?

"We can travel on our own. We have our ways." Shhkuk seemed to read my face.

It looks like I had no choice.

For the next hour, we discussed the details. My skin crawled like fire ants burning at the skin's surface. It wasn't to shift, but to get back to Emm. I had promised to be by her side tonight and start opening myself up to her. It had to be done—no more secrets.

Plus, my knot was going to explode if I kept it out of her body much longer.

The mission would have to go on without me, and I couldn't stand that I wasn't able to be with my club to support them. I felt like a failure as a president. It was like my ruthless bastard of a father, who would send off his warriors to be slaughtered, while he stayed behind enemy lines and watched the bloodshed.

I had to think about the members here. They were weak—just as I was. I couldn't leave them powerless as well. Hawke would be the only one mated, truly able to heal from wounds quickly, until I was fully mated with Emm. I needed her to complete the bond with me and soon.

And mating with my mate was no hardship. I knew how important a mate was. I dreamed of it when I was just a pup. The stories my mother told me about how your true mate was your one and only.

And when that dream was crushed, I never thought I would have a second chance. I was going to fucking cherish Emm.

Maybe in a fucked-up way, because Mordecai ruined the shit out of my wolf and me.

But she is her own kind of crazy.

After recording the last few notes from the meeting, Switched gathered his notebook and gently tucked it away in his bag. As he departed, he acknowledged me with a quick nod, prompting me to offer a comforting pat on his back.

"This will be successful. Even though the mated numbers are small, my clan will help in the retrieval," Shhkuk said, gaining back my attention.

I hummed in agreement, rubbing the scruff on my chin.

"You are distracted, President. Is it because your mate is hiding in our forest?" I raised a brow and Shhkuk chuckled. "Sorry, your forest."

I let out a huff of irritation. "It is ours. I bought it for all who wanted peace. I'm just—"

"Territorial," Shhkuk interrupted. "I understand. She is a fine female, and Luna, for the new pack you will create once the bond is completed."

I rubbed my hands over the large knife at my side. "And how do you know so much about her?" My agitation grew with Shhkuk. I wasn't particularly fond of the fae. It didn't matter what race of fae they were. All could be smooth talkers, filled with riddles and lies.

It wouldn't be the first time I thought about slitting Shhkuk's throat. Especially, given that he sent Nadia away from her clan as a baby, because she was born mostly human all those years ago. Even if it was for the betterment of his clan, I would leave no member behind in mine.

"The foliage talks to the summer and spring fae when we ask. They speak of her beauty, curiousness and wonder of the world around her. I do not believe she has been around nature much in her life."

I shook my head. "No, I don't believe she has. She's adapted nicely, however."

Shhkuk's head bobbed up and down in a quick nod of understanding. "Now that we know her true intentions, and she does not seek to harm any of us, we have the three intruders who intended to get into her trailer. Only two are in your dungeon. One of my clan members just recently received their magic and was... overzealous."

I clenched my teeth, digging my claws into my skin, desperate to release my pent-up emotions. True to his nature, my wolf had remained mostly silent, as he usually does. He rarely opened his mouth, except to voice his dissatisfaction.

"They all hail from the southern region. Darker skin, a language I am not familiar with."

"Spanish. Humans have different languages spread throughout the Earth."

"I thought there were only two." Shhkuk tilted his head.

The fae hid in Russia for many years, concealing their powers to avoid detection from Duke Idris. They interacted with Russians on a need-be basis. They learned their language, but only enough to get by.

Not wanting to explain everything to the fae, I brushed it off and we silently walked back to the bar. Despite the fae's beautiful appearance, they possessed an evil streak and a torture technique that left me quite impressed. Their vines strangled the intruders just enough to subdue them and get the answers we all sought.

And I wanted to know who the fuck was after my mate.

Shhkuk and I found ourselves in the basement. There was no crowd this time. Everyone was preparing for their departure and the unmated had jobs to do. This was for me and my sick, twisted pleasure.

Thick, gnarled vines coiled tightly around two of the men, constricting their bodies like a vice. The lifeless tendrils clung to their flesh, their broken, thorny branches piercing through their clothes, causing crimson droplets to seep through. With every futile struggle, the thorns embedded deeper into their skin, a cruel reminder of their entrapment. The scene was filled with the faint rustling of the vines, the acrid scent of crushed foliage mingling with the metallic tang of blood, and the agonizing sensation of the thorns mercilessly piercing their flesh.

"Well, well, what do we have here?" I circled them both as they sat on the floor. I noticed that someone had used the vines to wrap around their mouths and keep them quiet. I tsked, continuing my fun little game.

I squatted before the first one. His hair was dark, streaked with hints of grey to show his age. His older eyes widened in fear when I pulled out my knife and quickly broke the hard branches from his face. "You gonna talk? Or are we going to make this difficult. I'm good either way." I said with a smile.

With each sputter, blood trickled down his cheek, leaving a trail of crimson against his tanned skin. "W-what is going on?" His thick Spanish accent was hard to understand. "The, the branches. They got me!"

"A lot more is going to happen if you don't start talking. Why were you going to the RV? Who sent you here? I firmly grasped my knife and used its sharp edge to lift his chin, forcing him to look up.

His breathing grew rapid and his throat bobbed. The smell of ammonia grew and I looked down into his lap. "I-I was hired by Emmanuel Juderías."

I raised a brow and glanced at Skkush. He shrugged his shoulders and smiled. "Humans are pathetic."

"What for?" I trailed my knife across his cheek, pushing it into one of the holes a thorn had left in its wake.

"No! Stop please!"

I licked my lips, pushing it in deeper, and groaned when the blade hit his teeth.

Fuck, why do the guilty's screams sound so good?

Shhkuk cleared his throat. "President, do you think it's necessary?"

I chuckled darkly and pulled the blade from his cheek. "Of course it is. He tried to get my mate. Wouldn't you do the same?"

Shhkuk swallowed and nodded, standing back.

"And, who is this Emmanuel Juderías," I drawled. "What does he want to do with Emm?"

Tears ran down the intruder's face. He leaned his head back, trying not to move the cheek where fresh blood wept down his face. "He wants his daughter— he needs her back in Mexico."

A viscous smile crossed my face. "Her father." I bit my lip. "This is certainly interesting. And what does the father want to do with her? You know, having some random male come in the middle of the night to... what? Capture her? Kill her?"

I emitted a deep, guttural growl, baring my sharp, gleaming fangs as I tightly clasped the male's neck. The sound of his desperate gasps and chokes filtered into the basement. His eyes widened in terror as he witnessed my body transforming into a wild, untamed creature.

The other man behind him could only whimper, keeping his eyes closed from the sight.

"Ah-ah!" He tried to speak, but my anger took over and I squeezed him harder.

Shhkuk stood beside me, nudging me and clearing his throat. "President, maybe I should finish. I have interesting news."

I snarled louder, my fangs distending and fur growing down my neck and arms. I wanted his blood on my hands, to feel the taste of his life force in my mouth.

They almost touched her.

"Your mate is showing signs of a heat."

I lunged forward, my teeth piercing through the prisoner's shoulder. I savored the metallic taste of his blood as my venom seeped into his skin. His agonized screams echoed, blending with the intense, foreign words he cried out. With a slow, deliberate retreat, I ran my tongue across my lips, relishing the lingering essence of his blood.

Shhkuk stood back. "I do not have herbs to cure an alpha's bite."

"Good." I licked the remaining blood from my lips. "You aren't supposed to. Now, what about my mate?"

"Do you not wish to give them a second chance?" Shhkuk tilted his head.

I snarled and stepped toward him. "Their choice was to not take the job. Once you enter my territory and threaten my mate—your life is over."

Shhkuk swallowed. "Your mate. Her body temperature is rising. It is still early, but the trees can sense her pheromones."

Kraven stood in the doorway, his arms folded behind his back. Most likely the one who brought the news.

"We can take care of the prisoners, Hawke is on his way to accompany us in extracting information." Shhkuk said as his eyes glowed yellow, and he leaned his head back. "As I have said before, it would be an honor to help the male, who has given my clan hope, again, for peace to live.

I eyed him warily. I knew little about this male, but it seemed he must have been a warrior in his past life, or he is as psychotic as me.

I stared down at our prisoners. They were petrified; I did not believe it would take long to break the human. Which would not quench my thirst of a good torture.

I was slightly disappointed I could not do it myself, but Emm needed me and she was the priority.

"Do not kill the second. Put him in a cell so I can play with him later. Extract information from this one." I nod to the male, withering in pain from my bite. "I want to know everything. Who this father is, and why they want her. If they don't know, have Switch put out a search," I yelled over his pathetic whimpers.

I snarled and ripped my shirt over my head. I was ready to shift. I needed this since I didn't have chance to finish my interrogation. It's my favorite part. To hear them scream, to get justice for what they have done.

I groaned and grabbed my cock through my jeans. Fucking hell!

"Have the unmated run-in shifts. Look out for any unfamiliar faces." I ordered Hawke. I threw my shirt at him and jogged past.

"Have fun wooing the bad-ass female," he sang.

"Does everyone have to know my business?" As I sprinted up the stairs, Hawke's laughter filled the air with joyous barks.

"When it comes to a female coming into her first heat, yes. Again, good luck with that. I sure wouldn't want to deal with that Luna," he mumbled.

CHAPTER
TWENTY-THREE

Emm

I stoked the fire with a stick. I didn't feel like going back into town and having to explain to Delilah why I ran away from Locke—again.

Twice, I've run from him! I've never run away from my problems. I ran at them straight on—and hard. This time I did not know how to react to Locke. He would be the key to my family coming to the States, but obviously, I can't take him in.

I got emotional. I had sex with the target, and I grew an attachment to him that I couldn't explain. He was a complicated man, but my heart was in it—I was missing him even now, and my body couldn't stop reacting when I thought of him.

As I settled by the crackling fire, its warm glow illuminated my surroundings. The vibrant hues of the sunset having faded, leaving only the dancing flames as my sole source of light. Suddenly, the distant sound of a twig snapping caught my attention, causing me to rise from my seat. My hand instinctively reached for the cool metal of my gun nestled on my hip.

Please, let it be Fenrir.

It wasn't Fenrir. Of course it wasn't, because I have shitty luck. It was Locke and he came out of the woods, his feet bare, just a pair of black shorts and no shirt. Of course, he wouldn't have a shirt on—he was just trying to distract me.

I stood and straightened my back, only looking into his eyes and he let out a huff of amusement. "You look beautiful, Princess."

I tilted my head and shuffled my feet from side to side. There had never been a man who called me 'beautiful' as much as him. My stomach fluttered and I wanted to pinch myself to make it stop.

"It's alright, I come in peace." He kept his hands high and sat on the log away from me.

I was disappointed he didn't come closer, but I sat across from him. The fire crackled and the silence enveloped us until it was uncomfortable.

"There have been secrets between us—a lot of secrets, Emm, and I'm ready to come clean on my side, if you will come clean on yours. But I need you to promise me something, and it's important that you follow through with it," he said seriously.

I raised my jaw and nodded for him to continue. To keep that promise or not, I still wasn't sure.

"Do not run. Because if you run, I will chase after you. My instincts will be to chase you, subdue you and," he chuckled darkly, "make sure you never run from me again."

Instead of feeling fear, a thrill of excitement ran through me at his words. I have always been attracted to danger and the unknown, and Locke embodied both in a way that made my heart race. As much as I tried to deny it, there was a magnetic pull between us, that neither of us could seem to resist.

Damn him!

Locke's intense gaze held mine captive, and I could see the sincerity in his eyes despite the dangerous edge to his words. I knew he meant what he said, and a part of me was both terrified and exhilarated by the prospect of being caught by him.

Taking a deep breath, I steeled myself and replied in a low voice, "I won't run. Not anymore."

Locke's lips quirked up in a half-smile, and he nodded slowly. "We'll see."

He leaned back and put his forearms on his legs. "Grim is not the leader of the Iron Fang. I am," he admitted.

My eyes widened. "You? Then, why did they say Grim was?"

"Because he was the leader while I was absent. I have not been present for a while. I've been indisposed." Locke stood and walked away from the fire, but never took his eyes off it. "You see, I'm different. I'm not fully human."

Great, he really is psycho. Not that there isn't anything wrong with that. I like a little crazy in bed, but it's good to know for future Emm to deal with.

I shifted in my seat. "Okay, so tell me. What are you exactly? Is this your alter ego we are talking about?"

Locke stared at me, plainly and maybe a bit miffed. "No, Emm. It isn't an alter ego. I am—different. I am a shifter. A wolf. My bones break, my hair turns to fur and I walk on all fours. I am an animal. An alpha. I take care of the club, where most of the other shifters live and survive as a pack amongst humans. I've been more animal than human of late."

I stared at him for a long moment, blinking. "Are you high?" I squinted my eyes and stood from the fire.

He gave a crooked smile. "No, Princess, I'm not high, and please watch your movements."

I stared down at myself and moved my hand toward my gun.

"Why, are you going to attack me or something?" I stepped back, and

Locke stepped forward.

Locke radiated a low growl from his throat, and I stiffened. I'd heard that growl before. From the club on the night that guy touched me.

"I would never, ever hurt you. But, my wolf will make sure of your safety, even if that means preventing you from hurting yourself, when I take the gun off your hip."

"Then stay back." I raised my jaw. "And I won't have to use it."

Locke cleared his throat and stayed in place. "Fine, just, don't shoot me. Hurts like a bitch, and I'd prefer not to have the fae come running in here, and throwing you up against the tree."

I snorted. "Fae? There are faes now?"

"In this forest, yes, there are. They have saved you three times from intruders, besides the one I killed and buried behind your RV."

My heart stopped and the breath from my lungs was sucked out of me. I don't think I had known genuine fear until he confessed he knew about the male buried behind my trailer.

"E-excuse me?"

Locke smiled—like he always does. "Yeah, remember the hand I brought to you? Your little gift? I was disappointed you didn't at least pet me for a job well done, Emmie. You should have heard him cry out when I spilled his blood on the forest floor. I did it all—for you."

I felt the blood drain from my face as Locke's words sank in. The hand he had given me as a grisly token whisked on a whole new level of horror. My mind raced, trying to make sense of everything he was revealing to me.

No—he wasn't — Couldn't possibly.

Locke watched me intently, his gaze never wavering as if he were waiting for a specific reaction from me. The revelation of his true identity as a – wolf, the buried body behind my RV, fae in the forest – it was all too much to process at once. Almost.

I thought my grandmother was crazy. She pretended to be a witch for so long. Was she really a witch, then? Was Tajah really one, too?

Swallowing hard, I tried to maintain a façade of calm despite the turmoil churning inside me. "Why?" I choked out, my voice barely above a whisper. "Why are you telling me all of this, now?"

Locke's expression softened slightly at my question, a glimmer of regret flickering in his eyes. "Because you deserve to know the truth, Emmie. It's wrong of me to play this game I've been playing. Besides, I'm ready to claim you and show you the reality of the world that you are now a part of."

What. The. Fuck.

I swallowed heavily. The man I had been drawn to, captivated by, was not just a dangerous biker but a shifter with primal instincts lurking beneath the surface. Fae, witches—

But then, my mind clicked. Gone was the fear of the unknown. It all made sense now. The magic of this forest that I felt, the town, the shroud over the town. Of course, it had to be magical; of course, it was filled with something other than normal.

The real kicker was—Locke. He'd lied from the beginning.

"You—You are Fenrir." I wagged my finger at him, taking bold steps toward him.

Locke licked his lips and tilted his head toward me. "Guilty."

"You have watched me bathe, you have watched me dress and have intimate moments with myself; you gnawed on my fucking dildo!"

He bit his bottom lip and grabbed me by the hip to pull me closer to him. He took the gun from my hip and threw it away from us, hitting the forest floor with a soft thud.

"I couldn't resist tasting you. With your scent, your arousal right there at my disposal, what was I supposed to do? So, I licked up the sloppy seconds so I could have a sweet appetizer. So, yeah, I've done all those things—and what are you going to do about it, Princess?"

I narrowed my eyes and opened my hand, rearing back to slap him. He caught it, his powerful hand wrapping around my wrist. Power and strength came from it, far more than when we wrestled in the ring hours before.

This man played me the whole time!

I didn't know if I should be utterly turned on by being impressed, or just fucking mad.

Locke puts his mouth toward my ear, his lips grazing my ear lobe. He tsked. "Now don't tell me it makes you angry because we both know that is a lie." His hot breath fanned down my neck. I felt the breeze flow between my breasts and my nipples stiffen upon impact. "You like it that I've watched you all this time. That I have licked you in my wolf form, that I have comforted you, that I have stayed with you when you were lonely."

The heaviness in my chest was stifling.

"I can smell you, you know. All those nights where you were so needy. You wanted to run those fingers through those slick folds and you didn't know why. It was because of me— even though you hadn't met me yet, there was a connection there."

I shook my head and tried to pull away from him. He kept one arm wrapped around my waist and the other around the back of my neck. "Don't deny it. You were hot and needy. You just didn't know your mate was right there. In an animal form. Far too taboo for a human to understand."

"Locke—" My face heated with embarrassment.

He clicked his tongue. "There is no need for that, my sweet mate." He ran a finger down my cheek. "Humans don't know any better. You weren't aware of the bond that was settling into place. I knew, know, it is difficult to understand. But it was me—I am your wolf, your crazy. That is why your body has such a strong connection to me. My Goddess has paired you to me."

I reared my head back the best I could to stare at him in the eyes. The same eyes as Fenrir. *Why was I so blind not to see it before?*

Shit—it was him. I could feel it. The same smell, the same touch—the heat.

"Goddess? Goddess?" I tried to sound skeptical, but that word had already become ingrained in me. Don't ask me how. I wanted to say it was because of Abuela and her dancing half-naked in the forest when I was young. She had Elena and I dance in the forest, and pray to a Moon Goddess for a pairing— of soul mates that would love and protect us so fiercely it would near strangle us.

Now, it was Locke's hold that was strangling me.

I thought it was just a fairy tale. There were no fated mates.

"I mean, it's just—it can't be real, right?" I said to myself.

Locke laughed, the sound low and deep. He grazed his thumb over my lips, making me part them slightly. "Oh, my sweet mate, it's very real. Our bond... it's strong. Our connection... it's ancient and unbreakable. We were destined for each other."

I shook my head, trying to get my bearings. "So I have no choice? I just have to be with you? I'm just going to be horny for you, you cocky bastard?"

Locke gently took me by the shoulders before his hands gripped around my face. "No, you don't have a choice."

I shuddered, my nipples hardening into sharp points.

Locke's eyes darkened and he took a deep breath. He leaned in closer, his breath hot on my face. "It's a gift, Emmie. You are the other half of my soul. I will never hurt or forsake you. I will protect you, love you fiercely and fucking kill anything that gets in the way of that."

My thighs tightened together.

"And, I am going to claim you, Emmie. I want to seal our souls together to make us one. You are in danger, and I need to know where you are at all times. I've kept these secrets not because I wanted to, but because I had no choice. Now that I can control my human form we are doing this for your safety. I am strong enough to take you, knot you, show you what a real male does to protect his female; it's time for you to accept your new reality. And you are a warrior, strong enough for this."

I ground my teeth together and jerked away from him. "You don't tell me what to do."

His eyes narrowed as he moved closer to me with purposeful strides. "Emm, do not run."

"I'm not going to run." I planted my feet firmly into the ground. "But I would love to kick your ass."

Threw his head back and laughed. The cocky dick was not even paying attention to me when I lunged forward and right-hooked him to the face. He stumbled backward with me on top of him and I pushed his arms above his head.

He continued laughing, as I rained down punch after punch to his gorgeous face until my knuckles were sore and bleeding. He grabbed them when I winced and held my wrists. I tried to rip them away from him, but my grunts and cries to get away from him were absolutely useless.

"That is enough. Stop! You are hurting yourself!" he yelled, but I continued to fight.

I wasn't going to stop either. I was fucking pissed.

He rolled on top of me, our favorite way to subdue each other, pinned my arms back and he straddled my waist. He took one look between my breasts and wiggled his brows. "Now, are you ready to calm down or am I going to spank your ass to teach you to behave?"

I spat in his face. "I am no one's property."

He let out a huff and wiped away the spit from his eye. "Sweetheart, I belong to you as much as you belong to me. There is no head of the relationship here—we are equals."

"Seems like there is because you are making all the decisions with all this 'your mine' shit," I sneered.

"No, no, no, my sweet little mate. The Goddess is the one that paired us together. Two puzzle pieces that fit quite nicely together. I don't know if you have noticed, but your arousal has fucking drenched my cock, and I can smell your heat approaching."

The deep sounds of the purr in his body were felt between my legs.

Heat? That is an animal thing.

"No—"

"I don't tolerate lying," he growled, his face inches from mine. "Say that you want me. Say that you want this thick, juicy cock shoved in your tight cunt. And if you do, I will reward you with a knot to sate that hunger of yours that wasn't sated earlier."

I tried to squeeze my legs together, but he pushed his knee between my legs.

"The hell is a *knot*?" I snapped.

Locke pulled down the front of his shorts. The picture he sent me earlier had his hand covering the base of the monstrosity that I was now seeing. There it was, a large bulge at the base of his dick, right below his last piercing.

Locke ran his hand up and down his shaft. "This is my knot. All wolf shifters have it," he groaned. "When I am ready to fill you with my seed, I will shove it inside you. Fill you up with my come and lock it inside you. It will make sure that none of my seed escapes you."

And, instead of feeling fear, my pussy fluttered with anticipation.

I wanted him more than I cared to admit, and I knew I was being a grade-a-bitch. But how else was I to process it? My chest heaved and my body shuddered when he rubbed his thick cock against my most sensitive clothed parts.

"What is a '*heat*'?" I moaned, pushing my breasts toward him. "That is for animals, I'm not—I'm not—"

Locke licked my shoulder where he bit me earlier. "Ah, that might be my fault. I sped up our bond by biting you. But you just looked so delicious." He licked my cheek.

I panted, feeling his teeth graze my shoulder. I was feeling drunk—not myself at all the more he touched me, kissed me and now I wanted him to sink his teeth into my skin again.

Locke chuckled. "Finally calming down? Don't worry, I'll be submitting to you plenty in this relationship. But first, let me take care of you—I've waited far, far too long for this moment."

CHAPTER TWENTY-FOUR

Locke

She was taking it remarkably well. Especially, considering how strong of a luna she was going to be.

I placed kisses down her neck and over her mark once more. I released my scent allowing it to envelope her and it acted like an aphrodisiac. Sure, I was cheating a little bit, but I think every one of my men has cheated in some way.

"I still can't believe you're a wolf." She panted. "I need some sort of proof. Can you shift into your wolf or something? It still doesn't seem real."

I tsked "I don't think so." I enjoyed having both my hands on her, thank-you-very-much. Instead, I let my claws from my lycan form flow from my fingertips. As the sharp claws grazed her skin, she gasped.

"That is not from your wolf,." she muttered. "What the fuck are those.?"

I smiled mischievously. "Yeah, they're not. These are part of another form that I can take. No other wolf shifters can take this form and, in fact, no one else knows of this form." I frowned and gazed down at the enormous claws.

She stared up at me and for the first time ever, she looked so damn innocent. Her eyes were wide, filled with curiosity as her fingers played with mine; my mate, as she examined the claws.

"You mean there are things you haven't told your club; your friends?" She said it so softly, so tender I felt my heart weep.

"We all have our own secrets. I may have the most. They don't get to choose what to know about me. I'm the one that protects them, and gives them shelter. They just know I am the one in charge. But not with you, Emm, I'll tell you everything."

My mate's breathing came in soft pants.

Perhaps she didn't want to be tough all the time.

"The form I take, I believe humans and in their fairy tales would call me a werewolf, but it is in fact Lycan."

My mate's arousal seeped around us as my scent covered us. My fingers curved around her ass, sinking them into the soft flesh. I pressed my hips against hers and let her feel my shaft rub against her mound. I couldn't hold much longer. I don't know how many questions she was gonna ask, but to gain her trust I was going to do what I could.

"Dios mio."

My wolf let out a thunderous purr. Her body shivered against me as my lips pressed hastily against her. I couldn't get enough. I needed to devour her, take her. I didn't want to wait any longer.

"Let's get you in the RV, I will not take you on the ground," I grumbled into her mouth.

Believe it or not, I cared about my mate's wellbeing.

Her dilated eyes blinked several times before she came out of her lustful gaze. "And what if I want you to take me here?"

So fucking feisty.

I chuckled. "As exotic and exquisite your tastes are, the first time you take my knot, you will not want to be laying in the dirt and sticks. Now, get in the RV before I put you in it."

I stood and pulled her up, but she pushed me away once she was standing.

"Is that so, Mr. Lycan? Are you going to tell me what I will and will not like?"

"Emm. Do. Not. Run." I gritted my teeth.

My mate looked behind her, and I swear I saw the leaves beckoning for her to enter.

I swear to the Goddess, those damn fae.

"Princess!" I growled in warning.

"I wanna see this Lycan." She licked her lips. "And, I want to see what he's packing, too."

This female!

"My lycan form is much larger than my human form. You do not know what you are asking for."

"I think I do," she laughed. "And I would love to see how big that cock can be, too."

I grabbed myself, feeling my cock dripping with seed. To take her in such a beastly form? I tilted my head back to imagine it.

"I would take you in my beast form. Do you understand that?" I questioned. "There would be no mercy. I will bite you, I will mark you and I will not stop even if you asked."

Emm continued to back away, going deeper into the forest. "Oh, I'm counting on it. You have no idea how much monster smut I have read in my lifetime. And, with a monster dick being pierced and all? I think I'm ready for it."

Goddess above.

My companion swiftly disappeared into the depths of the woods, disregarding any clear path and venturing into the dense tangle of thicket. As she pushed through, the branches rustled against her delicate skin, their rough texture leaving a faint sensation. In that moment, my mind was consumed with a desire to leave my own imprints upon her beautiful body - to etch my own scars, and create my own marks.

My wolf snarled, pissed off that I even let her attempt to flee from us. He was still broken from our previous rejection. He didn't like Emm being out of our sight at all.

"Get her!" he snarled.

My bones shattered, the excruciating pain surpassing that in my wolf form. I could hear the sickening crunch as they splintered into minuscule fragments, rearranging themselves into intricate structures.

When my back broke, I slung my body back. That's when I let out an enormous howl letting everyone in the vicinity know that they needed to get the fuck out. The elves would be surely hiding in their homes, in their village, somewhere on the property. The club members were cheering and having another beer at the bar.

I dug my claws deep into the soil, feeling the earth yield beneath my paws as I gave my mate just a precious few more moments to escape before I took off. Patience was never a virtue that I possessed.

I charged through the dense thicket, the sound of snapping branches and rustling leaves filling my ears. The earthy scent of freshly broken foliage wafted up, mingling with the dampness of the forest floor. As I moved, the small trees and shrubs magically regenerated, their wounded limbs mending with the help of intertwining vines. Towering trees gracefully arched away from my path, their supple branches gently guiding me forward.

Like I needed it.

My mate's scent was hefty and heady from her arousal. She was easy to find, and I darted far enough away from her to get ahead. I took the long way around to a clearing so I would be stood in front of her.

The trees gracefully bent and swayed, creating a natural path that led her to a tranquil clearing. It was like fate leading her to me, ready for me to take her as mine.

Emm stopped, panting, a sheen of sweat covered her forehead. The surrounding area was quiet, no doubt the other forest animals, feeling my power, decided to stay away.

"Shit," she mumbled.

At least she knew that I was near. Now, do I play with my food or do I devour her whole?

"Are you done running, pet?" I taunted.

My mate jerked her head in my direction. "You can talk. You can talk like that?"

"I may be in beast form, but I am as coherent as a human. Is that so shocking?" I licked my maw, letting my fangs drip with venom.

My venom was not poisonous to my mate. I was taught this from a very young age. It was the same for all alphas. The only person immune was her.

I stepped from the shadows where I hid. I let the moonlight cast its gentle glow upon my body. Her eyes widened not in fear but pure, pure fascination.

"Holy shit, you're huge."

I chuckled. "I didn't exaggerate." My hand ran down my furred muscular body until it reached my cock. "And this will be a tight fit."

Come dripped from the angry head. My knot pulsed, heavy with need.

Emm's eyes widened, her breaths quickening as she thrust out her chest, allowing her breasts to heave with desire. She took a step forward and I couldn't help but rise to the occasion, the muscles in my body tensing. I shivered as the power of the full moon reverberated through me, binding me to my primal nature.

Her eyes locked onto mine, and I watched as her hesitation flickered away, replaced by a fierce determination. She took another step, and I mirrored her, matching her pace and stalking her like a predator toying with its prey.

"Do I, though?" she asked, her voice thick with anticipation. "Are you sure you can handle me?"

A smirk tugged at the corner of my maw. "I promise you, I will take you harder and rougher than you've ever experienced, pet."

She hesitated, her eyes locked onto the sheer size of my cock, straining against my fur as it pulsed with need. However, before she could back away, I lunged forward, my body slamming into hers with a force that sent her stumbling against the trunk of a tree.

"I'm not going to be gentle," I warned, my breath hot against her ear as I spoke. My powerful arms wrapped around her waist, pulling her close, and I nuzzled my face against the side of her neck, my scent mingling with hers.

"I claim you as mine," I growled. "There will be no turning back."

Emm's eyes fluttered shut, her fingers digging into my fur for surrender.

With a growl that shook the very trees around us, my muscles bulged, my fur darkened until it appeared a deep obsidian, and my eyes glowed, reflecting the moonlight with an eerie, otherworldly glow.

"Mine," I snarled.

I used my claws to rip at her clothing, gentle nicks ripped at her skin. Her body trembled, her soft whimpers only fueled Fenrir and his desire to claim.

Once she was laid bare to me, I took in the sight of her body. Minor scratches highlighted against her skin, but there was one more spot that remained positively clean. The tiny bite I left her just hours ago.

I purred against her, my hand cupping her pussy and licking at the mark I left her.

"So wet." I nibbled at her mark.

I let my two claws retract and shoved them deep into her cunt. I wasn't a complete asshole. I would make sure she was ready.

As I nibbled her mark with my sharp teeth, I let her arousal coat me. Fenrir, wild with desire, had had enough, he would not give her the pleasure she wanted for defying and running from us.

He forcefully pulled our fingers from her body and she cried out, pulling on our furred arm.

"No!" she tried to lead us back to her dripping pussy.

My hand reached around her neck. "You ran, you don't get a say!" Fenrir snapped.

My mate's face changed from desire to fear when she heard the new, deeper voice. "I am Fenrir, your wolf. You ran from me."

Emm tilted her head when he eased up on his hold around her neck.

"You never run from me." He tilted his head low and pressed it to her forehead, taking in long deep breaths before he tapped our cock against her entrance.

She grunted, holding onto the wrist that gripped her neck. "You hid from me." She gritted her teeth. "Only fair."

Fenrir smirked, pushing the head of our cock in her body and then pulling it out again. "Then, we play."

Emm groaned, whining for mercy as he slowly edged our cock inside her. He tortured her, and I felt every fucking bit of it until I slowly took our control back. That sadistic fuck was too damn much.

Once I fully seated myself inside her, knowing I would not rip her apart, this was where the fun began.

"Get ready." I let the low growl in my throat overtake the sound of the forest. "Because this is something we both fucking need."

I withdrew from her, only to thrust forcefully back into my mate. A cry escaped her lips as her tightness gripped me. The sensation of the ladder's ridges gliding within her tight cunt.

"So big!" she breathed. "Shit, I'm going to be ripped in half!"

I panted, my breath blowing steam across her face.

But I would not hold back. I told her this.

I wanted to claim her like this. A fucking animal. I'm showing her the true strength of what I am. I claim her as my mate, strong and capable.

As my hairy chest heaved and brushed against her breasts, her eyes flashed with desire. She craved it; she wanted more. I thrust deeper into her.

The moonlight shone on her face, casting eerie shadows on the forest floor. Her eyes were wide with a mix of fear and pleasure as her body arched beneath me. I kept myself embedded into her and laid her on top of a log. I could see the pleasure coursing through her veins, feel the intense emotions surging between us.

"Fuck me!" she cried, her voice hoarse with passion. "Fuck me harder!"

And so I did. I thrust into her relentlessly, my power and strength over-taking her, consuming her in a whirlwind of lust and domination. With every stroke, I claimed her as mine, marking her as my own. My wolf and hers, becoming one in the process.

The night was alive with our primal screams, our bodies moving in perfect sync, lost in the intense, animalistic grunts and snarls I created. We were wild creatures of the night, and in this moment, I finally felt alive again.

As my sharp claws dragged down her delicate skin, crimson marks bloomed on her soft flesh. Her fingers tightly gripped my thick fur, and her legs entwined around my powerful body. In this moment of ecstasy, sights blurred, the sound of our entangled breaths echoed into the night. This was fucking heaven.

As the intensity of our rutting reached its peak, I could feel her tightening around me, her body quivering with the waves of pleasure I was sending her. And then, just as the stars aligned, I felt the explosion within me, the release of control and power that only comes with true submission.

She screamed again, another orgasm taking over her. My knot was aching to be inside. It was time to burrow its way in.

My mate groaned, her fingers gripping hold of my fur. It was going to be a tighter fit. I knew it was. I could smell the tinge of copper mixed with her arousal as I tried to burrow my way in.

"I know, it's going to be tight," I grunted.

I continued to wedge my knot inside her, and shifted her gently to make her more comfortable with one arm, while the other pulled her off the log.

The soft moss, with its vibrant green hue, grew abundantly in this once peaceful clearing. I watched it as it suddenly appeared and carpeted the forest floor, creating a welcoming and comfortable space for us to rest. As I gently laid us down on the cushiony surface, the coolness of the moss seeped through our bodies, giving comfort to our aching muscles.

She whined, letting out a cry as I settled her in front of me. With a few small thrusts, my knot lodged itself inside. I groaned, moving my hips several times before, finally, it was my turn to feel my pleasure.

"Fuck," I groaned and pumped my hips, feeling my knot wedge in and out of her entrance.

My mate shuddered, a cry of another orgasm, and that was when I sealed it all together—with my bite.

She screamed; her arousal soaking the both of us. I don't know where our liquids were going, but they would not come out of her.

My body let out a comforting purr, when we both felt utter and complete pleasure as the bond wove itself, tying us together. Slight tremors of pleasure fueled the both of us as we settled on the moss.

"Maybe I wasn't ready," she mumbled, half asleep. "Still would do it again, though."

I chuckled and licked the bite on her shoulder. The blood was fresh, but the full bite of the bond would heal far faster than the half bite I left her earlier.

I let my hand run up and down her body, cupping her breast as I felt her breath even and her heart rate slow. My knot still throbbed, pumping more come into her body. I groaned, feeling her pussy milking me.

Was it awful that I didn't want her to sleep? That I wanted to do it again?

As time passed, my knot softened and I slipped my cock from her body. I felt our fluids leak from her and my wolf panicked, feeling it pour onto our furred leg where we were holding her.

"Put it back," he sneered. *"Now!"*

I shook my head and nuzzled against her cheek.

"We can fuck her again in a minute, just let me have this." I took in a deep breath, taking in her scent. She smelled like me now. She was mine, and no one else could have her.

"I don't like her out in the woods. We are vulnerable." Fenrir snapped and took the time to listen to our surroundings.

My hand rubbed up and down our mate, feeling her body.

Will she love me in time? Will she have the same feelings I have toward her?

She had some knowledge of the Goddess, otherwise she wouldn't have been brought to me, for me to claim her. Her grandmother made sure of that many years ago. The question was, was I too broken to be loved?

I put those thoughts away, for now. It was for another day. Now, it was time to show her what a suitable mate I could be—for her.

To sate Fenrir, I took our finger and wiped the come from my mate's inner thigh. I shoved it back inside her and watched her body squirm. I inspected her folds. Her folds appeared swollen, puffy, and with blood-tinged on the outside of her lips.

My chest puffed with pride how well she took me, especially for a human that does not heal quickly.

Fenrir growled. "*More, take her again.*"

I chuckled and scooped my mate up into my arms.

We would take her more, but our mate's pussy was tender, I would not damage and make her hurt any more than I had to. "I think fucking in human form might be better. Your cock is too large to take her like this again," I said, and cradled her into my arms for the walk to our new home.

CHAPTER TWENTY-FIVE

Locke

"Tell us about mates, again," Amaryllis sat promptly up in her tiny cot.

We shared a bedroom, much to our father's dissatisfaction, but my mother knew how important it was for twins to stay close to one another as pups. Amaryllis and I **were** very close. We did everything together. From playing, to learning, sparing and even sharing the same room.

"Not tonight," our mother sighed, "I still have dishes to scrub."

Amaryllis pouted, her lip quivering. "Please. Father isn't here."

Our father had yet another alpha meeting and wasn't due back until late. Mother put us in bed early on the nights he was gone. It was to make up for lost sleep time; Father would force us to stay up late and quiz us on battle techniques and formations, or teach our bodies to run on less sleep.

Mother huffed, sat on my cot and rubbed both of our arms lovingly. It wasn't common for Mothers to show affection in the Blood Rose pack, especially out in the open. In the confines in our home, Mother let us know we were loved, when the watchful eye of our father wasn't near.

"Mates are gifts given to us by the Moon Goddess. They are the other half of your soul. They will make you feel complete in all ways and make you feel so loved and full." My mother smiled sadly and squeezed our hands. "You will find your mate when you are a full-grown wolf. Their smell will draw you in and once you look them in the eyes, there will be no one else in the entire world that will matter. It will just be you and your other half. It is all-consuming, all-powerful. They will make your heart flutter, your soul sing, and your spirit soar. Finding your mate is the most precious gift a wolf can receive, and you must cherish and protect that bond above all else. Your mate will be your rock, your confidant, your partner in every sense of the word. And when you find them, you will know in your heart that they are meant for you, destined to walk by your side for eternity."

Amaryllis' smile widened. Her toothy grin aiming at me. "Can't you wait, Koen? To find your mate?"

I shrugged my shoulders. My face heated.

"Stop embarrassing your brother." My mother swatted my sister. "Boys do not wish for those sorts of things so young."

Amaryllis threw her head back and laughed. "What about you, Mother? What was it like meeting Father?" My sister's voice grew solemn when she spoke.

Our father was neither a patient nor a kind man. We never spoke ill of him in front of him or anyone else. We were to respect him being the alpha of our pack, but it wasn't respect I had for him. It was fear.

To go against the alpha was treason. According to the by-laws, the alpha has the authority to tear a child to pieces in front of their parents, if they speak badly about their leaders.

Mother rolled her lips, her heart raced.

As I reached out and held my mother's arm, her body stilled as she rested against me. I could feel her heartbeat slow against my fingertips. "What's wrong? You don't want to answer?"

My intuition was stronger than my sister's. I was the second born. My sister was strong and extroverted, while I liked to stay by myself. Amaryllis could be bold in her questions, but me—I read the room.

My mother's throat bobbed and she nodded. "A story best for another day."

Amaryllis growled, her tiny eight-year-old body shook in the bed. "I heard an elder say he isn't your true mate."

Mother snapped her head to my sister and narrowed her eyes. "It is treason against your father and alpha. You best not utter those words aloud, again."

Amaryllis narrowed her shoulders. "Don't care. Is it true?"

My mother stood up, her footsteps resonating softly on the wooden floor as she made her way towards the doorway to our room. With worry in her eyes, she gently pushed the door open, allowing a sliver of light to filter in from the hearth of the kitchen. After a brief moment, she closed it with a gentle click, shutting out the outside world. Returning to us, she gracefully lowered herself to the floor before us.

"This does not leave this room, nor is it repeated, my sweet pups." Her hand cupped both of our faces. "I think it is why I teach you about mates, so much, because I want you to find your own—your true mates. Your grandparents wanted the same for me."

My heart seized in my chest with sorrow, but my sister exuded anger.

"A long time ago, our pack was peaceful, until your father—a single alpha male - came along. His pack was strong, and was envious of our territory and how well we took care of the forest. He wanted it for himself. He visited our pack many times, offering my father an alliance. That alliance would be to mate with me and join the packs together. One day his patience grew thin and he gave an ultimatum. Submit or there would be a war.

"My father refused. He believed in the mate bond, but your father wanted me for my body and for the land. That was when war broke out, at the

negotiations table." A tear ran down my mother's cheek.

I climbed down from my cot and sat on her lap. My sister did the same as we held onto her.

"The battle was brutal. We weren't ready for such bloodshed, but Mordecai was. It lasted for days. Our resources were depleted and many of us took to the forest. That was when I caught a smell that relaxed my body and nearly drifted me to sleep."

"Your mate," Amaryllis gasped.

Mother nodded. "Yes, and he was so handsome." She brushed my sister's hair away from her face. "He was a warrior for Mordecai, but 'sides' blurred at that moment because we were both instantly drawn to one another. We both shifted and, naked, ran to each other, holding one another."

"Ew," I squirmed in my mother's seat.

She laughed and kissed my cheek.

"Our happiness was short-lived, though." Her voice grew soft. "Because Mordecai found us. Our happiness blinded us to the danger surrounding us, and it tore us apart. Your father gave me a choice. Accept his mark and bite him in return, or my pack, and my family would be murdered."

My mother stared at the blank wall, as if she was living every moment.

"I cried for him." Her lip wobbled. "I wanted him. I chose him. But my mate—trying to be the hero— took Mordecai's dagger from his side and stabbed himself in the chest."

My sister and I both stared at my mother in complete devastation.

"He did it so I could save my pack and family."

My sister and I sat silently clinging to our mother.

"Do not be a hero," Mother whispered to the both of us. "Do not be a hero, because look at me now. Our pack has turned evil, pups are discarded, there is no love, and mates be damned. The only good that has come out of it is the two of you. Without you both, I am nothing but a husk of my former self."

"Then, what are we supposed to be if we can't be a hero?" My sister asked.

I swallowed and leaned against my mother and sister. "A villain. That's all that's left."

We sat in silence while my mother silently cried.

"I didn't even know his name," she muttered.

My sister and I sat at our favorite spot. It was on the far side of the lake, away from where the pack would gather their water and fish.

"I heard Mother and Father arguing last night," I sat and whittled the block of wood I held in my hand. It was my favorite pastime. I enjoyed making small animals, people and even furniture. My sister and I had a full trunk of the creations I'd made, and would play with them during the rainy seasons.

"When do they not?" My sister swung on a vine from a tree and landed on both her feet with steady precision. "I don't even want to call him Father or my alpha anymore, after hearing what Mother told us about him."

I twisted my lips and concentrated on my carving. "Nothing we can do now. Not until we are stronger, or you take over the pack," I said.

I was glad that Amaryllis was the firstborn. It meant I had more time to do things I wanted. I didn't have the expectations of upholding a pack, to protect it and help it grow. Amaryllis had all those qualities a proper alpha should have; better qualities than Mordecai ever possessed.

"I'll turn this place around." Amaryllis put her hands on her hips. "Back how Mother said it was. Where the water was so clean so you didn't have to boil it, the animals so scared that we have to hunt miles away."

I smirked. My sister knew how to go off on her tangents. I think that is what I liked most about her. Her confidence and her desire for a change.

"I'll support you anyway I can. Your training starts tomorrow for alpha, right?"

Mordecai expected training from pups as young as eight years old. It was no different for his children. However, it felt earlier for us. At night, he taught us things a pup shouldn't know. About war, blood, and who to trust.

There were nights where he would send Amaryllis to bed and make me stay awake. He would drone for hours about alpha duties. Strength, bravery, determination, and to do what one can to win a fight.

I didn't understand why he would tell me these things. I was not meant to be alpha.

"Yes, on the morrow. Will you stand and watch my first training?" She stood over me, blocking the sun from my sight.

"Yes, now move, you are in the way." I pushed her leg and she laughed, falling over to my side. As she sat, she nudged me and gazed down at the wood that still had yet to take shape.

"And once I change things in years to come, what will you do? Will you be a warrior, be my beta?"

I shook my head and held up the block. "No, I will be none of those things."

"Then what?" My sister acted appalled.

It was rather odd to think of anything other than sparring, fighting, or becoming a warrior or hunter within the pack. It was all we did in the Blood Rose. However, before our time, Mother said that every wolf had a job, and it didn't have to involve fighting and blood. There were clothes makers, homebuilders and bakers. Things we didn't have to outsource or trade.

"I would want to be a toy maker." I smiled. "I'd want to make toys for all the pups. Toys we never got to go play with much because we were too busy trying to—" I stared at the other side of the lake. Children were gathering water, or fighting over food and scraps. They were encouraged to fight with one another. "—I want pups to know what it means to play. Like Mother explained."

My sister laughed. "And you will explain how to play? Become their creepy uncle and lead them into your toy shop?"

"Hey!" I snorted and pushed her away from me. "I will not be creepy! I'd be the fun uncle."

Amaryllis cried out when I lunged at her. "That isn't any better! Mercy, mercy!" She cried. I continued to tickle her, and we rolled into the dirt, laughing. My whittling knife and block of wood were long gone as we rolled into the tall grasses.

I gasped, feeling the cool droplets of sweat forming on my forehead. Slowly, I lifted my head from the rumpled sheets, my eyes scanning the room, desperately seeking reassurance that I hadn't been transported back there.

Once I took a deep breath, smelling my mate's scent, my heart slowed and my body relaxed. I snuggled my body around hers, in the blankets that served as our nest.

Watching scenes replay of my past— feeling my sister's touch and hearing her laughter made my heart seize in my chest. We were both so young and innocent, and she was so damn fierce.

I felt my throat bob, and I buried my nose into my mate's neck. Her body didn't move, and I pushed myself closer to her, enveloping her.

Soon, my mate would know everything about me. Who I am, where I came from, why I am the way I am.

Will she run in fear? Will she understand at all?

I fucking hated the unknown.

I squeezed her tighter, my body covering hers.

I would not let her go. She would not leave me.

I will not lose another person I loved.

Mine.

CHAPTER TWENTY-SIX

Locke

I don't know how long I lay there holding her. I haven't felt the skin of any female since my mother and my sister.

My ruts have been painful in my time alone. I sought no relief from another female and endured them with no sort of medication, although I carried it for others close to me, trying to help ease their pain.

Now, I felt the heat of my body rise. My cock was constantly hard and I had yet to gain permission to take my mate's body while she was sleeping. Now that I had claimed her, I felt my scattered and irrational thoughts fade, and now I wanted nothing but consent from her.

I think it was part of the old me shining through. The broken pieces of my mind being pieced together. Those cracks would be sealed through the bond. I wouldn't achieve perfect healing, as it was impossible with the memories I held. I don't think any god or goddess could make me forget. The pain made me the wolf I was today and I needed it to help this pack survive.

My wolf stirred, his ears twitching as he rose from deep within my mind.

"*A pack,*" he muttered. "*It is the first time you referred to our club with that term and meant it.*"

I took a deep breath, nuzzling my face further into my mate's neck. It *was* the first time I had thought of the club as a pack, or at least felt that it was the right word. Was this the turning point for those who fought to be inside the Iron Fang?

Would there be differences within the pack, now that I thought of them as a pack rather than a club since, Emm's and my mating?

Thoughts about what I have created in this world circled in my mind when I should have been concentrating on my mate. Yet here I was, worrying about everyone else.

There was no time to enjoy the pleasantries. I had to ensure that the rest of the shifters and fae were taken care of as well.

I rearranged the cozy blankets, ensuring that my scent enveloped them completely. As I held my mate close, I could feel her shivering slightly. It was crucial for her to stay warm, as her body would soon undergo significant changes. I wanted to relieve her immune system of the need to regulate her body temperature.

When I pulled away and saw her sleeping form, I couldn't help but feel gratefulness toward the Goddess. For so long, I damned her for what she had done to me and to my friends.

My mother never told me a mate could reject you. It was either she didn't know, or just refused to tell me. There was so much darkness in Blood Rose, maybe she wanted to give me hope.

Regretfully, I pulled away from my mate and took my phone off the nightstand.

I'd brought my mate to the new packhouse, still being constructed, after I ravaged her on the forest floor.

The third floor of the large mansion reminded me of packhouses I had traveled past in the Elysian realm. They were for the more developed packs, ones that had a heavy export in textiles, armor or other items that were considered luxurious. I hadn't seen anything like it before until I finally left the ashes of Blood Rose.

I wanted that for a pack of my own.

The Iron Fang's packhouse stood tall and imposing, even though the first and second floors were partially incomplete. The sturdy walls were constructed from the finest stone and reinforced with iron. However, what set it apart from other packhouses I have ever seen, was the touch of nature that adorned its exterior.

Lush green vines cascaded down the walls, intertwining with the logs and creating a harmonious blend of human construction and the fae's natural influence. The foliage seemed to have a life of its own, as if the fae had carefully chosen it to complement the surrounding scenery. It was as if the packhouse was not just a home for the alpha but for the unmated wolves that had yet to build their own families. The mated had their own cabins being constructed. This sanctuary was integrated into the wilderness. The combination of modern strength and fae magic made the Iron Fang's packhouse truly unique.

Once the packhouse was completed, we could bring them here. Emm and I would watch over them until they were mated and had their own cabins to retreat too.

I took several deep breaths.

Time. All in good time.

My phone had several messages, mostly from Bones and updates from the club.

> **Bones**: "The crew is set up at the mansion. They are currently delayed but are taking time to scout out patterns of their security."

I tilt my head and rub my chin as I read it. *Why the hell would they be delayed?*

> **Locke**: *"Why is it delayed?"*

The response was quick.

> **Bones:** *"Nadia and Bear have a headache."*

I raised a brow.

> **Locke:** "Explain."

The phone vibrated in my hand and I answered. I stepped out of our bedroom, but kept the door open to monitor her.

"Sorry, I didn't want to disturb you," Bones cleared his throat. "It's being taken care of; I told them some meds to pick up. Bear said they would resume once they've kicked in."

"Why the hell would they get a headache? Shifters don't get a fucking headache, not unless-." My heart stopped beating in my chest. "Fucking shit." I ran my hand through my messy hair. "The link—a pack-link. There is a link trying to form."

"What? Nadia's had a headache before. I figured Bear might be feeling hers through their bond. Humans have medication for this sort of pain. I'm hoping it will help with theirs."

I shook my head. Nadia and Bear were a mated couple. There's way human medication would touch them. Bones didn't know shit about links and how they formed.

"They need to pull out," I growled. "Tell them to back off and come home."

"Alpha, they are already there. They are so close—"

I balled my fist and banged it on the table. "I said get them the fuck home. All shifters need to get back to home base. The ones who are going to feel this the most are the mated couples, Bones. It's going to get worse."

Bones wouldn't know that even for a doctor; few shifters did. Alphas were taught how links were created; tiny wires inside the mind, hunting and searching to connect their threads to a wired system. Bear and Nadia didn't have our pack close enough to connect with anyone—to a leader. Their animals wouldn't connect to just anyone, they would only connect with someone they have submitted to or trusted.

I just hoped that was me.

"Get them out," I snapped. "We will have to find another way."

"The vampires?" Bones questioned. "The ones that offered their help. Bear can have them come in and take their place."

As much as I wanted to leave out that damn coven, it was a suitable substitute. I clenched my jaw. "Do we have maps available? What about the Moonlight Outcasts that helped Bear rescue Nadia? Are they willing to negotiate with the coven and lead the operation?"

Bones repeated what I asked. I heard Switch's confirmation and the repeated tapping of the keys on a keyboard. The Moonlight Outcasts were a bunch of vampires and a werewolf, who'd formed some sort of friendship bond before finding me. They held each other together and helped Bear rescue Nadia. They would know that mansion inside and out, as much as Bear.

"Any other mated pair cannot take part in this rescue," I snapped. "That's an order. I want this done in six hours."

Bones said nothing on the other line.

"I said it was an order. Do you understand?" I growled.

"Y-yes, Alpha."

He said Alpha! And it wasn't in a derogatory or joking manner. It was in reverence, in hope.

I took a deep breath and sat in the chair. My eyes darted to Emm who was still sleeping soundly, undisturbed.

My body craved to be near her, but I couldn't let this go. Not yet, not when we were close.

For the next hour I made phone calls. One to Bear to check on their health, and the other to Hawke. I felt stupid that I would forget such a huge detail about pack-links, but shit, it had been so many years since any of us had been a part of a pack.

Mates, in general, were stronger, of course, their animals wanted to establish a connection. The pain in their mind, searching for its home pack, would get stronger until it was relieved. The mated needed to be returned home quickly to establish the connection.

As for the unmated; a ceremony performed by a witch would have to be established. It would pull their animals from going rabid and establish a formal connection. At least, I hoped; it was what I read in books I had found many years ago.

It was never an easy process for shifters to move from pack to pack. It was painful and downright dangerous. Some could lose their life with the pain, and if the soul was not strong enough— they may not make it.

Before performing such a ceremony, we would have to check each soul.

And, who the hell was going to check a soul to make sure a member wasn't going to be in danger of dying?

Journey?

I ran my hand down my face. If they are too far gone, if they have been rogue long enough, I can't help; only their mates can.

At least some individuals, who have been recently rejected within the past few years, had a better chance.

"We are getting there," my wolf mumbled. *"You are doing everything in your power."*

I chuckled and pulled at my hair. *"My sister would be better at this."*

He hummed. *"Probably."*

Asshole.

Two days passed. I had been rearranging our new living quarters on the third floor of the packhouse. It was not completely furnished, still, but I didn't think it would be. At least someone had the idea of finishing the alpha suit first - walls, a bed, a table and kitchen supplies. Hell, it even had food.

Journey, she had a sixth sense about this stuff—or the Goddess inside her head. I don't know which.

And they all think I'm crazy.

Emm has moved very little and was still laying in bed. I constantly checked on her, keeping her warm and covering her with blankets again, while trying to make our home more like—a home. Adjusting the drapes, fluffing the pillows, all that.

Gods, I fluff pillows!

I ordered so much shit, and wolves kept dropping it off just outside the door. Too scared to even knock on the double doors, afraid I would come out and bite their heads off.

They should have been scared; their luna was transitioning, and my fucking shaft was raw as fuck.

Luckily in one of the boxes, Bones had the decency to put in some lube and a damn fleshlight inside. He even put in the infamous rutting root, that he had told me time and time again not to use, but I know I will not use it. I think it was as a joke, but a fucking terrible one.

The rut was getting worse, but I did what I could to keep my mind off of it. And, that was to decorate.

Our home would look much better than the shitty RV she was staying in. She's lived in that thing for almost fifteen years. Flashes of her past life flickered in my head constantly, and the more I see, the more I realize just how strong she is.

The Goddess didn't make a mistake, that was for sure. Emm was a real fighter. Taking men, twice her size, down with single blows. Her combat skills are incomparable, even for when I trained. For a female—hell for a human - she had more skills than most of our pack.

She wouldn't be the timid Luna you often see hosting boring tea parties. She would be a warrior and the backbone of the pack.

I did something unspeakable—but being the possessive bastard I was, I did it anyway. Bonded mates can look inside each other's minds. Emm wouldn't be able to do it as well as me yet, but hell, I could pry inside hers without her noticing.

I dug deep, wanting to know every last detail about her while I fucked her. I saw things I shouldn't have, like flashes of past lovers, and that was when my rut became worse. Fenrir hated it. His claws would grow, our fangs would descend, but our mate wasn't in our life then. I had to remind him of that.

My mate didn't fully understand what she prayed for, all those years ago. Her grandmother told her what to say, how to feel and, like an innocent child my mate was, she hung on her every word.

We owed her grandmother much.

Now, I fear my mate will worry about my true intentions. Yes, our mating will save The Iron Fang, form them into a pack and save countless lives. But it wasn't just about that—

If I knew that my mating to Emm would have destroyed everything I had built for these souls— I would have let it happen.

I would have let the Iron Fang burn.

Because, as my mother said, it is best to be the villain and get your happiness.

CHAPTER
TWENTY-SEVEN

Emm

I drifted in and out of consciousness, like waves lapping against the shore. Amidst the haze, I could discern Locke's voice. I think he was yelling at someone on the phone. His urgent commands echoed in my ears, piercing the silence. Each time, my body would shudder with distress, as if an electric current jolted through my veins. Overwhelmed, I would surrender once again, plunging deep into the abyss of sleep's obsidian embrace.

There are other times I'm watching a scene of a movie. Two children playing in a primitive village. When I say primitive, I mean it was just that. Dirt roads, log cabins, there wasn't any electricity, and there was an obvious caste system to the dreary town.

The two children I felt the urge to follow each day, had it better than the rest. They looked healthier, stronger. They didn't fight like the rest. They didn't look— so feral. And the little boy's eyes were just so green and lively I could easily get lost in them

I knew I was sleeping, I kept trying to wake myself with a pinch or a shake of my body, but my mind would bury itself deeper into the dream, more immersed in it.

Right now, I was watching these children on the day where the girl called Amaryllis would start her training to be alpha. It was an important day, I figured, by the announcement that the large male yelled over the crowd.

Koen, the young boy with a beaming smile, settled on the sidelines, perched on a rough log. I observed Amaryllis, a determined little girl, brimming with pride. However, as I observed the other children of the pack I saw them to be undernourished. A nagging sense of unease washed over me.

It was a loveless—pack; that was the word often used. These were horrible creatures—the wolves that I saw trotting through the town. The warriors of the pack would kick and hurt the weak, and when I first came here, I often tried to push them away.

My efforts were in vain. My hand would fall right through. I knew one thing, though, I didn't want to have anything to do with a pack if this is how it was run.

I waited, stood in the crowd full of children and adults, watching as Amaryllis stood before her father, the alpha. My panic rose when the alpha waved his hand on the other side of the crowds and easily made a circle.

"Something is not right," I muttered to myself, my head swept through the crowd. I couldn't understand why no one else could sense it, but I certainly did.

A person walked up beside me; I felt the cool wind that accompanied them, but didn't turn to see who they were. No one answered me when I tried to talk to them.

"You are correct. Something isn't right."

Startled, I jumped, my heart racing as I swiftly turned my head towards her. She stood before me, adorned in a pristine white dress that flowed elegantly around her. Her hair, a shade of white so pure that it seemed to possess a faint bluish tint, glimmered under the sun. As her gaze met mine, her ethereal blue eyes locked onto me, captivating and mysterious.

I opened my mouth to speak but closed it again. *She didn't belong here. Hell, neither did I.*

"This is the Blood Rose pack. The pack was named after the blood-red roses that would grow inside its territory, before it was tainted."

I still couldn't find words to speak, which was rare for me. I just continued to stare at this woman who didn't look human at all.

"It's overwhelming, isn't it? Seeing where your mate had grown up?"

I let a strangled puff of air out of my throat and glanced at the little boy sitting on the log, with a knife and a block of wood in his hand. He didn't look at all like Locke. Sure, he had the same dirty blonde hair, maybe, the same colored eyes, but this boy looked loved despite the pack he lived in.

This boy was shy. He had dreams of making toys. He didn't look like he had a malicious bone in his body.

"I'm going to witness something terrible, aren't I?" I whispered, as I watched the alpha of the pack put his hand on Amaryllis.

The woman folded her hands in front of her, a frown forming on her lips. "I don't normally allow humans to be shown the past of their mates while they are being woven into the bond. Transitioning into a shifter is quite delicate. However, this is a special circumstance."

Excuse me?

Before I could explode with questions, the crowd grew quiet when the alpha hovered over his daughter and pushed her into the ring. There was no love in his eyes, as he ordered her to take on the challenge of a male child, twice her size.

The male was tall and muscular in his build. I would say about fifteen and being paired up against an eight-year-old child was crazy. It was fucking suicide. This was supposed to be her first day of training.

And there was nothing I could do about it.

The powerful alpha remained unfazed, not a muscle twitching, as Amaryllis confidently advanced and unleashed a swift strike. The air crackled with determination as Amaryllis continued to rein blow after blow.

That was until the teenager struck back.

Her mother cried out from the crowd, her hands over her cheeks.

"Why am I a special circumstance? Why am I being shown Locke's past?"

The woman took in a breath. "To show you how Locke used to be, before he was tainted. He may have ultimately beaten his father many, many years later, but it was a rough road to get there. His body, mind and wolf were broken, and they will always remain so, no matter how much the bond tries to mend it."

There was that word again.

The crowd cheered as the male hit Amaryllis again. Koen, who I now knew to be Locke, stood and pushed people away from him to enter the ring. His father yelled and pointed for young Locke to stay back. It distracted the opponent enough for Amaryllis to jump and swing her leg to kick her attacker in the head.

Her much taller opponent, with a resounding crash, stumbled and collapsed onto the unforgiving ground. The impact reverberated through the air, accompanied by a chorus of gasps from the spectators. A moment of stunned silence ensued as the defeated figure remained motionless, defeated. Amaryllis, smiled and basked in the sweet taste of victory.

The crowd had a mixture of cheers and groans they handed money to each other.

The fight was quick, and it took everyone by surprise.

Amaryllis stood tall and pulled her shoulders back. Locke's shoulders slumped in relief and he began walking towards her to congratulate her. Amaryllis skipped, a wide smile on her face as she opened her arms to hug her brother.

The tension in my body left too soon, because I heard Locke scream. Amaryllis' mouth hung open, her eyes filling with tears. She stumbled forward, landing in Locke's arms. He screamed again and the crowd roared with confusion and chaos.

I ran through the bodies, trying to get a better look. When I came to the clearing, there was a weeping young Locke, cradling his gasping sister in his arms.

"No, don't go. Please don't!" He held her tightly.

His mother rushed beside him, screaming her name, "Amaryllis! Amarillys! No! Gods no, please don't take my pup. Gods, please no!"

I stood over them, trying to hold back the sobs. *What the fuck happened?*

"Mother, what do I do?" Locke was covered in blood. He was holding his sister at an angle so the knife in his sister's back would not go in deeper, as he sat on the ground.

"I don't know!" his mother cried. "A healer! I need a healer!" She gazed over the crowd, but no one stepped forward. They silently traded off their money from their ruthless gambling.

"Why isn't anyone coming!?" I cried. I felt the woman behind me. "Where is their healer?!"

The woman gently shook her head. "There were no healers in Blood Rose. The alpha believed if you were weak enough to become injured, you deserved to die."

My heart constricted, aching with a heaviness that suffocated. I was enveloped in Locke's agony, as if it were my own, feeling the sharp sting of sorrow piercing through my soul.

Locke's anguished cry pierced the air, echoing like a mournful howl.

Trembling uncontrollably, he gently pressed his quivering lips against his sister's cooling forehead.

The unbearable pain seared through my chest, tears ran down my cheeks and my body shook. I didn't know I could feel a pain like this.

"Now that his twin has left the living plane, he will unlock the alpha blood within himself," the woman said. "He will take all her strength and multiply it by two."

"Oh my god," I gasped, covering my mouth. "Did—did their father know that?" I pointed to the alpha who stood off at the edge of the fighting ring, with his arms crossed. There was a twitch in his lips.

"Yes," she said angrily. "He did. But he made sure that her death looked like an accident."

The alpha stomped over to the opponent who had fought against Amaryllis. The male had a smile on his face and bowed to his alpha. "I have beaten the alpha's daughter, I have earned—" The alpha gripped the teenager by the neck, his hand wrapping around his throat, and squeezed. A crack echoed through the crowd, and the people stood back in shock, watching the lifeless body fall to the dirt.

"This was hand-to-hand combat. No knives were to be used. You break the rules, you suffer the consequences." His glare went around the ring. "And let this be a lesson to you all. Never turn your back on an opponent, even when they are down."

The alpha's expression remained cold and impassive as he silently made his way towards his wife and his only remaining child. His gaze fixated on his son, deliberately avoiding the sight of his lifeless daughter lying nearby.

"Stand," he commanded Locke.

Locke's eyes narrowed, and the grip on his sister tightened.

"I said stand," he snarled. "Your training starts today."

I hadn't had a chance to look up close at Locke's father, but he was a terrifying male. Tribal tattoos littered his entire body, bulging muscles and a face that was not at all handsome. Luckily, a beard covered most of his face, that held beads and shells.

Locke still did not waver. Instead, his father had to pull Locke away from his sister's body by the arm.

His mother cried out, catching Amaryllis in her embrace.

Locke's face contorted in anger; his lips curled back as he snarled. With a swift, forceful motion, he yanked his arm away from his father's grasp. The gathered crowd stood frozen, their eyes fixed on the intense standoff, their anticipation palpable in the air. The atmosphere was charged with tension, as if a storm was brewing just beneath the surface.

"As I thought," the alpha whispered. "You will be the strongest alpha to lead this pack, once you are old enough. Now," he purred, "you best listen, or your mother will be next."

Locke glanced at his mother, who was still rocking Amaryllis in her arms, crying silently. Locke swallowed and nodded once in confirmation.

The alpha turned to the crowd and held up his hand. "Blood Rose, I give you your future alpha. A powerful *male* that will be worthy of your protection. Koen. His name meaning bold and brave. What this pack will need in the coming years to be in favor to the king."

The crowd cheered, long forgetting Amaryllis, the former alpha heir.

The crowd dispersed, and I stood there watching Locke's mother cry for the dead child in her arms.

I wiped away the tears and still felt the woman beside me. "I didn't need to see this. Locke could have just told me."

"He wouldn't have told you about it. And if he had, would you had believed him? Would you have trusted him enough?" She said with a smooth, velvet voice.

The surrounding area disappeared, and we found ourselves in a meadow.

Darkness fell and the large moon rose above us.

"I have shown you the *beginning* of your mate's pain. He only suffered more throughout his adolescent and young adult years." The woman walked in front of me and I followed behind her.

I gritted my teeth, trying to listen and not interrupt. I'd been alone for days it seemed and at least I was getting answers. I could not believe I was thrown into this shit show.

"Locke has told you he has claimed you, but I don't believe you realize what that means. Locke can get ahead of himself, especially since his mind was half rabid."

"Half rabid? You mean crazy? I think we both know he has problems, but I'm guessing it was because of his shitty childhood."

I rubbed my hand up and down my arm. I felt so damn bad for him, but I had a feeling that Locke didn't like pity, and I would not give it to him. I would be fucking pissed for him though. He lost his family, and I had a feeling he also lost his mother.

"No, rabid is when your soul is too broken and you begin to die." She looked into the distance. "That is a story for him to tell you about later, but I am just telling you that—you are on the path to mend his soul." The woman turned back to me. She was shockingly beautiful, with skin as pale as the moon itself.

I tilted my head. "Me? How do I mend him?"

"You are his soul mate. You've heard him say that before. You've even heard his mother speak about it."

I bit my lip. The way his mother said what soul mates were was so poetic. Did Locke feel all those feelings when he saw me? Or was it simply lust and desire? There was no doubt I felt a pull, but I tried to force any sort of romantic feelings away. Romance, feelings— just didn't work in the real world.

I swallowed. "I did, and it was beautiful. But, Locke wouldn't feel that way toward me."

The woman smiled and nodded. "He does. He might have a different way of showing it. As do you—you are one tough human, Emmie. Your pairing was quite easy once I saw your soul light up on this Earth."

I blinked several times. "Are you—"

"The Moon Goddess?" She hummed. "You can call me Selene. And just so you know, you have, well, *had* a choice to accept Locke. You could have rejected him. All souls have the option."

I scoffed. "Locke said I didn't!"

"And would you have rejected him?" She put her hand on her hip.

No. Probably not. He had the mix of danger, desire and hot monster-sex I've always wanted.

Selene giggled and played with the tips of her hair. "Not only are you perfect for each other, but perfect for the Iron Fang. The Iron Fang will transform from a club into a pack of once-lost souls, who will be guided to a better path."

I grabbed her hand, feeling the coolness of her touch. "A pack? Like Blood Rose?"

Selene's eyes narrowed. "Nothing like Blood Rose. You and Locke will create a thriving pack, completely opposite. You will be the protectors of the weak. But I really need you to promise me you will stay, Emm. You need to stay with the Iron Fang. Protect them, fight for them." Selene grabbed my other hand and held it to her chest.

I felt pride that she would ask *me,* but she was the one that dealt with souls. *Couldn't she protect them? Why would she care if I stayed to help protect everyone?*

"Because if you don't stay, Locke will follow you. He will let the Iron Fang fall and all the souls with it." Selene gripped my hands tighter.

"He would leave it all if I left? Why would he do such a thing? He built all of this, didn't he?"

Selene nodded quickly. "He did but he would burn the world for you. His friends, his family—all for you. You are the rock, the luna of the Iron Fang. You must stay so we can continue to help the rogues, the ones that will go rabid if they don't find their other half."

"Lost souls? Rabid? I still don't understand." I shook my head.

Heat engulfed my body, it wrapped around my back, to my chest and between my legs. I let out a shaky breath and forced my hands out of her hold.

"What about my family?" I pressed, backing away. "They are far away. I need my family here with me."

"Emm, you must promise me you will stay." Selene's voice faded.

I whimpered, feeling the heat grow. I was so hot, and I was feeling—horny. My nipples hardened and a moan escaped my lips. I needed to touch myself.

How embarrassing.

"I—what about my sister, m-my nephew? Abuela?" I dropped to my knees into the grass. Selene followed, but all I saw was her long hair sweep in front of me. I couldn't hear her voice, just the rushing sounds of the wind.

CHAPTER TWENTY-EIGHT

Emm

Instead of waking peacefully in bed, I woke and my body ached with desire—no, it was more. My body was lit on fire, and it burned with an intensity so strong I thought I would burn to ash. It was painful. I thought I was dying. If this Goddess was truly real, maybe I was being thrown into the depths of the underworld, where I would burn instead of waking and returning to Locke.

I'd burn for my sins of lusting after a lycan and being fucked by one in the forest.

I could feel myself writhing in pleasure and pain while I remembered the wolfish beast pounding into me. His breath was hot and ragged against my neck, his teeth gnashing at my fragile skin. I knew this wasn't just about lust. Something primal and ancient was at play. My body responded instinctively to the otherworldly nature of the creature, and I could feel the transformation happening within me.

It was like he was there, I could feel his breath on my skin.

"I can't take much more." I heard Locke's guttural groan. The rapid slick, slurping sound coming from behind gave me some damn dirty visions in my head.

Was he masturbating?

I let out a low, pleasurable moan as I arched my back, savoring the sensation. Beads of perspiration glistened on my skin, making my legs feel damp and sticky. I could feel a steady trickle of warmth escaping from between my thighs, heightening my desire. With a longing touch, my hand glided over my stomach, then ventured into the intimate depths of my folds, igniting a wave of intense pleasure.

"Fuck, Princess, are you awake?" he rasped. "Your heat is driving me wild and I can't keep back. Please let me sink into that slick."

Dios mio, he was a dirty bastard.

I moaned again and pressed my fingers to my clit to gather some relief from the burning pain. When I touched myself, there was no relief, I thought I would orgasm easily as my pussy throbbed for a climax, but there was none to be had.

"Please," I whimpered, fucking my hand. "I—I can't get there."

Locke let out a huff of excitement and pulled the covers away from my body. "Princess, you are just soaked. Let me help you."

As I gazed up at him, I noticed a subtle widening of his nostrils, and a deepening darkness in his eyes.

"Yes," I whispered, my voice barely a breath. "Help me, please."

Locke smiled, a dark and predatory grin that sent a shiver down my spine. He spread my legs his hard length pressing against my damp core. His hands gripped my ankles and put them over his shoulders. He drew up his cock, rubbed it against me, and coated himself in my slick arousal.

"I will," he promised, his voice rough and commanding. "We both fucking need this." He grabbed onto one of my breasts and pinched the nipple.

With a sudden force, he thrust into me, burying himself to the hilt in a single, powerful stroke. I gasped, my eyes wide as I felt his thickness stretch me open. He moved, a slow, deliberate rhythm that built in intensity with each deep thrust.

"Fuck, you feel so good," he growled, his eyes never leaving mine as he continued to pound into me. My body responded instinctively, my hips rising to meet his every thrust. The pleasurable pain from before now transformed into pure, unadulterated ecstasy.

"Yes," I cried.

"You're so damned tight," he groaned, pulling out and thrusting back in with increasing speed. "I can feel your heat surrounding me, pulling me in deeper."

And I could feel every inch of him. The rough, cold metal of the barbells scraping against my walls, creating a pleasure I haven't felt before. All of this was just so—intense.

My body shook, and goosebumps rose on my skin when Locke continued to slap his hips against my body.

"That's it, come. I will not make you hold in your orgasms, not when you are in heat."

I shook my head and used my legs to push on Locke's shoulders to get a better angle. He picked up the pace to jackhammer me.

I cried out and felt the pain leave my body as the orgasm took over. But it was only a quick relief because once the orgasm was over, the pain returned.

"Why does it hurt?" I cried, when Locke pulled out of my pussy.

"You need my knot," he panted, a sheen of sweat glistened over his forehead. "And I'm going to give it to you. It will give you relief before we need to do it again."

I let out a soft moan, my fingers expertly tracing their path back to my throbbing clit. With an urgent pace, I continued to rub myself—I couldn't just lay there waiting.

"Damn, it's so hot seeing you play with yourself like that." Locke lowered his head and took a long tentative lick. I threw my head back and clamped my thick legs over his head. His claws raked down my thighs while he continued to bury himself into my pussy.

I orgasmed again and once I finished, with a quick movement, he rolled me onto my stomach and slapped my backside. I squealed at the sting while he pulled my ass and lined up his cock. "I'm going to knot you so many times in the next few days. You're pussy is going to crave it."

Gripping the sheets tightly, I could feel the texture of the fabric beneath my fingertips. I remembered his Lycan's knot, and it was almost too much.

Locke rubbed my back and rested his hand on my hip. "It won't be as big as in my lycan form, but it will still stretch you so good, Princess, trust me."

His cock slipped inside easily, with my arousal continuing to drip, and I pushed myself toward him to get more.

"Fuck, like a glove. And so needy."

"You'd be needy, too, if you were on fire," I retort.

"Princess, you have no idea." His fingers dug deeper into my ass with one hand and the other was on my shoulder. His cock went in and out of me; the bars on his Jacob's ladder rubbed so nicely on my throbbing clit that I moaned like a dirty whore with how good it felt.

Timidly, I glanced back at him, my eyes wide with anticipation. "Please, Locke, do it." I begged, my breaths coming in short, quick gasps. "Give me the relief I need."

I'm not normally a beggar, but apparently with Locke I am.

Without speaking, Locke continued the rhythm, his cock sliding in and out of me. I could feel his knot stretching, growing with each thrust. My body arched and contorted, yearning for the release he promised. The pleasure was building, growing like a tempest, tossing me about as he fucked me.

"Yes, you are going to take it!" Locke growled, his grip tightening on my hip and shoulder. "You need me, and I'm going to give it to you."

And then, like a strike of lightning, my relief hit me. It coursed through my body, setting every nerve off with pleasure. I shuddered and screamed, clenching around Locke's cock as his shaft throbbed. Locke let out a grunt and forced his knot inside me. The pain of the stretch morphed into bliss, a searing wave of ecstasy that washed over me.

The knot, not as large as his Lycan was still painful as he pushed it deeper inside. It swelled, pulsing, prolonging the pleasure.

If someone makes knotted dildos, they really need to up their marketing.

I sighed in relief, feeling more and more of his come filling my body. My stomach felt distended as his cock pulsed and emptied into me. The shudder of an aftershock cooled my body and my shoulders slumped in relief.

Locke's powerful purr, reminiscent of his wolf's when he slept with me each night, reverberated through the softness of the bed. In that moment, my body surrendered to the comforting sensation, the tension melted away and relieved by his gentle touch.

Locke leaned close, his warm breath tickling my skin, as he left a trail of tender kisses down the curve of my spine, each one sending shivers of pleasure through me. The soft touch of his lips gradually made its way back up to my shoulder, and he gently pressed his tongue against the spot where he had previously bitten me. A delicious mix of sensations flooded my body, causing my senses to heighten. I could feel the tightening of my pussy intensify on his cock and another shiver of aftershock made me moan into the pillow.

"Mmm," he groaned in my ear, "I could get used to this."

My body was exhausted even with the sleep, but would I do it again? Absolutely.

Locke gently rolled us to the side, his knot lodged deeply inside me as we lay on the bed contentedly. Occasionally, it would pulse and my body would spasm into bliss.

None of it was normal. Not a single bit. Even if I left out the *heat* and the knot; the cuddling wasn't a thing that was normal to me either. Locke held onto me. He was petting my hair, placing kisses on my neck and rubbing my arm tenderly. If there was no knot, I was sure he would still do the same.

And I think back to that little boy in my dream, who listened to his mother about mates. How his mother said you never give up on a mate, you hold on to them, fight for them and never give them up. Locke would never give me up. The Goddess herself said so.

And in this moment, I firmly believed it.

"Locke?" I whispered, and daringly, placed my hand on top of his hand, which was caressing my breast.

He mumbled, mid-kissing my neck. "I think you should explain a couple things to me," I chuckled and felt this cock pulse again.

He groaned and held me tighter. "Yes, I think I owe you explanations about some things. How about over dinner?" He moved his hips to push his cock in and out of me, just enough not to dislodge his knot.

I let out a cry, and again I felt another spurt of his come. "Ugh, I needed that," he sighed."

"My god, how can you come so much?" I turned my head to see a sated look on his face.

"Princess, I've been in a rut since you fell asleep. You have no idea how much I have come since you have slept for three days."

My head fell back on the pillow. "Three days?" I whispered, and then my eyes widened. "Three days!? I haven't called my fam— I need to go—"

Locke tightened his hold, and we both groaned when I jerked our bodies.

"No one is going anywhere until my knot releases you, mate. Now calm down," he growled.

"But I can't!" I panicked. "I have to make a call. Where is my phone? Where the hell are we?"

I quickly scanned the room, my eyes darting from one corner to another, only to realize that we were nowhere near my familiar RV. The room had a quaint, rustic charm, its simplicity evident in the minimal furnishings; a solitary bed, a modest nightstand and a plain dresser. A modern-looking cabin is the only way to describe it.

"I have all your things," he calmly said. "Like I said, I'll explain everything. We have time because we aren't going anywhere for a few days."

"A few days?" I squealed and my pussy fluttered. We both moaned, and I fisted the sheets.

"Yes, days. You are in your heat because I claimed you. I am in my rut and need to have my knot emptied frequently. It's a gift to the both of us that it happened at the same time."

I narrowed my eyes at him but he only grabbed my breast in reply. "We help each other and it is the perfect time to get to know one another. Really, know each other because—"

I shook my head. He didn't understand. He didn't know about my family, didn't know about all of them in Venezuela. He didn't know about the bounty on his head—what if he found out about that?

How was I to tell him all this? He would be angry, furious. And what about the men chasing me?

If he gets pissed enough, he'd leave me to deal with this *heat* alone. I did not even know what a *heat* or a *rut* is! Or why it was happening!

And that was when I did something I never do; I began to cry.

CHAPTER TWENTY-NINE

Locke

If there was one thing in this world that could instantly deflate my knot, it was the sound of her tearful cries. The sight of a woman shedding tears was unbearable to me, their faces flushed with anguish, the glistening trails of sorrow streaming down their cheeks.

It was why I had my men take care of the women after a mission. Women saw me as a dick. I was stone-faced around them, ordering the men to take care of the weeping women after rescue missions. My men were better capable.

I couldn't handle seeing women in distress.

My mate was now sobbing in front of me while my knot was lodged deep inside her. It was softening more quickly than I ever thought it could. My body was shutting down, my heart breaking. I could hear the cries of my mother when my sister died, and I had to make her stop.

The only tears I wanted to see from her were of pleasure, not of pain.

"Baby, I'm so sorry." I pulled on my cock. My knot was still hard, but it had softened enough to dislodge from her cunt. It made a slick pop when it fell from her body. My wolf was protesting. He wanted to shove it back inside her, but damn it, I would not have my princess cry.

I climbed over her, letting my skin feel the dampness on the sheets. I brought her body closer to me and let her head rest into my neck. "Fuck, I know I'm a lot sometimes but I swear it's to keep you safe. But you crying like this is gonna break me."

She sobbed again, gasping for air. "I-I am not crying. My eyes are sweating."

As my wolf snorted, a soft snore filled the air, causing a smile to slowly spread across my face. I observed her face, which turned a deep shade of red, while her nose twitched and sniffed with each breath.

When my mother cried, my father would try to beat her. I'd always be around to stop him; tell him if he laid a hand on her, I'd do everything in my power to ruin what he had built. He would stop, but still, I would cross the line if I comforted my mother in his presence.

Mordecai saw me as nothing but a walking, emotional, weak wolf. I was weak in my father's eyes because I had feelings toward my mother. I wanted to protect her from the bastard, but that didn't stop the insults, the punches and blows I took for her.

"An alpha isn't allowed to have feelings. Females are to bear children for the betterment of the pack."

I cleared my throat and continued to stroke her face as she continued. *What does one say to comfort a female?*

"Emmie, let me fix it. What do you want?" I pleaded.

I fucking pleaded!

"I—I need to call someone," she said.

I raised my head and looked for the phones that sat on the nightstand. I reached over her, bringing the phone between us and laid it on the pillow.

"Here, it's right here. You can call whoever you want." I very well knew it was her family. She was worried sick now that the reality of it all was crashing down on her.

Emm sniffed and stared up at me. "Can I have privacy?"

She looked so hopeful I almost let her win.

"No," I shook my head. "You're my mate, no secrets between us. You are finding out mine through the bond we share—"

Her eyebrows raised, and her lips parted.

"I know you've seen some shitty parts of me. And soon I'll be able to see all the shitty parts of you. I know some Emmie; I've seen that you have been with other men, and how you've worked hard to be who you have become."

Her lip wobbled, but she tried to set her lip into a pressed thin line to hide it.

"But you are mine. The Goddess decided, I decided, and you accepted my bite and my knot. Nothing about your past, what you have done, will deter me."

This made her roll her face into the pillow and cry even harder. An overwhelming power of guilt radiated off her. I was surprised the bond was this strong even without her bite to claim me fully.

I growled and shook her shoulder. "Stop crying!" My wolf had his hackles up inside my mind. Fur was sprouting over my arms. "You cannot cry in my presence. Not when it breaks my damn soul to see you this way."

She sobbed again and rolled on her back. Her breasts heave and I tried my damnedest not to look. I was trying to make my mate stop crying, this powerful female does not cry, and I feared I'd fucking broke her.

My mouth instantly went to her nipple, forgetting all logic. She cried out in shock and she ran her fingers through my hair. My come that was still leaking from her body mixed with the fresh scent of arousal.

"Locke," she whined and I sat her up in the bed. I made her straddle my lap, my hands dug through her hair, and I gripped her scalp firmly to keep her looking at me.

"Nothing-nothing about you will keep me away. And everything I have done—" I chuckled darkly, "I don't give a fuck if you don't' like it."

She giggled and wiped away the tear with her hand.

"I am the president of the club. My members are vigilant. They knew where you lived, every move you made, tried to get into your laptop—"

Emm tilted her head, her wild hair tickling my skin.

"And why do you think that is? Hmm? Why do you think they know all that? I trained them and also—" I leaned forward, letting my lips graze her ear. "I've heard almost every phone call you've made since you got to town, my mate. And I know who you have spoken to."

My mate's eyes widened. "What?" she muttered. "Y-you could hear—you know?"

I nodded, pressing kisses down her neck. "You have a family in Venezuela. You're desperate to get them up here, aren't you, Princess?" My arm wrapped around her waist, pulling her closer to my cock. I was ready to sink into her again, my rut not giving me an easy time.

Her heat was building as well—so much for feeding my mate actual food. Now, she's just going to need a shot of protein.

"My little hunter was on the job." My hand traced between her legs and I stroked her clit. "My hunter, my luna, my mate was hunting me. I was a difficult target for you, wasn't I?"

Emm's breaths came in rapid pants. Her fingers tightened on my shoulders and she tried to push me away. I held onto her tighter, pulling her so her pussy rubbed up against my shaft. She groaned, her breasts pushing against my trimmed chest.

"You were gonna turn me in. Collect the money and save your family, weren't you, baby?"

Emm's once rhythmic movements on my cock came to a halt, leaving us in an eerie silence. The taste of her skin lingered on my tongue as I delicately traced a path from her collarbone to her neck.

"H-how does that not make you angry? I scouted this place, got to know your club. To search for you to—turn you in?"

I chuckled against her shoulder. "It was the best foreplay I've ever had. Touching the enemy, licking the enemy in front of the bar. Fuck, Princess, I say we do more of that roleplaying shit."

Emm pulled away from me, her mouth opened in shock. Her eyes were still puffy and swollen. "It wasn't foreplay, it was real, Locke. I was going to take you in—for the money to save my family. And now—I can't." Her eyes softened and looked at my cock standing to attention between my legs.

"I feel so guilty for it," she whispered. "I told my family I'd get them here and I fell for the—"

My shit-eating grin exploded on my face. "Yeah, baby. You fell? Fell for who?"

Emm slapped me on the shoulder and covered her breasts. "Stop, you're being such a bastard."

I pushed her back into the bed and planted kisses down her neck. "Last person that called me a bastard I ripped their heart out. When you say it, though, it really gets me fucking hard."

"You're always hard!" she squealed, as I sunk my cock back into her body.

My mate relaxed and let me touch her where I wanted.

"We need to talk," she said with a pleasurable gasp. "I need to talk to my fam—"

My knot lodged inside and I pulsed it in her pussy. My hips pump into her gently, letting my knot push in and out of her opening.

"Shit, you can't do this to calm me down." She cried out as her back arched.

I very well can damn try.

I left Emm lying in the bed, filled with furs to keep her warm. I still needed to explain to her about her upcoming change, the heat, and the other secrets I have kept from her.

I had so many surprises for her, but getting her through her heat, her transformation and the brief history lessons on the pack was enough to worry about. I was so giddy with all my surprises I didn't know how I was going to keep them from her.

"Just hope she doesn't learn how to enter your mind," my wolf drawled. *"Then, we're fucked.*

"You always were a mood killer," I mumbled back to him.

I was fucking trying to be communitive and shit. I'd even bought a book on it.

I flipped the last of the dozen eggs on the pan. I heard my mate's gentle footsteps and I turned around, seeing her in one of my shirts. Her breasts were tightly pressed against the fabric, her nipple piercings showing through the dark color - I could spot them a mile away - and oddly, I'm not so hungry for eggs anymore.

I turned back to the eggs and cleared my throat.

We've done enough, let her pussy rest.

"She can fucking handle it," my wolf growled appreciatively. *"I think she*

wants more, just do it on the table," my wolf panted.

I switched off the gas stove with a quick flick of my wrist and turned around to brace myself. "Sorry I didn't ask before, but you were sleeping. But how do you like your eggs?" I let the fried eggs slide off the pan and onto a plate.

"Fertilized," she purred.

Instantly my cock pressed up against my sweats, and Emm laughed softly. "It's so easy to get you riled up, huh, Alpha?"

I rolled my eyes to the back of my head when she referred to me with that title. I never thought I would like it. It was a power title, one I refused to take while me and my members were rogues. We took it in jest, as a joke. Because I fucking didn't feel like an alpha after I destroyed a pack that was supposed mine.

The way she said it though—maybe I could be an alpha. A real one, with her by my side.

"I'm guessing you like being called that?" She raised a brow and strolled toward the table.

"Only when you say it. It's like Dom or Master."

Emm rolled her eyes and padded over to me. "You're something else. You know that?"

I wrapped my arms around her waist. "I think people use more colorful words, but, ah, yes, I am quite different, huh?"

She hummed, her fingers grazing down my torso. "Yeah, you are. I went from a crying mess to being fuck-comforted. Anytime I get upset, I'll be sure to come to you."

My chest swelled with pride. "You always come to me. I'll fix it."

Emm backed away and looked at the table, filled with eggs, sausages, pancakes. One day, everyone in this massive home would be served a basic packhouse breakfast.

"This is a lot." she grabbed a sausage from the plate and took a bite. "Mm, that tastes so good." She sat down and didn't look at me as she grabbed food and barely put it on her own plate before she'd started to inhale it.

I watched her in awe at how the smallest things made me love her more. Yes love, I fucking craved her. The smallest things she did made me obsessed with her.

A feeling of contentment washed over me; I had provided for her, for my mate. Of course I had, because I was going to be the best mate.

She choked and panic rose in my throat.

"Slow down," I barked at her.

My mate narrowed her eyes and shoved another forkful into her mouth. "Hey, if I'm going to keep up this bod, I'm going to need some calories." She shimmied her breasts.

Ignoring her enormous globes, I took the fork from her. She looked absolutely appalled when I took her plate and held it in my hand. She watched me, still chewing the food left in her mouth, and a look of amusement washed over her. Once she'd swallowed, I held the fork up to her.

"You-you're going to feed me?" Her quiet voice entered my heart.

I scooted my chair closer to her, our knees touching.

I knew she'd got a lot of emotions running through her right now. She cried in my arms, because she'd seen my past; I could feel her heart squeeze in mine when she looked at me. It isn't pity, it's—an understanding of why I'm the way I am. On top of it all, she was in heat, and I'd heard from my men that is fucking awful.

All I wanted to do was to protect her, be the mate my mother would want me to be.

A male that showed her protection and care, not just give her the severed hands of her enemies.

Wait, no, I'd still do that.

I held the fork up to her and she tilted her head. I let my eyes plead with her just to take the food. I didn't feel like explaining to her why I needed to do this—that this was the way of a shifter; to provide food and substance.

I didn't want any smart-ass remarks, no joking, no—-none of that. My heart just wanted her acceptance.

And she did.

Because she is perfect.

My mate leaned forward and took the bite I had ready for her. We stared into each other's eyes. It was such an intimate moment that I felt my heart grow two sizes. She finished her plate, and I wiped her clean. The only sounds we could hear were the birds outside and the rustling of the trees.

My throat constricted when I pulled her into my lap from the kitchen chair. "Thank you." I rubbed my cheek against hers.

"For what?" she whispered, her hand touching my chest.

"Letting me feed you. It is a high honor when a female eats the food that a male provides." My voice was quiet while I said this, soaking up every moment. She really was my church, and I wanted to be reverent to it—for now.

My mate ran her finger over my cheek. "And what else do shifters do? To please their mate? Are there other traditions?" Her voice was so understanding. There wasn't a hint of malice or anything condescending.

I swallowed, my throat bobbing as I nodded. "Yes, one is to make a proper nest. Especially when their female is in heat and it's their first time." My hand trailed up her side and tickled the underside of her breast.

"You are having a heat because of me. My bite, not only helped solidify the bond between us but also—it's going to change you, Emmie."

Emmie's nails raked across my back, sending shivers up my spine.

"You will be a shifter. I don't think you will be Lycan, but a wolf. Like what I was. I'm sorry—I should have told you." I turned my head away, too fucking embarrassed to see her yell at me. But she grabbed my chin firmly in her hand and brought it toward her face.

Instead of seeing anger, I was met with her soft eyes and a gentle kiss on my lips. "I had a feeling. I don't know how to explain it. I'm just glad you confirmed it." She took a long, steady breath.

"You aren't angry?" I squeezed her thigh.

She shook her head. "I'm more relieved you found out I was hunting you. That I was going to sell you off to get my family." She winced and looked at the time on the wall.

"I need to call them, but—"

I could feel her dampness already pooling on my leg.

"And, so you know, I'm on birth control. I'm not ready to have any babies."

"Pups," I corrected. "And no, human birth control won't work. Now that you are changing, human contraceptives aren't a thing."

Her mouth opened slightly.

I kissed her cheek. "Don't worry, I'm taking my contraceptive. Males are usually in charge of the reproduction control, if they are proper mates."

Emm blushed and smiled. "That's amazing. I hated that stupid shot."

"But, Emm," I said and tilted her chin back to me. "I need you to do something this time. It will solidify our bond, more. Just so you know, if you do this, I will see everything in your mind just as you can see everything in mine. I've only been able to see fragments, just as you have with my life. After your teeth sink into my skin," I shuddered, "we will see each other's—everything."

She looked away and fiddled with her fingers. "That's intense," she finally said. "Just—don't go digging into when I was a teenager, when I had a crush on Jonathan Taylor Thomas. It's kind of embarrassing."

I barked out in laughter, put one arm under her legs and the other behind her back. It was going to be official now, I was going to be claimed.

CHAPTER THIRTY

Emm

My legs ached from the different positions he put me in. I didn't know there were that many ways to have sex, so I guess my originality was lacking. My pussy was swollen, damp but hell, I wouldn't say no if he asked to do it again.

I lost count of the euphoric peaks we'd reached, soaring on wave after wave of pleasure. The fatigue in Locke's body was clear as he pressed his knot inside me for the fifth time, releasing his sinful essence inside me. He pulled me to his chest to get me to stop the small tremors afterward whenever I moved. It was like he was begging me to stop.

Ha—finally outdid him in something.

I hadn't bitten him during this session of intense erotic pleasure. I was still too far into my head, trying to figure out how I exactly fit into his life.

I was a human, and I was becoming a wolf.

I loved scratching, biting, and bruising, during sex, but the bite he was talking about —he wanted it deep into the muscle, and the human side of me wasn't ready.

For the very first time, I had the privilege of witnessing Locke in slumber. His tousled hair cascaded over his forehead, casting playful shadows on his peaceful face. As I gently extricated myself from his tight hold, I paused, savoring the moment, and allowed my gaze to linger on him.

He lay sprawled on his stomach, his chiseled back physique exposed, untouched by any covers or bedding. The nest, as he referred to it, was a chaotic jumble of tangled sheets. The room carried a faint scent of musk, and the disheveled bed emitted a soft rustling sound as he shifted his weight to become more comfortable.

I could hear soft pants, a faint smile on his face. He looked happy, content and his heavy breathing made me realize what a deep sleep he was in.

He was like a cute, psychotic, death puppy.

I grabbed a blanket from the floor and wrapped it around me. I felt guilty leaving, but I really needed to call my sister. My phone sat on the nightstand, charged and ready to go. He gave it to me earlier, it meant I was allowed to use it, right?

What do I mean allowed? Of course I was.

For blackmail, and for me to remember this sweet moment, I took a picture of Locke's naked body sprawled on the bed. *Mmhm, he was a fine specimen.*

I left the room afterward, quickly dialing on the burner phone. My main phone for other calls sat on the kitchen counter, charging.

He really had thought of everything.

The phone rang once, and Elena picked up with a breathy hello.

"Hey, sorry I haven't called." I started and picked at my fingernail. As I strolled into the living room, I relished the sensation of the plush rug carpet caressing my bare feet. The room extended before me, amplified by the luminous high beams above, but it was not this grandeur that seized my attention. Rather, it was the colossal windows, revealing the beautiful view.

The forest was thick, lush and vines with flowers. Before I stumbled across this town and this MC, it had been so long since I spent time in the woods or a forest. The foliage here was different than what it should be in the northeast, but who was I to question about the plants?

I was turning into a werewolf, I shouldn't worry about freaking plants. A shifter's soul was intertwined with mine, so I had other things to worry about.

I held the blanket tighter around my shoulders and listened to Elena.

"So, how have you been?" she prodded. "Has anything interesting happened to you in the past few days? I bet it has been—exciting."

The sarcastic voice put me off, but I ignored it.

"Yeah, it's been something. I have something to tell you."

"No, no, no. Let me guess!" She got excited. "You stopped pursuing Locke as a bounty and fucked him into oblivion. In the forest, no less."

My heart stopped.

"And, and!" she screamed excitedly, "you took that big nasty knot and let him come all up in you raw."

What. The. Fuck.

"Elena!" I screamed, and covered my mouth. "How the hell?"

Had she been eating Abuela's mushrooms? But, how would she know about the knot?

While I was worried for her health and sanity, I couldn't understand how the fuck she would know.

"Emmie, I am fine! Just a headache, though. So are Luis and Abuela. We are all doing great. Better than ever."

"Then, how did you know? About a knot? How—"

Elena laughed on the other line, hysterical. "I'm sorry, it's just that I've never been so happy for you. Have you bitten him, yet?"

Mary and Joseph.

I sank into the plush, oversized, padded rocking chair, feeling its comforting embrace. Through the window, my gaze fixed on the world outside. The ominous rumble of thunder reverberated in the air, as raindrops cascaded from the heavens. Each drop plummeted onto the broad, lustrous leaves, creating a mesmerizing display before falling off onto the next.

"Elena, what's going on?" a growl left my throat.

Elena stopped laughing. "All the things Abuela told us as children are coming true, Emmie. We have soul mates. I'm just so happy for you. That you are letting this happen."

I rubbed my forehead. "But you guys are still in Venezuela. Our family is apart and now that I am with Locke, I can't leave." I rubbed my chest, feeling a longing for something so unfamiliar. The friends I made here had become my family.

My only problem is that my blood was left behind. I had to get them here where it was safe.

"I don't know how I'm going to get you all out of there. I'll raise the money. I'll work at the bar here in town. I'm not hunting or doing bounties."

Elena was silent for a long moment. "Emmie, are you feeling guilty?"

I bit my lip. "Yes. And I think that was why I haven't bitten Locke, yet, to complete the madness."

"It's so hot, you should have done it already," Elena whispered.

"You act like you know everything that has happened to me!" I snapped. "Do you know about wolves, knots, biting, where have you—wait." I stood from the rocking chair and paced the room, "Like you have been through it?"

My heart pounded in my chest. Locke has heard every conversation I've had with my family. He had my burner phone; he said Switch was great with computers; she knows everything that has happened to me.

He. Did. Not.

"Where the fuck are you?" I screamed into the phone.

Elena smacked her lips. "I can't tell you that right now. You are in the middle of your mating thing, and you are in heat. Which - let me tell you—"

"Shut up! What the fuck! Where is Abuela? You two monsters have kept secrets from me!"

"Emmie, we had to. You were still coming to terms with Locke and—"

"Don't Emmie me!" I shook my head. "You knew things were weird and said nothing!"

"Because I couldn't!" Elena screamed back. "Locke wanted to keep it from you. He wanted to tell you himself. You wouldn't have believed me. And, anyway...I needed my time, too."

Her time? Her *time*? What the hell? Does that mean she is someone's soul mate, too? I wasn't mad about that, on the contrary. I was happy she found love, but she kept it from me. They all did, and here I am feeling guilty as shit falling for a lycan.

Fury consumed me as I let out a feral growl, my face contorting in anger. With a forceful motion, I hurled the phone across the room, its trajectory slicing through the air with a whooshing sound. The device collided with the wall, shattering into a burst of splintering fragments.

All this time I was protecting my family, trying to get them here, and it sounded like she didn't want to come back at all.

I let the blanket fall and pounded my fist into the sturdy coffee table. It was a hardwood, I don't know what it was called, but I wanted to break it.

I continued to pound my fist into it. I felt my bones crack and my fingernails lengthen. I made one long scratch down the table as I growled into the room, and suddenly a warm, naked body surrounded me and pulled me away.

"Let me go!" I bared my teeth and hit at his arms, that were gathered around my stomach.

"You've got some of my anger, Princess. I need you to take some deep breaths."

"No!" I screamed, trying to fight and get away from him. "You told my family not to talk to me. Where is my sister? Get off me!"

Locke's powerful grip tightened around me, his fingers digging into my skin as he expertly maneuvered me, flinging me around and pushing me into the wall with brute force. The sound of our heavy breathing filled the air, mixing with the thuds and scrapes against the wall.

"If you would behave for a minute—" he raised his finger at me.

I pulled up my knee to hit him in his knot, but he grabbed my wrists, pinned them above my head and pinned my hips with his.

"Listen!" He growled deeply and my body betrayed me.

My nipples hardened and he took his thumb to flick the bar on my breast. It shot desire straight down to my pussy and I let out a moan.

Locke's hand snaked up my chest and grabbed me by the throat, not even using his full strength to keep me plastered to the wall. I very well knew he would beat me in a fight—especially now knowing what he is.

I knew he wouldn't, though. Because I could still see the fire burning in those eyes. Not of anger, but with desire.

As Locke held me against the wall, our eyes locked and I felt my resolve crumble. I couldn't deny the attraction I felt towards him, and the thought of being with him sent a shiver down my spine.

But, I was still fucking pissed. More so than I normally would be. I was just trying to protect my family and I felt lost. Was Elena in Venezuela? Was Locke just telling them what was going on with me? Where the hell was everyone?

"Locke, I don't know what's happening to me," I admitted, my voice barely audible because of his grip. "I'm so angry, I'm—" I rubbed my legs together, feeling my pussy pulse again. "My family—"

"I had to get them to a safer place. If you were to be mine, I needed them where I could see them. They are safe, and yes, your sister has someone who will take care of her."

I let one of my legs wrap around him.

"You seem to think you have secrets from me," he chuckled and ran a finger over my jawline. "You don't. And I'll know even more once we are bonded. Family is family. I will protect yours, and you'll protect mine. We are in this together, Princess."

"Where—?"

"They are safe!" he growled. "You will not leave this cabin. Not until we are both sated."

I felt the hard ridge of his cock press against my mound. He let my wrists go and I slid my hands down his body to grab his toned ass.

Locke relaxed, sending a resounding purr through both of our bodies. He took his shaft and coated it in the arousal leaking down my leg.

"Be a good girl and spread your legs for your mate." His cock dripped with his come, and he slipped it between my folds. He pushed in hard against me and seated himself deep, groaning. "That's it, takes this big, fat cock in that tight, little cunt."

My eyes fluttered shut as his thick cock filled me, and I let out a loud moan, feeling the strength in every part of his body. He was powerful, and I had never felt so electric with anyone like this. The feelings inside me were overwhelming, a mix of anger, desire, and love. I wrapped my ankles around his firm ass, pulling him closer to me.

"Locke," I panted, "I want to be with you, but I'm scared."

He pulled out in a slow, steady motion and then thrust back into me, going deeper this time.

"Don't be scared, Emmie. I promise I will take care of you and your family. We will be together, and no one will ever hurt you again."

Did he know about my father too?

Locke winked and I bit my cheek to hold in that eye roll I wanted to do.

His gentle reassurance brought warmth to my heart, and I could feel myself surrendering to the pleasure he was giving me.

"Harder, Locke," I whispered, knowing that I was about to complete the bond that had grown stronger through this fierce connection.

His movements became more erratic as he came closer to his release, and I felt his teeth graze my neck, a silent claim on me. As he thrust into me, I could feel his orgasm building and I reached up, grabbing at his hair, pulling his head to the side, and staring at his shoulder.

"Come for me, Emmie," he growled, and I knew he was right there with me, locked in this moment, angry, passionate and loving all at once. "Come all over this dick. It's your dick, claim it!"

I cried out as my climax hit me and it took no more hesitation to bite into the thick muscle of his shoulder. Locke's body shook as he joined me, releasing himself deep inside me. Locke held me up, letting his knot nudge further inside me.

He held me like I was light as a feather, caressing my ass while he continued to shallowly pump his knot in and out of my entrance.

"I'm yours," he whispered, panting at my neck. "You really claimed me!"

I let go of his shoulder and I saw the blood run down his torso, but the bite I had given him was already healing.

A darker, more animalistic urge had me lowering my head again and licking the crimson liquid off his shoulder.

Locke shuddered and while he was still connected to me, kneeled on the floor, and held me in his arms.

"Thank you," he petted my hair, running kisses up my neck. "Thank you for accepting me."

CHAPTER THIRTY-ONE

Locke

I observed Emm meticulously arranging and rearranging the bed, expertly placing the freshly laundered blankets and plump pillows that had just been delivered. I could see her face light up with delight as she pressed her cheek against the velvety softness of the linens. The sound of the fabric rustling filled the room as she skillfully blended the old blankets with the new ones.

She didn't understand what she was doing. Her body went on autopilot, and I hung back and watched her. It was like every other female brought to the Iron Fang. Their nesting instincts took over and my mate's were taking over quickly.

My bite might have something to do with it, the fact that I needed her to step up and take a role in leadership. I was fine with that because I knew she could do it. She already had a handle on me and she very well knew it.

So, I was savoring this moment. I never thought I would have a mate—not after what the first one did to me. I thought I was over and done with. Grim gave me small hope but I thought my own sins were too much to be redeemed. Look at me now, a lucky bastard indeed.

Here I was, watching my mate make our nest, so the next time we slept, it would be ready. Ready for her to take my knot over and over.

I adjusted myself as I thought about sinking back into her tight cunt. I swear she was sculpted by the gods just for me.

We showered in the massive bathroom made for us. I went all out on the third-floor blueprints of this packhouse. If it was going to be for me or some other alpha, in case I didn't make it, there was to be enough room for a few pups and a guest room. Unless she wanted to fill the whole floor with our miniature selves.

That might not be a good idea.

When Emm finished, she put her hands on her hips, turned to me and smiled. It was a rare smile, one I'd only seen from her when she was truly happy, not the forced, awkward social smile I'd seen so many times before at the club..

I held my hand out to her and she took it gladly. I led her out of our floor, and down the stairs to the second. Now, that our heat and rut had calmed, to just fucking every couple hours instead of minutes, I felt we could walk away from our nest for a time. I was still rock hard and couldn't keep my hands off of her. I didn't think that would ever go away, and now I knew how the other men felt when I'd seen them always looking, touching, and pulling their mates into a darkened hallway in the club.

"This is where the unmated and recently turned rogue will stay," I explained, as I flicked the switch; filling the room with a soft, yellow glow. The light revealed a dimly lit corridor, lined with empty rooms. I guided her through, the floor creaking beneath our feet. The sight of the shells of rooms awaiting completion was eerie - walls stripped bare, exposed wiring hanging from the ceiling like mechanical vines. The air carried a musty scent, a mix of dust and wood. As we walked, a faint echo of our footsteps reverberated, adding to the sense of emptiness. These rooms, although empty, would hold the promise of shelter for those who hadn't succumbed entirely to despair.

"Recently rogue? You mean recently rejected from their mates?" There was sadness in her voice, and she squeezed my arm.

"Yes, if they have been rejected recently, Journey believes we can still bring them into the pack and have them stay integrated with healthy wolves. It will help them not forget who they are." I said sadly, squeezing her arm in return. "Being connected to a pack alpha will slow their decline, and they won't go rabid as fast as the rest of us who had no pack."

"And what of the ones too far gone?" Emm gazed down the empty hallway once more and we walked toward the balcony following the railing to the grand staircase.

I sighed. "They will have to remain at the bar, in the apartments there. You and I will need to stay there with them during the week, and then my second, also known as my beta—Grim- will switch with us over the weekends."

"But why keep them apart? Wouldn't the most restless rogues want to stay in the forest? Would they be more comfortable?"

I wrapped my hand around Emm's waist and led her down the grand staircase, onto the main floor. The stones were laid by contracted bear shifters that usually work on the packhouse. I'd sent them away until I had fully claimed my mate. I couldn't have them around when Emm and I were here, I'd go too fucking crazy.

"They are dangerous, too far gone. They don't listen well and can be hard to handle. Those rogues could put others in danger if they decide to defy me. There are cabins surrounding this packhouse now that hold the mated, such as Hawke and Delilah, and their pup. At the club house there are more security cameras and there are lockdown capabilities if needed. I just have to keep everyone safe."

Emm nodded. "And, they might go rabid in the packhouse?"

I sighed and gritted my teeth. "Bones and Journey will do frequent check-ups here at the packhouse. Bones will check the healthy ones' physical body, while Journey will check their souls and see if they are fading. If they have to, they will move to the bar apartments where they can be monitored more closely."

Emm shook her head. "I can't believe so many women rejected all of those men. Did any of them deserve it?"

I stopped at the double doors at the base of the stairs, and held both of her hands. "I don't know all their stories. I don't go digging into people's pasts, but I ask them questions so I can figure out if they are good enough to be a part of this pack. There are rogues that deserve to be rogues."

"Like Duke Idris and his followers?" Emm's throat let out a growl.

I chuckled and rubbed her jaw with my thumb. "Exactly. They want the power rather than living peacefully. Money, greed, the ability to control monetary things that shouldn't matter. The gods put our souls here, made the lands for us to prosper and live in peace, and gave us abilities to make our lives easier."

"And some shifters took advantage," Emm continued.

"Not just shifters—but fae, and other magical beings as well." I squeezed her hand and took her outside. I wanted her to see what a real pack was to look like.

I had never grown up in one myself, but I have had visions. I read plenty of utopian pack fiction, although that would never work for men and women like us. We have seen too much darkness to fully trust anyone, but we were going to get as close as we could get.

As we stepped outside, my mates' eyes widened in awe. They took in the sight of the cabins, still in the process of being built; their frames standing tall against the backdrop of the fading daylight. The unlit bonfire in the center caught her attention, its wood stacked neatly, ready to ignite. I watched as she saw the paths taking shape, a blend of gravel and cement, under her feet. The air carried the scent of freshly cut wood and the faint hint of wet cement. It was a reminder of the ongoing construction.

"H-how are you guys building all of this?" My mate half laughed as we walked by.

"Bears." I shrugged my shoulders. "Bear's former sleuth works in construction. I'm paying them to do everything."

Emm blinked and saw several cabins with lights inside; trucks, cars, even motorcycles sat outside the open garages.

"So, you are making your own commune, maybe even a cult."

"A cult?" I raised a brow.

Emm laughed. "A bunch of like-minded people getting together, living, thriving, and sharing responsibilities together. Maybe even worshiping someone, or something?"

I tilted my head to the side and continued to walk with her until I pulled her off the maintained path, and took her down one not yet completed. "No, we are a pack. We can take care of ourselves, individually, but if someone needs help, I am here. You are here. We protect them."

"It's a cult," she muttered and continued to follow me. "Because of the way some of them talk about you, it's like they worship you."

I shrugged my shoulders. "I wouldn't tell them not to worship me. I'm pretty kick ass."

Emm threw her head back, her laughter echoing through the tranquil forest, and she playfully called me a cocky bastard as I guided her further into the dense wilderness. As we meandered, a comfortable silence enveloped us, interrupted only by the rustle of leaves beneath our feet. I noticed her wide-eyed gaze, studying the vibrant foliage surrounding us. The lush greens and exotic flowers, unseen anywhere else on Earth, captivated her attention. Despite her awe, she remained silent, lost in the uniqueness of Elysian beauty.

I wondered how far back she's seen into my mind. How much she knew about the other realm where I came from. Does she want to go there? Does she hate where I come from? All these questions swirled in my head as we ventured further to our destination, until she finally squeezed my hand and made me stop.

"How—how did you get here, exactly?" Her voice was soft.

I let go of her hand and left her leaning on a tree, and playing with a flower that flickered back and forth in the gentle breeze.

"How much have you seen, Princess?" I squatted, then sat down on a log across from her, resting my elbows on my thighs. The less I had to explain to her, the better.

My mate licked her lips and pressed her hands to her face. "I've seen a lot," she bobbed her head. "When you were a boy; your sister and mother. How you gained your title," she whispered the last part, and I balled my hand up into fists. "After I bit you, I saw you destroy your father, Mordecai. You destroyed everything—the whole pack. I don't know why you did it though and don't know how you ended up here."

I let out a huff and ran my hands through my hair.

"Well, you were right; I destroyed everything. Every damn thing that was left of Blood Rose." I licked my lips. "Except, all the blood money from Mordecai. I took all that. I wouldn't let anyone else have it." I sniffed and picked up a rock, tossing it in my hand.

"Blood money?" She stepped forward, unafraid.

I could feel my anger building just remembering the betrayal and deceit that had consumed my old pack. The memory of Mordecai's treachery, the schemes he concocted behind my back, all to further his own power and control. My grip tightened on the rock in my hand as I felt the rage bubbling inside me.

"Blood money," I repeated, the words tasting bitter on my tongue. "Mordecai lined his pockets with the suffering of others, with deals made in shadows and alliances forged in lies."

Emm watched me intently, her eyes never wavering from mine. I could see the questions forming in her mind, the curiosity about my past and the darkness that lurked within it.

"I had to destroy it all," I continued, my voice low and with a raw edge. "The corruption ran too deep, the rot too pervasive. Blood Rose was tainted beyond redemption. As much as I warned them behind my father's back, they didn't listen. They wanted power as much as he did."

My mate frowned and took steps toward me.

"Mordecai entered a treaty with the Emerald Pack. It was a neighboring territory that desperately needed protection. There were ogres that coveted the shiny stones that the Emerald Pack mined and used to export for the king. This pack's territory was located in the mountains, they had few exports, so this was their only means of making money."

Emm sat on the log beside me and wrapped her hand around my leg.

"Mordecai ordered me to lead our warriors to the attack against the ogres when they entered the Emerald Pack. When it was time to lead the attack, none of the warriors would listen to me. They stayed in position and watched the pack burn. I was so enraged, I went to fight on my own, but it was all in vain. The ogres were large. I did my best to help get the women and children out of there." I balled my hand into fists.

"You couldn't do anything." Emm said.

"I failed," I snapped. "I didn't save them. The ogres had everyone surrounded. I escaped, barely, just because they were distracted with loading up the gems into large wagons—with the king's seal."

My mate's mouth dropped.

I scoffed. "When I returned, the pack was filled with royal soldiers. A chest of gold was being unloaded from one of the wagons."

Emm snarled and stood from the log. "The king and your father, they—"

"Set them up to die." I finished. "Made it look like the ogres stole the gems so the Royal Council wouldn't suspect the king abusing his own kind."

When I explained to Emm that the Royal Council was just a round table, filled with the high royals of different species of the Elysian realm, she didn't like it. She said nothing good ever came of leaders coming together to discuss the 'betterment of the people or species.' Someone always got hurt and it was always the lesser people-never the leaders.

And she was right.

"I couldn't say anything—not then, anyway. My mother was still alive and—" I swallowed, "and my mate at the time was living within the pack. Mordecai would have killed them both."

Emm let out a low, jealous growl and I smirked, pulling her closer. "Emm—I never touched her. You are the first female to ride this cock, Princess."

The mood lightened considerably when her eyes widened. "Excuse me?"

I nodded and grabbed her ass. "Yeah, I was, uh, not sure about her. My mother said I would be head over heels for her, but I never got that pull she was talking about. I guess my wolf realized she was betraying me and didn't understand how to convey it to me. My wolf is, uh—" I scratched the back of my head, "very, traumatized."

Emm leaned in and kissed me on the cheek. A sweet gesture that seemed very out of character for my mate. "Tell Fenrir I will never hurt him," she whispered. "Ever."

I stared down into her big eyes, those long lashes kissing my chin. "He heard you." I swallowed. "We both did."

I leaned in closer to my mate. Our eyes locked, filled with desire. The world around us seemed to fade away as our lips finally met. The touch was gentle, yet electric, sending a shock wave through my body. We explored each other's mouths, our tongues dancing in a passionate rhythm. Every movement was deliberate, every caress a declaration of our love. Time seemed to stand still as we savored the taste and warmth of each other's lips, losing ourselves in the intoxicating sensation of the moment. It was a kiss that spoke volumes without the need for words.

This wasn't lust, it was so damn—fuck, it was love. It was everything my mother ever spoke about.

She cupped my cheek and pecked it several times. "Are you okay, handsome?"

I nodded, feeling my throat tighten. I didn't know if I could continue.

As if reading my thoughts, "We can stop. You don't have to talk anymore." She caressed my face. "You've done so well talking to me."

And fuck, if I didn't just get so bitterly hard. I let out a hoarse grunt and shook my head. "Let me finish."

My mate frowned but understood and continued to massage my leg.

"You see, I wanted it to be more traditional. I wanted to woo her—not just fuck and bite. It was an old, old tradition. I'd visit her, bring her gifts and visit her family. It was supposed to make the bond stronger, the mating more intense."

Emm growled, and she rubbed her chest, looking embarrassed.

"What you are feeling is normal. You are going to be jealous and possessive. And trust me, I'm a possessive bastard." I chuckled and nuzzled into her neck. "But please know this baby, I could not imagine having anything more intense than what we have. Our bond is—gods, it's stronger than I ever could have imagined."

"Yeah, you brought me a hand. I'd say that is a deep level of commit-ment."

"Just wait, I'm going to bring every guy's dick who you have ever looked, at once I get in that pretty little mind of yours."

"Ahh, a bouquet of dicks. That sounds awesome." She grinned wildly.

I rolled my tongue over my lips and bit at her neck. "Just so fucking perfect."

"Continue your story, Alpha. I want to know it all." She laid her head on my shoulder while I drew circles on her leg.

"Yeah, well, I guess she didn't like me teasing her. She got fed up, maybe she thought I died, or whatever, and she didn't wait around to find out. There was a baron that helped deliver the chest of gold. Let's just say he was immediately interested, and she took him to the cabin I had built for the both of us."

Emm's mouth dropped, and a growl resonated within her. "Please tell me she is alive, so I can kill her."

I brushed a lock of my mate's hair behind her ear. "My sweet mate, you don't want to hear that story."

"I do," she whispered. "Please," her breath tickled my ear.

"Later," I brushed my lips with hers. "Besides, you want to know how all this came to be, right?"

Emm huffed in irritation. I loved her jealousy, wanting to know if my ex-mate was still alive. Keeping the information from her was going to be fun. I had plans for that later, too.

"Fine," she rolled her eyes. "Keep going."

"When I found out about my mate's betrayal, my body underwent a transformation that hasn't been seen in a thousand years. My body broke and molded into the Lycan that you saw. For the first time I had ever seen,

Mordecai was scared out of his mind. I couldn't stop it, it was painful. I thought I was dying." I held my mate tighter, remembering how fucking frightened I was.

"When I stood up on two legs, Mordecai had my mother and gripped her around the neck. He told me to change back into my wolf form, but I didn't know how," I whispered. "I backed away and he—"

"Don't—" Emm straddled me and held me. "Don't say anything else."

I buried my face into her shoulder and let out a long, deep breath. "He took her from me."

For a long time, we sat there as I held my mate. She let me bury my nose in her neck, nuzzling the mark on her shoulder.

I wanted to fucking cry—and I hadn't cried since I lost my sister. I couldn't. I was beaten when I even looked like I was going to shed one ounce of emotion. When my mother's neck broke and she stared up at me from the dirt, the tears would not come.

My chest tightened, constricting my breath as I desperately fought back the overwhelming surge of emotions. The weight of grief bore down on me, threatening to crush my soul. I could feel the burning ache behind my eyes, a telltale sign that tears were desperately clawing their way to the surface. But I had learned, through years of beatings, to bury those tears deep within me, to lock them away behind an impenetrable fortress.

The rawness of the memories flooded my mind, intensifying the ache within my heart. I saw my sister's face, her laughter and warmth that had once filled our lives, now haunting my every waking moment. The guilt gnawed at me, echoing through the corridors of my mind, reminding me of the time I had failed to protect her.

And then, the image of my mother, lifeless and broken, flashed before my eyes. The shock of that moment, the sheer brutality of her untimely demise, threatened to shatter the heavy walls I had built around my emotions.

Sitting here with Emm, though, I wanted to let go, to surrender to the torrent of tears that threatened to escape me. I craved the release, but the fear of punishment, maybe not physical, just that of my mate seeing me as weak, was too strong.

"She—she smiled, though, when he held her by the neck." I let out a heavy breath into my mate's hair. "She smiled and whispered she loved me," my voice trembled.

"Koen," my mate whispered in my ear. "Let it out. I'm here for you, my sweet Koen."

I gritted my teeth and let out a loud sob. My fingers pushed into her skin enough to bruise her. I couldn't stop, could not let go of her for fear she would fade away.

I let out a wail. "That fucking bastard!"

CHAPTER THIRTY-TWO

Emm

I was seated on his lap, feeling the weight of his body beneath me. His grip tightened, his hands dug into my skin, igniting a mix of pleasure and pain. As I stroked his back with one hand, I lost myself in the sensation of his muscles beneath my touch. My other hand became entangled in his hair, relishing the softness between my fingers.

He was sobbing, uncontrollably sobbing, and my heart tightened in my chest. I'd only seen a few men cry in my life—usually for their lives. They begged me not to take their life, but they were cowards, saying they had too much to live for.

They didn't.

Locke did, though.

Images of his life flickered before my eyes; a rapid succession of memories that filled my vision with a sense of overwhelming weight. The sight was a painful reminder of the tormented past that he had lived through. Though invisible to my eyes, a presence lingered, its ethereal essence permeating the atmosphere, as if a Goddess herself watched over us, trying to show me this man, even through pain, was worth loving.

And, damn, he was.

The haunting visions played in my mind, vivid and tormenting. *I* could see him as a young boy, the sight of his feet in the wrong stance during training. The sound of his father's harsh voice filled his ears, criticizing his every move. The stench of fear lingering in that young boy as he was beaten by a rival alpha in his teenage years, the pain coursing through his body like a raging fire. His father's presence was suffocating, exuding cruelty and offering not even a trace of pity or mercy.

Despite the pain, Locke maintained his composure in front of his father. He masked the turmoil within, concealing his shattered spirit. Each blow, every punch, claw, and scar etched into his skin, disappeared as if they had never existed, leaving no trace.

My body ached every time my eyes blinked, watching Locke suffer. No wonder he was different, no wonder he clung to me. He lost his family; his sister, and then his mother. All those years he was beaten to protect his mother from his father's wrath, and it was all for nothing.

I don't even remember my mother. My abuela was my mother. I couldn't imagine if I lost her.

Locke let out another sob and I held on to him tighter. I rested my head on his and rocked him gently. Women may find men crying to be the most unmasculine thing to behold, but fuck them. This man has been through hell, and he continued to tread through the fires with bare feet.

"My sweet Koen, you aren't alone anymore." I let my fingers tangle through his hair and kissed his head. "I'm here now and I'm not going anywhere."

If it were even possible, Locke squeezed me tighter and I let out a sad laugh. Locke squeezed me tighter, pressing my breasts against his body and making it hard for me to breathe. I was shocked when my body involuntarily purred. But I let it, not wanting to stop it because it calmed my mate down instantly. *Yes, my mate!*

His grip loosened, but not enough to let go.

"I'm here, never leaving," I promise him again, my words whispered gently into his ear as I released my grip on his head. As he tilted his head upwards, I observed his face, flushed and red, the aftermath of his relentless crying. His tear-stained cheeks glisten with moisture, a testament to his anguish.

"You must think I'm weak," he rasped.

I shook my head vigorously.

"Never." I swallowed the large lump in my throat. "You have every right to show your emotion. You have every right to let this out, especially to me. I will safeguard all of your worries, and your pain."

Locke closed his eyes and pressed his forehead against mine. "I am supposed to be strong. And I have shown you weakness. You will not find me attractive enough too—"

I pressed my lips firmly against his, savoring the subtle hint of salt on his mouth. As our lips met, a gentle sigh escaped him. With a slight tilt of my head, I deepened the connection, seeking a heightened sensation. Sensing my desire, he opened his mouth, allowing my tongue to delicately explore and caress his own.

Locke groaned into my mouth, while I hastily worked at the belt of his pants.

"Emmie, what?"

I continued to kiss him, unbuttoning his pants and pulling his raging cock free.

"You are my mate, and I will always find you attractive." I let out a heavy sigh into his neck. "Let me show you."

I kissed down his neck, leaving hickies in my wake. They healed quickly, his skin far too superior to leave any sort of bruising. I lifted his shirt, tracing his happy trail with my tongue. He gasped and his fingers threaded through my hair.

"Emmie—no, you don't. I shouldn't— I've been weak, I—."

I grabbed his shaft with one hand, letting my thumb rub on one barbell near his knot. He groaned as I took a lap at the head. I gazed up at him, letting him see the desire, the heat in my eyes, how much I still wanted him even with him breaking down in front of me.

He showed me a side no one has ever seen, and I found that to be the hottest, most desirable thing in my life. A secret only that I would be shown.

His cock was constantly leaking. He wasn't coming but it sure looked like it. I continued to lick at the head, my hand wrapping around his large girth and thumbing against the bars of his Jacob's Ladder.

He sucked in a quick breath through his teeth when I wrapped my mouth around the giant head, and took him all in at once. My bottom teeth grazed the bars and I opened my mouth wider to accommodate them.

"Goddess Almighty, you took all of me."

I felt his dripping come running down my throat. It wasn't salty or musky but sweet. I swallowed continuously because he is just one needy little wolf.

Locke's hand threaded through my hair but he didn't push me. It irritated me, so I put my hand on top of his and had him push on my head.

"Fuck, gods, you're perfect." He got the idea and began to pump my head to the rhythm he wanted.

He fucked my mouth, and I fondled the knot that was expanding. I didn't realize just how large it gets and I opened my eyes watching it fill with his seed.

My pussy fluttered, pulsing as he took what he wanted. He knew I liked it rough and when his head pushed to the back of my throat, I gagged.

My breasts felt heavy as I gagged and I grabbed one of my tits and pinched.

"You fucking like it rough, don't you, Princess?"

I moaned into his cock, letting him hit me in the back of the throat again.

"My pretty little luna loves this cock, doesn't she?" He groaned and pushed me lower as his shaft expanded. He let off a low groan and I felt his come spurt into my mouth. I swallowed spurt after spurt. It kept coming, and I knew it would take ages before it stopped.

I pulled my shirt up over my breasts and unfastened my bra, keeping my mouth on his shaft. My thankful breasts fell from their confinement and touched the cooler air. It took me a moment to maneuver, but he wasn't paying attention. He was relishing my mouth on his cock, sucking him down.

Once I was ready, I let the come, that had gathered in my mouth, dribble out between my breasts. Locke whined pitifully, but I was able to situate his cock between my tits and rubbed it between them.

"Holy hell," he leaned his head back and thrust his hips, while I squeezed my breasts together, "this is so fucking hot!"

He was still coming, spurting on my neck and chin, dripping between my breasts causing it to easily slide between my cleavage.

"Shit, shit, shit," he chanted as he grabbed my shoulder to use for leverage, while he pumped his cock in and out of breasts. The top of his cock bumped my chin and I let his come drip down my neck. "You look so good, painted with my seed." He groaned again and let off one more spurt that covered the top of my breasts.

We were both panting, his hand that had held onto my shoulder fell to my chest, rubbing his come over my skin.

"They will smell me on you for days," he murmured to himself. "Even when we wash it off."

My pussy pulsed. I knew he just came an obscene amount, but the way he talked so dirty, how I was covered in his come and he fucking loving it made me want to ride him so damn much, right now.

He tilted his chin up, his eyes gazing down at me. His knot pulsed and more of his come slipped from the tip.

Lock gritted his teeth. "Come here, Princess, get on my dick."

I shook my head and rubbed my breasts up and down his cock again, causing him to spurt more. "This was about you. I wanted to make you happy," I purred and licked the head.

The sensitivity was too much, the red, angry knot made him double over when my breasts grazed it too hard. His hand gripped my hair and his heavy pants ran down my back.

"Fuck!"

Somehow, I knew his knot was far too sensitive right now to take me. He knew it too, but wanted to please me, knowing I was so turned on. It wasn't about me though; it was about giving him comfort, knowing I was always going to be there for him.

And I was. For the first time in my life, for someone other than my family, I was promising to stay and be with him. I was promising him and the other lost souls he was trying to help.

As his knot emptied, the sun was setting, and the cool air dried his arousal on my chest. He slowly slipped his cock from my breasts and pulled me in for an intense, passionate kiss before letting me go. "Perfect," he whispered into my mouth. "I still owe you a good fucking."

I rolled my eyes and pulled on the hair at the back of his neck. "We are mates. We don't owe each other anything."

Locke's smile went from cocky to a wide, boyish smile. "Yeah, is that right? You are an expert in mate bonds, now?"

I shrugged my shoulders. "I'm an expert in many things. I figured I'd be an expert in this, too."

Locke threw his head back and laughed, tucking his cock back into his jeans. He pulled down my top, letting the dried come crackle under the fabric.

Any other time I think I'd be grossed out having dried come on my body, but since it was his, there was something deep inside me that was oddly satisfied about it.

"Let's get you cleaned up." He threw me over his shoulder and I squealed when he slapped my backside.

It didn't take us long to come up on a lake. It was a lake all too familiar to me. Across the clear waters I zeroed onto my RV on the other side. I reveled how I could see so far when, just days ago, I didn't think I could remember seeing anything across the lake before.

Locke kept me busy from thinking too hard, though, because he stripped me down and had me in the lake completely naked, fucking me in the water, while I moaned his name until we were both spent.

If that is his version of cleaning up, I think I could get used to it.

After we finished, the moon had already risen in the sky and the night air felt crisp. It wasn't cold on my wet skin as my hair dried. In fact, I felt warm and comfortable as we playfully chased each other, slapping each other's backsides while we headed back toward the packhouse—our home.

Once we came closer, Locke sniffed the air, then pulled on my hand to put me behind him and growled. A deep rumble in his chest rattled me to my core. It wasn't a playful, seductive growl but one of possession and anger. I grabbed onto his shirt behind him, and of course I gazed all around us, and kept my knees bent to jump and spring into action if need be.

"Stay back," Locke snapped.

I let out a growl in my own throat, one that I was becoming more and more familiar with. The hair on the back of my neck rose and I could feel my nails tingle.

"I will do what—"

"Them, not you," Locke spoke more gently and pulled me close to him, as out of the darkness I could somehow see Hawke and Delilah coming forth out of the bushes.

I furrowed my brow, seeing Hawke holding their sweet baby, Hannah, in their arms. She'd grown almost double in size since I last saw her, looking almost like a small toddler.

"Hi guys, what are you doing out here?" I let go of Locke to greet them, but he grabbed my arm and pulled me back.

"Mine! Get back!" Locke barked.

I blinked several times and jerked my head back and forth.

Hawke raised his arm in surrender. "I know this is a bad time. I know you don't want us here, but hear me out, Alpha." Hawke leaned his neck to the side, but Locke didn't falter. He gripped my arm tighter and fur sprouted all over his arms.

He was going to shift.

"Hey," I whispered to Locke and ran my fingers across his fur. "It's alright. It's your friends."

Locke didn't listen. He pulled me in close and took a deep breath into my shoulder. "Mine." A deep, guttural voice came from within. *Fenrir.*

"Listen, we—we need help. A lot of the mated do. We have these headaches—"

Locke's grip loosened slightly.

"We know you are still in your mating period, but our mates—we can't stand seeing them in pain."

Locke mumbled to himself, his hand running down his face.

"Can you help them?" I stared up at him. "Is there a way we can help?

Why do they have headaches? Shifters can get headaches? I thought they weren't prone to illnesses?"

Locke ran the back of his hand down my cheek and nodded. "Yeah, we can help."

Sorrow hit me, and I wasn't sure why.

"Get Tajah and Bram. Bring every mated couple to the bonfire here at the packhouse. Are Bear and Journey back?"

Hawke put his arm around Delilah, who looked miserable. "Yeah, they did this morning. All the rescued humans have been put up in our apartments or sent back to where they came from, if that is where they wanted to go."

Locke let out a sigh and steered me toward the packhouse. "Have everyone here in an hour. Don't be late."

As always, I had more questions than answers, but I kept quiet and tried to shift through the jumbled mess inside Locke's head.

CHAPTER
THIRTY-THREE

Locke

I grabbed my mate's hand and whisked her past the large pit. It contained logs, old timber, and trash from the cabins. I swallowed, aware that fire would soon consume me, but it wasn't my first time being surrounded by flames recently. Months ago, I was in a burning building and I did just fine when Grim and Journey dealt with Idris.

"Keep telling yourself that," my wolf grumbled.

I had nightmares for weeks and my smoking and drinking picked up, not that anyone noticed with everyone getting mates and all.

Emm stumbled and I slowed down. Her body was burning up but I wasn't sensing any arousal from her. I wrapped my hand on her arm and gave her a worried glance, but her eyebrows shot up.

"Are you going to explain to me what's happening or am I going to have to try to figure out this head thing?" She tapped her temple and gave me a smile.

I shook my head, and gently tugged her along. With a firm grip, I pushed the heavy double doors to the packhouse open. As they creaked, a sliver of light flooded in, revealing the vastness of the space. The sudden flicker of fluorescent lights illuminated the bare walls, casting long shadows. The silence was broken by the sound of my voice reverberating through the hollow halls, echoing with each syllable.

"You understand we were a club, just a bunch of rogues coming together. We were helping one another, but we weren't really a pack." I led her up to the third floor and took her to our room. I pulled out the drawers and gave her fresh new clothes.

I cursed myself that I wasn't able to do more for her. With the Law of Ares I would have supplied her with our own rutting cabin, clothing, food, gifts and supplies. All the things I wanted to give to my mate were flickering to a distant memory, but being an alpha I wasn't allowed such luxury to spoil a luna.

"Being a part of a pack also means you are bound to one another. You are together not just as a group with common interests, but also in mind and spirit. A large family unit. You can speak to one another through a link common link. It comes in handy when you are in your animal form and need to communicate."

Emm put on a pair of black leggings and I did my best not to stare. The bruises that I left on her body were fading—far faster than I thought they would. I tilted my head to get a better look and she swatted my ass.

"Hey, don't get distracted," she giggled.

"Anyway, it's called mind-linking. A mind-link breaks when you become rogue. Your wolf is helpless. It needs an alpha to guide the wolf, to make them feel safe and secure. The only way you can have a pack is with an alpha, and alphas are not made; they are born. In combination with my alpha blood and my sister's death—" I took in a deep breath and immediately my mate was beside me. "I have double the strength of an alpha. But with no mate, I am nothing but an ordinary man."

"You are more than an ordinary man. You have lasted longer than a lot of these rogues, Locke. You've saved many."

I shook my head and pulled up my jeans, fiddling with the belt. "But not enough. I felt like a failure, but no more. Since I've found you, I've been given hope not just for me, but for everyone." I pulled her body flush with mine and whispered into her lips. "But, if you told me to run away with you, I would. I'd leave them all—"

"Don't say that." She narrowed her eyes. "You care for these people, your pack—"

"I want you to know that I love you because you are my soul, Emmie. Not just because I'm trying to put a pack together."

Her eyes widened. "It never crossed my mind that you would only be with me to save your pack, Locke. I feel your intentions are true, in here." She laid her hand on her chest. "It's a weird feeling but I believe it. And any person with a heart would naturally want to help others in need."

I chuckled darkly, and grabbed my boots from the floor. "Baby, I don't have a heart. You should know that by now." I roughly tied my boots while I sat in the chair and she knelt beside me.

"I know you don't have a heart, because you gave it to me," her voice rasped.

I stopped tying my boot and looked at her.

"Now I'm giving you mine, and that means we are going to help them," she pointed to the window. "We aren't gonna run away, so don't keep telling me that like I'm gonna do it. They are my family now, too."

"You love me?"

"Is that all you got out of that?" she sighed heavily.

I smirked. "Yup."

I pulled her up for a kiss and threw her on our nest, pinning her between my arms. "You love me."

"Alright, alright, don't get your panties in a twist. Now, come on, we have to go cure some mind-link headaches."

I placed a kiss on her shoulder and let her rise from the bed. As painful as it was to do so, I let her stand and looked longingly at our nest. This should be our time, but as always, according to Ares' Law, a luna is always the most thoughtful one.

Maybe I could enjoy some parts of the old ways.

I continued to explain the basics of the mind-link to Emm as we descended the stairs. The mind-link is what makes the pack. No other pack can infiltrate it. It's strong and sacred.

What I failed to see before was that we were creating a new pack. It wasn't just a matter of the wolves pledging allegiance to an alpha and a luna. We were creating a whole new pack, and it wasn't as simple as the link 'strings' coming together to form between Emm and me. We had to create the center.

Emm and I were the conductors, while our pack members were like roaring electrical charges and currents. Their electricity was zooming through the air, ready to find common ground. While they were close enough to us to keep their pain at bay, they needed guidance to find us, and that is where Tajah and Bram had to come in.

Establishing a pack needed guidance by a powerful witch or warlock.

When Emm and I entered the middle of the courtyard, the blazing fire already hot and ready, my mate snarled toward Tajah. I had almost forgotten Emm's dislike for her, but I knew Emm could handle her own.

"I don't like her," Emm said loud enough over the roaring flames. "I don't trust someone who deliberately bullies another."

Tajah jutted her chin towards Emm. "I'm sorry. It wasn't intentional. I was making sure your intentions were just."

"By forcing a male, who isn't used to it, to be in the field?" Emm stomped forward nearly chest to chest with Tajah. I didn't pull her back, I was actually quite turned on by the spectacle.

It was then I realized my mistake by not stopping my mate, when Emm reared her arm back and gave Tajah a right hook to the face. The small group that gathered all gasped and watch Tajah tumble to the ground. Beretta hissed, her fangs bared and lunged forward to cover her mate.

Fuck, that was hot.

Grim grunted in approval.

Emm bared fangs in return, and fuck if I didn't get hard at the sight. "Never force someone to do your own bidding. You knew it made Switch uncomfortable, and you defied orders."

I crossed my arms and covered my smile with my hand. It seems Emm has dug deeper in my mind than I cared to admit. *What else did she know?*

Tajah stumbled as she stood, wiping away the blood on the corner of her lip. "As I said before, I misjudged you. But, when you first entered our territory, your intentions were not, let's just say, positive. I sensed your deceit. We all could. I was trying to protect what Locke had built, in his absence."

My mate stared at everyone around the fire. The mated, even Sizzle, Bones and Switch, who had come for security all watched to see what the two strong females would do.

"You could have backed down," Emm continued. "When Journey entered our conversation at the bar, telling you to chill out, you didn't. With Journey being a priestess to the goddess of pairing I'm surprised you didn't. If you had chased me off, which - by the way, you wouldn't have," my mate looked Tajah up and down, "this club wouldn't be a pack. You could have destroyed all of it with *your* intentions."

Tajah's stern face softens, and her fists unclench. "You're right. It was a poor choice."

"And using Switch? You are supposed to be a family, not using him to do your fucking bidding."

Tajah winced again and crossed her arms. "Again, trying to find out your lies. But, obviously I was mistaken—"

"Tajah has been punished," I interrupted Tajah, taking my mate by the arm. "I didn't go as far as hitting her in the face, but she has served time."

My mate scrunched her nose. "It's two strikes in my book. A third, and I can't promise what I'll do to you," my mate smirked and put out her hand for Tajah. "And, by the way, I do have my own secrets, but they are to keep people safe. In time, you will know who they are."

Tajah gave a playful smile and shook Emm's hand. "I like her," she said to me. "The Goddess did well. A perfect pairing."

"What the fuck just happened?" Hawke said from the sidelines. "Are they friends or—"

"More like frienemies," Delilah said. "Like they understand each other, but I don't think they will be sharing nail polish anytime soon."

Thank fuck Emm hadn't dug too far into my head. If she had she would know that Tajah knew her secret about her family, and where they were located.

I let off a low growl, pulled my mate into my arms and whispered into her ear. "Look at you being a luna and shit. That was hot as hell." I rub my shaft against her pussy and she let off a whimper.

"Don't do that, I'm sensitive still." She grabbed my vest and held it tight.

I licked the underside of her ear. "I don't know. Fucking you in front of them might be kinda hot. Show them just how we don't give a damn."

"We can hear you!" Bear grunts. "Can we get this done? My mate has had about enough."

Nadia, the smallest of the females, was being carried by Bear. Her hands covered her ears and fuck if it didn't make me feel like a bastard.

"You're right, let's proceed." I adjusted myself and turned to Tajah, who held a large leather-bound book in her hand. Bram stood beside her in a long cloak, which covered his face. He held it with her and pointed to several places in the book. His voice was so low that mated pairs wouldn't be able to hear him, but I could and it appeared that Emm could too.

"It's powerful enough to reach Luna's sister and her mate, so they don't have to be present."

"Wait, what!" Emm pulled away from me and ran toward the sorcerers. "My sister, she said she had a headache. So, she—she really is mated? And she's close? Where is she?"

I leaned my head back in exasperation and pulled her away from them so they could continue talking. "She's fine, but she cannot be here right now."

"Why?" My mate hissed. "I haven't seen her. I want to know where she is."

"She's indisposed," Bones says. "She can't be present, but I promise you she is alright."

"Why?" My mate demanded.

I grabbed my mate's chin. "She will be a distraction, and I need your full attention. This is serious, Emm."

"Indeed, it is." Tajah let out a long breath, "because we can't perform this unless our luna is a full shifter and of the same strength as our alpha."

My body stiffened, and my eyes narrowed. "What do you mean?"

"I meant what I said; to form a pack, we need an alpha and luna of the same strength to form the ties of a new pack. This means that Emm will need to force shift into a wolf of equal caliber. That's why you didn't see many new packs formed in Elysian. It was difficult to find lunas and alphas of the same strength. In fact, it was hardly heard of."

I growled and stomped toward Tajah. "No, I won't allow it. That is fucking painful, ask Journey. She almost fucking died when she forced a shift."

And this time, Emm wouldn't be force-shifting into a wolf—but a Lycan. The highest form.

Journey stepped forward, Grim beside her with his arm around her. "It's true, she will have to shift." Journey's eyes glazed over bright blue until they faded back to their normal color and she gasped. "Goddess!" She covered her mouth.

"The Goddess must have shown her what you truly are," My wolf spoke, deeply. *Our secret will finally be set free."*

I forcefully ran my fingers through my disheveled hair, feeling the strands tangle and knot beneath my touch. With each step I took around the crackling fire, the ground trembled beneath my feet, echoing the fury that consumed me. My eyes, ablaze with an inferno of rage, reflected the torment that awaited her.

The impending shift would put her in an enormous amount of unimaginable pain. I dread the thought of witnessing her agony, of seeing her body contort and transform from human to wolf, and then to Lycan. It was an ordeal I had endured before as a pup, being an adult is a whole new experience they say.

But when I made the transition to Lycan, it felt like a death sentence. The excruciating torment was beyond anything I had ever known, a visceral torment that tested the limits of my endurance. I couldn't bear the thought of subjecting my mate to such suffering, to watch her endure the same indescribable pain that had nearly broken me.

Emm has undergone enough emotional trauma of my past in just a few days, and now I'm asking her to go through physical pain as well?

I gazed over the mated and the unmated. I started this club for them, to give them hope. A part of me wanted to save those that were like me—rejected and alone. I'd give it all up for her, I've told her many times, but now that my mate has given me her heart, part of her soul—I still wanted to save them too.

Emm stared at me from across the fire. She showed no weakness, just determination in her eyes. She slowly walked around the fire, her gaze set on me.

"You don't have to do this," I linked her. *"They can live with the pain just a while longer until you can shift into a wolf. We can get you used to that form and then—"*

Her eyes fluttered when I first used our own personal link. And understanding how it worked quickly filtered through her mind.

"I don't half-ass things," she said back to me, *"and I will not start now."*

"You have no idea how much fucking pain you are going to be in." My wolf snarled when she came closer. The air was thick with tension, and everyone who had surrounded the fire backed away. *"Like your body is glass and then rearranges itself—"*

"Stop," she whispered to me. *"It's sweet you are trying to save me from the pain, but I said we are in this together, didn't I? My sister is a part of this, our friends, our family. We need to do this. What if Idris comes?"*

She was right. We were vulnerable with the mated experiencing pain, but what about my mate?

Emm rubbed her hand up my cheek. *"You've been through pain, I'm here to match it. We are supposed to be equals, right?"* she chuckled.

I wrapped my hand around her throat and gave her a rough kiss. It was desperate, and it was painful, but I needed it. "I'll be here. Through all of it." I rasped into her lips.

"I know."

CHAPTER
THIRTY-FOUR

Emm

I sucked in a breath, making sure my bravado didn't waver.

I knew I was in over my head, but I wasn't a quitter.

Locke snaked his arm around my waist and gave a nod to Tajah. She and Bram were doing their magical duties, I supposed. They were pouring salt, sugar, cocaine- hell if I knew, in a circle near the fire while the rest of the group were talking amongst themselves.

Grim and Journey exchanged anxious whispers, their voices barely audible. The sound of their words reached my ears, crackling like distant static. Desperate to hear, I instinctively reached up to my ears, tugging and massaging them. As my fingers explored, a damp liquid trickled down my lobes. Trembling, I slowly withdrew my hand, revealing a sticky residue-stained crimson with blood.

"It's normal." Locke held my wrist looking at the blood. "Your hearing is acclimating to a wolf's. It's also why your body heat is rising quickly as well."

Ah, okay. Glad to know that.

Grim's scowl deepened when he approached. "When were you going to tell me you were a fucking lycan, Locke?" Grim hissed. "You're like my brother."

Locke shrugged his shoulders. "Never came up in conversation?" He smiled and hugged my shoulders.

Locke continued to smile, that crazy psychotic one where I could see how people perceive him as a damn lunatic. And he partially was. He was unpredictable. Hell, now that I was in his head, I could see he's one complicated guy.

His mind would jump from one idea to the next, not truly fixating on one problem but many. When Locke saw a problem, he attacked it from every angle and anticipated every move from his opponent. I didn't know how to keep up. He truly was an apex predator.

For now, I'll stay out of it and ask my questions when I need to.

"You going to make an announcement or something?" Grim raised his brow.

Locke shook his head. "Nah, It will be a fun surprise. Then, I'll shift too, and everyone can see what an exceptional power couple we are. Right, babe?" Locke stared down at me with such adoration, while I pulled my hand away from my ear that dripped with blood.

I agreed that I could take this, and I would not say no.

"We got this." It was said a little weaker than I intended, and my body heated, not with arousal like I was accustomed to, but a roaring fire of needles and piercing pain.

I gritted my teeth and tried to push through the agony, but it was like a thousand knives stabbing into every fiber of my being. I could feel my bones shifting, stretching, reforming beneath my skin, and the sensation was excruciating.

Locke's firm grip on my arm tightened, sending a shiver down my spine.

The intensity of his gaze locked onto mine, as if peering into the depths of my soul. I could almost hear the sound of his steady breaths, intermingled with the faint rustle of leaves in the nearby trees. The scent of earth and Locke's overpowering one calmed me enough to concentrate on the road ahead. In that moment, I felt the weight of his concern, and unwavering determination seeped into my very being. "Hold on, love. You got this," he urged, his voice a soothing balm amidst the chaos raging within me.

Tajah and Bram had paused their preparations, their attention now fully on me. Tajah's eyes glowed with a fierce intensity, her hands crackling with arcane energy as she prepared her area of magic. Bram's expression was grim, his features etched with worry, most likely for my well-being.

Did he know?

Grim and Journey exchanged a knowing look, their expressions unreadable as they observed the beginnings of a pain I'd surely never forget. Grim clenched his jaw, his gaze hitting me, then to Locke.

I roared out, doubled over in pain. It was a human scream which morphed into an animistic roar that echoed into the night air, cutting through the quiet night. The sound echoed in my ears, resonating deep within my body's changing form. I felt a surge of power coursing through me, overwhelming and raw in its intensity.

"Let's get started," I heard Tajah's words settle over the roaring fire.

Locke held me in his arms so I wouldn't lie in the dirt, but the ground looked so inviting. The softness of the earth, its coolness would feel so good against my bare skin.

"I want my clothes off—" I barely said before Locke had already ripped them off with his claws.

Being stripped naked in front of everyone didn't bother me, all I wanted was to be comfortable. Damn it all to hell if everyone saw my ass and tits, since they'd already seen me have an orgasm in the bar.

I could hear Tajah's rhythmic chanting echoing in the background, filling the air with a melodic energy. As I lay there, my senses became increasingly heightened, every sound and movement magnified. Locke, towering above me, seemed to float effortlessly, his gaze fixated on the others, as if expecting an imminent threat.

He was protecting me, I realized. I was in a vulnerable state. Naked, shifting, transforming. The gun that was strapped to my thigh when I got dressed earlier was snapped off my leg when Locke ripped off my clothes. I really was utterly fucking helpless.

"Keep her comfortable, just like it was any other shift," Bram said gruffly.

I stared up at him and noticed his hood had come even lower to cover his face.

"When she shifts into her lycan form, she's going to beg you for death. You cannot lose control because of your mate's pain. And, I can't give her any pain relief. She must live through the same pain you have suffered." I felt his eyes on me and with the fire blazing, I could see his lips pursed into a thin line. "And I mean every bit of pain, when you completed your lycan form."

Locke gave a jerked nod, his hand resting on my shoulder. His hand that should feel warm— burned my skin and I screamed out in pain.

"She will get through this. Our luna is strong," Locke said with conviction.

"I know this" Bram said. He stepped away and returned to Tajah.

"How does he know about your lycan? I thought no one knew?" I linked Locke as I let out another cry.

"Bram is a powerful warlock. He's old and a rogue himself, I'm surprised he can do most of the things he can."

As I plunged my fingers into the damp soil, my nails transformed into sharp, menacing claws. The sight of my once sun-kissed skin morphing into a deep, rich brown fur filled me with a nauseating dread. The earthy scent of the dirt mingled with the musty odor of the newly grown fur.

I couldn't concentrate on anything except the lightning of pain. My forearm snapped and I saw the bone poking out under the skin.

Maybe I couldn't really handle this?

I frantically pawed at the moist earth, feeling the decaying leaves crumble beneath my body. Raising my gaze, I was greeted by the radiant glow of the round moon, casting its ethereal light upon me. The once-dazzling stars were beginning to vanish, dark clouds appearing. The moon was too stubborn its rays breaking through. Bolts of lightning weaved through the ominous growing clouds.

As the wind intensified, a cool breeze brushed against my burning skin, offering a momentary relief.

"You're doing great, Princess. Keep going, don't fight it, it makes it worse." Locke tried to soothed, but like a birthing mother, his words only irritated me.

I couldn't speak as another bone broke, this time my femur. You could hear it snap above the roaring flames and the thunder that followed the lightning.

The girls all cried out, their hands covering their mouths as they watched me.

"It wasn't that bad for me. Is it supposed to be like that?" I heard Delilah shout to Journey, who leaned her head on Grim's chest.

"A forced-shift, yeah, but—"

Journey silenced herself and wrapped her arms around Grim. Delilah tried to leave Hawke and her baby, but Hawke quickly grabbed his mate by the arm, holding her tight.

"You got this." Locke leaned into my ear. "You're strong. You're my fighter. You are my equal, and you will do this quickly. Let your wolf rise."

His words were harsh, no longer soothing.

My lip went into a snarl, and I snapped my elongating teeth. "Shut up."

"No," he growled back. "Shift. You're slowing down. I know my mate can do better than this."

Pardon me, but after my leg broke, I wasn't really in the mood.

A low, guttural growl reverberated in the depths of my chest, sending shivers down my spine. With a swift motion, my arm lunged forward, slashing through the air towards Locke. His sinister grin widened as he threw his head back, releasing a maniacal laugh that echoed through the room.

Horror-stricken, the others watched our confrontation unfold, their eyes wide with disbelief. Yet, amidst the chaos, Locke understood what I needed. He knew how to push me to my limits. In his sadistic and twisted manner, he became the catalyst for my growth and transformation.

I continued to push through the shift as time went on. Tajah waved a candle in front of her face calling upon higher powers, or whatnot. I was still laying on the ground, my body convulsing, as I continued to sprout fur on my body.

"We got a problem." I heard Switch's voice come from above me.

"Keep going," Locke barked at me. "Don't you pause just because I'm not telling you every damn breath to breathe."

My face had elongated at this point, and I scooted forward and put his ankle between my teeth, not breaking the skin. He let out a bark of laughter and pried my mouth off of him. "What a good girl." He patted my head, which was still sprouting thick fur.

"Alpha, club's in the dark, and the fae aren't in the village."

I grunted, the last of my hind legs taking shape. I stood on my two front legs and pushed my body against Locke's.

Instead of everyone sighing with relief that I made it to my wolf form, they were paying attention to Switch, which I was glad about.

"Cameras," Locke barked.

Switch held out his phone and swiped it several times. Tajah's chanting continued and I dropped to the ground again, letting out a howl, and my temporary reprieve from pain was over, as it started again.

"What the hell is happening?" Nadia broke away from Bear's arms and ran toward me.

Locke's lips curled up into a snarl as he lunged forward, positioning himself in front of her. The sharp clicking sound of his claws unsheathing makes the fur on my body stand. Locke's arm raised, ready to slash at her, but before he could make contact Bear swiftly yanked Nadia back.

"Nadia!" Bear roared at her. "Never approach the alpha and luna! Especially, when one is down."

Nadia whimpered and hid her face in Bear's neck. I wanted to comfort Nadia. She'd been nothing but a good friend, but the pain had me shaking, and trembling. I didn't know if I could keep going on like this. My body was breaking all over again, but the pain was ten times worse.

Bram was right. I wanted to die.

Locke stared down at me and back to Switch, who didn't know how to approach the situation.

Help me or help the pack?

"*Phone,*" I linked him. "*Look, phone.*"

I've been on my own for years. I've taken care of myself. If the Goddess said I had to go through a pain like this, be equal to Locke, in order for a pack to be formed, then I knew there was an end of this. I just had to take the journey to get there.

Locke reluctantly took the phone from Switch. Locke's eyes glazed over with fury, his grip tightening over the phone. "Shit," he hissed, handing it back to Switch. "Got a problem," he announced.

I curled my body in on itself, keeping myself in the fetal position. Tajah was concentrating heavily on the book that was floating in front of her. Whisps of blue and purple light surrounded her while she held a cream-colored candle, drawing a pattern in the air with the light.

My stomach rolled, and my tongue lolled out of my maw. My teeth wept, I didn't know if it was saliva or stomach acid but it burned as it left my mouth.

"It's your venom," a deep voice entered my head. *Fenrir.*

Locke was barking out orders, yelling on the phone to get the Iron Fang members here and have weapons loaded.

"Pay attention to me, my luna. Don't worry about Locke. He can handle himself."

I whined when I felt my rib cage crack and lengthen.

"You're strong, but to become stronger, one must break into a thousand pieces. The bones become tougher than they ever were in the beginning."

My mouth continued to leak venom, soaking the ground in front of me. I felt the fur on my face sizzle and the venom land on my bare skin.

"Your skin and fur will be impenetrable by any human bullets, not even silver will burn you in your lycan form."

I concentrated on his voice, holding onto him like an anchor through the pain.

"You are gaining your own wolf. She will teach you the ways of your forms. Tonight, you will have to concentrate without her, follow your instincts."

"Why?" I screamed out loud, unable to concentrate to link back.

Locke's eyes darted to me but quickly but masked his concern when he yelled at Bones and Sizzle to get guns from the bunker.

"I said follow your instincts, female. You know how to fight," Fenrir growled back at me and my body shuddered in response.

My heart pounded relentlessly within my chest, its rhythmic thuds reverberating in my ears, as if echoing through a cavern. In that moment, an overwhelming wave of anguish washed over me, gripping my being like iron. A searing pain ripped through my back, as if every bone was snapping one by one, causing me to emit a guttural roar that boomed through the air, silencing the clamor of voices around the crackling fire.

The next thing I heard were trucks entering the clearing, surrounding us, all while my body continued to break into a thousand pieces, shifting into the lycan I needed to be to make this club into a pack.

CHAPTER
THIRTY-FIVE

Locke

As if things weren't stressful enough, we had to add another problem to the equation. My mate was dealing with an unbearable amount of pain. It was unfair to her, morphing from human to wolf to Lycan, and having to deal with it alone.

Now we deal with Idris. A threat that I've only briefly discussed with her because the problem felt so far away. Except it wasn't. It had followed us here to the Iron Fang.

Idris, the banished fae necromancer from the Elysian realm, and his followers had entered the territory right from under our noses.

"How could this have happened?" I stomped over to Bear who was still dealing with the pain in his mind.

Bear shook his head. "I don't know, I swear we covered our tracks. With that many people we rescued, maybe we missed one that had a tracker?"

I gritted my teeth and swore. "The Moonlight Outcasts, they were to check for trackers. Were there any on the humans?"

"I think that's irrelevant at this point. Idris is already here." Hawke pointed out, scrolling his phone. "Idris' followers came in the daylight. They were fast, too. They didn't look like rogues."

"Maybe they weren't rogues," Sizzle joined the conversation. "Think of all those humans he's been experimenting on. He might have been converting all of the human guards from Delilah's ex-husband's crime syndicate, giving them vampiric, fae, and hell, maybe shifter qualities. He's got control over all the east coast right now."

"Shit." I ran my hand through my hair. "He made his own army, then. We won't be strong enough, not with the few mated pairs we have."

Besides most of the inner circle, we had a few randomly mated pairs around the club. Being mated strengthens them more than the average single shifter. We even had a vampiric couple from the Moonlight Outcasts. Cyran found his mate when they were rescuing Nadia. She was bloodthirsty and has been held up in an apartment feeding. Releasing her would be beneficial.

Bram limped up to the group. "The mated will not have their animals in top condition. Their animals are trying to connect to the pack-link that is being established by Tajah right now. Once Emm has completely transformed, you will all be stronger than those genetically mutated monstrosities, but, before then—"

Hawke got on the phone and handed it to me. I yelled into it, demanding whoever was on the other line to get everyone to the packhouse. Mated, unmated, almost rabid. We needed all the reinforcements we could get.

The bunker was here, full of guns and ammo, but anything they had on hand they needed to bring. Guns, knives, we needed it all.

I stared at my mate. She was trying to keep her cries to a minimum, but fuck, I remember what it was like. Emm was fucking strong, but all I wanted to do was to comfort her. This is not how I wanted my mate to be introduced to this life. This wasn't how I pictured having her join my world.

Sure, I wanted it memorable, but it wasn't this. I was going to make it romantic, I swear to the gods. This was fucking different. Every plan, everything I wanted to do was crumbling right in front of me.

"Save the pack," Fenrir growled. *"I will tend to our mate."*

I pressed my lips to a thin line, staring at her morphing face. Her eyes meet mine, pleading.

"Go," she howled, withering into the dirt.

"If you don't, there will be no mate."

With a fierce growl, I tore my shirt apart, the fabric surrendering to my raw strength. The distant rumble of roaring engines filled the forest as trucks, motorcycles and cars invaded the landscape, their presence felt through the rustling of trees and the crunching of dirt and gravel beneath their tires.

They raced towards the packhouse. The sound of screeching tires and roaring engines filled the air. The urgency of the situation weighed heavily on my shoulders as I navigated through the surrounding chaos. Pack members quickly gathered, leaping out of the back of trucks and through the windows of cars. They armed themselves with whatever weapons they could find, their faces etched with a mix of determination and fear.

Most of them hadn't seen the packhouse. Only the mated could be here. Their faces were of both awe and fascination, looking up at the big structure, but Hawke, Sizzle and Bear had already spouted out orders, organizing everyone into groups.

Those who still had some capability to shift transformed into their animal forms, vampires flashed their fangs, and a sense of unity pulsated through the air despite the imminent danger lurking on our doorstep.

Fenrir wasted no time intending to Emm from my mind. I pushed back his words as he spoke to her, urging her to keep going. My heart ached at the sight of her pain, but I knew she was strong and resilient. She would fight through this; we all would.

As I stepped forward in front of the club, a hush fell over the crowd, enveloping it in silence. The crackling fire behind me sent waves of intense heat searing my exposed back. Before me, the club stood, its imposing presence commanding attention. Though our numbers were not vast, the strength of our training was apparent, even though most members were rogue and unable to shift.

"I have mated with my luna." There was no cheer, but there were looks of relief on everyone's faces. "She is undergoing her transformation, and only then, can we create our pack."

I could hear the haunting sound of her guttural cries as she tightly held in her pain. The blinding lightning cut through the darkened sky, followed by the deafening rumble of thunder echoing through the towering mountains.

A chilling enemy howl echoed through the air, originating from a distant hilltop. Its piercing sound served as an unmistakable warning, indicating that the enemy was drawing nearer.

Time was not on our side.

"Your objective is to protect your luna and Tajah. Without them this club will not form a pack, do you understand?" I screamed at them, my face red with anger.

The pack members nodded in unison, their expressions hardening with determination. They knew the gravity of the situation at hand, and the importance of protecting their alpha's mate, and the future luna. The howls of the approaching enemy grew louder, signaling that the impending battle was upon us.

We were ill prepared, and no fae to help with oncoming attacks. Who even knew if they were still alive.

Hawke, Sizzle and Bear moved swiftly, organizing the pack into defensive positions. Those in animal forms were situated in the forests. Hawke grabbed his snipers and positioned themselves in trees and on top of cabins. The few vampires had positioned themselves strategically, ready to strike at a moment's notice. The air crackled with tension as everyone braced themselves for the onslaught.

Fenrir continued to support Emm through her agonizing transformation, his voice rough and commanding; so she could concentrate. She had to do this fast, but it also could not be rushed. Emm's primal screams echoed through the night, a symphony of pain and rebirth, that resonated with every member of the pack.

"Don't pay attention to her screams, you protect the luna!" I roared.

I pulled on my belt and dropped it to the ground. My unbuttoned pants ripped, and I let my lycan form's muscles bulge as I hunched over. My fur burst out from my skin and covered my entire body. The transformation was swift and powerful. My shoulders rolled back, my posture becoming more upright, and I stood in my full lycan form. I let out a fierce howl, revealing rows of sharp teeth and bright green eyes that glinted in the moonlight.

I felt the gaze of my future pack upon me. I snarled and gazed at all of them before I swished my claws into the air. "Protect your future pack and Luna, or face me!" I scraped my claws on my chest letting the blood drip down my torso.

As the first wave of enemies emerged from the shadows, I took one last look at my mate. We shared a silent understanding of our roles in this pivotal moment. She would concentrate on shifting, and from the looks of it, Delilah and her pup would be by her side.

I would protect Emm with my life. I wouldn't stray far from this center. I would lead our pack into battle, fueled by the fierce determination to keep our loved ones safe. For peace, like I have always wanted.

With a primal roar, I let my venom fall from my maw. The pack stood united behind me, a formidable force ready to defend their alpha, their luna and their home.

The clash was imminent, but we were ready. As one cohesive unit, we charged towards the enemy horde, who broke from the trees on the other side of the clearing. Our battle cries reverberating through the night sky that continued to be webbed with lightning. This fight would test our strength, our courage and our loyalty to each other.

The ground trembled beneath our feet as I stood at the forefront. I tried to look for Idris, but of course, the coward was nowhere to be found—yet.

With a determined growl, I signaled to my pack members, readying them for the impending clash. We were outnumbered and outmatched, but our determination was strong enough.

As the first wave of Idris's followers descended upon us, a primal roar ripped through the air, signaling the beginning of a battle that would determine the fate of our kind.

Fangs bared, claws unsheathed, we met our enemies head-on. The clash of fur and claws filled the clearing with a cacophony of grunts and snarls. Bodies fell on both sides, the scent of blood thick in the air as we fought relentlessly to protect what was ours. I could feel the raw power of my pack members beside me, their loyalty and bravery unwavering in the face of danger.

I locked eyes with a particularly vicious opponent, his snarl matching mine as we circled each other, waiting for the perfect moment to strike. With a swift movement, I lunged forward, sinking my teeth into his shoulder and feeling the satisfying crunch of bone beneath my jaws. He let out a pained howl before collapsing to the ground, defeated.

I punched my fist into his chest cavity, pulling out his still-beating heart.

I lift it up into air and roared violently. The enemy that had surrounded me, attacking me from all sides, retreated. I laughed maniacally and bit into the muscle, letting the crimson drops soak my face and neck.

"Fight me!!!" I roared, spitting out the piece of the heart.

It was a quick death; every single opponent was. As it should be. I was a fucking monster, and with one swipe I could take down one, then another.

Some of my brothers were not as lucky. I pulled witches, warlocks and shifters off my future pack, one by one. We were in defense mode, just trying to save them all.

I snarled through the hordes of souls fighting. Bones was picking up bodies, trying to find heartbeats, trying to save those that couldn't be saved.

Gunshots were ringing out, Hawke's snipers were particularly helpful. Especially with the rigorous training Hawke had put them through. Most bullets had been soaked in my venom, and that appeared to be what had been saving us.

I took a quick swipe at one body and noticed how quickly it fell. Human.

Humans were mixed against the men fighting against us. They weren't all genetically mutated. It was a blessing in itself, of poor planning by Idris. My guess was that he was trying to get here more quickly than he had intended.

When I saw the human laying before me and I cocked my head to the side. If he didn't have time to change them all before he arrived, then he must know—

Know that I had found my mate and we had intended to create a pack. A pack that would strengthen us and make us harder to defeat.

My vision immediately went to Emm, and that is where I saw Duke Idris come out of the distant wood. He was wearing a long cloak, and something bulky was beneath it. His face was uncovered, and his chin was tilted upward like a cocky bastard. He had two warlocks in front of him, holding their hands up, using ruins of gold papers to cast their spells.

Bram stood between the women and Idris. His magic emanated a faint shimmer, forming a forcefield that enveloped him, Tajah, Emm, Delilah and her child. The air crackled with a subtle energy as they all remained in his protected space.

Bram's shield wasn't gonna hold.

Shit, shit, shit.

Idris knew about Emm and was going to try kill her.

I roared to Hawke, pointing toward Idris. Hawke yelled to his men, and to the new target, as they took aim and fired, but, the bullets bounced off his own invisible forcefield.

Idris's determined strides brought him nearer to Emm, intensifying the surge of fury coursing through my veins. I sprinted with a vengeance, viciously tearing into our adversaries, the sound of my claws ripping through the air.

I rushed towards Idris, my heart pounding with determination and rage. I leapt onto an enormous wolf, taking them down with a single swipe of my claws. As I tore through the remaining enemies blocking my path, I could feel the temperature around me drop when Hawke's men opened fire.

Suddenly, a blast of energy exploded from Idris, knocking several of our pack members to the ground. I snarled, shoving my feet into the soil and using it to leap toward him. Idris held out his hand, and my teeth wrapped around his white hand with long black nails. I crunched into the bones of his hand, and he groaned.

His grip tightens around my lower jaw, causing it to tremble under his forceful shake. Suddenly, a surge of electricity coursed through, jolting every nerve inside me. The intense shockwave rippled through my body, unleashing a deafening sonic boom that reverberated deep within my stomach. In an instant, I was propelled past Tajah, hurtling through the raging flames, and crashing through the walls of the sturdy packhouse.

I was stunned when I finally landed at the back of the nearly empty main floor of the packhouse, and shook my head, letting the glass fall from my fur.

No, that fucker didn't.

Struggling to rise, I scrambled to my feet, momentarily unsteady until I regained my balance. As I rushed outside, gasping for breath, I was confronted by a gruesome sight. The air was heavy with the metallic scent of blood, and the ground was painted crimson, evidence of the fierce battle that had consumed my territory.

This was not what I had wanted.

My lip curled into a snarl and I leapt off the steps. However, before I could rescue my mate, I froze, I fearing if I took one more step I would see a repeat of my fucking past.

CHAPTER
THIRTY-SIX

Emm

As I forced my eyes open, the blinding lightning seared through my vision, intensifying the throbbing pain. Lost in the abyss, I struggled to distinguish whether I was sprawled in the gritty dirt, hunched on all fours, or cradled within the embrace of unknown arms.

I told Locke to go. I told him to take care of everyone else. And I'm glad he did, I am. But now I'm breaking, not in the emotional sense, but my whole damn body.

"You are not going to give up now, are you?" I could see bright green eyes glowing in the dark recess of my mind. Fangs came from within the depths, and enormous paws smeared with blood pounded toward me. *"You're just getting started."*

As my body contorted, I could feel my spine stretching, causing me to involuntarily let out a sharp cry. The pain was unbearable, shooting through every fiber of my being. I clenched my fists, determined not to cause a scene, but the agony was too intense. I couldn't help but curse under my breath, vowing to break every one of Locke's bones for not warning me how bad this truly was.

"*Fight.*"

Fenrir circled me in the darkness. I watched the paw I had just recently gained morph into something terrifying. Long-boned fingers, with razor sharp nails to complete the transformation. Blood dripped from cuticles where it cut through the skin.

I let out another cry while I lay in my darkness.

Fenrir stood over me, I felt his fur against my back. "*You have this. You are the luna, the leader of this pack.*"

I let out a snarl, continuing to keep my eyes squeezed shut.

The deafening thunder reverberated around me, accompanied by the piercing sound of gunshots whizzing past. The air was filled with screams, roars and haunting howls, creating a cacophony of terror. My heightened hearing detected every sound with precision, while my senses seemed to amplify, allowing me to feel the scorching heat of burning embers that singed my nostrils.

A surge of raw, pulsating power invaded my body, infusing each and every breath with a newfound strength. It was as if I could feel the energy coursing through my veins, electrifying me from within. The pain that had once consumed me was now gone, replaced by a sense of invincibility. But there was no time to revel in this newfound bliss. The urgency of the situation demanded my attention, and I pushed on with renewed determination.

The fight was just beginning.

"*That's it, good girl.*" I felt Fenrir's body hover over mine, his breath tickling my pointed ears, and his nose nuzzling into my neck. "*You've done well, but it isn't over yet. Open your eyes and let them see what you have become.*"

I threw open my eyes and the darkness that covered me was filled with light. The moon glowed in the sky; the clouds parted just enough for it to shine down.

The bullets that continued to pop off in the distance sounded closer than they were. Yells and screams of pain perked my ears up, and I slowly stood on just two feet. I had easily grown a foot and a half and stood over Delilah, who was shaking beside me.

Delilah held onto her pup, who was buried deep in her chest. She wasn't even looking at me, but what was behind me.

As I turned, Tajah was still chanting, her hair flying in all directions. When she opened her eyes, they glowed a bright yellow and she drew a pattern in the air with a candle. Bram stood before her, his hands out in front of him. A weak sliver of a barrier confined us all. I jerked my head to where Bram and Delilah were staring, and I saw the fae that Locke had talked about.

Duke Idris, the dark fae that ha taken it upon himself to learn dark magic and necromancy, and take over the humans of Earth.

I tilted my head as he came closer, watching him in slow motion.

Why did he give humans powers? Why is he genetically mutating them? Doesn't he want them weak?

With a sharp blast of power from the enemy, the warlock beside him broke through Bram's shield, causing Bram to stumble backward and fall into Tajah. Tajah's body lit up with a fierce purple aura, protecting her from the attack. But another warlock quickly followed suit, unleashing an electrical charge aimed at Tajah. Yet, she glowed brighter still, as if the hit had never even fazed her. The air crackled and sparks flew as the two powerful forces collided in a dazzling display of magic and strength. Bram could only watch in awe as Tajah stood her ground, unfaltering and confident in her abilities.

With a mighty roar, Beretta burst forth from the flames as a strong and sleek black panther. Her movements were graceful yet powerful, her sharp claws leaving deep gashes on the two warlocks who stood before Idris. But, before she could make another move, Idris' face twisted into a wicked grin. His pale skin seemed to glow in the firelight, as his pointed features and the shimmering white, silver and black glitter on his cheeks gave him a menacing appearance. With a flick of his finger, he sent Beretta flying, slamming her against a nearby tree with a loud thud.

"Get out of here," I spoke out loud to Delilah, my eyes not leaving Idris. "Delilah, run!" My voice was deep and slurred with my longer tongue, but I was pleased I could still speak. "Now!"

Delilah shook herself from her stupor and bolted.

"Hello, there, Emm. What a pleasant surprise," Idris purred. His voice was sickly sweet, and condescending.

This wasn't a pleasant surprise.

I could still hear Tajah. She was still chanting away. *How much longer does it need to take?*

"I'll make this quick." He opened his large cloak that was covering something or someone, and revealed a body.

Abuela!

Her hands were tied, a cloth around her mouth and eyes filled with anger.

Oh my gods! She's pissed.

"Stop the ceremony and she lives." Idris' eyes narrow at me, and then to Tajah.

Tajah kept chanting. Her vision flickered to me and back to the book.

I gritted my teeth, letting off a low growl. "How do I know you won't just kill her, anyway," I snarled, and saliva dripped from my teeth.

Idris chuckled darkly. "You do not have the upper hand, darling, your bond, your tiny pack and the rest of your pathetic little rogues are dying.

You are only delaying the inevitable."

I balled my hands into fists.

"You know, if any of these animals had half of a brain, they would have taken up some necromancy. Figure out how to live without half their soul." He wrapped a finger around Abuela's hair. "Sure, it makes you a little manic, but you know what that's like. Being mated to Locke, leader of this monstrosity." His lip curled. "If I hadn't lost my memory in that damned fire, I would have come back a lot sooner, but that is where you came in."

I tilted my head, stepping forward, slowly while he villain monologued.

"Yes, yes, you were the one that responded to that bounty ad. Took some time to crack through your computer and that stupid firewall. But, with a little magic, and a little this a little that," he giggled, "we found you. You led us right here." He waved his hand around us like it was a magical trick.

My breath caught in my throat. *I led them here?*

Idris wagged his finger at me. "I knew Locke would meet his mate soon, but wasn't sure how you both would meet. You know, magic can be limited." He petted his hand until he pricked it with his sharp nail. He watched the blood run until it dropped onto the ground. "It's rather poetic, I think. To think you could have captured him and brought him right to me?" He clapped his hands. "Gods, that would have been delightful! I should have just had you murder him, though."

I snarled, my fur rising on my back.

"But you fell for it. You fell for that bond. It's sickening, isn't it?" His voice rose. "You still had a choice. I'm disappointed you didn't choose your family, no, instead you chose THEM!" He roared and grabbed my abuela by her hair.

His eyes grew manic, his cool tones in his voice had long vanished. The air crackled around him with anger. He gripped her hair and his teeth bared at her with contempt. "You just couldn't help it. You had to fall for your soul mate. You chose him and he trusted you so willingly. So fucking sickening. All of you!"

I held out my arm, and I lunged forward to reach her. Idris already had his long sharp nail across her neck, ready to swipe.

Using my enhanced vision, I watched in slow motion as Abuela's eyes softened. Her eyes closed and opened again, and tried my best to stare into her soul, to know what she wanted to say. But I didn't know, not truly. She was standing here, staring at me. Did she really know it was me? I looked like a monster.

My heart thumped, one, two and before the third thump—

Idris' razor-sharp nail, gleaming in the dim light, glided effortlessly across Abuela's delicate throat, leaving a faint trail of crimson.

I could smell her scent entrapped into the blood as it dripped slowly. Then, like a roaring waterfall spilled down her neck.

I felt a surge of emotions coursing through my veins, causing a physical reaction that was impossible to ignore. My heart, once beating steadily, now seemed to pause, as if captivated by the sight of her. It was as if the world around me had frozen in time, the chaos and noise fading into the background.

Every hair on my body stood on end, as if reaching out to connect with the overwhelming love and gratitude I felt towards her. Goosebumps formed on my arms, a tangible testament to the depth of my emotions. It was a powerful reminder of the impact she had on my life, the indelible mark she left upon my very soul.

As my gaze locked onto her, all other distractions vanished. The worries and anxieties that often plagued me were momentarily silenced. In that instant, I saw her not just as the woman who took me in, but as a pillar of strength, a guardian angel who had selflessly dedicated herself to my well-being.

I couldn't help but be overwhelmed by a flood of memories, each one etched vividly in my mind. I saw her wiping away my tears when I stumbled and fell as a child, her comforting words acting as a balm to my pain. She was there through the ups and downs of my teenage years, providing a safe haven when my heart felt broken and lost.

She had given me everything she had, pouring her love, time and energy into helping make me the person I had become. Her unwavering protection had shielded me from the harsh realities of the world, allowing me to grow and thrive in a safe and nurturing environment.

In that moment, I realized how truly blessed I was to have her in my life. She was not just a caretaker, but a mother figure who had selflessly stepped into the void left by my own parents. Her presence filled my heart with a profound sense of gratitude and admiration.

With her, I had found a sense of belonging; a home where I felt loved and cherished. She had become the embodiment of unconditional love, a beacon of hope in times of darkness. As I stood there, my heart paused, my fur standing on end, I realized I hadn't protected her like I promised.

Abuela's eyes rolled into the back of her head and Idris let go of her hair, as she promptly fell to the forest floor like she was nothing but a speck.

The. Bastard.

Without uttering a single cry of pain, I found myself consumed by an overwhelming sense of rage. The world around me transformed into a fiery crimson haze. In the depths of my mind, a faint tickle sent shivers down my spine, while a pair of piercing scarlet eyes locked onto mine. Slowly, two paws emerged from the darkness, accompanied by the ominous descent of gleaming ivory fangs.

My wolf.

I launched forward, not caring for the consequences. Abuela's heart was no longer beating, her body turning colder by the second. Idris' smile was still on my grandmother, and I watched as he slowly came to face me.

His hand raised, most likely to press his power into me, and a snap echoed inside my head. Dozens of voices reverberated inside. It was overpowering with the echoes, but not enough to deter me from what I was about to do.

The surrounding air crackled with a powerful energy, like blue lightning running through my fur. I could see the electrical charge jumping from me and spreading the area in my peripheral.

But I wasn't stopping.

Idris' hand swirled a grey light and pushed it out of his hand. Without any movement of his arm, the light propelled toward me, landing me straight into the chest. I waited for the impact, but my body absorbed the shock.

"You mother-fucking bastard!" I roared and slung my claws right across his chest.

Idris' tall, muscular form stumbled backward, his hair falling messily across his face. His dark, slicked-back locks were now ruffled and wild, pushed out of place by the force of the attack. His jaw clenched as he bared his sharp, white teeth in a ferocious snarl. Drops of blood trickled down from the deep claw marks on his chest, staining his pristine white shirt. The veins in his arms bulged as he struggled to stay upright, still reeling from the impact. His eyes flashed with anger and pain as he prepared to retaliate.

I didn't wait for him to be ready. I didn't even take a second look at Abuela's body on the ground. I no longer could hear her heartbeat, or her breathing. I sucked in every bit of emotion I could. That had to wait, I couldn't fall apart now.

This prick was going to pay.

"Behind you!" I heard Beretta's voice echo in my head.

A warlock that had been knocked off their feet by Beretta slung a bolt of electricity toward me. I dodged it easily, but it gave Idris ample opportunity to get up.

He stared at me and then to Tajah, who was no longer chanting. She closed the book with a loud thud and smiled. "Too late, it's done, but you already knew that, didn't you?"

Idris' face, which was already contorted to anger, turned to a bitter understanding.

The battle would shift.

The trees rustled and shook as a massive grizzly bear emerged from the cover of the forest. Its thick, brown fur glistened in the sunlight, and its sharp claws extended as it swiped at the men with ease. Behind it, a smaller but equally vicious bear followed suit, its teeth bared and eyes full of fury. Despite its size, it took down men with incredible strength and agility, tearing at their throats with its powerful jaws.

"We are kick-ass, right?" I heard Nadia inside my mind.

The link— it was complete. We could hear each other, talk to each other in our animal forms.

"Pay attention; reinforcements are coming," Bear grumbled. *"Hawke to the west, and the fae are approaching."*

The mysterious figures emerged from the shadows, their silhouettes illuminated by the blazing fire nearby. Piercing gazes swept across the battlefield taking in the bloodied sight. Arrows, swords and vines? Vines came from the trees and snatched up men and wrapped them tightly, choking them.

I darted my attention back to Idris, who was backing away into the woods. The coward wasn't even going to help his men. I steadied myself and bolted toward him as he ducked into the darkness of the forest.

The rustling of the leaves above me seemed to echo my own footsteps, as I felt the pain of Abuela fade into the background. My focus was set on Idris, and nothing would stop me from avenging her death. My eyes glowed with an intensity that reflected the fiery passion burning within me.

The forest seemed to bend and twist around me as if it was molding itself to my every movement. It was as though the very fabric of nature was conspiring to help me bring justice to this treacherous man. As I pushed deeper into the shadows, the sounds of the battle faded behind me, replaced by the silent whispers of the trees and the howling of wolves in the distance.

I would not stop, I wouldn't give up. I would destroy him and take away everything he has taken from Locke, and from me.

We reached a clearing, where we stopped at the lake that was all too familiar. Idris turned, his chest already healed and only blood stained his dark clothes.

"I have to say, I did not expect this." He pulled on the collar of this cloak. It fluttered to the ground. "That the daughter of a drunk gambler would become what she is today."

I stomped toward him and gripped my giant hand around his neck. I squeezed, and he sputtered, but he didn't fight me. One squeeze and I would have him, he would be dead, lying in the dirt like Abuela. I could let the buzzards eat out his eyes, let the worms feast on his flesh.

"The cartel will be upset to know that you are unavailable, but at least your sister can take your spot."

My eyes widened, and I let off a warning growl. "You know nothing." I let the hot spit dribble from my maw.

Idris chuckled. "But I do, darling. And I know where your sister is. Why do you think I had dear old grandma, hmm?" He stared at me knowingly. "I don't go into battle without a back-up plan. It's just, not wise."

I set him back down in the dirt and he tugged on his clothes that were not yet ripped. "Now, if you want nothing to happen to your sister, Elena, and her son, who was it, Luis?-"

I stared at him, breathing hard.

"- then, you will do as I say, little pup. Otherwise, you will never know their location."

CHAPTER THIRTY-SEVEN

Locke

I prowled on the edge of the woods. She was there—I could see her put Idris down and let him go. As their conversation continued, it made my heart thump harder and harder.

The lies he spat, the fucking audacity.

My lip curled, my fangs dripping. My cock was hard, I couldn't help it. I was a sick fuck wanting to sink my fangs into his throat and let my mate watch me rip him to pieces. She'd watch me slowly dismember him, take him piece by piece until I took out his heart. I'd swallow it whole and let his blood smear on my body.

Then I'd take her, I'd fuck her over his corpse.

My body shuddered, and I leaned my head back against the tree.

Fenrir purred with me, our hand stroking our shaft.

Our mate watched her enemy with intent to strike. She was listening to the bastard's monologue, while he tried to sway her against me.

That would never happen.

She was far too deep within my grasp, too far deep into my soul. It was an idea that Idris would never know. Bonds cannot be broken.

"He's lying," I linked her. *"I have your sister and she is being protected by one of my most trusted men."*

My mate didn't move, didn't show any signs that she heard me. *Good girl.*

"Remember that male that got too friendly with you at the bar? Mr. Lucky Charms?" Idris circled my mate.

Emm didn't show any interest, she just kept her eyes narrowed.

"He took the tiniest lock of your hair. You didn't even know it!" Idris snorted. "He did it for your father, just to make sure it was you. I guess you have changed a lot over the years." Idris looked my mate up and down. "He kept sending his men to your camper, to see if they could find an idea where your sister was so he could pay off the cartel with her, but I don't think they were expecting your guard dog."

"And where is my father, now?" Emm's voice remained eerily calm.

Idris clasped his hands together. "Far from here. Once he realized there were beasts in the area, and who exactly I was, he stayed far away. We do, though, have an arrangement." Idris winked at her.

"And, that is?" My mate walked closer. Her fur bristled on her back, her claws lengthened.

Idris remained motionless, as vibrant sparks of electricity crackled and danced along his fingertips. "Easy there, now that you are away from your pack, you are weaker. I'm sure you have learned little from your mate now, have you?"

"I'm here, near you," I told her. "As long as your mate is near you can absorb that small charge, but it's going to fucking hurt."

"I'll take my chances," Emm snapped. "What is the arrangement?"

Idris grinned. "I like your spunk. The arrangement is that you come with me. I will leave your sister and her son alone. You will leave your mate and his pack here. What happens to the pack is no longer your concern. You will be given to the cartel to pay off your father's debts only this time instead of marrying into the cartel, you will be their weapon."

"And if I refuse?" My mate raised an eyebrow.

Idris threw his head back. "Then, everyone you know and love will perish. Brutally, slowly, and I'll leave your mate for last so you feel every bit of pain he does." Idris' smile grew wide enough to reach his pointed ears.

"How do I know you will keep your word?" Emm tilted her head.

I crossed my arms and leaned against the tree.

"A binding contract. Just a handshake, the magic will weave itself." Idris held out his hand, his nails long and creepy as shit.

Emm stared at it a long moment and I read the thoughts swirling in her head. She would not shake it and I almost chuckled about what she was going to do next.

Emm reached out her hand, pretending to take it. Idris was fucking giddy, watching her reach closer until Emm instead balled up her fists and punched Idris right in the nose.

Idris sent over a ball of light so strong it pushed my mate back onto her ass. I leaped forward and used my arms to run a four-legged sprint and jumped on the bastard.

My claws dug into Idris' back, and I could feel his electrifying charge flow through me. I growled in rage and pain as I clung to him. Emm charged at us, her fur standing on end, her teeth bared in a vicious snarl.

Her fangs bit into his shoulder and Idris let out a blood-curdling scream like the fucking bitch he was. He threw out his arm, and his electricity seemed to multiply, zapping my mate and me both. It was like being shocked by the entire power grid. I could feel my muscles spasming, my bones rattling, and my consciousness slipping away.

He blasted both of us from his body. I shook my head and jumped back onto my feet, ready to tackle him again.

Idris held onto his shoulder, as black tar oozed from his skin where Emm had latched on from earlier. The venom was working. It looked just as it did when Journey had bitten him the first time. It would weaken him just enough to deliver some final blows.

"You fat cunt, you'll pay for that."

Idris' hands swirled in the air and I charged. His one hand came down and a red glow blasted from his fingertips and enveloped my body. It felt like every muscle and nerve was being pulled and twisted at the same time, I let out a piercing roar as it held me in the air.

Emm lay in the dirt, still getting over the previous blast. She may have force-shifted into Lycan, and she thinks she is fucking unstoppable, but she is still weak. She can't fight for long.

With a sudden jolt, her eyes snapped wide open as Idris released a bolt from his other hand. The deafening crack fills the air, causing her to startle. The bolt missed and hurtled towards the ground. She jumped away just in time as the bolt met the dirt, and a cloud of dust and debris erupts.

"Hold fucking still," he growled. Idris lowers his hand. I was still unable to move with a red glow around me.

"You can't fight forever, Emm, you're going to become weak. Run back to the pack."

Emm snorted and circled Idris, who was pulling shit from his pockets.

"Nope, not leaving you here," she snapped. *"I've already lost one person, I can't lose anyone else,"* her voice cracked in the link.

Idris' gaze flickered to his pocket and Emm took the shot. She darted one way and then another using her lycan speed. Her claws ripped into his other arm and she pulled, causing his right arm to be pulled out of its socket. She sank her teeth into the limp arm and, again, his body became an electrical charge and knocked her off.

Emm, again, was thrown, this time at my feet.

When I tried to move, the inside of my body pulled and tugged, straining the sinews of my muscles. I couldn't even lean down to pick her up.

Idris narrowed his eyes and smirked. "Well, if it's a game you want, little wolf, then let's play."

Shit.

"Get up, Emm. Now!"

Emm blinked immediately and looked up at Idris.

Idris pulled out a pair of long, sharp knives from his belt and held them in his hands. He blew on one and it floated into the air. Emm took a deep breath.

"Just a knife. I can dodge those easily," she mumbled.

"Not these," Idris taunted.

"They're enchanted, they won't stop coming at you. Fucking leave and get back to the pack!" I roared inside the link.

"If you are going to talk out of your ass, at least turn around so I can hear you better," she snapped at me.

Emm lunged at Idris with the lycan speed she possessed. It was slower than it should have been had she had been trained and not recently shifted, but she was still fast. Idris was quicker, his magical daggers proving to be a lethal asset.

He dodged her attacks, his legs working just fine. He held out the dagger again and it rose into the air. The pointed end aimed for Emm and flew with outstanding speed. Emm gasped, feeling it hit her shoulder, and hissed.

"NO!" I was able to roar, pulling and twisting in the red bonds that tied me.

Idris's menacing laughter echoed through the air as he retrieved a gleaming dagger from his concealed stash. Gripping it tightly, he held it aloft, watching as it hovered weightlessly. With a forceful exhale, he blew on the blade, causing it to slice through the atmosphere and find its mark on Emm's shoulder, eliciting a sharp and agonizing pain.

I roared again, this time the bonds that held me faltered and I began to break free.

"You fucking bastard, you fight me!" I yelled at him.

Despite Idris' ability to heal, he was bitten twice. Venom was running through his body. His skin was grey and he was having trouble, even with his magic. He could throw the knives, try to heal, or keep me pinned. He couldn't do all three.

Idris snickered, and walked closer to Emm, pulling another knife from his sash.

Amid their matched chaos, Emm's body shifted back to her human form. I knew she couldn't maintain the lycan form. Her body was giving up.

Idris' sinister laughter echoed through the air as he maliciously hurled yet another blade towards her. With a surge of adrenaline, I managed to break free from the restraints that held me captive, his weakening magic granting me freedom. Instinctively, I positioned myself to shield her from further harm, bracing as the blade pierced my shoulder. The searing pain shot through my body, accompanied by the metallic scent of blood that began to flow down my arm.

I turned my head slowly, my fangs dripping with anticipation. "My turn."

Idris backed up several steps toward the lake, and bubbles came to the surface. I smirked and let my claws clink together, as Idris let another dagger rise from his hand. He blew on it and as soon as it went into the air, my hand raised and I caught it with ease.

"Someone has become weak—again." I taunted.

Idris smirked despite being cornered. "Is that so? Go ahead, kill me." Idris opened his arms. The last few remanding daggers dropped to the ground. "Rip out my heart. See if I care?" He laughed again, and I wondered if I really was the crazy one here.

If it was a trap, I didn't know but I didn't really care. I was ready to sink my teeth into his throat and end him for good. To kill him with my bare hands, feel his blood on my teeth.

I took a determined step forward. His eyes flashed with malice as he lunged towards me, his nails slashing across my abdomen. The sharp pain seared through me, but I refused to show weakness. I clenched my jaw, feeling the warm trickle of blood down my side, and locked my gaze on him. With a swift motion, I raised my arm, the metallic scent of sweat and anticipation filled my nose ready to end this once and for all.

My mate was slowly healing behind me. I could feel her. But to keep her safe, I needed to end him quicker than I really wanted to. As my hand reared back, the bubbles behind him gave way to two blow-holes. A large snake-like head rose above the water, and Idris and I both stood back.

A magnificent blue dragon, its towering form covered with shimmering silver scales and adorned with vibrant yellow accents, loomed above us. As it gracefully opened its nostrils, a refreshing cascade of water poured down upon us.

I could smell Anaki's scent, his recently-mated scent. *"Anaki?"* I linked

Without hesitation, Anaki launched into action, moving swiftly and silently like a cobra. With lightning speed, Anaki's powerful grip ensnared Idris by the torso, pulling him forcefully into the depths of the water. The surrounding waves trembled violently, echoing with the tumultuous commotion. As the chaotic struggle unfolded, Anaki's sleek body twisted and turned, mimicking movements of a crocodile.

I stood in shock until the waters calmed and I could no longer see Anaki or the Idris.

The hell?

Sadness hit my chest, a new feeling since starting the fight here next to the lake, and I realized I needed to tend to my mate. I dashed toward Emm who was laying naked in the dirt in her human form. Blood was drying on her skin, tears streaming down her face.

Her body was healed, but definately not her heart.

I gently lifted her and cradled her in my arms, feeling the warmth of her body against mine.

"Princess, it's okay." I rocked her in my lycan form. "Everything is going to be alright, I'm here now. He's gone. Your sister and nephew are safe."

But your grandmother isn't.

I didn't say it, but she knew it that was what I was thinking. Guilt consumed me more than anything. If I hadn't brought them here, then maybe she would still be alive?

"Don't." She sobbed into my furred chest. "Don't you dare say it's your fault."

My mate's fingers clutched my fur tightly to the point it hurt. "They would have found someone; they found my father. I mean—gods, I wish I had paid attention." She shook her head. "I wish I had listened to her more closely, understood her better."

"What do you mean?" I tilted her head up with my claw.

She looked so damn beautiful, but when she cried—fuck, I don't know—she looked even more so.

"She said once we found our soul mates, that we didn't need her any-more. That they would protect us. At the time I didn't believe her, didn't believe in—"

"Mates. You didn't believe I'd find you."

"Didn't believe in any of it." She heaved in a breath. "I wish I could go back and tell her I loved her. Tell her she isn't crazy; tell her I believed her."

I pulled my mate to my chest and rocked her slowly. "I'm sure she knows. Why else do you think she was in the duke's clutches? She knew her fate, Princess."

My mate cried harder, and I held her.

It then clicked for me. As it always did, much later, with the cryptic words of a priestess, and the words of a witch or a warlock. Emm had to suffer as I did when I became Lycan. She had to know what pain I went through when I became what I was. I lost my mother and Emm's grandmother was as close to a mother as she could get.

I gritted my teeth, my cheek resting on her head.

I still think we are just pawns that the gods like to play with in this damned world, but what did it matter? Nothing, nothing mattered to a mortal soul like mine. There would still be pain and suffering no matter what I did to this pack.

Once Emm's grandmother died, that was when the pack-link was established. I could link everyone that was mated, and soon, those who were healthy enough could join the pack. Those that were too far gone, I suppose cell phones would still have to be our primary source of communication.

"Everything alright?" Hawke linked as I let my mate sob.

"Yeah, we're good. Idris is gone."

"Gone or dead?" Hawke's heartbeat was loud through the link.

"Goddess, I hope he's dead."

CHAPTER
THIRTY-EIGHT

Locke

My mate cried until she passed out in my arms. I sat there for a while longer mulling over what the hell happened. It all happened so fast, I'm not sure if I could explain it.

Idris was there, and then he was not. Was he dead? We thought he was when the fire consumed him, but now he was taken into the lake. Anaki came the fuck out of nowhere and drowned the fucker.

"Anaki?" I linked. I waited for him to respond. Now he was mated, and to make it even more surprising, he was mated to my mate's sister. I'm going to be honest. I thought it was a great pairing. The two of them were made for each other. Anaki was overly helpful to her, even when she was trying to push him away. The dragon never learned how to take a hint.

Did any of us?

I waited a little longer before I reached out to him again. It has been a while since either of us established a connection and I was not sure if it was even possible between a wolf and a dragon. I heard Bear quite well, but Anaki—he was a reptile. Reptiles and mammals were different.

Their mating practices, and their mannerisms. I've never indulged in my curiosities with him. None of us really do.

"*Alpha-*" His voice was deeper than it usually was. More serious. "*I apologize, it's been a while since I've had to control my instinctual side.*"

I inhaled, feeling the crisp air fill my lungs, and shifted my posture to face the tranquil lake. Gradually, his head emerged from the water, its sheer size obscuring the moon's delicate glow and the fading wisps of clouds.

"I get it. But where the hell is Idris? He better be buried underneath a rock in the deepest part of the lake." I spoke aloud.

Anaki's large serpentine head looked back. "*His heart stopped beating and I held him in my mouth, but he disintegrated. Is that how the fae die?*"

I snarled and ran my claws through the fur between my ears. "I don't know. We will have to speak to Bram. He knows more. Where is your mate, and her son?"

Anaki's long forked tongue whipped across his lips. "*Safe within my cave. Her grandmother ran off and said she must fulfil her destiny. I tried to stop her—*"

I shook my head and held up my hand. "She fulfilled it. But, she is no longer with us."

Anaki's dragon slumped and turned away. "*I failed her.*"

"No—" I shook my head. "It had to be done. It was her destiny and I'm sure the Goddess will bless her in the afterlife."

Anaki left me on the shore. I held my mate for a few minutes longer as I prepared myself for the aftermath. All that we have worked so hard for, I knew, would be gone.

The trek back was far quicker than I wanted it to be. All I wanted was my mate in my arms and a nest to hold her in. Her body was weak, her mind even more so and my rage was still brewing below the surface.

I would have to take care of my needs later, and the only solution seemed to be having sex with her. I was a simple male, but now that I was mated, I had to think of her.

As I approached the clearing, I knew I needed to assess the damage of the cabins and the packhouse, but first I took in the men and women that I once called a club—now formed as a pack.

As I looked around, the sight of many individuals, their bodies bleeding and fighting for their lives, was disheartening. However, there was a glimmer of hope as they were recovering, at a swifter pace than usual. The air was filled with the sound of murmurs, groans and the occasional gasp of pain. The scent of antiseptic and medicine lingered. Despite the progress, we still had a long and challenging journey ahead.

Grim sauntered up to me, Journey by his side, as always. "It was won as soon as the link was established."

As I surveyed the cabins, a somber sight greeted my eyes. The vast majority lay in ruin, particularly the unclaimed ones, leaving behind a sense of time and energy. However, the true devastation unfolded before me as I approached the packhouse. The third floor, where I had painstakingly crafted my den in the past few days during my mate's heat, and my rut, was fucking ruined. All efforts were in vain.

"My old sleuth will be here at dawn. They will help put it back together. They work fast, you know that." Bear came up beside me and patted my back. "We can't have our alpha and luna without a proper place to stay."

Nadia placed a blanket over my naked mate's body, and I nodded my head in thanks.

Any other time I believe I would have snarled and slashed anyone for looking at my mate's body, but I had too many things on my mind.

My wolf was terribly silent—pacing inside me. He wanted more blood. He wanted Idris' head. An unsettling feeling settled in my stomach.

Pack members continued to take the dead bodies of the enemy and put them into the fire. To my surprise, we didn't lose manyif any. Sizzle was still counting, and Bones was patching up the wounded.

"Everyone did well, especially when the fae arrived. If we didn't have them, I don't know if we would have lasted until the link was established." Hawke said. "That headache was so bad we couldn't even shift."

I continued to walk with my mate in my arms to survey the damage.

"Where were the fae, what happened with them?"

Hawke picked up a broken limb in our path and threw it into the forest. "Idris rounded them up, his men and witches had fire torches, and threatened to burn up the whole place. You know fae and nature. They don't want to see nature suffer because of them."

I hummed in agreement; spring and summer fae had a weakness for nature. Flooding or fire to any of their creations and they throw a fit. They must have realized they were outnumbered and under-prepared. Fae don't have the muscle power, and they liked to plan strategically.

"There were magical cages just out of the camera's view and the enemy locked them up so they couldn't join the fight."

"Sneaky bastard," I mumbled under my breath. "So, who freed them?"

"Emm's grandmother," Hawke said in surprise. "Don't ask me how." He threw his hands up. "But she did."

My mate groaned in my arms, and I sighed heavily. I needed to tend to her. "Anything else?"

"I think we can handle everything. Bones and Nadia are tending to the weak. The fae are helping with the cleanup. They are getting the forest to pick up shit." He rubs the back of his neck. "The clubhouse is quiet. Are you going to take the luna back there? I can make an effort to keep people's noise level to a minimum, until the cabins are rebuilt and the packhouse is somewhat livable.

I stared back at the packhouse. The outside was finished, but now there were smashed windows with burn marks up the side, and the third floor was completely missing. Even if the bear shifters worked their asses off, it would take at least two weeks.

With a link established, those who had never had a link before would have trouble filtering out thoughts. Their minds will not have learned to pull certain 'communication wires' in the brain. Especially with Emm, when her wolf has not yet surfaced to help guide her. She will need to stay away from the packhouse so she doesn't hear everyone's thoughts.

I needed her to be resting and to mourn the loss of her grandmother, and reestablish our own connection.

"I've got a place where we can go. I'll need some supplies, though."

"Anything," Hawke said, glancing at his mate and pup. "You know, your mate ordered mine to get out of there. Delilah was in such shock. I don't think she would have moved away and who knows what would have happened to her."

I gave a smirk and rubbed my nose into Emm's hair. "That's what she's here for, to protect everyone."

"Just like you, huh? Crazy bastard." Hawke shoved my shoulder. "Even though you don't act much like one anymore."

I raised a brow. "Trust me, the crazy is still there. I'm just showing my best self for her."

"And I'm not good enough for you to show your best self?" Hawke ran his hand down his bare chest.

I glanced at Grim who was scowling at us and crossing his arms. "No, Grim is the only one that matches my vibe."

Hawke rolled his eyes and flipped me the bird. "You guys have a weird relationship, I fucking swear. You barely talk to each other but act like you fuck each other in the dark."

I shrugged my shoulders. "Don't knock it till you try it."

Hawke stepped away. "Fuck you, man." Hawke walked past Grim and stopped to stare at him.

Grim wiggled his eyebrows and Hawke gasped.

I threw my head back and laughed. Then laughed some more, thinking how ridiculous I probably looked standing in my lycan form laughing at some sick jokes.

Grim stepped up and jutted out his chin. "I stocked the cabin, after you switched back to being human."

While I was rabid and had to seek shelter from snow and rain, now sometimes I would wake up in the old cabin Grim and I built out of a scrap of logs when we first moved here. It wasn't much at first but we had a king bed, blankets, a kitchen and such, while we'd fixed up the bar.

From time to time there would be meat, and clean blankets for me to make a nest, while I was rabid. It calmed me enough smelling his scent, even though we were not blood brothers—we were brothers. He was the closest thing to my sister that I had.

I smiled, grabbed his forearm and shook it. "Thanks, brother. I owe you."

"Nah, I think I owe you. You helped give me a second chance. I'm just glad you got yours."

I nodded and grunted in agreement. "It's far from over. We have to help everyone else. Are you still in for that?"

Grim gazed around the scene, with every male and female helping each other.

"Never thought it would get this big, but yeah. I think so. Journey wouldn't have it any other way."

I huffed. "Yeah, neither would I."

We departed and I let my inner circle take care of the mess. I felt like an ass for leaving, but taking care of their luna was my priority. She'd been through hell and back today, and I would take care of what was mine.

So, I took the long trek up the hill, closer to the bar, where our old cabin sat. The forest was quiet besides the soft rustle of the leaves beneath my bare feet. I was grateful for the silence because could hear the small murmurs of my pack trying to understand how to use a link again.

As I neared the cabin, my eyes fixated on its weathered state. In my wolf form, I had never truly observed it from the outside. Time had not been kind to it, evident in its deterioration, yet it remained strong. Drawing closer, I observed the slithering vines, like serpents, coaxing through the broken windows, filling the gaps and weaving in and out from each other.

I shook my head and chuckled. Shhkuk was a saint, but I think he was going to get on my fucking nerves one day trying to help out my mate when it was my fucking job. The vines weaved in and out of the windows, giving me enough light so I could see inside. When I stepped in, dried leaves and dirt were scattered about, but the bed was clean with fresh linens and blankets.

I tilted my head in question, laying my mate's body on the bed and wrapping her body with the blankets. An envelope sat at the base of the mattress with a golden scale, a feather on one side, and gold coins on the other.

I hadn't seen an envelope like this since we had rescued Journey. Before I started having PTSD from seeing the damn thing, I snatched it up and ripped it open with my claw, to see neatly written scripted writing.

"Congratulations on your success, Alpha. Your efforts have not gone unnoticed by the Gods. Continue your valiant efforts, and in the afterlife, you will be justly rewarded."

My lip curled, and I crumbled the letter in my hands. I changed back into my human form. My mate and I were dirty, but I was too exhausted to care to clean either of us, or the cabin. Instead, I wrapped my body around my mate, my purr resonating loudly in the room. My wolf stopped his pacing, and he curled up in the back of my mind.

He remained unsatisfied. His thirst for blood was forever stronger. We still could not rest, would not rest.

Because we did not believe that Duke Idris was dead.

Thoughts of him remaining alive swirled in my mind as I held onto my mate. My hand slithered up her chest and onto her right breast, to remain calm.

I growled, my nose nuzzling into her mark. *"My mate, my pack. We will destroy all who dare threaten them."*

CHAPTER
THIRTY-NINE

Emm

I stretched on the plush bed, sinking into its softness and relishing the sensation of the fuzzy pillow against my face, gently stroking it up and down. The pillow carried the lingering scent of Locke, filling my lungs and instantly soothing me. As I nestled deeper into the cozy blankets, my skin warmed, prompting me to burrow further, seeking maximum comfort.

The cabin was smaller than the master bedroom of the pack-house and I almost preferred it. I felt safer here, more confined. Especially when Locke would join me on the bed and wrap me up in his arms.

I never thought I would be a cuddler, but he has made me a cuddle slut.

I've lost count how many days we have been at the cabin. I'm guessing about a week, only because our scents have intermingled with the nest and the cabin, which is a stark difference from what it was in the beginning.

When I first woke, the floor was covered in dirt, leaves and twigs. An animal may have lived here, because there were hunks of fur, rats, nests and old blankets on the floor. The bed, however, was new, as were the mattress, blankets and pillows.

Inside was a small kitchen, a bathroom with a toilet and a generator that gave us just enough electricity to fuel the lights. We mostly used candles, and the ambiance of that was comforting.

Despite the desolate cabin, I found solace in Locke's embrace. Tears were constant when I lay awake. Even as I wrestled with my emotions and attempted to distance myself, he remained steadfast by my side.

He let out growls of protest when I tried to push him away. He would pull me to his chest and pet my hair. His purrs grew so loud that the entire bed would shake and it echoed in the room. But it was what I needed. I was stubborn, and he knew what I needed even more than I knew myself.

"You need comfort. I'm here for that," he would say.

I'd sniff and cry, telling him to leave and to go help his pack. He never would, told me his beta, Grim, would be in charge until he returned. His gamma was Hawke, and his delta would be Sizzle, once his dragon returned.

I was still getting used to the lingo and what all of those terms meant, but it was just a social ladder of who was in charge when one was not present.

Locke left periodically, mostly when I slept and wasn't thrashing through the night. The guilt ate at me; tore at me, not just because of Abuela's death, but because I couldn't get up and help the newly formed pack.

I had sunk into a depression, and I worried if I would ever get out.

Locke cleaned up the cabin as I lay in bed sleeping. I've never seen a man clean in my life, but Locke wasn't just a man. He was an alpha and I believe he was making do with the den we had because he had set it up quickly. The next time I woke from a nap, it was a cozy cottage in the woods, near the bar.

He even hung up the damn curtains.

A small bouquet of flowers sat on the table. There was always a loaf of bread and food in a small icebox. It was so fucking endearing that it would make me cry all over again.

And that would set him off.

He went from my psycho stalker, gnawing off my enemy's hand and leaving it at my doorstep, to an over-brooding mother hen. He picked me up, held me in his arms and rocked me, petting my cheek with his thumb, letting his thick musk scent envelope me and crush me until I was a big pile of goo.

How this scenting thing worked, I wasn't sure. Could women do it? I wanted to do it to him when he got upset.

But he wasn't even upset, right now. He was holding onto me, keeping me grounded. It was almost annoying.

"It's alright, baby. I gotcha." He heard me sniffing. With my back turned to him, he immediately came over to the bed and scooped me up. I was naked; that way the entire time I'd been here, and I hadn't minded it at all.

"Hey, how's my princess doing today?"

"Better," I linked, not wanting to speak. *"I need to get out of bed and stop this self-pity."*

Locke hummed and set me on his thigh. He pushed my hair away and pressed kisses up my shoulder. When I moved, I felt something hard move against me, and that was the first time I felt something up my ass.

My eyes widened and I moved around some more, then jumped up off his lap. Locke smirked and rubbed my ass tentatively.

"Something wrong, Princess? What's got you standing?"

I glared at him. "There's something in my ass."

Locke chuckled and bit his lip. "Is there now? I wonder what it could be?"

Locke tried several things to lift my spirits, even though he knew mourning was part of the process. He said, even to this day he gets upset about his sister and his mother, and there isn't a day that goes by that he doesn't think about them, but he tries to keep the pain away.

He'd told me stories, even though I could reach into his mind and find them myself. I found it so invasive; I didn't want to do that, nor did I have the skill. So, he told me bedtime stories about him and Grim, and how the club came to be.

After Blood Rose was no more, he took the carriage that held massive amounts of gold, and the horses, and took the long trek to the nearest portal. Along the way, he found Grim, just as beat up and lost as he was.

Their smells were similar then, the smell of rogues with no pack. They decided that since their situations were the similar, they would travel together to the Earth realm and die in peace on Earth.

That vision changed when they saw others just like them dying off along their journey. Many deserved to be rogues. They had refused any sort of bond or were wicked. What Locke and Grim noticed was that the rogues who paired together didn't go rabid as quickly.

As they pondered those findings, they concocted the idea in their heads about making a group of rogues under the disguise of an MC. The more rogues together, the longer they could last before they went rabid.

Because all living things want to survive, why couldn't they?

And motorcycles seemed like the logical choice. It was the perfect cover for roughnecks like them. Plus, they could ride, go fast and feel the wind in their hair. They couldn't very well run through the forest like they used to.

Locke had the most hope that one day they would achieve redemption, maybe even a second chance, but they knew very well that it was a far-fetched idea, especially Grim. They didn't know where to start in the beginning, until one day he found a letter with a gold weighted scale embossed on the front, with feathers on one side and coins on the other.

Locke said, at first, he thought it was a joke and threw away the letter, but it appeared back on his desk the moment he turned his back. He figured he'd humor whatever ghost, god or entity had thrown it back there, and took some of his stronger men to a site that had women held in cages. It was their first mission.

It was sloppy, he said. They should have been caught, but the enemy didn't know they were coming. They were a small group but after that night they took it more seriously, and the letters kept coming; the missions larger and more complicated.

They never lost.

Not once did Locke and his men turn down a mission, even though he took his men to *church* and asked if they wanted to complete it. His members had to do something; they couldn't sit on their asses. No shifter, rogue or any other supernatural could sit on their ass and do nothing. Thus, they started the Iron Fang. The one percent of MCs that took care of the weak, especially women.

Locke and Grim used the gold stolen from the Blood Rose pack to get started. The left-over gold still buried underneath this cabin. If we are ever in any financial need, Locke told me that beneath the rug and floorboard, we would find twenty more gold bars and that would keep the club running.

The club was self-sufficient, now, though. With Locke's investments in the human world—we didn't need to use the gold from his home realm of Elysian. It was just back-up gold at this point.

He was resourceful. I'd give him that.

There was a mirror in the small bathroom, and I sauntered over to it. The mirror was too high to see the thing poking my asshole and I groaned, trying to bend my ass over and see what was back there. But I had a good idea what it was.

"Did—did you plug me?" I tried not to smile, but it spread across my face anyway.

"Maybe," he drawled. "Figured it was one way to get you outta bed."

I bit my lip and walked back toward him. Luckily, I kept up with my hygiene by taking a dip in the lake. Locke cleaned up the dried blood, dirty sweat, and tears from the first few days while I was passed out from exhaustion, but I was determined not to let him see me as a hairy human.

"Sorry, a lot happened at once. I should have gotten up, especially with the pack I—"

"Shh, shh," Locke soothed, and pulled on me, so I straddled his legs. "My luna needs to take care of her physical and emotional health first, before she can tackle a pack. Besides, the mind-link was a mess. I've been detangling all that for the pack while staying in here with you. It isn't like I was sittin' pretty either."

Guilt hung heavy in my chest.

"Fucking gods, Emmie, don't do that." He pulled on my hips and kissed my soft stomach. "Before I set off from Blood Rose, you wanna know how long I stayed in that barren wasteland before I took off with all that gold? Two months."

My heart skipped a beat.

"It broke me losing my mother. You have every right to grieve. The only difference is you've got me, your family is this pack and your sister. And that sister of yours keeps pestering me to see you." He rolled his eyes. "By the way, that nephew of yours, he's cute as fuck."

I giggled and wrapped my arms around my mate. "Yeah, he's cute. When I talked to him on the phone, the other day he said he was ready to go to an actual school. Are you sure it's safe for him around here?"

Locke gave me a look, one that I knew would get me in a heap of trouble later for even thinking the area around here isn't safe.

He better not edge me. My poor body can't take it.

"Of course it is. It's one school building for all grades. Police are there and if it makes you feel more comfortable, we can station some prospects out there until things die down."

I nodded and took a breath. "Until my father is caught, the cartel and all, I think it would be for the best."

Locke smirked, a fang descending from his lip. "Baby, you don't need to worry about that. Your alpha has that all taken care of."

I raised a brow, and he pulled me down over the bed. My ass was in the air and he landed a large slap to it. I could feel it ripple and Locke massaged away the sting. "Now, let me have some fun with this.

Locke stood and I heard him put his hand in his jeans, listening to the fabric between his fingers. I could hear everything so much clearer now, it was multiplied times twenty.

"That's it, don't move. In fact—" he went to the drawer and pulled out a set of handcuffs.

I picked my head off the bed. "Hey those are—"

"From your RV? Yeah, I had someone grab them. Amongst other things." His voice was dark, and I heard the clink of the cuffs. He grabbed my wrists, firmly planting them behind my back and locked them in place. I heard them click and my breath hitched.

Locke's dominant side was coming to the surface, and a shiver of anticipation ran down my spine as I lay there, helpless and at his mercy. His touch was firm, yet gentle as he explored every inch of my exposed skin. His lips trailed fiery kisses along my back, igniting a hunger deep within me that only he could satisfy.

"Hold still," he rasped and picked up the phone from the bed. He parted my cheeks and I heard the click of his phone. "Perfect."

He. Did. Not.

"Have a look." He brought the phone up to me and showed the picture he just took. Of course, it was my backside with a plug, and at the base it said, 'Luna' on it. "You like it? I'll get you more."

I rolled my eyes and wiggled. He gave me another hard smack, and I squealed.

My body was already responding. It always did. Even in the nights where we slept together in this cabin. I couldn't recall how many times I woke up with his face between my thighs, his tongue licking my slit like a starved man, then knotting me over and over.

Depression did not slow down my sex drive, and the sex was a great distraction. Abuela would have been happy for me.

This plug, though, this was something new.

"If you are a good girl, I'll let you come."

I arched my back, wordlessly begging for more. His painfully hard erection dug into my ass as he kissed my back, licking, sucking and trailing painfully slow kisses down my skin.

"Locke," I whined and wiggled my ass.

"I haven't even got to the middle of your back and I can already smell you. You've stunk up the whole room, haven't you?" One hand rested on my hip, the other trailed up my inner thigh. He stood back and watched his painstakingly slow hands reach up to my slit.

"My gods, you are just dripping. What a sweet luna you are, getting all wet for your alpha to knot you."

I panted, my back arching off the bed. I could feel the usually soft blankets feel rough on my pierced nipples.

"Locke, please," I begged.

He hummed, swirling his finger around my arousal and placing the pad of his finger on my clit. "You beg so prettily. You only beg for my knot, don't you? Never for anything else."

I whined and pushed back.

He tsked. "I want to do something different, if you are up for it, Princess."

Locke backed away and went to the nightstand drawer. It was rickety and made a loud creaking noise. There was a towel, and wrapped up inside was another version of my old dildo, the one I nicknamed The Prolapser.

"I wanna stick this in your luscious ass while I knot your pussy."

My breath hitched, and my eyes hooded. I've never been done in the ass.

Locke, able to read my thoughts, grabbed a bottle of lube and sauntered back over. I eyed him as he dropped it on the bed and took off his shirt. "I'll go slow. I wanna fill you up real good, baby."

My heart thrummed with excitement and nervousness. Since I was Lycan, I could take this right?

Locke chuckled, and I heard the zipper of his fly go down and his pants drop. "This won't be painful. Uncomfortable, yes. But I put a big ass plug in you and you accepted it just fine. Let's get you to come first."

I mewled like a damn cat when I felt two of his fingers push inside me and he pumped them along with his hips, pushing me into the mattress.

"That's it, take these fingers. I want you nice and wet. I'm thirsty and need something to drink."

Locke was playing with the plug, pulling it half out and pushing it back in. Between his fingers and the plug, my body was tensing, feeling the strange sensation in my ass and in my clit.

"You're so tense, let me see you squirt, baby."

His dirty words had me coming faster than I intended and I cried out his name. My wrists tightened around the cuffs and my sensitive breasts rubbed against the sheets.

Gods.

I wanted more.

My mate ran his fingers up my leg, pushing them deep inside me again and pulled them out, along with the plug. I watched over my shoulder as his fingers entered his mouth and heard him slurp up my arousal.

"Fucking delicious, baby. No squirting yet, but we will get there."

My empty ass contracted. After having a plug, I felt so utterly empty, but I knew it wouldn't be long before I was filled again.

He reached for the lubricant next to him on the bed, opening it with one hand, while maintaining the rhythm with the other. I could feel my body ease into his touch, my muscles yielding to the familiar sensation of being claimed. Locke's eyes met mine when I turned around briefly, heat in his eyes.

As he lubed up the toy and his fingers, I couldn't help but worry about the size of it. My eyes trailed down to the dildo wrapped in the towel, and a shiver ran down my spine. I wasn't sure if I was ready for this, but the anticipation was turning me on.

Locke positioned the lubed-up toy at the entrance of my ass, and I held my breath, not knowing what to expect. He looked at me, his eyes filled with warmth and understanding. "Don't worry, I'll be gentle. We'll take it slow."

With those comforting words, he pushed the tip of the toy inside me, and I let out a sharp intake of breath. The feeling was unlike anything I had experienced before - a mix of pain and pleasure that sent my senses reeling. I clenched my hands into fists, my eyes were staring straight ahead as Locke continued to inch the toy deeper into my ass.

He stopped momentarily, letting me adjust to the sensation. "Are you okay?" he asked, his concern clear in his voice. "Say 'tamale' if you want me to stop."

"Okay," I croaked, nearly laughing. My throat felt dry suddenly with unease, but I felt through our bond how he was trying to lighten my spirits.

It was all still an unfamiliar feeling, but I knew trusting Locke was the key to this new experience.

With a nod, he resumed pushing the toy inside. It felt like an eternity before the length was inside me, stretching my ass in a way I never knew was possible. My body protested at first, but soon it accepted the sensation, and I let out a low moan.

Locke pulled out the toy halfway, leaving a void that I knew was about to be filled. He positioned his shaft near my pussy, grabbed my hips with his free hand and nudged his cock against my entrance. Taking a deep breath, I steeled myself for what was to come.

"Ready?" Locke asked.

"As I'll ever be."

He thrust inside me, filling me in a way I had never known before. The pain and pleasure intermingled, and I felt my body respond to his touch. Locke began to move in and out, driving both the toy and his cock further into my body with every thrust. I couldn't help but feel completely full, and it was exhilarating.

"Are you alright?" Locke asked, concerned.

"Yes," I panted, my breaths coming in quick gasps. "I'm fine."

He picked up the pace, his cock pounding into me while the toy remained buried deep in my ass. Every thrust sent electric shocks through my body, and I felt the familiar sensation of being on the edge of climax.

"Locke!"

"That's it. You are all full. Fuck, I can feel how stuffed you are."

Locke's choked voice had me speechless, and I pushed back against every one of his thrusts. "I think I'm going to—"

"Come!" Locke roared, shoving his knot inside me. Once his knot was inside he pulled it in and out, letting it stretch in and out of my entrance. All the while he continued to deeply thrust the dildo in my ass.

I felt my arousal coat his shaft as his come was filling my body. I couldn't hold myself up because of the cuffs and I felt my face move against the fabric. Surely, I would have a fabric burn against my face.

Locke's thrusts slowed, his knot and shaft still pulsing in my body. He slipped the dildo out of me, and I moaned when he dropped it on the towel to wrap it up.

"What a good fucking luna you are. Taking all those dicks in your body," he purred.

Locke laid on his side, keeping his knot buried inside me as it continued to spurt. "My sweet luna, my brave, beautiful Emmie."

CHAPTER FORTY

Locke

"I'm not surprised your menstrual cycle hasn't begun. You've been through a lot, Luna." Bones said matter-of-factly.

Emm's cheeks turned a few shades darker and my cock pressed against my jeans. She was wearing a simple oversized medical gown. Her body wasn't to be seen by Bones, but he needed easy access to get blood, take her blood pressure, and all that other shit doctors wanted from their patients.

Since things had died down with Idris and the threat was nearly down to zero, my possessiveness had skyrocketed. Now that I haven't been stretched thin, trying to take care of myself, the pack, the club and my mate, I can now concentrate all my focus on my luna.

And my wolf was savage.

Once she felt up to leaving the cabin, she hadn't left our sight. No more going to the bathroom alone, not even walking or eating. We were there, and she fucking hated it. I even offered to wipe her ass, and she threw her shoe at me.

I'm only trying to help.

I let out a low growl when Bones turned my mate's head and gazed at the bite on her shoulder. Bones looked at it longingly and gave a small smile.

Poor guy needed his mate.

"Good clean bite. I'm surprised he didn't rip your shoulder out, though, when he was in his lycan form. His teeth looked massive."

"Locke knows what kind of pain I can take." Emm's eyes glitter with excitement.

Yeah, I do. This morning, I edged her until I had her crying and sobbing for an orgasm. She almost said her safe word. Key word was *almost*. I had her tumbling over, squirting all over my face until I lapped every bit up with my long tongue.

Lycan tongue fucking was a thing, and she begged for it. Listening to her beg was the second-best thing. The best thing was biting all over her body. She loved a good bruising, and it still takes a few hours for them to go away. When her wolf comes, I'll teach her and her wolf not to heal them, so they last all day.

I groaned, rubbing my dick again through my pants. My marks on her just looked so damn good. Seeing my claws around her neck, scrapes around her throat. I licked my lips and I saw Emm shuffle on the medical table.

Bones shook his head. "Easy, I don't need you guys fucking in the office. I only get one and I need it open to remove some stitches later." Bones eyed me and I raised a brow at the challenge. "Anyway, you are safe to shift into your wolf, Lycan, but I would wait. Your body is still healing. Any signs of your wolf coming forward? There isn't a worry if you haven't seen her. Journey's took some time, too, when she shifted because of stress."

Journey's forced shift was because of Idris. Idris was fighting against Grim and when Journey saw it on the security cameras, her body short-circuited and knew she had to save her mate. Her body shifted—too early-and she didn't have her wolf to guide her, but Journey did fine. Goddess, helping her and all. But now, Journey's wolf was strong and apparently quite the talker, teaching her the ways of the wolf.

Emm hummed and rubbed the back of her neck. "She's there, I can see her. It's like she doesn't know what to do."

Bones scratched the base of his beard and hummed. "You shifted from wolf to Lycan. Kind of a big jump. She's just getting her bearings. I'm no expert in wolf shifting or in lycanthropy. I'll do some research of my own."

"Thanks, doc." Emm readjusted her gown. "By the way, how did you get your medical licence and stay here at the club? That had to be difficult." Bones didn't meet her eyes. She was too busy staring at me, well, rather at the tent in my pants.

Both of us froze and Emm raised an eyebrow at Bones. "You have a medical license, right?" She grabbed the front of her dressing gown.

Bones let out a long breath. "I was a doctor in Elysian. Shamans, priests, and elders who have used trial and error, have trained me over the years."

Emm blinked, and I chuckled, sauntering into the room and wrapping my arm around her waist. I took in her smell and let my scent take over, covering her while my purr tried to calm her.

While Bones pissed me off from time to time; took things too far, he did things for the betterment of the pack. Bones and I were close in age, despite how different we looked. We were hovering close to mid-fifties, but alphas age slower.

Time wasn't on Bones' side, however. In the time he spent researching the human body, how medical practices worked here on Earth, his body was deteriorating and fast. He wasn't taking care of himself, too busy trying to take care of everyone else.

"Princess, I trust him with my life."

Bones hanging head lifted quickly, and his eyes widened in surprise. "You do?"

I huffed and pressed my mate's body next to me. "I do, even if I get pissed at some of the shit you pull. You do it for the pack. Just make sure you run it by me first." I let out a growl in warning and he nodded his head quickly.

"Do you know about my sister's condition, then?" Emm questions. "Has she been taken care of? She needs special—"

Bones held up his hand and shook his head. "I've done plenty of research, and watched a ton of YouTube videos."

Emm's face paled.

Bones let out a bark of laughter. "Kidding, but yes. I have taken care of your sister, but since you are no longer the next of kin and she has a mate, I cannot disclose her care to you."

Emm growled and jumped off the table. "What do you mean? I'm her sister!"

Bones backed up and held up his hands. "It's patient, privacy stuff. I've read up on that, too."

Emm narrowed her eyes and wagged her finger at him. "Of all the things you gotta read, you read that shit?"

Bones shrugged his shoulders. "I told you, I'm thorough," he winked.

"As long as she's taken care of. Is she taken care of?"

Bones nodded. "Of course she is. I would tell you if she wasn't."

Emm jutted her chin out and nodded. "That goes with any other female in this pack. If there is any trouble—"

"—You will know about it," Bones promised.

We then got on the subject of the pack and the rest of their health. We spoke of the pack members, who were saved mainly thanks to Bones, and the fae with their herbs, grown in the secluded section of the forest which they'd made home.

The rabid were healing, some slower than others. The slowest ones were the ones growing near rabid, and I hated to hear some of the members I was closer to, were the ones who were getting closer to becoming rabid.

We stayed in the small exam room for a while longer. Bones gave a briefing on how she needed to be eating more meat and how her body would l still undergo changes. Her depression and guilt were brought up as well. With the bond, I could detect if it was becoming too much for her and if we needed to take any other steps to ensure her comfort.

I didn't need my luna to be blood- and torture-dependent like me.

I could feel her guilt inside the bond, but she knew, as well as I did, that her grandmother's destiny was for her to die. Her sacrifice made the pack, and Emm understood that. I just wish they had more closure, but when a loved one dies, is there ever really closure?

I led Emm to the bar downstairs. She still hasn't seen her sister, and I doubted she would for a while. Anaki had accrued a lot of time off and he had put in for it to get to know his mate. Dragons were notorious for hoarding, and mates were no different.

Wolves, we wanted to be around the pack, and even Emm was itching to get out of the cabin after a week of sulking.

The secluded cabin was a great oasis for us. We could stay there during her heats or any time we wanted to get away. For now, we would be staying in the packhouse. They were making progress on the third floor, just as Bear had promised, and they would be close to finishing it in two weeks.

Damn bear shifters were fucking fast. Emm asked for a few modifications, and one of them was to make the master bedroom smaller. She wanted it cozy, like the cabin. Instead of a bed, she wanted big mattresses, pillows, blankets and furs. My mouth nearly dropped to the floor at what she wanted.

It was all of the things I wanted to provide her. All of the things that the Law of Ares would have proclaimed that I bring for the perfect nest. I couldn't before because of bad timing and Idris—that fucker. But my mate, she wanted it to be a giant nest. Just for her and me, and any pups we wanted in the future.

I've never known my wolf to leap and bark, but Fenrir was fucking prancing like a pup all over my head.

I'd do anything for that sweet pussy of hers, and I will give her everything.

"She looked in your head, you dumb shit," Fenrir snorted. "Our mate wants us happy."

I didn't think my cheeks could hurt from smiling but, apparently, they could.

When we descended the stairs, a loud ear-piercing scream came from across the room. Emm darted her head to the noise and a wide smile spread across her face.

"Mijo!" She gracefully skipped the final steps, her footsteps slamming against the concrete floor. Elena's little boy, Luis, with his jet-black hair and deeply mysterious eyes, dashed towards her with unrestrained excitement. The vibrant energy enveloped them as she embraced him tightly. Giggles and laughter filled the air as my mate playfully spun the boy around, capturing the attention of the bar's patrons, who momentarily paused their lively conversations to witness the heartwarming spectacle.

"Emmie! You are okay!" Luis laughed into her chest.

My wolf growled, watching the boy bury his face in my mate's breasts. I tried to stifle it with a clearing of a throat, but my mate heard it. She sent back a beautiful smile and bit her lip.

"Luis, are you okay? Did you get hurt?" Emm patted the boy's arms down, and turned him around like he was a rag doll.

Luis laughed and swatted her hands. "I'm okay! I've had so much fun! I saw a dragon, Emmie! A real dragon! And I saw wolves and elves and flowers, and vines choking people!"

Emm's eyes grew wide, and she slung her head back toward me. I shrugged my shoulders and stuck my hands in my pockets.

The boy was safe. He would survive.

"Aaaand!" Luis said. "I have new best friends! Tajah and Beretta. Have you met them? Tajah knows magic and Beretta showed me all her guns, and she's a panther!"

I stifled a laugh as I tried to hunt through Emm's mind. She wasn't angry but shocked that Tajah would be so caring for a child. I suppose she thought since Tajah was a bitch to her, she wouldn't be loving to her nephew.

Tajah and Beretta were good people. Sure, they make mistakes like any other soul, hell, I know all about mistakes.

There is one thing Tajah and Beretta have been wanting for a while now. With the new link established and Tajah weaved in a bond with Beretta, I could hear their thoughts. They wanted a child.

I'm surprised that Emm hadn't felt it. Or maybe she refused to see it. Alphas and lunas can see and feel more of their pack's wants, desires and ill-intent through links. It isn't widely known among the pack members. It is to help us guide them and make the pack strong.

Unfortunately, some alphas can turn their packs into a terrible place. Like my father did to the Blood Rose. Either way, Blood Rose's pack members still had the ability to reject the words of their alpha, if they felt his words to be wrong.

Now, Tajah and Beretta didn't want to steal Luis away from his mother, but they had found an opportunity to mother and care for a child, while a newly mated couple could get to know one another, and Luis could still get the care he needed.

Tajah stood from a nearby table and walked up behind Luis. "This is Tajah," Luis said and pulled on Tajah's arm. "She's been watching me while Madre has been getting to know my new dad." Luis made an exaggerated wink. "I like him a lot. Did you know he can dance?"

I smirked, came up behind Emm and wrapped my arm around her waist. "Is this your mate?" Luis pointed.

"Mate? You know about mates?" Emm laughed.

Luis shrugged his shoulders. "Yeah, Abuela made me do some funny dance in the woods when Madre and Dad were *getting to know* each other." Luis snickered and then paled. "She got naked. If I close my eyes too long, I can still see it!"

Emm rubbed her hand down her face. "Me too, mijo."

Tajah gave a sheepish smile and put her hand on Luis' shoulder. He smiled up at her and gave her a hug. Tears brimmed Tajah's eyes and, fuck, if it wasn't making me fucking emotional. I wondered if Emm's grandmother asked her to take care of him.

"She loves him, doesn't she?" Emm said through the link.

I hummed. *"They both do, they've been watching over him."*

"And my sister is okay with this?" Emm studied them as Luis pulled on Tajah's cloak and pulled her down to whisper in her ear.

"Your sister is still Luis' mother. They are just watching Luis. I wouldn't be surprised if they blessed him."

Emm cocked her head.

I chuckled and pressed a kiss to her forehead. *"There's a lot to learn about our world, but you've got plenty of time."*

Emm huffed. *"I'm past my mid-thirties. I don't have that much time."*

I bit her earlobe. If she only knew how much time she had. Her life was extended now, and she wouldn't experience any further aging. If I would let her spend time in the bathroom alone and really let her look at herself, she would see her age was reversing.

I'd explain another time.

Emm stepped out of my hold and my fingers itched to pull her back. Even my wolf snarled at the look Tajah gave me, silently asking permission to talk to my mate.

But I didn't want her out of my sight.

Seeing Emm with Idris, having to fight on her own—correction, letting her fight on her own, because I knew it was what she needed— about damn near killed me. Now that he was out of the picture, I didn't want to force myself back from not protecting her. I wanted to keep her safe, like a proper male.

I reached for my mates' hand and pulled her back. "Mine," I bared my teeth at Tajah and she rolled her eyes.

"I only want to talk to her for a moment. Our luna has questions for me."

The witches and warlocks don't usually share a mind-link. They can enter minds on their own. Our pack wouldn't be able to mind-link them directly. Any future magical entities would lack the link. Since Tajah created this link she was bonded to this pack, as was Bram.

Mind-link problem solved.

Emm rolled her lips and nodded. "I do. You wanna join, Alpha?" She elbowed me and my face softened. Maybe she didn't want to be away from me either, and that brought my wolf's stiffened fur down. He snorted, but still hovered close to the surface.

"If you'd let me?" I gave her the option for me to back off, but I think she knew I'd come, anyway.

Beretta snarled and slapped a board game that hung over one of the tables near the bar. The board went flying, fake money and pieces of the game flying in the air. "This is not fair! You took all of my money!" Beretta hissed.

Luis was counting the colored bills in his hand, giggling. "I can't count this high. Can you count it for me?" He waved the money in front of her face and her fangs lengthened to hiss at him again. Luis burst into a fit of giggles, and my grin grew wide.

Yeah, I think I like that kid.

Emm shook her head. "Do not play Monopoly with that kid." Emm pointed at Beretta. "I taught him everything he knows, and he is vicious."

CHAPTER FORTY-ONE

Emm

The bar was bustling with life. Mostly the club was in attendance, but a few of the locals in the town came in to say hello, and to grab a drink or some bar food.

Most of the pack were still healing. The ones that had their animals buried deep inside them were suffering the most. Their healing was slow, human-paced, as I have heard Bones define it. Some of them should have bandages over their stitches, but of course they kept them removed, wearing them like badges of honor.

The women swooned over them, asking where they got such battle scars, but the pack remained tight-lipped about the altercation that happened in the woods just a week ago. We didn't need the town knowing that there was an evil, dark fae fight just on the outskirts of town. They wouldn't have believed it anyway, not with a magical spell that keeps most of the humans clueless.

The atmosphere in the bar was different from before - no longer filled with a hazy cloud of smoke. The faint scent of tobacco, which used to linger, had faded away. The windows were wide open, allowing the re-freshing summer breeze to enter, along with the enticing aromas of sizzling steaks, burgers and various other meats being cooked in the kitchen.

I took my fry, stirred it into the mayo and ketchup sauce I'd created, and popped it into my mouth. Locke made an unsatisfied grunt behind me, squeezed his arm around my waist, and tapped my lip with a fork full of steak.

I rolled my eyes and opened, chomping down on the medium rare steak. I bobbed my head back and forth, and waited for him to put another mouthful in.

"More meat, fewer carbs," Locke grumbled behind me. "Your wolf needs the iron and blood. If you don't, then when you shift into your animal form, she's going to go crazy and hunt down a deer."

I wrinkled my nose in disgust and opened my mouth again. Locke purred, satisfied I didn't argue back. There were just some things I was not ready to do, wolf shifter or not, and killing a deer with my teeth, ripping into the fur and bones and devouring it was one.

Tajah drank her water. She wasn't much of a drinker, but we all sat in silence after she dropped the bombshell; that I should have known all along.

Abuela was a witch. Well, rather, she was Wiccan. I was in denial for years. I thought it was the mushrooms or whatever she smoked that week. It had been a long time since I had really spent time with her, but Elena said nothing about Abuela or any of her antics.

Elena didn't want me to worry!

Abuela wanted us to have happily ever afters. She was a romantic. She didn't have a great one, and neither did her son, which ultimately destroyed him. I thought her little ceremony was a way to say, 'I've done everything I could.' I wasn't sure if she thought it would involve supernaturals in the beginning. Surely, she didn't mean to put us in the middle of all this danger.

Tajah explained, that after the death of Abuela's husband, she had to shop at second-hand stores for my father's clothing. While looking, she found a book that 'spoke' to her and it ended up being a spell book, just tossed into a bin.

Luckily, most of it was English, which Abuela knew very well. She read a spell about unlocking the power of oneself, and the rest was history. Somewhere along our bloodline there was magic. It was just a matter of unlocking it with a simple incantation, and Abuela had opened it.

Tajah said she was Wiccan because she taught herself. Other Wiccans could help and teach each other. You could only gain witch or sorceress status if you were an apprentice or were taught in a witchery school.

Wiccans could do basic spells, nothing overly powerful. However, Tajah said that Abuela was one of the more powerful Wiccans she had ever come in contact with.

Of course she was.

Abuela did everything possible to get her hands on every spell book she could. Oftentimes they were counterfeits. Humans trying to profit off of dark art enthusiasts. As the years went on, she practiced and she became strong for a Wiccan. Once my mother died, Abuela moved in to take care of my sister and me.

I didn't realize how much I hadn't remembered a lot of my childhood, and that included my father; because of her. Tajah said my father truly was evil, and the only reason I remembered my father when I turned eighteen was because I needed to run.

And like an impending storm, lightning crossed through the vision of my past. The night I was promised to be the head of the cartel's son's bride; to pay off the debt my father had.

Throughout the entire explanation, Locke was growling in my ear and his claws were digging into my hips. I hadn't had the time to explain everything about my past, but he knew enough now, I supposed.

The son who was to inherit the cartel was dead, because of me. I went through with the wedding, and the night of the consummation I plunged a knife in the bastard's heart.

My first kill.

And I didn't regret it.

I'll never forget hearing the knife crack through his chest and watching the blood soak through the white-collared shirt. The once dark eyes that bore into mine with desire, thinking he was about to take some eighteen-year-old's virginity, became lifeless. Being the son of the cartel, the next in line, you'd think he would be in his twenties. But no, he was a forty-year-old pervert.

Ever since then, I've been on the run.

How my father was still alive, I wasn't sure. Still working off a debt?

I licked my lips, trying to catch the warm semi-cooked blood that gathered at the corner. Locke beat me to it and sucked the side of my cheek.

"It might make me sound like a vampire, but I'd love to suck some blood off of you."

My nipples tightened against my bra and my ass wiggled in his hold. He was hard, he always was, but I could feel his knot expanding beneath my pussy as I leaned more on the bar.

"Aw, fuck, Emm." His fingers dug into my hips and gave them a squeeze.

"I'm sensing that you have a lot on your mind." Tajah took another sip of her water and gazed at Beretta.

Beretta was playing another game with Luis, one where, hopefully, they wouldn't have pieces all over the floor.

Before I could open my mouth to speak, someone placed two Pina

Coladas in front of Locke and me. My eyebrows raised at Surkash, who had taken Anaki's spot, and he shrugged his shoulders.

"Anaki called, said you guys needed it. He also wanted me to let Emm know that a Pina Colada is Locke's favorite drink."

Locke scoffed and shook his head. "Asshole."

Locke accepted the drink, raising it to his lips with a slight hesitation. When he finally finished, his chilled lips brushed against my neck, sending a shiver down my spine. The contrast between his cool touch and the warmth of my neck created an electrifying sensation, intensifying my arousal.

Tajah shook her head. "I've given you as much knowledge as I have about how your grandmother got her magic. Any other sort of secrets she has, ask your sister. I only knew your grandmother for a short time."

I pushed Locke back with my ass. His groan was loud enough to draw attention. I grabbed Tajah by the arm, and tried to push the arousal away that would soon take over.

"But, what about her? Did Abuela dance, and pray for the Goddess too?"

My grandmother chanted late into the night, dancing around a fire until my sister and I fell asleep in the tent. Now I know she really was getting soulmates for my sister and I, but did she try and get one for her too? Did she give up her soulmate for us?

My heart dropped at that thought.

Tajah smiled wildly. "Ah, I guess I left something important out. If your mate wasn't so distracting, making a spectacle out of your bonding, I would have remembered."

Locke scoffed, biting my shoulder where the bonding bite sat, and I let out a whimper.

Damn him.

Tajah scoffed and waved her hand. "Your self-sacrificing Abuela gave you and your sister the chance for soulmates. However, when she asked for her own soulmate, she found that he was not on the living plane." Tajah looked away and stared at a new picture on the wall. It was of Elena, Abuela and Luis standing in front of the cabin where they stayed when Locke kept them hidden on the property; unbeknownst to me!

My heart sank further. Her soulmate wasn't alive.

Tajah lifted her finger and pointed at me. "However, the Goddess made a deal. If she would sacrifice her life for you at the right moment, she would get her chance. Reincarnation and her chance to have her soulmate."

The faintest of a smile appeared on my face as Tajah rose from the barstool. She patted my hand and turned to go back to the table with Beretta and Luis.

Locke rubbed my arm, his purr loud enough for everyone around us to hear. There wasn't a doubt in my mind that the people around us heard.

Locke nuzzled into my shoulder again, his hands running over my arms.

It was all bittersweet. Abuela would get her happy ending, but her granddaughters wouldn't be a part of it.

Locke did his best to keep me occupied. He kept grinding his dick against my ass while we drank, and members of the pack that I hadn't met came by to say hello. The pack was much larger than I'd realized, and it was only going to get bigger with the prospect list that had grown since Locke's absence.

Locke hummed, his hand running up my hip. "You don't know how many times I've pictured myself with my luna on this dance floor."

Locke swayed behind me, one hand on my hip, the other just underneath my breast. His purr was constant and I could feel Fenrir right there with him. The bar was packed now, even though it was late, and the party didn't show any signs of stopping.

The lights where the band played shone across the small dance floor. It was shoulder to shoulder. They should think about moving some tables back to give everyone more room.

But then, you wouldn't have the same privacy. The fevered bodies hovering around us as Locke's fingers tickled the waistband of my knit mini skirt. Locke wouldn't have cared. I bet he would have finger fucked me in front of his entire pack, if he knew it would get me off.

And it would.

Locke's nose trailed up my neck and down my shoulder. He'd already ripped the side of my shirt tonight, to show off my mark to the entire bar. The humans that had no clue what we were, thought it was just a cool tattoo, a rite of passage to become the old lady, as most MC's called their women, but of course this MC called them mates.

I huffed at that. Any sane person, not put under the spell that Tajah had cast over the town once she gained her mate, would think it was downright crazy. The spell that kept the humans safe, made them forget the supernatural events that happened in the town, or write them off as a conspiracy. The only way they could know is if they were mates or were directly told by another supernatural.

It was a way to keep the Royal Council of Elysian out of the Earth realm. If they caught wind that humans knew about supernaturals, the humans who knew and every supernatural would be at risk.

The beat of the music dropped, and so did Locke's fingers. They tickled over my mound and my arm went back to grab the back of his neck.

"Fuck, you're gorgeous," he growled, the pad of his finger rubbing my clit.

I pressed my back firmly against his warm body, feeling the heat radiating through our clothes. The soft glow of dimmed lights danced around us, casting flickering shadows on the walls. His hand slowly traced a path down, grazing lightly over my sensitive skin, sending shivers down my spine. His strong scent filled my lungs, making my body shiver with arousal. As his touch intensified, my hips involuntarily arched, seeking more of his teasing caress. A soft moan escaped my lips, blending with the loud beat of the music playing in the background. My head fell back, finding support against his strong shoulder, as I surrendered to the intoxicating sensations.

Locke nuzzled my neck, his breath warm against my skin. "There's only one thing better than seeing you dance," he whispered. "It's hearing you beg for me."

The words sent shivers down my body, and I felt myself growing wetter for him. I wanted him inside me so badly, I needed his cock, his knot.

Gods, I really wanted that knot.

As I pushed back against him, his fingers continued their exploration. He trailed them lower, teasing my entrance with the tip of his finger before gently sliding inside. His touch was so intimate, so potent, that I felt like I was breaking apart under the weight of the bond we shared.

He was seriously psychotic sometimes, but one thing was for sure, we were crazy for each other.

The band's lively melody reverberated through the air, its pulsating rhythm forming an electrifying background to Locke's relentless teasing.

With each motion, his fingers swirled, rubbed, and flicked, intensifying the sensations that coursed through me. The anticipation brought me to the very edge of ecstasy, only for him to skillfully withdraw, leaving me longing for more.

I whined and dug my claws into his forearm. He chuckled, licking the bond mark, only to drive me more insane.

Finally, he slipped a second finger into me, twisting them inside my weeping cunt as his thumb rubbed my clit. It was too much, the pleasure building while I gripped his hair and bit my lip.

"Come for me," he growled in my ear.

And like the good girl he sometimes liked to call me, I did.

Locke held me close, his fingers still buried deep inside me, as we rode out the aftershocks of my orgasm. His purr was still strong, a rumbling presence that reminded me of his strength and his claim on me.

When he finally slipped his fingers out and put them in front of my face. He chuckled darkly. "Open, taste yourself."

I didn't hesitate, I licked his fingers clean, tasting the arousal that only he could bring from me.

"Mmm, my luna. you drive me absolutely insane." He turned me around to face him and leaned down to kiss me. His mouth was hot and demanding as he tasted my sweet release. I wrapped my arms around him, pulling him closer, wanting nothing more than to surrender to his touch.

We stood there, in the middle of the dance floor while other bodies rubbed and ground into each other. He licked my cheek and massaged the bond mark on my shoulder. I nuzzled into his mark and he let out a whimper.

I guess my alpha needed tending to as well.

"Damn straight I do." He pulled away, his green eyes turning dark with desire. "And I've got just the spot."

CHAPTER FORTY-TWO

Locke

I grabbed my mate's hand and pulled her from the crowd of sweaty bodies. No one paid attention; either they were too busy trying to rub one out on their potential mates or dance partner for the night or wishing for a mate like mine.

I held in a prideful smirk when I pushed back a table to get the fuck out of there and nodded to Hawke, who was palming Delilah's ass. Her nose was buried in the crook of his neck, a baby monitor on his hip, and fuck it looked domestic.

"Where are you taking me?" My mate yelled over the music.

I palmed my raging boner and pulled her to my side, wrapping my arm around her neck and nipping at her ear. "I've got a surprise for you. Another gift."

Emm rolled her eyes and put her hand in my back pocket.

She was getting sick of 'the gifts'. First, it was all the nesting blankets, pillows, fairy lights and other oddities I thought would make an amazing nest for her. She deserved the best, so I got her a bit of everything. Our new packhouse alpha suit wasn't as large, per her request, but that didn't mean I would not supply it with everything my mate deserved.

I even got her new clothes, weapons and sex toys. She said if I got her anything else, she was going to plug me.

Fat fucking chance.

"I told you no more gifts." She gave my ass a squeeze as we went out the door. The breeze picked up, and her scent surrounded me. It was muted inside the bar with everyone else's scent surrounding us, but now hers was more potent, away from everyone else. That tropical smell wrapped around my cock and my Albert's piercing was covered in my come already.

"Ares' Law allows me. You don't get a say in it, female."

My mate shivered, her tit piercings poked through her thin white top, and I stopped to stare and stroked one with my thumb. "Besides, I think you've enjoyed being covered in gifts."

She looked away and crossed her arms, it made her tits look just as tempting.

"I don't know what you are talking about."

I hummed, delighted. Ares' Law was superior. I couldn't believe the aged law had fizzled out. It has made my mate near compliant, whether she knew it or not.

I pulled her around the back of the bar. Even though we were a pack, now, we were still an MC, too. The Iron Fang MC would always be the disguise of who we are in this town, and where we would always hide. In the short time I have known my mate, bonded or not, I still had yet to take her for a ride on my bike.

Hammer and some of his crew were drinking beers in the back. He jutted his chin in welcome and continued his conversation, as I grabbed my keys and led her down the rows of bikes in the garage.

The air was cool, but with both of our bodies' heat in-sync with one another, I knew we would stay warm.

"Locke, seriously, what are we doing? I thought we were going to go fu—"

I pressed my lips to hers to silence her. "We are, but we won't do it at the bar, yet." That was a promise; I had wicked things to do with her there later. First, I wanted to fuck her elsewhere.

I tossed the helmet off the bike, letting it crash to the concrete, and straddled the bike. She put her hands on her hips and watched the helmet roll away.

"Isn't it safer with a helmet?" she chided.

I turned the key and revved the bike. "We are fucking shifters. We will heal just fine. Besides, you think I'm gonna let something happen to my fucking mate?" I growled at her, pulled her closer to me and bit my teeth into her bottom lip. "Now, get on."

She huffed out in response and when she lifted the leg of her miniskirt, I realized I'd forgotten she wasn't wearing any panties.

"Fuck," I groaned when she flashed me.

"That's what you get."

"Damn tease," I retorted, and threw the throttle on the bike, to shoot out my frustration.

As I revved the throttle too forcefully, my mate's piercing scream filled the air. Her arms instinctively encircled my waist, tightening like a vice. A joyful laugh escaped my lips as she squeezed me around the middle, her touch sending delightful shivers down my spine. The tires screeched relentlessly as we burst out of the garage, the smell of burning rubber intermingling with the exhilaration in the air.

As the tires connected with the smooth, black asphalt, the familiar sensation of wind rushing through my hair flooded back. It was a feeling I had almost forgotten as a human, but now it was exhilarating once again. Grim and I had first discovered motorcycles when we arrived on Earth and saw humans riding these small, powerful engines. They looked dangerous, but that only added to our attraction. We were drawn to the speed and agility these machines offered, knowing that one false move could result in a fatal fall.

That was the allure - the thrill of going fast and pushing ourselves to the limit. There were no safety barriers to protect us, no shapeshifting abilities to heal us from harm. It was a risk we willingly took, relishing in the rush of adrenaline that came with it. Dying while engaging in such a daring activity only added to the excitement - it was like a final ride into the unknown.

Now, we couldn't die, not from a simple crash. Our wolves would heal, and it wasn't like I would let my mate suffer, not when she was on the back of my bike.

I slowed down, now that she wasn't gripping onto me for dear life, and let her feel the wind in her own hair. It was flying around us, wrapping around my head, and I took in her scent.

The bumps in the road, her hands around my waist, my tightened shaft still wasn't going down. It never did, because around her I was always damn hard. I wouldn't be surprised if I went into another rut soon. She drove me so wild.

My shirt rode up my back as the wind tore around us and my mate was becoming brave. *"Mm, your skin is so warm,"* she said through the link.

I shivered, feeling her nails scratch my skin, enough to leave marks on my body.

Fuck, she knew exactly what I needed, or wanted.

We were both pain sluts.

But, then she traveled lower, her fingers playing with the button of my low-rise jeans. My hands gripped the handlebars, the growl in my chest became just as loud as the engine between our legs.

"Female," I growled. "What the hell do you think you are doing?"

A soft, tinkling giggle escaped her lips, and it felt like my heart had skipped a beat. My mate's laughter was a rare gift since losing her grandmother, filled with mischief and joy. It brought a warmth to my chest that I rarely felt. She had been through so much in the past few weeks - navigating my mind games, adjusting to the chaos of my pack, and mourning the loss of a loved one, while gaining a whole new family. And, yet, in that moment, she shone like a diamond, her beauty and strength radiating from within. It was both heartbreaking and breathtaking to witness.

I let her continue, until I felt her unroll the leather and heard the clink of my belt buckle over the roar of the engine.

Shit!

I tried not to close my eyes, but the feel of her warm hand sliding beneath my happy trail, her hand wrapping around my knot that wanted to fill her with my seed, made me feel fucking euphoric.

Gods, don't come.

"Now I have you at my mercy." She licked my ear and my heart pounded in my chest.

She bit my earlobe gently, sending a shiver down my spine. "I'm not sure that's such a good idea, Princess." I warned, trying to keep the heat out of my voice. "If you're not careful, one of us is going to be eating dirt before we can even think about where to find some privacy."

She laughed softly, a sound that was both enticing and dangerous. "Then, we'll just have to make sure that doesn't happen, won't we?"

I couldn't help but growl, a low rumble that reverberated through my chest. "You better not crash my bike. If you crash my bike, Hammer will be pissed off.

My mate put her warm hand all over my shaft, rubbing, playing with the barbells and stoking her thumb over my Albert's piercing. I groaned, my knot filling. My hips jerked when her hands went down to cup my heavy balls filled with seed, and she laughed wickedly, when she pulled my shirt to the side to lick at my mark.

She was getting me back for messing with her at the bar.

Fuck, I loved her.

"I love you," I said into the wind, my head leaning back into her shoulder.

I felt the smile on her lips as she bit into her mark.

"I know you do," she linked.

As we neared the pack-house, she released my shaft and quickly buttoned up my pants. I could sense her confusion through our bond, but I couldn't reveal the surprise just yet.

I adjusted myself, my jeans were too damn tight to be comfortable. My mate gave me a smug smile, and I narrowed my gaze at her.

I turned off the engine to the bike, the light going out with it. It plunged us into darkness and we accepted the distant chirping of crickets and croaking of frogs. The moon cast a soft glow over the surrounding trees, creating a peaceful atmosphere, despite my mate's apprehension to the newest surprise.

I pulled on her arm, making sure I got a magnificent view of her cunt as she got off. She slapped my arm at the blatant peek, but I was her mate. It didn't exactly matter.

I pulled her to the pack doors; brand new, made with reinforced steel. These babies weren't coming down, even if a lycan was thrown into them.

Not that I would know or anything.

We made our way up the stairs to our new home, which was nearly done, with just a few more finishing touches. We moved on to a special place, a *special room.*

I tugged on her arm, her eyes everywhere, taking in the sights, but where I wanted to show her. We had the whole third floor to ourselves, but she only wanted so much for a living space, for our future family. She didn't want to have a large living quarters.

I should have known, she was used to a simpler life, and so was I. Hell, everyone here in the Iron Fang was, but like an idiot, I wanted to show off for her.

But, what was I going to do with the extra space of the third floor?

Being the genius that I am and working with the contractors, I decided to build something wicked. It would take away all our itches, our cravings, and all our desires. A place to get away from our future pups, a place where we could experiment and fulfill every naughty fucking thing we wanted to do, without leaving the confines of the packhouse when our family needed us.

I unbuttoned my pants when we came to the double doors.

Emm's arousal heightened when she saw the head of my cock spring out of my pants and I let out a haggard breath.

"I think it's time for some payback, huh?" I tugged on my cock and slipped the key in the hole.

It clicked, and when I pushed open the door, automatic low lights came on in the room.

The plush, deep red carpet stretched across the entire room, softening each step we took. The walls were painted a velvety black, creating a sense of mystery and intrigue. In each corner, LED lights glowed, casting a spectrum of hues to match our desired mood. My eclectic taste in furniture was on full display, carefully selected and quickly shipped to create the perfect atmosphere for our evening.

I wanted it all - every experience, every sensation - with her by my side. And I knew Emm would revel in it all; after discovering the hidden trove of books in her RV. From sex swings and stockades, to stools and rockers, I had spared no expense in furnishing our playroom.

Large chests were filled with feathers, nipple clamps, butt plugs, dildos and vibrators. This was the ultimate sex room.

Emm stepped into the room on her own accord. Her mouth hung open as her fingers grazed the leather that hung from the ceiling. She continued on, touching the caged bed, letting the silk sheets rub between her fingers. In the very back, a hot tub sat waiting, steam rising from the waters, and the various oils she could add to soothe those aching muscles after I had my way with her.

"What do you think?" I stalked forward, pushing my jeans to the floor. My cut was next, along with my shirt.

Emm stood, not horrified, but simply astonished.

"This is what you came up with, with all the extra space?" She was nearly speechless.

This is good.

"Yes," I purred.

Her eyes drifted to my cock. It was weeping. I've been hard all night, and it was time for her to give it up.

"Pick what you want to use first, because it won't happen often," I growled.

But, as soon as the words left my mouth, Grim's voice entered the link. *"Alpha, your other present has arrived, a few days early."*

I snarled and grabbed hold of my cock.

Those bastards are going to die slower than they already were.

Emm stared at me in confusion and walked toward me.

"Princess, unfortunately, this present is going to have to wait."

I'm going to have a blue knot forever.

"But why?" She made a sympathetic look toward my cock.

"Your other present has arrived, and unfortunately, we cannot put it on hold."

CHAPTER
FORTY-THREE

Emm

I couldn't keep up with him.

One minute my pussy clenched, wanting his cock and the next he left me cold and wanting.

Maybe that was why I craved him so much. He kept me chasing after him.

He left his clothes in a heap on the floor and my slick of arousal, which had become a constant drip since being more than the average human, had dried then rubbed against my inner thighs.

I groaned as he pulled me down the stairs. He instantly sensed my discomfort and grunted, his thick, long cock slapping against his hips and upper thighs and slung me over his shoulders.

"Sorry, Princess, but you will want this present." I sensed his excitement through our bond despite the desperation in his dick.

"And then we get to try out the sex room?"

The wolf had some serious taste. He thought of everything, down to the tiniest of details. He had wrestling mats, padded the corners of the furniture, hell, I think he even had a scratching post, for when he shifted into his lycan form. The ceilings were built with a vaulted structure, enabling us to shift.

Oh, Lycan sex?

My body shivered when we hit the cool air outside, and his body heaved in a large breath.

"Princess, you're fucking killing me here," he growled and stomped off into the thickest part of the woods.

"How do you think I feel? I'm fucking chafing. Us girls with thick thighs have trouble with all this moisture." I rubbed my thighs together. My clit pulsed, on the verge of an orgasm. This wolf was a fucking tease and always had me going.

Locke slid his hand up my ass, underneath the fabric, and took a firm hold. "Calm down, I don't need Sizzle smelling the fresh stuff. Just hang on."

I groaned, let my head hang limply over his back and watched his toned ass flex while he walked.

It was such a nice ass.

How could this surprise be any better than the sex room?

Locke picked up the pace, my weight doing nothing to slow him down. If my calculations were correct, we were heading closer to where my old RV was.

I sniffed and smelled Sizzle's familiar smell of burned wood and ink. Before I could get a good look, Locke flipped me over and I saw Sizzle with an AK-47 draped over his shoulder and his eyes rolling.

"You guys fuck like rabbits; more than Grim and Journey. It's kinda disgusting." He pinched his nose. "I can't smell that great, but damn."

Locke grinned, not even bothered that Sizzle, who I knew to be another dragon, could smell my arousal.

Journey told me in passing that shifters don't normally like their mates being on display for others to see or smell. Their arousal, their bodies or anything of that sort. Locke was the exception in all ways, apparently, he was happy to display me; and honestly, I loved it!

I felt sorry for any bastard who tried to touch me, though, because I think that may be when Locke would really snap.

"She smells like fucking heaven, doesn't she?" Locke buried his nose into my neck, his hand hiking up my skirt. "You wanna see some damn good pussy? I bet you haven't seen any in a while."

Sizzle turned up his nose, his mouth frowned into a sneer. "No, and no offense to you, Luna. Pussy doesn't do it for me."

"He's gay?" I whispered to Locke, and he barked out a laugh.

Not that there was anything wrong with that, I was just curious.

Sizzle's face heated and ran his hand through his dirty blonde hair. "Fuck, no, I'm just. Females—ugh. Just no. Females are trouble. I don't need any of that shit."

Locke hummed and shook his head. "Sizzle has sworn off women, especially any second chance he might have. Stubborn dragon," Locke huffed and pulled away, showing his bouncing cock. "He'll fall for his mate soon enough when she comes into his life."

"Fat chance," Sizzle growled and pulled out a pair of shorts. "Now, put these on so they don't stare at that monster dick, with all your hack job piercings, or they won't pay attention to anything you say."

Hack job?

"Our level-headed alpha wanted to pierce himself," Sizzle said, eyeing Locke as he put on the black pair of shorts. "I told him to let me do it but of course he wanted to torture himself, and I lined up the spots where he should pierce his tiny dick, but if you look at it close enough, it's crooked."

I shrugged my shoulders. I didn't sit there and stare at his cock. I put it to good use.

As if reading my mind, Locke smirked and pulled me close by my waist, "She doesn't care."

Sizzle rolled his eyes. "Yeah, well, if you need back-up. Link someone, we will be around, but I think you got this handled."

I raised an eyebrow in question, but Locke steered me away from Sizzle, and through a thick grove of trees. The forest was quiet over here, no crickets or frogs could be heard, but then I heard the murmurs of unfamiliar voices, until a taunting voice came through the fold.

"Elena? Are you in there?"

The rapping on the door was quick and my heart stopped when I heard the voice. It had been years since I heard it, but it was like a torrent of memories that swept me up from the past.

"Elena? Emm? Hello?" I heard the creak of the door open, and I peeked through the bushes to see the RV surrounded by men in dark jeans and button-down flannels, like they were trying to fit into their surroundings.

Cars and trucks were parked up the path, no way to escape if there was a car here, not that there was.

"Elena? Emm?" The voice was more irritated now, stomps came out of the RV, and there was the face I hadn't seen in years.

He was older now, salt-and-pepper hair, worry lines stretched across his brow and a nice crease between the eyes.

Instantly, I growled and the men that surrounded the RV, all armed with guns at their side, pulled them from their holsters and took off the safety.

Locke chuckled beside me. "Happy Mating present, Princess. Think you can shift into your wolf, at least?"

My growl rumbled through my chest, and when I looked inward, I saw the wolf that had been hiding within me for the past week. She'd been shy, almost afraid to come forward, but when she saw my father, I saw her take a step forward.

Her jaw snapped, her nose curled and drips of venom fell from her maw.

"Definitely," I whispered to him.

I stepped out from the bushes and the men all had their guns on me.

My father's eyes widened in shock, his face a mixture of astonishment and confusion. "Emm? Is that really you?"

"What the hell is that?" one of his men yelled, noticing the venom dripping from my sharp canines extending past my lips.

"Lower your guns," I warned.

My father let out a nervous laugh and waved his hands in a downward motion to his men. "Put them away. My daughter wouldn't hurt me."

Is that what he thought?

They hesitantly put their guns down, but they didn't let their fingers off the triggers. Locke stood behind me in the brush. He knew I wanted to face this alone, and I was glad for it.

"What are you doing here?" I asked.

My father gazed around his men, as if he was looking for an answer, until his eyes met mine again.

"Just wanted to see you," he smiled. "We haven't seen each other in so long. The head of the cartel is dead. They have a much more... forgiving leader. You can come back to Mexico, now." His heart sped up and I instantly knew it was a lie.

I hummed and stepped forward, observing the men around him.

"And why did they keep you alive?" I asked, pinning my eyes on him.

He chuckled nervously. "I had an enormous debt. It was all a mistake. I was so heartbroken over your mother's death I did things I shouldn't have..."

It was a poor excuse for an apology.

"And they don't just kill those who owe a debt, they make them work.

I've been working off my debt. Doing what they wanted, their bidding; anything. The new cartel boss said I was done," his eyes brightened. "He said I could find my daughter and bring her back to Mexico, to be a familia."

I looked away from him and crossed my arms.

"Emm, I am so sorry. You have to understand, I was under so much pressure. Please, mija. Please, forgive me."

Lies! His heart was racing, and not with excitement. His forehead perspired and his scent was off.

"Good job, Luna." Locke intercepted my thoughts. *"He is lying. The cartel still wants you dead. They want Elena, now, and they don't know about her son. Don't worry, I've got a pack down south that is taking care of that little cartel problem. Your father and these fuckers, are yours."*

I rolled my shoulders back and tilted my head from side to side, to hear it crack.

"Emm, what is wrong with your teeth? Are those... some sort of enhancement?" My father gave me a wobbled smile and I touched them delicately.

"They are. Would you like to see them? After, we can go find Elena and catch up? I'm sure she will be excited to hear about the cartel not being a part of your life anymore."

My father took several steps toward me, his scent of fear dissipating more the longer I stood there. Even his men relaxed when his arms opened and I went into his embrace. I held my nose, the smell of tobacco and burnt almonds stifling, and when I let go I gave him a large fanged smile.

"It's silly, really," I shook my head. My father raised an eyebrow while I let the claws on my fingertips grow, "that you really thought I would forgive you after all these years?"

My father's eyes widened as I lowered myself to the balls of my feet and cut the tendons on the back of his knees. My claws were strong enough to break through the jeans, through the skin and the sinew of any human.

His scream echoed through the night, as he clutched the back of his leg. He wasn't going anywhere, even if he somehow managed to drag himself with his arms.

Open gunfire rained down on me, pegging me in the back and at my side. Despite being a wolf, I still felt every hit.

Locke roared, jumping through the trees, his muscles glistening in the moonlight. His muscles rippled across his skin as he disarmed the twelve men that accompanied my father.

The air was thick with smoke and the stench of gunpowder as the remaining men ricocheted bullets off the ground in wild desperation. I knew that they were only moments away from being overwhelmed by Locke, who was now standing triumphantly over them, his eyes glowing like green embers in the darkness.

Locke, with his own thirst for blood, took out two. Plunging his fist inside each chest and ripping out hearts. He licked his hand after each one, and watching him rip limbs, meat and bone from the weak humans... damn, it turned me on.

Locke shot me a knowing look, and I shook my head as I punched and elbowed the other men. Two shot off into the dark, unarmed, and I felt my wolf nudge me to chase.

The memory, of how Locke told me not to run when I found out he was a wolf, came to me, and here I was with my wolf. Instincts to hunt and catch prey overpowered me. I couldn't help but grin, my face glowing in the moonlight as I transformed into my wolf. I took off after the men, my instincts kicking in.

The chase was exhilarating, and I could feel the rush of adrenaline as I pursued my prey. The wolf inside me reveled in the hunt, and I knew Locke would be proud. I leapt over bushes and ravines, my nimble paws and sleek body making easy work of the pursuit.

As the men stumbled, trying to evade my powerful jaws. One male looked back, terror filling his eyes and I didn't wait. I lunged for the softer part of his neck, heard a satisfying crunch and dropped his body to the ground. There was nothing quite like the feeling of being a predator in its natural element, and I knew that right now, I was exactly where I was meant to be.

The last human thought it would be smart to climb a tree to evade my hunt. I sniffed around the base and stared up into his fearful eyes. He smelled of fear and ammonia, and the wolf inside me only felt satisfied at the thought of bringing him down.

"No, please!" He cried out, holding onto the branch he was perched on.

Bones' warning, to keep my lycan body inside and let it rest, was long gone. I was never one to listen anyway. I let my bones crack. It felt worse than shifting into a wolf, but I did it anyway. The pain felt good, as I let my back arch and howled into the darkness, only to see my mate dragging my father behind him in his own lycan form.

I snarled in satisfaction and gazed up the tree. My claws gripped hold and I took to climbing. The bark fell, and it wasn't just the scream from the human I was hunting that I heard, but my bastard father who I wasn't chasing at that moment.

Because he was next.

The human climbed onto the outer part of the limb, thinking I wouldn't climb out so far. He was mistaken because I took the challenge. I licked my lips for good effect until the limb broke and I leapt, gripping hold of his leg.

We both fell to the ground and he howled in pain when his arm fell out of its socket.

I didn't let him suffer for long, because it was my father that I wanted to see suffer the most, so I snapped his neck. I felt his lifeless body go limp and turned to my father, who was upside down, held by my mate's claws.

My father was reciting the Lord's Prayer. Like he would go anywhere near heaven. I chuckled, coming closer to Locke, covered in the rest of my enemy's blood.

I thought it was damn sexy. Did that make me psychotic, too?

"Yes," Locke breathed heavily. The cock between his legs bobbed in agreement and I tried to hold back a whimper, because I would not fuck him in front of my father.

Did I want to say something cliche' before I ended his life? Or just get on with it?

I gripped my father by the neck, my claws sinking into his throat, and pulled him right side up.

"Bet you didn't see this coming?" I breathed, my hot breath in his face. "Thought your little girl was weak, huh?"

I took my claw and let it run down his arm, touching the bone as I went.

He screamed and tried to push me away.

"Well, Daddy, allow me to show you how wrong you were." With a swift motion, I plunged my claws into his chest, just missing his heart. I felt the warmth of his blood against my palms. His eyes widened in shock and fear, and for a moment, I saw the same expression I'd mirrored in his eyes when he tried to marry me off to a cold-blooded killer.

At that moment, I couldn't take it anymore. I'd had so many ideas about how I wanted to make him suffer, but I just wanted to end it all, quickly and swiftly. So, I slit his throat with a swipe of my two claws.

He gargled, unable to form words. I watched the blood trail down his neck and onto the leaves of the forest floor.

It was done. No more running.

I was safe. Elena and Luis were safe.

My body, tired from running and shifting, cracked. I winced, feeling myself shifting from that of Lycan, back into my fleshed human form. Again, standing naked in the woods.

I felt Locke approach me from my periphery, in his human form. His cock still throbbed, and his eyes were filled with pride, and desire.

Without a word, we turned to each other, our bodies glistening in the moonlight, covered in blood and sweat. He licked the side of my face, tasting drops of blood, until our lips met.

Passionately, our tongues entwined as we savored the taste of our enemies and the thrill of a hunt, a kill and a fucking victory.

CHAPTER
FORTY-FOUR

Locke

I firmly struck the gavel on the polished wooden pulpit, its sharp thud reverberating through the room. The restless chatter persisted, and my impatience grew. No one knew when to shut the fuck up.

Idris wasn't dead.

Bram explained it simply that since there was no body, a necromancer was still alive.

Of course he was, Idris was a damn cockroach.

Later, we were having a meeting to discuss further but right now I had another issue to deal with, and it was a bunch of naggy pack members that had the attention span of a goldfish.

I had no MC members strong enough to go through the ritual to become bonded to the pack and be given a link. Only the mated were sealed to the pack. Their souls were strong enough to take the magic that Tajah had weaved, bonding the pack together with Emm and I.

The few that were strong enough were the prospects. They were freshly rejected, and they fought alongside us dealing with Idris and his followers.

"What the fuck do we do now?" I said, as Morpheus stood in the middle of the crowd.

The pews were a little worse for wear now. The roof was collapsing, holes let the moon shine in, and bats had taken up home in the attic. I guess, since we were staying here longer than any of us ever planned, the bear shifters might need to get in here and fix the place up.

I sighed. More money out of our pockets.

I dropped the gavel, rubbed my hands together and pressed my index fingers to my lips. "If you don't sit the fuck down, I'll give you something to do, Morpheus."

The crowd shut up after that, the pews groaning under the pressure of the added weight.

My luna, who sat beside me, nudged my leg. She gazed up at me, shaking her head. Emm was a leader now, and she was trying to keep me grounded - ey word was trying. I usually hid behind a mask of indifference, or a smile that would ward people away from me, but now I was just irritated.

Q and A was not my forte and everyone had questions.

"We don't know what we are going to do." My claws lengthened, and I scratched the end of the pulpit. My pack watched on as I let the curls of the wood fall to the floor. "I'm meeting with Bram and Tajah, and they might have some insight into what we are dealing with."

We hadn't had a debriefing from the fight. I was too busy taking care of my mate, the pack rebuilding and healing. None of that was as important as dealing with the *right now*.

"Any other questions?" I raised an eyebrow, but the fidgeting in the pack's seats was enough for me to know that they didn't want to tick me off further.

I didn't have a lot of answers, I just knew we were safe. Idris wouldn't fucking step foot here again. He wouldn't be as stupid as to lose his memory again, like he did the first time. We were a pack. The strong ones had mind-links. We had the fae here. If there was any fighting going on, we would have to go to them.

A small hand raised in the crowd, it waved high as it stretched. A smile came to my lips, and I nodded in its direction. "Yes, Luis, you got somethin' to say?"

Luis stood up beside Surkash, and put a hand on the naga's shoulder to steady himself. He stood up tall, not giving a damn that everyone in the room wasn't human. He knew of everyone's past, that most of them were broken, just like his new father was.

And that was why he latched onto all the men here.

And, he was one of the only humans, who may never be mated, who could know that shifters were real. Damn the Royal Council if they found out, because he had a whole pack that would fight for this kid. Rogue, rabid, mated, didn't matter.

Luis pushed his shoulders back and saluted. Everyone chuckled while Emm's fanged smile spread across her face.

"I was just wondering when everyone was going to hurry and find their mates, so they can do that link thing. It makes everyone stronger, too, so you can kick that Idris dude's butt, right?"

The crowd murmured, shoving each other. Surkash adjusted his shirt and cleared his throat.

"Well, some men and women here haven't met them yet, it takes time. And when they do, they'll claim 'em and make them theirs." I smiled down at my mate, rubbing the mark on her shoulder.

"But Surkash keeps starin' at one girl's butt and won't do nothin' about it!" Luis yelled over the crowd.

The pack roared with laughter as Surkash covered Luis' mouth and had him sit down. He whispered in Luis' ear whose face lit up. "You'll give me your old snake skins! Cool!"

Ahh, way to shut up a kid.

We adjourned the meeting. Luis joined Emm and I on the stage and I picked him up, to settle on my arm. He played with the patch on my cut, staring at the logo embroidered into the fabric.

"Why do you call your vest a cut?" Luis asked, when we went into the old bishop's office.

I shrugged my shoulders. "I don't know, that's what bikers called them. I just picked up on the lingo."

Satisfied with my answer, I set him down and he ran to Beretta, who had a handheld video game contraption in her hand. He climbed on her lap and grabbed it, as she put a set of headphones on his ears.

"You know, you're hot when you take care of kids." Emm nudged me when I sat down at the round table.

The inner circle was here, with their mates sitting in their laps.

"Yeah, you wanting some pups soon?"

Emm's face went pale and she shook her head. "Ah, uh, no, I haven't—"

I placed a tender kiss on her lips and rubbed my hand over her soft belly. "It's alright, I never saw myself as a family man. If you ever want them, I'll give you a pup and be the best father. If not, I'm happy with that, too."

Emm physically relaxed and leaned into me.

"I'd like to take things slower. I'm not saying yes and I'm not saying no."

I got it. Hell, she went from a loner to a luna of a pack in a month. But fuck, would she look good with a rounded belly and milk dripping from her tits.

When she orgasms, I bet they would just leak and I could lick every drop that ran down the underside of her—

"Alpha!" Sizzle snapped and ran his hand down his face. "We are all here."

I looked around the room and saw Bram pulling on his collared shirt and clearing his throat.

"My bad, my mate is just stunning today." I lifted her hand and pressed a kiss to it.

Delilah nudged Hawke and whispered in his ear, "You like the way my milk tastes, right?"

Oh fuck, did I say all that shit out loud?

"Yes, you did," Emm linked, "and have you ever heard of induced lactation?"

My body sat up straight in my chair when Bram pulled out a notebook from his back pocket. He twirled the pen in his hand, but all I could hear was lactation.

"Alpha Locke, you know that I can still hear inside shifters' minds, right? I'm not that far gone, yet."

My eyes narrowed, and I grabbed hold of my mate's breast. Emm squirmed in her seat when all the eyes were on her. "I don't mind you looking, but touching and drinking from my mate is a big no-no."

"Goddess help me," he ran a hand down his face. "No, Alpha, I'm trying to explain how to kill Idris."

Oh.

"Right, yes, uh. So, you did figure it all out. How to kill him? Properly, I mean?"

Bram cleared his throat again, his back leaning against the wall. The room was silent while we waited for him to begin.

Bram was old, and no one really knew just how old. He was rejected like the rest of us but, somehow, his power had kept him alive all this time. He was Tajah's professor and mentor. Having two sorcerers on our side was great, well, until Bram found his mate.

"I've gone through every scroll and parchment I own about necromancers, specifically ones with dark fae. There are several routes you can go to become a necromancer and I think I've discovered the path that he has taken, and which way to destroy him."

You could almost hear a pin drop, besides the buttons clicking in the corner where Luis was playing his game in Beretta's lap. She engulfed him, petting his hair, grooming him like a feline, licking her palm and then his hair.

"Necromancers can take several paths to grow and use their powers, but I will name just a few. One is to bring the dead back to life, take the soul once departed, and bring it to the living plane. Another is to bring demons from the underworld and have them possess a body. They can do up to five demons at once."

Nadia shifted in Bear's seat, and he held onto her tightly.

"The third and final one I want to talk about is the ability to bring oneself back. If Idris dies, then he will come back to life himself."

"And that, is the one he has learned to use," Tajah added. "Idris is powerful. He can take the hits. The venom weakens him, putting him in a weakened state. Such as with Journey's bite the first time. Once the fire consumed him, he died." She put her fingers in air quotations. "The next time he was weakened with Alpha and Luna's bites, with their venom. It was enough to drown him in the water with Anaki."

Sizzle put the Glock he was holding on his lap, onto the table. "It takes that much to weaken him enough, to be killed by a weak element." He shook his head. "That makes little sense."

Bram chuckled and looked at his paper. "But it does. He's weakened enough so an element can consume him. Even a necromancer has its limits, he cannot be brought back an infinite amount of times."

I leaned back in my seat and ran my hand down my face. "So, when he wanted me to push my hand into his chest, to take out his heart—"

"Your signature move," Grim grumbled.

"-it wouldn't have killed him?" I asked.

Bram huffed, "No, it wouldn't have counted as a kill. He needs to be killed by an element for it to count. His body would have dissipated and regenerated in his respawning designation."

Beretta growled in the corner. "I'd love to know where his respawning spot is. We could attack right when he bounced back."

Oh, that would be devilish.

"Alright, fire, water. What else?" Emm asked.

"Earth and air," Bram said.

Hawke shuffled Delilah and their daughter in his seat. "That's why we could get those humans out of the mansion so easily. The fae were all over the place." Hawke tapped the table with this knuckle. "Then he had his men trap all the fae before the fight. When they got loose, he retreated into the woods. He was scared of getting choked by a vine or something. Earth—the soil, the branches, anything that extends from it."

Bram and Tajah nodded.

"But he ran straight toward the lake," Emm said. "He was right there."

"He didn't know," I growled. "Idris didn't know the lake was there, and he was hoping we wouldn't figure it out, either. He wanted me to rip out his heart and crush it, and he could disappear. Then, he would have another chance."

"Damn him!" Grim growled and slammed his fist on the table. Journey jumped, then rubbed her hands over his face to calm him down.

Grim settled his nose into her shoulder to calm himself. He was pissed and hell, I was too, but no sense in losing our shit now. We couldn't do a damn thing about it.

"But what about that demon," Bear barked. "The one that messed with Nadia in her head?"

Bram looked at Nadia sympathetically and lowered his shoulders. "It was Idris that either ordered it or helped summon it, but it wasn't all him. He had help, and with enough sorcerers, they all could have used their magic to pull that demon out of the underworld."

Nadia swallowed, but she didn't show any fear. She looked relieved. Bear, however, looked crazed, like was ready to fuck her all over again to stake a claim.

Which was a great reason to end the meeting.

"Right," I said standing. "We need to kill the fucker. We know how, just when and where is the question. I say we take some time. It would be better if we could get more couples mated."

I wanted to call out Journey. Her connection with the Goddess was the one that would make all this shit go away. My mate nudged me and shook her head.

Fuck, I should have never taught her to crawl into my mind like that.

"Yeah well. People we need to look out for?" I raised an eyebrow and people spat out some names. Names I already knew. Bones, Surkash, Bram and Sizzle, who was pissed I even brought him up.

He flipped the bird and left in a huff.

"He'll come around," Emm rubbed her hand up and down my arm. "When he's ready."

"Well, the rest of us are," Bram mumbled and shoved his notebook in his back pocket.

Surkash was holding back taking his mate and Bones? Hell, I didn't see any prospects for him at all.

I rubbed my hand down my face while I watched everyone file out.

CHAPTER FORTY-FIVE

Emm

L ocke was utterly disappointed.

Forced lactation wasn't going to happen, according to Bones. Through the bond I witnessed his devastation, and I had to make it right.

If only I had the experience of shuffling my way through his mind to know exactly what he had in store for me.

When we approached Bones with my plan, he didn't hide his shock. I thought his mouth would catch flies, the way he kept it open as I explained humans often took supplements and medication to induce lactation for the adoption of babies.

But this was purely for Locke's fascination and kink, not for a baby.

Unfortunately, shifters don't take human medication well. The steroids he gave Locke while he was healing from his rabid state was enough to speed up the process for his healing, but once he was at an alpha state, no human supplement would touch him. Since we are at the same strength, through our bond, no lactation medication would touch me.

Now, I'm fulfilling another fantasy of Locke's, and it is borderline insane.

No, scratch that, it is insane.

Grim grumbled to my right while he made notes on his clipboard. "I cannot believe you are doing this. If I wasn't mated right now, I wouldn't be down here."

Locke chuckled, his hands roaming up and down my waist as I sat on his lap. "That's exactly why you *are* down here. I trust you. You know how I am."

Grim swore, and my face flushed with pure embarrassment. I could feel Locke's knot rubbing my clit from the inside. His knot was swollen, thick and he has already released his come once already.

One wrong move and I was going to cream all over that Jacob's Ladder.

"I would never let Journey do what you are doing. No one sees my female like that." Grim gave a bombastic side-eye to Locke.

Locke chuckled darkly, pulling my hair away from my neck and kissing my mark softly. "Of course you wouldn't, but my mate loves it. Turns me the fuck on. She will do what I want and will only do it for me. Isn't that right, Princess?"

I whimpered when he shifted my body; the knot sliding deeper inside.

"Besides, it's a great way to test the prospects. We already got the one traitor out of the way."

Locke nodded at the headless body in the corner. The basement didn't stink; it smelled of bleach and other cleaners, laced with artificial lavender. Like that would put the calm in these prospects.

This was a torture chamber with taxidermy heads on the wall for the Goddess' sake. No amount of artificial lavender smell was going to make this place any more comfortable.

Locke shifted my hips, and I moaned and lowered my head.

It was both embarrassing and a turn on.

Gods, we were sick.

"No, we are perfect for each other," Locke purred. "And this is the perfect test of the prospects and their loyalty."

Locke had already declared to the bar nights ago, that looking was okay when he fucked me up against the wall in a hallway where people walked by, but touching what was his was a 'no-no" as he liked to say. When the prospects came into this meeting, seeing me sitting on their alpha's cock, they kept their faces away from me and only looked to their future president slash alpha.

All except one; the one that Locke had had his eye on. He didn't buy it for a second that this wolf was rejected. In fact, he thought it was the other way around. It didn't take long to get the truth, and he was, in fact, a liar.

To make sure he had enough evidence, Locke offered me up on a platter; he offered to share me. I knew Locke didn't mean it, but the prospect took the bait. He stood up from the interrogation chair and took slow, steady steps toward Locke and I, but before the prospect could lay a finger on me, Grim had the prospect by the throat.

Grim took his time torturing the creep; torture *was* his specialty. Locke watched, growing impossibly hard as he did. He shifted his cock inside me, jerking his hips and let the seed push into my body.

Fuck, it was so delicious.

Sizzle stood in the back the entire time, his hands draped over his AK-47 and banged the back of his head on the concrete wall, muttering to himself. "Anywhere but here. Please, someone take me anywhere but here."

"Don't come, don't come." Locke chanted. I don't know if he was talking to himself or me, but we both came anyway.

"Last one, then I'm leaving," Grim wrote another note and Locke grabbed his wrist. Grim still had blood on his arm and Locke stuck out his tongue to lick up the blood from his best friend's skin.

Grim growled and pulled his arm away, laughing. "You sick fuck, lick blood off your own mate."

They both snickered and his cock jostled inside me.

Damn it.

As the last prospect entered, the small group's attention was drawn to a striking woman with short white hair that barely brushed her jawbone. Her piercing purple eyes seemed to capture the light and reflect it back in a mesmerizing glow. Clad head to toe in sleek black, her skin was so pale it almost appeared blue under the dim lights. Despite the dark attire, there was a sweetness and gentleness emanating from her that couldn't be hidden. It was as if she were a precious gem, waiting to be discovered in the darkness of her clothing.

Bear led her to the chair and instructed her to sit. She put her hands in her lap and stared at the both of us.

Her cheeks flared when she took a tentative sniff and gazed back down at her lap.

"Name?" Grim huffed, even though he very well knew who she was.

The woman gulped, her sharp cheekbones being a dead giveaway that she wasn't a shifter, but something else entirely.

"Nefeli," she said, louder than I thought she would. "Winter fae."

Grim hummed. "I saw you fight. You used some of your frost. Any other power you have?"

Nefeli shifted in her seat, her fingers rapping on the rickety chair. When she caught sight of the dead body in the corner, her eyes widened. "I can control the wind. Yes, the wind," she blurted.

I felt the excitement through the bond. Locke's thumbs rubbed up against my breasts.

"Really, that's interesting." Locke tilted his head toward her. "It is a terrible feeling, to be rejected?"

Locke's question confused me. Of course it was supposed to be painful, but he asked her this question?

Again, Nefeli gazed at the body.

"Best not lie," Grim grumbled. "End up like that one." Grim pointed his pen at the dead male in the corner.

Nefeli paled and a shiver of fear ran through her.

"I-I am technically not rejected," she wetted her lips. "I never completed the bond. I just left. And my heart... it felt wrong to take someone else's mate to break their bond." Wetness pooled in her eyes and my heart broke for her.

Locke's did too and his arms wrapped around me.

Oh, so he knew something I didn't.

"Why did you leave?" he asked, leaving no room for her to reject his question.

Her voice trembled as she spoke, her eyes filling with tears. "He... had a family before me," she began, her words barely audible. "But he didn't bond with the female, he killed them when he first met me." The weight of the revelation hung heavy in the air. "His son - he was just a baby." A single tear ran down her cheek, glistening in the moonlight. "I ran, I couldn't bear to be with a male like that."

The room was silent, even Sizzle was stunned into silence.

"And this male hasn't bonded with anyone else. You haven't felt the bond break? What about bond sickness?"

She shook her head. "The bond hasn't broken. As for bond sickness, the winter fae are known to have cold hearts," she chuckled to lighten the mood.

It didn't.

Nefeli reached in her pocket and pulled out a bag. Inside I could smell dried dirt, bones, and spices. "Some traveling sorceresses gave me a recipe to help with any sort of bond sickness. When female fae ovulate the bonding sickness is at its worst. I put it under my tongue, and the bitterness settles it. I've lived with the sickness so long I've become numb."

This poor woman. *"She needs to see Journey,"* I linked Locke, as I tried to concentrate with his dick deep inside me.

His thoughts were the same. He wanted to talk to Journey first and see what else we could find out about this mysterious woman joining our pack.

"We will have more questions for you later. For now, you are welcome. We will conduct a mind-linking ceremony. I understand fae are not used to mind-links and it can be difficult to understand it. I'm leaving it up to you if you want to complete a link or not. You are also welcome to join the spring and summer fae if you wish."

Nefeli shook her head. "No, they keep it rather warm over there. The coolness of the bar is nice," she smiled.

"Great! Bear will show you to your room," Locke said.

Nefeli's eyes brightened and she nodded enthusiastically. "Thank you, thank you so much. I'll do the best I can to help around here."

Locke nodded, but he didn't smile. Too many thoughts swirled in his head that even I couldn't decipher.

Locke

"Locke," my mate whined, fisting her hands in my hair. "I really can't take anymore."

My tongue generously flattened over her clit, sending her spiraling over the cliff of ecstasy. She fell forward before her body collapsed on my face. I was quick enough to pull away, so I didn't get clam-slammed.

My mate panted when I rolled her over. Her head shook back and forth when I slipped the blunt head of my cock between her folds and slid in easily. We both groaned when I filled her up with my thick cock.

"Oh, Princess, you are so wet. Such a pretty little luna."

She groaned, her hands gripping my forearms and pulling me close. Tonight wasn't about any kinky shit; it was about showing her how much I loved her. I've been crazy about her since we first met. I wanted to do everything with her.

But this, I wanted it slow.

I pulled my shaft out of her slowly and pushed it back in. Her pussy clamped around me and I gritted my teeth.

Do NOT come.

"I can't promise anything," she cried. "You're too good."

Damn, she knew how to stroke my ego.

"No, Princess, I'm just me. I want to give you everything."

"You already have. I need a break." She panted and wrapped her legs around me, digging her heels into my back.

"Your mouth says one thing, your body another." My thrusts got faster and my balls slapped her ass. I tilted her hips to get deeper access, getting ready to plug her with my knot.

Fucking heaven.

She groaned, writhing beneath me, her hips bucking to meet my thrusts. I quickened my pace, feeling the familiar pull in my balls. It was time.

I pulled out and mounted her faster; my cock angled just right against her clit as I thrust. She screamed as my knot breached her entrance, stretching her tight walls. Her nails dug into my back as I held myself above her, with my knot lodged painfully in her depths.

"Please, please, please," she begged, her voice shaking. I could feel her body trembling, begging for release. With one last thrust, I bottomed out, letting out a primal roar as my orgasm took over.

Her cries echoed in the room, mixing with the sound of my howls as we reached the peak of our bond. I felt her entire body convulse beneath me, her walls squeezing, clenching my knot as she reached her climax.

I held my body above her, her eyelids heavy with exhaustion. I pressed my lips against her. She didn't pause. She cradled my face to make sure I wasn't going anywhere.

"Fuck, I love you." I pulled the blankets from our nest around us, burying myself in her shoulder. I sighed heavily, nuzzling and feeling her scent surrounding us.

She hummed, her claws scratching up and down my back, then down to my ass where it felt the best. There was something about her claws that felt so fucking good against my skin.

Sometimes I have a nagging feeling in the back of my head that Emm is gonna leave. I was far from perfect. Yet, she always proves me wrong. I always have some kinky shit to put her through, but she always jumps right in, ready to give me what I want, what I crave.

One thing she wanted to know was what happened to my previous mate. Emm knew that my previous mate rejected me and bonded to another, but I'd left what happened to my previous out, on purpose.

This is where those who really know me find me truly psychotic and, to be honest, I didn't want to tell my mate. I've kept this part of me buried so deep I don't think Emm could find it inside me if she ever tried.

Reluctantly, I told her before our lovemaking. I think that is why I ultimately decided to make love to her as well as I did. Because I unconditionally fucking loved her. She understood me in ways no one did.

"I found them in the throes of passion, miles down the road after I had destroyed Blood Rose. I waited until they were locked and couldn't do anything to defend themselves. I took one claw and took my time, slowly cutting their

skin from their bodies, skinning them until they unlocked. Then, I tied them up while they watched each other turn into nothing but hunks of meat. I left them there, in the carriage that she would have taken to her new home. I took a torch and threw it inside. I watched as they cried for mercy, watched their hair singe, and the blood crackle on their skin. I threw more wood into the fire, making the blaze so hot no one would find a body worth recognizing."

My mate stared at me with no disgust or horror. She sat up on her knees in the nest while I sat there with no fucking regret for what I did. I waited for her to bolt to the door, to run and take time to process.

Emm never did. She cupped my face and placed a tender kiss on my lips. "Should have done more," she said.

Which led us to the tender lovemaking, or at least, tender for us.

My knot still pulsed but was soft enough to slip from her body. I watched my come slip out, and I took two fingers and shoved it back inside. Emm groaned as I took one nipple into my mouth, taking a tentative lick.

"Shh, we are gonna rest now," that was a promise. I'd kept her awake long enough.

I pulled my mate to my chest, my hand drifted to her hair and I let my fingers get caught in the long strands.

"That's nice, don't stop," she mumbled.

I grinned like a goofy fucker and waited until my mate's breath evened out. I don't think my life could get any better right now. I had my mate, my pack and some way we were going to kick Idris' ass.

But, for now, I was going to enjoy the life I had and the little peaceful moments that came with it.

Their story doesn't end here. Come back for the next book, 'Anaki', and learn about him, his and Elena's journey, and answer more of your many questions about Abuela.

BOOKS BY VERA

Under the Moon Series

Under the Moon
Clara and Kane's Story

The Alpha's Kitten
Charlotte and Wesley's Story

Finding Love with the Fae King
Osirus and Melina's Story

The Exiled Dragon
Creed and Odessa's Story

Under the Moon: The Dark War
Clara, Kane, Jasper and Taliyah's story

His True Beloved: A Vampire's Second Chance
Sebastian and Christine's Story

Alpha of her Dreams
Evelyn and Kit's Story

The Broken Alpha's Princess
Melody and Marcus' Story

Twinning and Sinning From Mutts to Mates
Dax, Dimitri, and Seraphina's Story

Under the Moon: God Series

Seeking Hades' Ember
Hades and Ember's Story

Lucifer's Redemption
Lucifer and Uriel's Story

Poseidon's Island Flower
Poseidon and Lani's Story

Thanatos' Craving
Thanatos and Juniper's Story

Saving Zeus—Coming soon!

Under the Moon: The Promised Mates of Monktona Wood Orcs

Thorn

Valpar —Coming soon!
Sugha —-Coming soon!

Iron Fang MC Series

Grim

Hawke

Bear

Locke

Anaki— coming soon!

Visit authorverafoxx.com for updates and future books!

Printed in Great Britain
by Amazon

50691908R00235